EXIT

A novel about dying

by

Jo Kline Cebuhar

EXIT

A novel about dying

by

Jo Kline Cebuhar

Published in the United States of America by
Murphy Publishing
P.O. Box 65370
West Des Moines, Iowa 50265-0370

ISBN: 978-0-615-92290-4

To my brother Wes.
He was one of the good guys.

Life is no brief candle to me.
It is a sort of splendid torch
which I've got a hold of for the moment
and I want to make it burn as brightly as possible
before handing it on to future generations.

George Bernard Shaw

Other books by Jo Kline Cebuhar, J.D.

Last things first, just in case...
The practical guide to Living Wills
and Durable Powers of Attorney for Health Care

SO GROWS THE TREE
Creating an Ethical Will
The legacy of your beliefs and values,
life lessons and hopes for the future

The Workshop Edition of
SO GROWS THE TREE
Creating an Ethical Will
The legacy of your beliefs and values,
life lessons and hopes for the future

Whose big idea was that?
Lessons in giving from the
pioneers of value-inspired philanthropy

Principles
of Tax-deferred Exchanging

EXIT

A novel about dying

by

Jo Kline Cebuhar

Lois

Ray Spaulding made the coffee, collected the morning newspaper and placed them both on a breakfast tray along with buttered toast, two slices of crisp bacon and a peeled orange. He'd done the same thing every weekday for something like forty-two years, and he couldn't see why he should chuck the ritual just because his wife Lois was now living at Rockaway House.

The breakfast custom was a holdover from their working years—Ray spent his career as editor of *The Chesterton Bee* and Lois as the office manager of an accounting firm. Back then, while she enjoyed breakfast, he read aloud the highlights of the newspaper. Sometimes Ray asked Lois for her opinion on a story or a headline and she was always glad to offer constructive criticism. Later, while he showered, she dressed and fixed him a go-cup of coffee. Ray had a donut with his coworkers once he got to *The Bee*.

Lois and Ray's morning routine had always had a logic and rhythm all its own.

When daughter Carlene came along five years into the marriage, grabbing extra minutes in bed to bank even a small portion of extra sleep was a tempting option. Carlene was a difficult baby. Lois told Ray he didn't need to keep bringing breakfast to her, but Ray didn't see it that way. "On the contrary," he said, "let's have this time to ourselves, Lois, before that little stinker wakes up."

As Carlene got older, Lois and Ray's schedule expanded and conformed to include the high drama that inevitably ensued each day in getting Carlene off to school. Carlene was a difficult young child. But Ray wouldn't hear of foregoing their breakfast habit, saying, "Now, more than ever, Lois, we need this bit of time together. I just don't want to give it up. Unless you do?"

Lois always laughed and said, "Not me!"

Over the years, Carlene never once intruded on Lois and Ray's special time alone. In fact, Carlene didn't stir until Lois had eaten, the dishes were cleared and both Lois and Ray had begged her at least three times to please, for the love of God, get up. Carlene was a difficult teenager. With her, breakfast was a grueling ordeal as her food preferences changed without warning, followed by the daily wardrobe kerfuffle. Nothing was ever easy with Carlene.

An unintended bonus of his daughter's everlasting petulance was that Ray, seemingly unable to shed his role as editor, developed the amusing habit of putting the lid on most situations with a fitting headline. For example: **Hurricane Carlene Wreaks Havoc On Spaulding Household**. Ray whispered his pithy captions to Lois once Carlene had stormed through the room/from the car/out the door. Over the years, Carlene was seemingly ignorant of these humorous sidebars along with her parents' private breakfasts. From time to time, Lois and Ray thought perhaps they relished their little secrets a bit more than they should.

Six months before her high school graduation, it came as no big surprise when Carlene announced she would be going to college in California, literally the furthest she could get from home without plummeting into the ocean. Lois and Ray weren't anxious for her to move so far away, but they wanted Carlene to have the life of her choosing. It was exactly why they had so judiciously saved for her higher education, and they accepted the news with their customary encouragement and resignation. They wanted what Carlene wanted. So there you go. **Daughter Announces Trans-continental Relocation**

Once Carlene earned her degree as an herbalist—or was she a herbologist, Lois and Ray could never quite remember—she stayed in California to pursue her career. The target market for Carlene's herbology salon, *Au Naturale!*, was in Larkfield-Wikiup, California, not Chesterton, Iowa. Everyone agreed; it only made sense.

As far as Lois and Ray could tell, Carlene's clientele was fiercely loyal and had an abundance of discretionary funds for herbal cures of everything from acne to irritable bowel syndrome. Carlene's shop was in a trendy neighborhood where the locals believed the planets had surely aligned themselves for a person of Carlene's expertise and wisdom to be dropped into their midst. **Finely Aged California Whine** Carlene lived above the shop in an apartment furnished with what she called "mid-century modern" and what Ray referred to as "you know, that stuff we grew up with."

Over the years, family communications and get-togethers were predictable even if infrequent. Cards and calls were dutifully sent and made on birthdays, Mother's Day and Father's Day, and Carlene always spent the obligatory Christmas season in Chesterton—well, except for this past year—using the funds that Ray inevitably sent for her plane ticket without Carlene even having to ask. Lois and Ray visited California just once. The fold-out couch in Carlene's living room left a semi-permanent dent in Ray's back and the strict vegan offerings—unless Ray suggested they dine out, his treat—left both Lois and Ray in bad sorts for days after their return. Ray and Lois talked about it afterwards and they were sure that from then on, Carlene would prefer to spend their time together in familiar surroundings, in Chesterton.

The months turned into years and then into more years.

When Ray approached age sixty-five, he and Lois considered the timing of his retirement, keeping in mind that he wanted to leave at the top of his game.

At breakfast one morning Ray said, "Honey, you know the paper's ripe for a buyout at any time. And when that happens, they'll do what they always do in these situations, they'll pick off the old and weak from the herd. That would be me. I'd rather go out on my own terms."

Lois didn't disagree. Their nephew Byron had been in charge of their investments for years and had done very well by Lois and Ray. They were financially secure and they had their health. Why not get started on living out those golden years of retirement they'd heard so much about?

The Assistant Editor Jake Elbert, just two years out of journalism school, was named as Ray's successor and on July 1, 2002, *The Bee* staff had a small going away party in Ray's honor. Lois and Ray departed the next morning for a ten-day cruise to Alaska. It had been their dream since Carlene left for college and the trip was all they hoped it would be.

Life in retirement was agreeable in its consistency for Lois and Ray. Each day still began with breakfast in bed for Lois, except Ray was no longer hurrying off to work. He doubled up on the toast and bacon and picked at the communal plate as they read *The Bee* together.

Lois was still his number one fan.

"Is it my imagination or is this newspaper just not as good as it used to be?" Ray frequently observed.

Lois agreed. "No, it is not your imagination. You were a darn good editor, Ray Spaulding, the best that paper ever had."

Ray sat on the edge of the bed and smiled at his bride of over four decades. "**Beautiful Ingénue Falls For Newspaper Nerd**."

"True, but you were still the best," Lois said.

Most days Lois and Ray took their time getting dressed and then headed out for errands or the day's activities. They maintained the unhurried pace of two people who had earned the right to take their own sweet time.

On the morning of January 10, 2011, Lois was still dozing when Ray brought the breakfast tray.

"Hey, there—breakfast is served."

Lois slowly opened her eyes and looked up at Ray. Even before she spoke, Ray knew they had a problem.

"Honey, I don't feel right. I must have a bug or something. My back aches—I ache all over." Ray didn't say what he was thinking. His wife's color did not look good.

Five days later, Lois and Ray found themselves sitting in front of a massive desk, with Dr. Randall Sims at a safe distance on the other side. After forty-eight hours in the Chesterton Medical Center, countless tests and a round of antibiotics, Lois had taken it easy at home for three days. She was convinced that whatever had caused her unscheduled trip to the doctor and on to the hospital had run its course. She was almost positive she felt better now.

The doctor asked if Lois had noticed being confused or having trouble concentrating. Lois and Ray looked at each other, laughed nervously and she said, yes, but they thought they were just having "senior moments." Dr. Sims flashed a fleeting smile and said that in Lois's case, it was more likely caused by *the disease.* Ray cringed. When Dr. Sims read a list of symptoms, Lois nodded to every one: decreased appetite, trouble sleeping, some swelling in her ankles, puffy eyes, backache.

What was Carlene pontificating about that time they were in California? "See it and be it." (She was fresh from a workshop on the Law of Attraction.) Lois concentrated on imagining healthy cells and looking and feeling hopeful while she answered the litany of questions. The Law of Attraction thing wasn't working. As the doctor continued, her hope turned into frustration, then anxiety.

Meanwhile, Ray was a get-to-the-point kind of guy, everybody said so. He couldn't take it any longer. "So what's all this mean, doctor?" he asked.

Dr. Sims removed his glasses—never a good sign—and placed both palms flat on the desk before him. Another bad sign.

"Mrs. Spaulding, do you have any history of kidney disease in your family?"

Ray's heart sank.

"Well, I can't really say, Dr. Sims—and please call me Lois. I was adopted and I don't know much about my birth parents. You see, back then we didn't have all the open records in an adoption like they do now." For some reason, Lois felt compelled to explain to Dr. Sims the cultural context for being so shamefully ignorant of her own family's health history. When she thought about it later, she thought that was probably because to her—and Ray had agreed—Dr. Sims looked like he was maybe nineteen years old.

"I see. In any case, Mrs. Spaulding, you have polycystic kidney disease. You have cysts in your kidneys and the damage is extensive. I'll get you scheduled with the dialysis clinic here at Chesterton Medical Center." Dr. Sims reached to pick up his phone. Ray calmly, deliberately and firmly placed his hand on top of the doctor's. Dr. Sims's head shot up. Ray paused a moment before speaking, his gaze locked on Dr. Sims.

"Young man," Ray said, "I don't know how much time your medical school professors spent talking about bedside manners, but it wasn't enough. You just told my wife and me that she has what I will assume is a life-threatening disease, so before you pass us off to the next expert, you need to explain just exactly what you know and what it means for us."

At that moment, Lois couldn't say if she was more shocked by the doctor's words or Ray's, but she did know that she had never been more grateful to have Ray Spaulding on her team. She couldn't speak.

Ray lifted his hand and the doctor slowly pulled his away, looking not quite sure how to proceed. "I come from a newspaper background, doctor. I'll make it very easy for you. We need to know who, what, why, when, where and how." Ray gave Lois's hand a reassuring squeeze. His grip was dry and warm. Lois took a breath and her heart stopped beating quite so fast.

Dr. Sims briefly considered Ray's words and then gave Lois and Ray the facts. He said, although he couldn't be positive, that Lois had probably inherited this disease. Her blood pressure was dangerously high and they would continue to address that with medication. A severe kidney infection had caused the back pain and was handled for the time being as well, but Lois needed to start dialysis straight away, three days a week to begin with, until they could evaluate how her body tolerated the treatments. As Ray later recounted this scene to his coffee buddies—using an expression Ray would normally never use—he said the doctor looked about as comfortable as a hooker in church.

Ray managed to keep his wits about him. He knew someone at *The Bee* who had a neighbor who had a sister who'd gotten a kidney transplant. Was that an option? Dr. Sims said Lois was most likely not a good candidate because of the hypertension and possible cardiac damage common with end-stage kidney disease. But—and Lois thought the doctor's manner softened a bit as he said this—he would schedule her for a comprehensive heart panel, just to make sure. Ray let the term "end-stage" pass without asking for further clarification, hoping Lois hadn't caught it at all.

Lois and Ray left the Chesterton Medical Center hand-in-hand, with a fistful of prescriptions and brochures and a reminder card for the first appointment at the dialysis center, two days later. As if Lois would forget.

On the way home, Ray finally remembered the one question he'd forgotten to ask Dr. Sims: *How long does my wife have?*

He could only hope that Lois would never remember.

EXIT - 6

Margaret

There they were—The Shoes. The Shoes that had become so much more than the sum of their parts. For instance, Margaret might be just going along, having an okay day, a day when she had actually noticed that the sun was shining, a day without a tearful fit, so far. Then, without thinking, she would open the closet door and her glance would fall upon The Shoes. A rapid jolt back to The New Reality.

Size nine and a half and once dazzling white with red trim, they were now justifiably scuffed, crusted with dried blades of grass and garden soil embedded with tiny pebbles. Margaret knew that for a fact because she'd spent the better part of an hour one day closely inspecting The Shoes.

They were Ernie's, his yard shoes. The shallow grooves of the soles were filled with the evidence of an afternoon spent pulling weeds in the garden. Was it on the last day before Ernie took to his bed for The Duration? Margaret couldn't recall for sure. That bothered her because what sort of person wasn't able to remember such a thing?

"Enough already with The Shoes." Margaret snatched her house sweater from the hook just inside the closet and gave the door a resounding slam shut. The echo bounced through the house. She gently donned the faded cardigan, one arm after the other in measured moves, slowed by what she hoped was just a touch of arthritis in the general area of her left shoulder. Like her reaction to the other little ailments that had surfaced over the past few months, she'd considered a visit to her doctor. Maybe she'd get some sympathy. She should make an appointment—and she would, if she could say exactly where it hurt. But it was more of a vague achiness. That sounded lame even to Margaret—she could just imagine the look Doc Husted would give her. A great guy—the best—but he wasn't known to suffer fuzzy symptoms. Margaret decided to wait a while and see how the shoulder felt in a few days or weeks.

She stopped for a brief look in the full-length mirror that hung on the outside of the bathroom door. How many times in the past two decades had she regretted the day she insisted Ernie install that torture device? Peering back was a sixty-seven-year-old with a body type which—if absolutely forced to—she would describe as "square." Ernie had affectionately called her his "little pistachio nut." *While I was thinking 'How cute is that?' why didn't I ever ask him what in the world he meant?* Even when Margaret turned this way and that, her face seemed so one-dimensional, so plain and dull and uncomplicated. Other people had video faces. Hers was a snapshot face.

Ernie claimed he never could, but Margaret easily spotted the differences between the girl he had married and this image. For one thing, Margaret's mousey brown hair was now fully emancipated, doing its own thing nine days out of ten, and in 1971, she wasn't quite as short. Margaret took a moment to practice smiling. It came off cheesy looking, the kind of smile you give to a smart aleck right after he's said something smart. Not quite a grimace, just short of a sneer. Recently, it seemed that wearing a bona fide smile required an extraordinary amount of energy. Margaret made a mental note to work on that.

She studied her reflection. *Capable. Dependable.* These were words people had always used to describe Margaret. Did she still deserve those labels, she asked herself. Would she strike someone as worthy volunteer material, even considering that her services came for free? Did she seem like a person you could trust to carry out a task—any task—with minimal screw-ups? Margaret certainly couldn't say—her objectivity was long gone.

She turned, and a few steps further down the hall nearly tripped on her housemate, stretched full-length in line with a rod of sunshine on the floor, just outside the kitchen doorway. "Tell me again why this seemed like a good idea at the time, Maxine?" Margaret sighed as she stepped over the voluminous grey tabby. She remembered hearing someone say that talking to oneself was okay—it was the answering back that spelled trouble. *Does talking to a cat count? Is this answering back? Stop it.*

It was September 3, the day Margaret was due at Rockaway House. When first invited to volunteer—she'd noticed that they were oh so careful to use the word "invite"—Margaret had rejected the idea out of hand. Such a commitment had implied more effort than she could possibly muster. The routine of dragging herself around the house, dusting imaginary dust, getting on Maxine's nerves with her relentless neediness and feeling weepy had become familiar, even comfortable to Margaret in a perverse way. Then unexpectedly, one day three weeks ago, out of nowhere Margaret knew she was overdue to get her derriere out of the chairrere. She gave herself a good talking-to.

How did I become this person? All itchy and cranky and looking forward to sundown just so I can rationalize going to bed?

The time had come. Margaret was momentarily open to the idea of planning ahead more than an hour at a time, having a reason to get up and looking forward to putting something on the calendar besides an "X" at the end of the day. Today's appointment had ticked off all the boxes. At least it had when she'd said "yes" three weeks ago.

Breakfast was a bowl of instant oatmeal, a small carton of low-fat yogurt and a handful of grapes at the table-for-two in the small kitchen. Fiber, dairy and fruit with a minimum investment of labor and time. Neat and tidy.

Margaret finished her cup of tea and hoisted herself up from the table.

A few household chores and then she'd be out the door. She glanced at the list she'd jotted on the back of a used envelope. Her eyes fell on the item "S.L." *Oh, good grief. What in the world does that mean?* Then she remembered she was supposed to take along a sack lunch. Margaret quickly threw together a ham and cheese sandwich and grabbed an apple. In an upper cupboard she spotted the insulated sack Ernie had used to carry his own lunch before retiring, the one with BROWN BAG screen-printed on its side.

"I suppose I thought it was clever when I sent poor Ernie out the door with that stupid thing in his hand," she mumbled.

After lugging the garbage can to the curb for the weekly pick-up, washing her few breakfast dishes and giving the countertop a swipe, Margaret let out a heavy sigh and dropped her sweater on the back of a kitchen chair.

Well, actually the sweater was Ernie's, not hers. "That thing could really use a trip to the laundry room," she used to say to him on a regular basis. Funny, because the cardigan hadn't been washed since long before Ernie's death. It still smelled like Ernie, and dirt and a little like celery. If anyone asked, Margaret would simply answer that it didn't yet need a trip to the laundry room. No one was going to ask. No one knew—it was one of Margaret's "dirty little secrets."

Now, that's funny.

"Okay, I said I'd do it, so I'm going. But if I don't enjoy it—and I really mean it—I'm not staying. So there!" An affectionate pat to the head of Maxine and Margaret was out the door, BROWN BAG in hand.

Down the driveway she backed the Le Sabre that Ernie had so loved, pointing its nose toward Rockaway House. She'd figured it would be seven minutes, door-to-door. Right turn at the end of Wilmoth Avenue, right again at 47th Street, then left onto Buchanan Avenue for three blocks. One more right and then it was a straight shot south on four-lane Marion Street to her destination.

Well, Margaret reflected, a tad self-satisfied, at least I know exactly where I'm headed today.

Actually, she had no idea.

EXIT - 10

Rockaway House

The route to Rockaway House on Marion Street was easily navigated from Margaret's cloistered neighborhood. That's because logistically, Marion Street ran north to south right through the center of Chesterton. And metaphorically, Rockaway House was smack dab where all roads ultimately lead: the end of the line.

Margaret slowed the Buick to a crawl in front of 1724 Marion Street. She'd lived in Chesterton her entire life. She was a product of the Chesterton Community School District, a dutiful subscriber to the *Buy Local* campaign and retired from one of two grocery stores in town. And yet, after logging thousands of miles travelling the streets of Chesterton for nearly seven decades, although Margaret had noticed this house—had even commented on its exceptional beauty—she had never realized what was going on inside and had never cared enough to wonder.

Home to those over the past century whose names had long been forgotten, its current function was simply stated on a white-on-black sign over the front door:

Rockaway House
Hospice Care

Margaret nosed her car into the driveway, craned her neck and could see there was most likely parking available in the rear, past the house and in front of the mammoth garage. *No thanks.* She opted instead for a space out on the street—*better for a fast getaway, just in case.* She sat for a moment in the car, ducking down to get a full view of the house through the front passenger window. *Holy moly.*

Rockaway House was a vast manmade monument, securely planted on an acre lot filled with centuries-old trees that dwarfed even its two-and-a-half story profile. Four twenty-foot fluted pillars bordered the front entrance, supporting a massive porch roof gripping tight onto the second story. There was little ornamentation to the exterior except the crown of hefty balusters that topped the porch, the solarium and the drive-under portico. The windows were adorned with only unfussy muntins and no shutters.

Margaret bent down further so she could see the orange tiled roof.

There was a compelling melancholy to the stately face of Rockaway House, but not from disrepair or neglect. No, the stucco exterior was in perfect condition, pale putty with white and green trim, immaculate. The neat lawn was mowed within an inch of its life with not a weed in sight. But flowers were conspicuously absent from the brick-bordered flower beds, filled only with fresh mulch. The few shrubs that adorned the foundation were healthy but spare.

Margaret didn't know it for a fact, but she supposed that Marion Street had been the main thoroughfare into Chesterton since the beginning of its days. No doubt, in this town now occupied by 12,800 attentive residents, this boulevard had always been the prime location for landed gentry to display the chief measure of their wealth: a noble home. Better than anyone else, Rockaway House seemed to know it had seen more glamorous days, but this home, without question still the most impressive on the block, had plenty yet to say for itself.

Whoever built this one must have hit the mother lode.

"Ernie, buddy, I hope you appreciate what I'm doing here." That sounded a little peeved—Margaret really hadn't meant it to. She smiled and gave the ring on her left hand a gentle pat. "And have a good one, sweetie. I'm sure you have somewhere to be—and today, so do I."

She stepped out of the car and walked up the sidewalk through the tidy lawn toward the massive entry. The house faced west so the morning sun was still somewhere in the backyard and the stone tile floor of the porch, spanning the full width of the house, was bathed in shade. Its only furnishings were two dismal plastic chairs. A simple brass plaque at the top of the door, *Rockaway House – 1922,* caught her eye. Margaret took a deep breath and walked in the front door, passing under a leaded glass eyebrow window.

Once inside, she let out a sigh of relief. She'd been worried it would smell like a hospital—worse yet, a nursing home. This was more like old wood and floor wax, and freshly brewed coffee. And a whiff of cinnamon rolls. *Good, someone's baking.*

Even though she hadn't consciously speculated about it ahead of time, somehow what Margaret found inside Rockaway House was disappointing. The reception hall was dark and cavernous, her vision aided by only a single bulb in a nondescript ceiling fixture. Even the open French doors that led to rooms on her left and right didn't help. The interiors beyond them were shadowy as well.

This is certainly lifting my spirits.

Fifteen feet ahead, wide stairs rose up, topped by a landing that took a turn out of sight. To the left of the staircase, at the end of a hallway, was another set of French doors, closed.

Margaret would never say the interior was dirty, or even dingy, just cheerless.

She took two tentative steps forward and peered through the doorway on the left. The living room? Paneling covered its walls but not the ubiquitous type that had lined every 1960s rumpus room and finished basement across America. This was of the 1920s variety: substantial quarter-sawn oak that ran two-thirds up the walls, topped with a decorative and utilitarian plate rail. There were no plates on it now, if there ever had been. Margaret's gaze followed the rich wood up to massive beams that crisscrossed the ceiling, dividing it into nine precise squares.

The room looked ordinary, a bit too ordinary, to Margaret's way of thinking. The furnishings were uninviting, an odd assortment of overstuffed chairs and a low table, covered with a smattering of magazines and newspapers. A red, green and brown couch was in one corner. A rug covered most of the floor, in colors that were similar—but not quite the same—as those in the couch. The germaphobe in Margaret was quick to note that everything seemed clean, albeit gloomy.

Shabby chic minus the chic.

On the far side of the living room, Margaret could make out another set of French doors leading to a solarium. When the house was built, this little room provided a buffer from the cold, a cool haven in the sweltering summers (being on the north side of the house), and lots of natural light—but no longer. Shades were now drawn tight on all three windowed walls. To the right, at the narrow end of the living room, Margaret spotted something that might be interesting. She peered and her vision was adjusting to the dull lighting when she heard muted voices drifting down the stairs. She turned, about to announce her arrival as a voice called out, "Yoo hoo! Be down in a moment!"

"Okay," Margaret responded faintly. *Too slow.* The option of bolting for her car vanished when the owner of the voice appeared at her side.

"Maggie?" Margaret turned to face a fifty-something woman slightly shorter than her with flyaway salt-and-pepper hair, clipboard in hand.

"Well, it's actually Margaret. I always go by Margaret." Well played, Margaret thought with shame. *Ernie always called me Maggie. I'm lying to this nice lady. I have no reason to lie. I'm pathetic. And I'm a liar.*

"Oh, sorry. Of course. Margaret it is. I'm Rose Sears, the volunteer coordinator. So nice to meet you. Let's get started, shall we? I haven't had my first cup of coffee, so the kitchen might be the best place to begin."

She commandeered Margaret through the French doors opposite the living room into what was probably the dining room at one time. To Margaret it was another drab, undefined space, outfitted with a few small tables, each surrounded by an assortment of unmatched chairs. Rose threw open drapes as she passed by.

Some sunlight certainly helps, Margaret thought as she trailed Rose through a butler's pantry. Without a butler, the demi-room was now without a purpose, and its glass-door cabinets were empty, hanging above vacant counter tops.

Then, in just a few short steps, they passed into another setting that was in such contrast with the front rooms, it nearly took Margaret's breath away. It was the bright and toasty warm kitchen. She first noticed the cupboards, much like the ones in her own home. Original to this house, they were painted a soft buttery cream and reached to the tall ceiling. The stove and refrigerator were new and institutional-sized, but even with shining granite countertops, it all worked—it looked and felt like 1922. At the center of the solarium, which was probably a more recent addition, was a table for eight and another small table in its corner with cushioned wicker chairs, bathed in sunlight. Lush ferns hung from the ceiling.

Margaret smiled as she looked around. *Oh my, this is just like Grandmother Grace's kitchen where everyone hung out. We used to hope for a dollop of cookie dough.*

Rose's voice interrupted Margaret's musing. "Coffee, tea, cocoa?"

"Tea would be fine, Rose. What a nice room!"

"It is, isn't it? Meals are prepared off-site, so this is for the families' use and, of course, any special requests from the residents. Have a seat," Rose said.

Turning, Margaret found a young girl already at the large table, drinking a cup of cocoa while texting. "May I join you?" Margaret softly asked. The girl looked up, a smile breaking across her face.

"Absolutely! I'm Tracy." She put her hand out to Margaret.

"I'm Margaret."

In a few moments, tea had appeared for Margaret; Rose had a cup of coffee in hand and joined them at the table. "It's pretty quiet down here in the mornings. All the action is upstairs. The patients' meals are delivered hot, so not much goes on down here until the visitors start to come—that's usually mid-morning," Rose said. "Most family members have things to take care of at home, so if they didn't spend the night, they start arriving about ten o'clock." Rose took a sip of coffee. "How did you come to volunteer with us, Margaret?"

Good question. I'm asking myself that.

"My husband Ernie had hospice—I mean, we used hospice at home when he was . . ." Margaret left the sentence hanging, not sure if the term "dying" was politically correct at Rockaway House. *Maybe the residents here "pass away" or "go to their reward" or "kick the bucket"—no, probably not that.* She'd already told a fib; she certainly didn't need to add insult within the first hour. But Rose rolled past Margaret's stumble without seeming to notice.

"Not surprising—most people volunteer because a family member had hospice care. That's how most people learn about us."

"How about you, Rose? Is that what brought you here?" Margaret asked.

"Oh yes. My James passed of pancreatic cancer seven years ago. He was one of the first to stay at Rockaway House. Seven years. Hard to believe . . ." Rose then turned to Tracy. "So, how is Caleb doing today?"

"He's pretty good, Rose, but he's having some trouble when he swallows. We're not sure what that's all about . . . " Tracy was looking past Margaret, her eyes unfocused. Rose gave the young girl's hand a gentle pat.

"I'm sorry, honey. Dr. Reese will know what can be done," Rose said. Tracy stood, rinsed her dishes and put them in the dishwasher. Margaret could now see the waif-like girl in full.

"Nice meeting you, Margaret. See you later, Rose." Tracy left through a swinging door at the back of the kitchen, and Margaret could hear her quick steps on wooden stairs.

She couldn't keep from asking, "How old is that girl?"

"Tracy? Probably seventeen. Her friend, Caleb, is seventeen, almost eighteen. You've signed all your volunteer paperwork, right?" It took Margaret a moment to understand what Rose was getting at.

"Oh, yes, the Confidentiality Agreement and all the HIPAA stuff. Yes, I did," Margaret assured her.

"Good. Caleb has ALL, Acute Lymphocytic Leukemia. It's in the final stages. His dad Jerry is probably upstairs with him now. His mom stays at night, then Jerry comes for a while in the morning and then Tracy stays during the day. There are three other children in the family, so they're trying to maintain some sort of normalcy around their house. You'll meet Caleb. He's a great kid."

Margaret shook her head. "I can't imagine dealing with death as a seventeen-year-old."

Rose tipped back the last of her coffee and smiled across at Margaret. "I think you'll find that being part of hospice from this side will be an eye-opener in many ways. Wanna see the rest of Rockaway House?" Margaret nodded as they stood and began to walk.

Rose led Margaret through the butler's pantry and back into the dining room as she began her tour patter. "Nine years ago Mrs. Sullivan—did you ever know Sullivan's Department Store downtown?" Rose interrupted herself.

Margaret nodded, remembering it fondly. Downtown Chesterton was at the town's center. Three blocks long with four cross streets, it was home to the business community's keystone fixtures: movie theater, drugstore, hardware store, bakery, grocery, bookstore, a couple of law offices, a bank or two, more recently a coffee shop, and—many years before—Sullivan's Department Store. Going there had been a big deal, a childhood treat. Margaret's senior prom dress and Ernie's first suit both came from Sullivan's.

Rose paused, engrossed in the telling. "Well, Mr. Sullivan died in 2003. Mrs. Sullivan kept him at home until the very end. Of course, they had the money to do that, but even so, it was a struggle to find the right help and to get the doctors to understand that Mr. Sullivan wanted to die at home. I'm told Mrs. Sullivan gave everyone quite a workout, right to the end," Rose said, stopping in the middle of the dining room. Now filling with morning sun, it was a bit more cheerful than Margaret's first impression.

"Right after Mr. Sullivan died, Mrs. Sullivan started bugging the doctors and the hospital to start providing hospice services. Of course, they'd both been on the hospital board and being the 'Sullivan' in the Sullivan Children's Clinic didn't hurt any. Then Mrs. Sullivan's granddaughter taught her to use the computer, and once she figured out how to get onto the Worldwide InterWeb, there was no stopping her." Rose took a breath as she landed at one of the small tables, motioned for Margaret to sit down across from her and then continued.

"She dragged them all along, insisting that Chesterton get with it and start talking about care for the dying. Anyway, one thing led to another and the medical center was soon certified to provide hospice care in people's homes and in the hospital and long-term care facilities. Eventually, the patients—and the doctors—got accustomed to the idea of *caring* instead of *curing* when the time was right. Once she got that far, Mrs. Sullivan started thinking about people who couldn't keep their dying patient at home—even if they wanted to—so she campaigned to open a place like this. She was driving past here on the way to her doctor's office a few blocks down the street and she saw it had a For Sale sign and she was off to the races!"

Margaret was only half listening to Rose. As if it was yesterday, she remembered exactly how it felt when Ernie's doctor said there was no point in further treating Ernie's cancer. Then Margaret's memory got a little fuzzy. That must have been when hospice entered the picture. She remembered someone had a hospital bed delivered to the house and at just the right time, a nurse started coming regularly, checking on Ernie and acting as a go-between with the hospice doctor. Throughout those six weeks, Margaret never thought about what their alternatives would have been without hospice because she didn't have to. Now she realized she'd taken it rather for granted. Not that Margaret hadn't been grateful—no day had gone by without words of gratitude to the hospice workers and prayers of gratitude to God. But until now she hadn't thought about how it all came to be. Every aid, every service, every person had just appeared when needed like guardian angels.

Margaret looked over at Rose and shook her head. "I had no idea, Rose. I never knew the history. Is Mrs. Sullivan still living? Do you know her?" Margaret wanted to personally thank this stranger who had made such a difference to Ernie—and to her.

"She died about four years ago, but yes, I did get to know her. She was one of the first volunteers here. In fact, I first met her while James was here. One day she brought some flowers into his room. She was just as down-to-earth as can be. So that's how we got Rockaway House." Rose was coming to her favorite part of the story and she got a big smile. "Except for the name. During renovation, the workmen discovered the brass plaque that's on the front door, the little one that says *Rockaway House – 1922*. It was painted over by someone a long time before. I guess Mrs. Sullivan took it as a sign. She said she just knew for a fact that it had meant something special to the people who built this home, so she had it stripped and re-installed at the top of the door, and she gave this place the official name of Rockaway House. Mrs. Sullivan was a real believer in 'God winks'."

That got Margaret's attention. "I'm sorry? 'God winks'?"

"Coincidences, serendipity, signs, kismet, when things happen for a reason. Anyway, that's how it got its name."

Margaret shook her head. "I can't believe I never knew any of this before. I can't imagine how this all went on without me knowing it. I've lived here all my life."

"Not surprising," Rose said as she stood to move the tour along, "we're a pretty well-kept secret, unfortunately—until you need us, of course. We better get moving. I'd sit and chat all day, if you let me."

Margaret stood, gave her legs and back a quick stretch and followed on Rose's heels through the reception hall beyond those closed French doors.

For the first time in many months, Margaret didn't feel unplugged. Her size eight Adidas didn't seem made of lead. For some reason—some reason she couldn't quite make out at the moment—she had a reassuring sense that she was right where she was supposed to be and that she had just taken the first steps in an extraordinary journey.

EXIT - 18

Victoria

Something woke her. Magda lay very still, holding her breath. Maybe the sound had been in a dream, but she didn't think so. It wasn't an intruder, she was pretty sure of that. She wasn't afraid. For some reason she thought the sound was familiar. Was it Victoria? She thought it might have been Victoria. Had Victoria called out from the guest room?

The baby monitor was on the bedside table. Magda reached over and instinctively tapped it, making sure it was turned on.

The green indicator light was a lifeless gray dot.

Twisting up in the covers as she tried to get out of bed, Magda nearly tumbled onto the floor. She grabbed wildly for the bedpost with her free hand, stopping her fall.

Then she remembered.

Of course the monitor wasn't turned on. There was no reason for the monitor to be turned on. Magda had taken Victoria to Rockaway House that morning—well, yesterday morning.

What time is it, anyway? The clock radio showed two fifteen. *Two fifteen—a.m.? I've been asleep for five hours? I haven't slept for five hours in a row for—what—six months?* Even so, Magda yawned and wanted nothing more at that moment than to lie down and go right back to sleep. But with her caregiver's brain now at Defcon 3, that wasn't very likely.

She untangled from the sheet and sat on the edge of the bed, taking a moment to get her bearings before she stood, although she was already wide-awake. Over the past six months, she'd become proficient at waking up fast and staying that way. Whenever Victoria needed her, Magda went from asleep to alert in a flash. Well, somebody had to have her act together for measuring meds or pouring a glass of water or cleaning up a mess, and it certainly wasn't going to be Victoria, was it?

I wonder how Vic's doing. Should I call Rockaway House and check on her? When I left yesterday they said I could come over or call anytime but people always say things like that. I wonder if they meant it. What if she has a nightmare or she's in a lot of pain? Maybe I don't want to know.

Magda recalled the advice she had given to Victoria a thousand times: *Be careful standing up. You might be dizzy.* In slow motion, she stood.

Magda wasn't dizzy but she was really thirsty. She stepped into her slippers and headed for the kitchen. Magda smiled as she reveled in flipping on every light switch between their bedroom and the kitchen, not having to think about whether she would disturb Victoria, who might have just finally gotten to sleep. It was wonderfully peculiar. Then she vacillated, went back and turned each and every one off again and returned to the kitchen led by the dim nightlights, the ones she'd plugged in months earlier along the familiar path.

Magda poured herself a glass of chocolate milk. She'd stopped at the grocery store on the way home from Rockaway House. They hadn't had chocolate milk in the frig for ages. The list of foods that Victoria could tolerate had grown dramatically short in the past few months and Magda had tried not to remind Victoria of what she was missing. She'd been very careful about what was kept in the house, even long after Victoria stepped foot in the kitchen for the last time. Instinctively, Magda felt a little guilty as she gulped the silky sweetness.

As she sat at the kitchen table, she glanced around the room. Her gaze stopped at the collection of photos pinned to the bulletin board, squinting to see them. She'd left her glasses back in their bedroom.

Victoria and Magda in Las Vegas two years ago. Magda had won two hundred dollars at the craps table. They'd seen *Jersey Boys.*

Victoria and Magda on the rim of the Grand Canyon a year ago. Victoria had pulled a folding camp chair from the back of the car and sat on the rim of the gorge until Magda said they really needed to get going to make it to the hotel by dark. Victoria hadn't wanted to leave and Magda kept having the uneasy feeling that Victoria was going to jump. Victoria said the Grand Canyon made her feel tiny and she said she liked the sensation of being flea-sized in the world, not having all the drama of being a human and having to be in charge of so much.

Victoria and Magda trekking up a desert path outside Sedona, Arizona. *When was that?* The calendar in Magda's head quickly flipped to the familiar marker of B.C. (Before Cancer) or A.C. (After Cure). Victoria was hiking, so it must have been B.C., prior to her finding that lump almost four years ago. Her breast cancer was cured three years ago—three years ago next month—at least that's what they were told three years ago. In any case, Victoria had never hiked again.

Then it hit the fan last January.

Victoria lost her appetite, then weight, then the scans showed the cancer was back. Metastatic breast cancer in her liver and bones. Magda still didn't quite get how you can have breast cancer in your liver or bones, but the doctor said it was because this was actually the same cancer Victoria had three years earlier.

So it wasn't cured after all?

No, no, it was cured, now it's returned.

So, it just went into hiding for a while and now it's turned up somewhere else? Like *Whac-a-mole?*

Well, yes, sort of. Well, no. It was gone, now it's back. In a different place.

So, why isn't it called liver cancer or bone cancer?

Because it's really breast cancer, but not in the breast any longer.

No, it's not likely to be since she doesn't have any breasts any longer. This is a stupid conversation.

Magda hadn't actually said those last two comments out loud to the doctor, she'd just kept them to herself, like so many other thoughts.

When the doctor told them the cancer was back, Magda was really pissed. Thinking back, she remembered how Victoria wasn't as angry as she was, which had made Magda even more pissed.

To hell with it. I'm calling. Magda reached over and picked up the wireless phone from the kitchen counter. She got the number for the nurses' station from the memo pad where she'd carefully written it down the day before. They answered on the second ring.

"Rockaway House, nurses' station. Trish speaking."

"Hello, this is Magda Stark. I wonder if you can tell me how Victoria King is doing?"

"Hi, Magda. She's very comfortable. We got ahead of the pain after you left yesterday afternoon and she's resting now. How are you doing?" Trish asked.

"Oh, I'm fine, I'm fine," Magda quickly responded.

"It's just that it's two in the morning, so I hope you're okay. It can be quite an adjustment for the caregiver."

"No, no, I'm fine. I just woke up and I thought I'd check on Victoria. I guess I'll see you tomorrow—no, I guess I mean later today."

"We'll be here. You take care of yourself, Magda. Good night."

"Good night." Magda punched the button and laid the phone down.

That's right, isn't it? I'm the caregiver. I am the caregiver. So, when there's no longer someone who needs to be taken care of, who am I?

EXIT - 22

Margaret

Margaret got home from Rockaway House and first thing made herself a cup of chamomile tea. She filled a Nippon saucer—Aunt Ione's good china—with Mint Milanos and traded her sneakers for her house slippers. Her dogs were killin' her. *What a day.*

Maxine wasn't really vested in how Margaret spent her time away from home and was in no mood to wait for dinner. Margaret hauled herself back up, shook out enough kibble to stop the relentless whining and plopped back down, putting her feet on Ernie's chair. Her head was bursting, but she was still eager to debrief herself and review what she'd learned that day at Rockaway House.

When it came to new volunteers, Rose Sears had a well-honed routine. With Margaret trailing by her side, Rose made quick introductions to the on-site staff and gave Margaret a brief overview of the hospice mission and an initiation on day-to-day functions. Most importantly, Rose peppered the time with brief stops in the patients' rooms. Margaret got to meet some of the residents and their family members and Rose got to discreetly observe Margaret. One of Rose's most important functions was to properly match volunteers and assignments, for everyone's sake. There were plenty of options for volunteer service, and she'd long ago recognized that not every person was equipped to work directly with dying patients. But, unless Rose had really missed the mark, Margaret, her newest volunteer, would be just fine.

Dipping a cookie into her tea, Margaret thought back on the remainder of the day. The tour of the first floor had ended in the rear of Rockaway House where Rose proudly showed off the elevator. That was a whole other story that Rose was delighted to tell.

"So, as soon as Mrs. Sullivan saw the For Sale sign, she contacted the real estate agent and arranged a tour for herself and—as she put it—'a few friends with big hearts and deep pockets.'"

Rockaway House was large enough to satisfy Mrs. Sullivan's vision for a residential hospice facility. As a bonus, 1724 Marion Street was ahead of its time when built and two of the five bedrooms already featured private baths. The other three bedrooms had space for half baths to be added.

The biggest obstacle to conversion was unavoidable and just inside the front door: the grand staircase. And grand it was—a great grand obstacle. High ceilings meant many steps between floors, and if any building demanded handicap-accessibility, it was this one. Besides concern for the patients who usually arrived on stretchers, common sense dictated that many of the visitors and family members would also be stairs-adverse.

As luck would have it, next door to the Chesterton home that J. H. "Bill" and Helen Sullivan had built and occupied for almost sixty years lived the Strawns. More than just neighbors, Patrick Strawn had been Mr. Sullivan's golf partner and closest friend. The wives met as young mothers with small children, each married to an ambitious entrepreneur, each maturing as a civic leader in her own right. Neighbors, friends and ultimately soul sisters, Helen Sullivan and Kathleen Strawn had joined forces to take on countless worthy causes, family crises and joyous occasions for nearly their entire adult lives.

Yes, it was lucky for Rockaway House, but maybe not quite so fortunate for Patrick Strawn who just happened to be the owner of Strawn Elevator Corp. A phone conversation between Helen and Kathleen was followed by a breakfast conversation between Kathleen and Patrick. Kathleen Strawn was one hundred percent on board to raise whatever funds were needed over and above what she and Patrick would, of course, personally donate. Kathleen considered the chairmanship of the hospice fundraising project a privilege and a rare opportunity to honor her dearest friend's late husband—a "God wink." The two-story addition to Rockaway House materialized, complete with a passenger-friendly freight elevator, courtesy of Strawn Elevator Corp., "*Chesterton's premier provider of quality elevators for over three-quarters of a century.*"

Rose continued the tale. To no one's real surprise, the plans for the addition went on steroids sometime between the Strawns' breakfast and when the contractor's shovel hit the ground. The Chesterton Medical Center's architect and the facilities manager reported that a second floor nurses' station, secure drug storage, clerical space and a patient bathing room with a lift were also needed. Mrs. Sullivan said that was fine by her. The additional square footage upstairs would justify enlarging the first floor addition to the kitchen.

Helen remembered well her husband Bill's last days in their home when the kitchen became the hub of activity. Every visit from a health care worker, friend or family member began there with a cup of coffee, a snack or a congregate meal. Every day ended in much the same way for Helen, a quiet moment shared with the night nurse or a lingering loved one. The kitchen needed to be big, much bigger, Helen had declared. The addition soon included a conference room on the first floor for training and grief support activities. It only made sense, she pointed out, to provide those Medicare-mandated hospice services on-site at Rockaway House.

The previous owners had been good stewards of the property but hadn't done much in the way of updating, so kitchen and bathroom renovations were added to the cost estimates. The number one priority was outfitting patient rooms with top-of-the-line beds, fold-out sleepers and soothing decor, while the first floor common areas were virtually untouched. That explained their appearance and Rose made no apologies. The comfort and care of the patients had to be—then, as now—the primary focus. Everything else was secondary.

Mrs. Sullivan visited Rockaway House often during and after the year-long construction phase. She marveled at how, of all houses, this house had appeared in just the right place, at just the right time. There was no question, it was meant to be.

At noon, Rose had left Margaret in the kitchen to enjoy her sack lunch. Tracy passed through once to grab paper plates and napkins; a pizza was on the way for her and a couple of Caleb's friends. Margaret met two other volunteers as they fetched snacks for patients and hurried back upstairs, and a nurse, Sheryl, when she came to the kitchen to microwave a bag of popcorn for the upstairs staff to snack on.

After eating, Margaret was standing in the sunroom addition, looking out at the back of the property when she heard Rose enter laughing.

"You're still here? Only kidding—no I'm not!" Rose said. "Once I actually had a volunteer who said she was going to use the restroom and never came back. Wasn't for her, I guess. People think they can do this, but then some get to worrying that being around the dying might be catching—not their diseases, just the possibility of dying. I guess it's more emotionally intimate than a lot of people care to be, if you know what I mean. What about you?" Rose sat down at the small table in the sunroom and Margaret joined her.

"I thought I knew about hospice from Ernie's death and all, but that was in our home—this is very different. Before I came here I was sort of afraid it would make me uncomfortable, but I can see myself in these family members and I see Ernie in the patients and it's not scary at all. I'm still not sure what I can do to help, but I'm glad I came, if that's what you mean," Margaret said.

"That's exactly what I mean." Rose looked relieved. "And we're very glad to have you, Margaret. This afternoon, I'm going to sit you down in front of the DVD player. There's a volunteer video I'd like you to watch and then I'll be available to answer any questions you have. Follow me."

Margaret was standing up, having a well-deserved stretch when Rose returned to collect her at four o'clock that afternoon. For two hours, Margaret had absorbed every fact about hospice that her brain could possibly hold. From its beginning in England when the physician Dame Cicely Saunders first cared for the dying, to 1982, when the Medicare hospice benefit began in the United States and on to today when forty-four percent of Americans die in the care of a hospice provider. To Margaret, the rest of the DVD was a blur of mind-numbing statistics and factoids.

God, I hope there's not going to be a test over this.

"Any questions?" Rose asked. Margaret said she'd need a chance to absorb it all—then she's sure she'd have some questions for Rose later. Right now, she was too tired to think. *Maybe later. And when I say later, I mean never.*

They said their goodbyes after Rose confirmed *again* that Margaret would be back the next day. Walking down the driveway, Margaret passed under the portico, in the same way that party goers or Sunday afternoon callers would have arrived at Rockaway House nearly a century earlier. Their Tin Lizzies would have pulled up under the open carport, protecting them and their finery from inclement weather and sheltering their delicate complexions on sunny days.

The lives of the family that built this house could not be further removed from the people who are here now, Margaret thought as she climbed into her car. *Like another galaxy.*

Now it was six-thirty p.m. and by the time Margaret sorted the mail and had her tea, going to bed already sounded like a good idea. And it was encouraging to consider it a welcome retreat after a long and fulfilling day, not just an excuse to escape reality. A bowl of soup leftover from Sunday dinner and a quick bath later, Margaret crawled under the covers, a book in her hand, although she didn't really believe she'd be awake long enough to read it.

Margaret was a fairly regular prayer while she was growing up. Then she wasn't. Then, when Ernie's cancer was diagnosed, she was. The habit had wavered a bit since then. She didn't know if God even realized it, but sometimes they weren't speaking—he and she. There'd been some hurt feelings over something she thought he might have done—or not prevented—although she couldn't be sure. Theirs was a complicated relationship.

Tonight, she really felt like checking in. All in all, Margaret would put this day in the Good column. She wasn't fully convinced of how she could be of service at Rockaway House, but she was glad she'd gone there. And that was something. Actually, that was a pretty big something for Margaret.

She closed her eyes and jumped right in. She wondered if God had noticed how long it'd been since she'd called, but she decided not to bring it up and make a big deal of it. She asked God to watch over all the people she loved and those who love her and to especially watch over the residents of Rockaway House.

Then Margaret took a deep breath and included something in her prayer for the very first time, something she had never before thought was missing in her life: she asked God to guide her path and help her to discover her true purpose, now that it was no longer being married to Ernie, which had been a very satisfying and worthy way to spend her life, until last spring. Just for good measure, she mentioned Ernie again by name at the end. She'd heard once that people who have died appreciate being prayed for, which made perfect sense. *Amen.*

Margaret had accepted Rose's suggestion to visit Rockaway House for a few days in a row until she got her feet wet. Then Margaret could decide on a regular schedule.

I won't be doing this more than one day in a row without a good night's sleep—which didn't seem to be happening. Just a few hours into the night, Margaret was wide awake, nowhere close to dozing off again. Not an infrequent event, but for the past few months she'd had the option to sleep in the next morning. That fallback plan wouldn't work this time. She was expected at Rockaway House at eight sharp.

She looked at the bedside alarm clock. Three a.m.

"Up for some television, Maxine?" Opening one eye and looking slightly perturbed, Maxine repositioned herself at the foot of the bed, turning her backside to Margaret. *Guess not.* Margaret sat up, propped Ernie's pillow behind her own, and clicked on the television that sat atop the dresser. Every time she did that, she remembered how it came to be there. With the side effects of the chemo treatments, Ernie had started spending most of his days in bed. Up until then, they'd never been ones for having a television in the bedroom, but Margaret had surprised Ernie with this twenty-one inch combination TV/DVD and Ernie hadn't protested.

"We've had plenty of surprises in the past year, haven't we, Ernie?" Margaret smiled as she spoke. "I'd be okay with things being normal for a while. How about you?" *Stupid question.*

A rerun of *Barney Miller* was just beginning. Margaret liked that show, Ernie had loved it. *Good, something we can both watch.* Margaret leaned back and smiled.

Lois

Not a lie, exactly. No, no, Lois was saying to Ray, only what was the point of worrying Carlene when they weren't sure how it would all shake out? She didn't have to twist Ray's arm. They told Carlene that Lois had "an issue" with her kidneys but they expected she'd be feeling much better soon. That was the truth. There was definitely an issue and they both had high expectations.

Three days a week Lois was hooked up to a dialyzer at the Chesterton Medical Center Renal Clinic. In essence, it was a remote artificial kidney that filtered her blood and returned it to her body. The rigid Monday/Wednesday/Friday schedule became the new normal for her and Ray. Lois no longer had much of an appetite first thing in the morning, so they spent that time reading the paper and having a chat before heading to the dialysis clinic or to the usual business of life on the off days.

Ray had every intention of staying with Lois during her four-hour treatments. She wouldn't hear of it. He was to go do something—anything. He agreed to keep his weekly coffee date with *The Bee* retirees at *Whole Latte' Love.* They talked politics, caught up on the illnesses and passing of acquaintances and critiqued the new generation of journalists. It was easy to see how the Internet had dramatically changed the role of print media. At least once every week one of them said, Thank God we retired when we did. The coffee klatch was just the sort of self-important, supportive diversion in the company of good friends that Ray needed.

On the other days, he sat alone on a bench in Chesterton Memorial Park across from the clinic. He sat and wondered about who the park memorialized since there was no plaque or statue of any kind. Or he thought about Lois and how glad he was that they had each other. Sometimes he meandered down Main Street, stopping in the local shops. He already knew practically every storeowner. He soon got to know the others.

As for Lois, she passed the time listening to audio books. Ray opened an account for her at the downtown bookstore, *Under the Covers,* and convinced one of the store's owners, Noah Smythe, to establish a trade-in program for books that Lois and other customers didn't care to keep. Readers got a small discount on their next audio book and Noah donated the used CDs to the Chesterton Library, which had a special place in the hearts of Noah and his business partner Lisbeth Jones. Good for the customers, good for the store, good for the library.

Lois felt better once the treatments began, no question about that. Then, about two months into it, a clinic nurse asked if Lois had considered home dialysis. It had to be done daily, but it only took about two hours each time. The nurse told Lois that with more frequent home sessions many patients experienced a lessening of side effects such as nausea and fatigue. She thought that overnight dialysis treatments might even be an option for Lois.

Lois got her hopes up until the nurse got to the part about Ray being the "care partner." He would need to take only a few weeks of training along with Lois, the nurse assured her, to be able to assist with every treatment. Lois said she'd think about it, but she never did. Ray had done enough.

When Christmas 2011 came, they told Carlene she needn't plan to come home that year. Ray and Lois had decided to take a Caribbean cruise over the holidays, the one they'd talked about for so long. That was a lie, but done to spare the feelings of a loved one, so more of a kindness than a transgression, if you really thought about it. Although Carlene couldn't recall her parents ever talking about taking a Caribbean cruise, she didn't argue. January was always a big month in the self-improvement/herbology/new age business. She could well use the time in late December to get ready for all the customers who would want to keep their New Year's resolutions by starting a healthy regimen right out of the gate on January 1.

Lois and Ray had a quiet Christmas at home. They invited their closest friends for an intimate Christmas Eve dinner, then just the two of them opened presents on Christmas morning. Since they were meant to be floating out on the open sea, bellied up to a buffet, they were pretty sure Carlene wasn't expecting a call, because it would have to be ship-to-shore, or something complicated like that, wouldn't it?

New Year's Eve was about the same. They had an early dinner out with friends then headed home, intending to watch the one hour-delayed rerun of the Times Square ball dropping at midnight. They didn't make it to midnight. As they headed to bed at eleven-fifteen, Lois reminded Ray that the last time they'd been awake to greet the New Year was December 31, 1999. Remember, because rolling over to the New Millennium had been a really big deal?

Things went pretty well for Lois and Ray for over a year and a half. Then they didn't.

Rockaway House

Too soon to ask for time off?

After only five hours of sleep the night before, Margaret wished she had just one single day of recovery before returning to Rockaway House. On the upside, if there was a difference between plain old fatigue and feeling like there was an anvil strapped to each ankle, this felt more like fatigue, which was good. *Maybe it's just from doing so little since Ernie died. I'm sure I'll get used to this. God, I hope I get used to this.* And for Margaret, a morning that began without all the mental drama of not knowing what might happen next was a welcome relief. One-on-one time with Rose was first on the agenda and they met in the kitchen of Rockaway House at eight o'clock on the dot.

Rooms have personalities, at least Margaret had always thought so. Some are warm and inviting and generous of spirit. Some are off-putting and downright annoying. As Rose led the way through the dining room, Margaret hoped they were headed to one of the former, perhaps the solarium just beyond the living room—with the blinds up—or even the plush conference room. No such luck.

Margaret was sorry to see that the living room's mood hadn't improved any since the day before. Even allowing that it was on the north side of the house, it was exceptionally dark and shadowy. On this visit, though, Margaret was finally able to see that interesting feature at the far end of the room.

"An inglenook!" she exclaimed as she pointed.

Rose followed her gaze. "A what?"

"An inglenook, that area with the benches on either side of the fireplace. What a great place to read a book. Do you have a fire in the winter?"

"No, sorry to say, the fireplaces in Rockaway House don't work. It's a safety hazard. Kinda sad, though, that is a nice spot, now that you point it out," Rose said as she shuffled her papers and found the form she was looking for. "Margaret, I'd like to visit a little about your impressions so far. We try our best to match volunteers with the duty they're most interested in and suited for."

Margaret hesitated. She wasn't accustomed to being asked for or offering her opinion. "Hmmm, I don't know, Rose. I'm pretty good at organizing things, but I liked meeting the patients and their family members. Is it all right if I say I'd rather not be assigned to stuffing envelopes or something like that?"

"It's all right to say anything you want," Rose assured her with a laugh. "I'd never ask a volunteer to do something he or she isn't excited about, and it wouldn't be smart if I did—you wouldn't stick with it. I could see you're comfortable with the dying part, Margaret—to put it a bit bluntly. We're going to have you and two other new volunteers go along tomorrow to visit a patient in a long term care facility, one at home and one in the hospital. We can talk again after that, but if it still sounds good to you, I'll have you work directly with patients."

"I'd like that, Rose. It's funny, because if you'd suggested that before Ernie died, I'd have said 'No way!' Now it seems right somehow," Margaret realized.

"If you ever change your mind, we provide lots of services besides patient care. There's volunteering in homes, and we offer grief counseling for the patients and their survivors. Family members and loved ones are eligible to get bereavement services for at least a year after the patient's death, if any of those interest you now or in the future."

"I've already been invited to join a grief support group." Margaret had been contacted by a hospice volunteer every two or three weeks after Ernie died, with the offer of bereavement group or individual counseling. Margaret had declined, with intention. She'd felt bad about it, like turning down a second helping from a hostess who'd obviously worked hard to prepare dinner. But she really did hope that issue was settled. Just to make sure, she added, "To be honest, it's just not my thing."

"We do ask that every volunteer sit in on a support group at least once, but that doesn't mean you have to permanently join. There's a five-thirty meeting for adults later this week. How about sitting in on it, then you'll know what it's all about if a family member ever asks you?" Rose gently prompted.

"Oh, sure. In the conference room?"

"Yes. And here are a couple more volunteers I'd like you to meet." In the living room door walked a woman in her forties, smiling widely, hand extended. Just behind her was another volunteer, younger and more reserved. Rose introduced Beverly and Amanda.

Beverly's seventy-nine-year-old mother-in-law had died in hospice care. She'd suffered a severe stroke, and once it was clear that her brain damage was extensive and irreversible, family members made the decision to remove her respirator and she passed away three weeks later. Until then, Beverly thought hospice was meant only for cancer patients. A stay-at-home mom, now an empty nester, Beverly was looking for some meaningful volunteer work. Today was her third visit to Rockaway House.

Amanda was twenty-eight and also a stay-at-home mother. Her children were small, three and four years old, and her husband had joined the staff of Chesterton Medical Center only four weeks earlier, the newest oncologist. When their second child was born, Amanda and her husband agreed that once he finished his residency and was working full-time, she would take one day a week for herself, hiring a sitter for the kids. Amanda's husband had been surprised, but not shocked, when Amanda told him she wanted to spend her free time volunteering at Rockaway House. She'd started coming there the week before.

Rose told the three women about the corporate structure of Chesterton Community Hospice (CCH). The whole operation was managed by the

Executive Director Lauren Dunlap (a bit of a spitfire, Rose said), who answered to a board of directors. All the medical and support staff not working at Rockaway House was in the corporate headquarters, adjacent to the Chesterton Medical Center (CMC). Rose added the editorial comment, "Far from the maddening crowd."

Margaret knew that hospice care was provided at Rockaway House, in patients' homes, nursing homes or in the hospital. But until Rose told them, Margaret didn't know that CCH also provided the Medicare respite benefit that allows a patient to come to Rockaway House for up to five days. It gives caregivers a chance to get away or at least have a break. And whenever Rose spoke of caregivers, her demeanor visibly changed. She had been one herself.

"I know that each of you has a personal history with the death of a loved one in hospice care. I wouldn't presume to speak for you, but for me, it was a great privilege to be there when my husband James died, and now I have the honor of helping others on their journey." Rose looked down, digging in her pile of papers to find her calendar. Margaret, Beverly and Amanda were lost in thought. Rose gave them a moment to reflect and then she asked them to share how they each came to be there that day.

For Margaret, experiencing Ernie's illness and death was, without question, the hardest thing she'd ever done, much worse than losing her parents, who both died after long, rewarding lives. But she'd never before thought of it as a privilege, more an obligation that she had willingly assumed. Yes, Rose was exactly right, it had been an honor to be with Ernie on his final journey.

Beverly's mother-in-law had lived two states away and, in spite of over twenty years of shared holidays, she and Beverly weren't really close. When her mother-in-law suffered the stroke, Beverly and her husband Gerry flew to Colorado to be at her side along with Gerry's siblings. The family accepted the irreversible nature of their mother's condition and made the group decision to remove her respirator. Once his mother was breathing on her own, Gerry needed to get home to his accounting business; it was mid-March. Other family members did the same. No one was more than a few hours away, but Beverly remembered well their torment as Gerry and his brothers and sister prepared to return to the pressing matters of daily life.

Without being asked, Beverly informed Gerry that she would remain in Colorado with his mother. Beverly didn't have a job to get back to and the kids were at college, so she could be the family's link to their mother, keeping Gerry and the in-laws apprised daily of her condition. Hourly, if need be.

Beverly sat with her mother-in-law each day, reading a book, talking to her, sometimes holding her hand. As the end approached, all the family members, even most of the grandchildren, returned before the matriarch drew her last breath. Beverly thought she and the in-laws would be closer afterwards. They were grateful for her presence—they said so many times—but when it was over, things went back to the way they'd been before and they weren't closer afterwards. But that was okay, Beverly had stayed behind because that's it was the right thing to do. And who would have guessed that in bearing witness to her mother-in-law's final days, Beverly had sensed the answer to the question she'd been asking since her children had left home: *What next?*

In September of 2011, Amanda's best friend since childhood, Wendy, died of ovarian cancer. It was the first funeral Amanda had ever attended. She still had her parents, grandparents and every one of her aunts, uncles and cousins. Leading up to that mind-numbing event, Amanda had visited Wendy every day, usually taking the two little ones along. They were always glad to see Aunt Wendy, even as she lay in a hospital bed in her parents' family room, under hospice care for the last three weeks of her life. Watching Wendy die a slow, sometimes painful, death changed Amanda forever and sharing her experience with her husband had changed the young oncologist forever as well.

When they finished, the three women looked at each other and smiled empathetically, then Rose spoke.

"At the top of the stairs, the room on the northwest corner of this house is where my husband James passed away. I've been in it a thousand times since he died seven years ago. Never once have I walked into that room without thanking him for dying with such courage and for bringing me here to have Rockaway House become such an important part of my life. I hope that one day you'll each feel the same, that your loved one's death was ultimately part of making your life more fulfilling."

At noon, the three volunteers filed silently to the kitchen. They hadn't expected to hear the stories they heard from each other because up until then, none had considered how anyone else came to volunteer at Rockaway House. Their journeys were different in many ways, but so similar in one essential aspect: they had all witnessed the passing of another person in compassionate hospice care. Much more than just a shared experience, it had been life changing for each one of them.

And secretly, until now all three had been dreading what they knew was coming the next day, the visit to a long-term care facility. Margaret had definite pre-conceived ideas about nursing homes. It was a frightening unknown for Amanda—she had never even been inside one before. And Beverly was convinced that the lovely facility where her mother-in-law died was the exception, not the rule. Now they could see that they needn't be anxious and they decided tomorrow's visits would probably turn out just fine. That was a relief. That was something they hadn't expected.

Margaret, Beverly and Amanda ate their lunches together and began to share more about themselves. When the conversation turned to the subject of pets, Margaret told them how she and Ernie had ended up with Maxine, and sitting there, in the kitchen of Rockaway House, they all laughed out loud. They hadn't expected that either.

Miss Lil

"The time of my end approaches. I have lately been subject to attacks of angina pectoris; and in the ordinary course of things, my physician tells me, I may fairly hope that my life will not be protracted many months. Unless, then, I am cursed with an exceptional physical constitution, as I am cursed with an exceptional mental character, I shall not much longer groan under the wearisome burden of this earthly existence." Her head slowly lowered to the pillow, her silver hair circling her face like a halo. Sheryl the nurse shook her head in amazement as she listened to the elderly woman.

"Now, now, Miss Lil, I hope you'll be with us for a while yet." Sheryl finished making notes on her tablet and turned to leave the room. "Is there anything I can do for you while I'm here?"

"No."

"Remember, I'm Sheryl, and if you push that little button there by your head, it will call me if you need anything. All right, Miss Lil?"

Lil nodded.

Sheryl left the door ajar. Alzheimer's is certainly an unpredictable disease, she thought to herself as she returned to the nurses' station.

Who was that? She looked so familiar. Everyone looks familiar. Little wonder. In ninety-four years, I've seen almost every possible combination of human features that God could come up with, so all faces look familiar to me. And just because I can't remember someone's name doesn't mean I'm off my rocker, does it?

They think I don't see it, but I see the look on their faces, the look that means they don't think I get what's going on here. But I do. Just because I'm ninety-four doesn't mean I have dementia. Who came up with that word? We used to just say people were 'getting on.' Dementia? Does that mean they think I'm demented? Doesn't that mean they think I'm 'crazy'? I'm not crazy. I'm ninety-four. Maybe they should walk even a little ways in my shoes. When they have all the memories and facts in their brains that I have, well, I'd just like to see how they'll perform. I doubt if I'll still be here, though.

This is a nice room. I don't recognize this room. I don't recognize anything in it. Where am I? I'm going to shut my eyes and imagine my own room in our house on Meadow Lane. I know that room. That's where I choose to be. I can be wherever I choose. All I have to do is close my eyes.

Rose paused in the hallway and shared some of Lillian Dexter's background before she sent Margaret into the room. "Miss Lil's been diagnosed with Alzheimer's disease for about five years. Her niece is her guardian—she doesn't have any other family in the area. She's been living at Rolling Hills Retirement Center for the past five years. Now her Alzheimer's is somewhat advanced, but the real issue is that she's been diagnosed with severe congestive heart failure and her niece brought her here to make sure she's comfortable at the end. She probably doesn't have much longer."

Rose went her way and Margaret stepped into the room. Not sure if Lil was asleep, she spoke softly, gently putting her hand on Lil's arm.

"Miss Lil? It's Margaret, a volunteer. Are you awake?"

Lil opened her eyes and looked up, smiling.

"Miss Lil, how are you doing? I wondered if you'd like me to read to you or if there's anything I can do for you."

I don't think I know this person. But she looks familiar. "Have we met before?"

"Yes, well, no, this is the first time I've visited you."

Well, she seems a bit confused. She still looks familiar. "If you would read to me, I would like that."

"Sure," Margaret said. "What would you like me to read?"

"There's a book right there. Yes, that one."

Margaret picked up the small volume on Lil's bedside table. "*The Lifted Veil*, by George Eliot? This looks interesting. Where would you like me to start?"

"It's always best to start at the beginning, don't you think, dear?"

"Yes, okay. Let's see," Margaret began to read from the tiny volume. "'*The time of my end approaches. I have lately been subject to attacks of angina pectoris; and in the ordinary course of things, my physician tells me, I may fairly hope that my life will not be protracted many months . . .*'"

Now, see, that's familiar. I know this passage. This lady has a nice voice. It sounds so familiar to me. "What's your name?" Miss Lil interrupted Margaret's reading.

"Margaret."

"Margaret. Margaret. Margaret, have you noticed how time goes faster the older you get?"

"I have absolutely noticed that, Miss Lil. What explains that, do you think?"

"I think it's the Bushel Basket of Apples Theory, Margaret."

"I don't think I'm familiar with that."

"Really? You're not? That's odd. When you have just one apple in your basket, it's one hundred percent of the apples. When you have a hundred apples, an apple is just *one* percent of the contents of the basket. So days are like apples, except there are thousands of them in your memory basket. So, the more you have, the smaller each one seems. That makes sense, doesn't it, Margaret?"

Actually, it does. "That does make sense, Miss Lil. I've noticed that myself."

"I had a visitor this morning."

"You did? Who was that?"

"My sister, Ivabelle. It was so odd, she had a turban on her head and I said 'What's under that thing on your head?' and she said, 'Oh Lil, you don't want to see my head, I look like Yul Brynner in *The King and I*.' And then she left. It was the oddest thing."

"Does your sister live close by?"

"No, she lives in . . . She lives . . . I can't remember where she lives." *See, this is what I mean. I know I know this but I just can't find the right word. But I know I know this.* Miss Lil began to softly sing, "*Meet me in St. Louie, Louie, meet at the fair.*" Margaret laughed aloud.

"Your sister lives in St. Louis? That's quite a trip to visit you. Is she still in town?"

"Who?"

"Your sister, Ivabelle."

"I don't know." Miss Lil spoke softly and her voice drifted off a bit.

Margaret waited a moment. She wasn't sure if the conversation had ended. She waited another moment, then she began to read again. "*Unless, then, I am cursed with an exceptional physical constitution, as I am cursed with an exceptional mental character, I shall not much longer groan under the wearisome burthen of this earthly existence. If it were to be otherwise—if I were to live on to the age most men desire and provide for—I should for once have known whether the miseries of delusive expectation can outweigh the miseries of true provision. For I foresee when I shall die, and everything that will happen in my last moments.*" Margaret glanced over at Miss Lil. She seemed to be listening intently, her head turned slightly in Margaret's direction. Margaret continued. "*Just a month from this day, on September 20, 1850, I shall be sitting in this chair, in this study, at ten o'clock at night, longing to die, weary of incessant insight and foresight, without delusions and without hope—*"

Miss Lil interrupted Margaret again. "Do you know how long I'm going to be here? I need to get home."

"No, I'm sorry, Miss Lil, I don't. Do you mean you need to go back to Rolling Hills?"

"Yes. No. I'm not sure. I just know I need to get home. Why doesn't someone come to take me home?"

"I don't know about that, Miss Lil. We're very glad to have you here with us right now." *Let me think. What's a good diversion?* "Miss Lil, do you have family here in town?" *Shoot, Rose told me they're all gone.* "Do you come from Chesterton originally?"

"I don't have family here anymore. I was born in Chicago. Mama died having my baby brother when I was eight. Papa's the luthier for the Chicago Symphony."

"I'm sorry, the 'luthier'?"

"He repairs all the string instruments. He works for Mr. Stock, the Musical Director. My brother and my sister and I each play the violin. But I don't like classical music, I like Broadway musicals. That makes Papa mad because he wants me to play with the symphony, but I don't want to. I want to be in *Porgy and Bess.* And you know what? Isaac Stern—he's a concert violinist, you know—he had dinner at our house when he played with the symphony, and Papa made me play my violin with him. He recorded *Bess, You Is My Woman Now* and it made me laugh when I heard that. Papa didn't get to hear it, but I can't remember why. My Aunt Sylvia moved in with us, she's a spinster, and she helps Papa take care of us." Lil was looking past Margaret, probably seeing faces from long ago. Then she came back to the present and turned her head in Margaret's direction.

"My husband, my children, my brother and every aunt, every uncle, every friend I've ever known are all dead. Soon I will be, too, and I can't wait to see them all and have my mother hug me and kiss my husband and my babies. I don't have family here anymore," Miss Lil said, finishing her look back at the decades.

Margaret hardly knew what to respond to first. She made a mental note to question Rose about Miss Lil's diagnosis. Margaret was no expert, but this didn't seem like any advanced Alzheimer's she'd ever known of.

"Has your husband been gone for long, Miss Lil?"

"Oh yes, Leroy died in the war on September 5, 1944. He was a pilot. I was twenty-six and he left me with two babies—not that he wanted to leave me. He's been gone a very long time. He was so handsome. Now every time something really big happens in my life, I lose him all over again. Why is that?"

The day after tomorrow is the anniversary of her husband's death, Margaret realized. She was very aware of such things these days. *I don't see any reason to point that out to her.* "I don't know, Miss Lil. I've been widowed for just a few months, so it's all new to me. Do you still miss him?" Margaret asked, not sure she wanted to hear the answer.

"Oh my, yes. Whenever something important happens, like our children growing up or moving away from home or getting married, I think about what it would be like if Leroy were here with us, or I wonder if things would have been different if Leroy hadn't died and it hurts all over again. I miss him every day."

"And your children, are they still living?" Margaret asked.

"No, they both went on ahead. My daughter, Esther, passed away on October 6, 1992—I was seventy-four—and my son, Richard, died on February 23, 1997—I was seventy-nine. They're right there!" Miss Lil pointed over Margaret's shoulder.

Oh my God. Margaret clutched. *I've heard of this, people who are dying being visited by those who have passed.* Margaret didn't know what to do. If she couldn't see the children as well, should she pretend she did? Margaret was guessing Miss Lil wasn't someone who would be easily fooled. Of course, if Margaret *did* see Miss Lil's dead children, that was a whole other issue. Margaret pivoted on her chair, slowing turning in the direction Miss Lil was pointing.

"The one on the left is my Esther. The other picture is of the two of them. Of course, they were very young then."

Margaret let her breath back out. She stood up, went to the dresser and brought the two framed photos back to Miss Lil. "They're certainly beautiful children, Miss Lil."

"It's not right, you know, it's out of order." Lil jabbed a finger in Margaret's direction for emphasis as she looked down at the pictures.

"Out of order? I'm sorry, I don't know what you mean."

"Children dying before parents. It's out of order. It defies logic. The order of things is out of order. Here I still am and they're gone. It's upside down, don't you see?"

"I'm sure it feels that way. My husband and I didn't have any children, but it must have been heartbreaking for you."

"I think it was. I'm not sure. Luckily, I can't remember," Miss Lil said with a shrug and a smile.

Never mind about talking to Rose.

"All I know is, they're all gone and I'm left here."

"Seeing them again is certainly something to look forward to, isn't it?" Margaret said as she reached out and took Lil's hand in hers. Lil smiled sweetly when Margaret touched her. Lil's hand was pale, veined, age-spotted. Margaret's was all those things, just not quite as vivid. She hoped someone would be holding her hand when her time came. She hoped she'd be in a place like Rockaway House with people like the ones she was getting to know.

Then it looked as if Miss Lil might have fallen asleep. Her eyes were closed, although her lips were moving ever so slightly.

Maybe she's having a sweet dream, Margaret thought. She tucked the covers around Miss Lil and tiptoed out. Margaret would try to stop back later. In fact, she was looking forward to it.

Summertime, and the livin' is easy. Fish are jumpin' and the cotton is high. Your daddy's rich and your mamma's good lookin'. So hush little baby, don't you cry.

Margaret

Margaret could've just bopped Ernie whenever he said, "It's all part of Nature's beautiful pageant," which had been one of his favorite expressions. Margaret didn't like to even acknowledge—let alone ponder—the whole pathetic deconstruction process that came along with getting older. From Margaret's perspective, Ernie had aged gracefully—like most men—not all lumpy and saggy and dull like most women. *Or is it just me?*

It was shortly after Margaret turned sixty, which was six years after Ernie turned sixty. She told him there was something they needed to discuss, because, you see, she'd just finished watching *Driving Miss Daisy.* That was the day they swore that neither one would ever send the other one to a nursing home, the old-school term they'd grown up with. The memories of visits to parents and grandparents were tattooed onto Ernie and Margaret's brains. Now they were called "long-term care facilities," "retirement communities with continuum of care" or "God's waiting rooms" but the indelible impressions hadn't changed: sad, smelly, impersonal, disrespectful, undignified, hopeless, depressing. Ernie and Margaret shook hands on their pledge. Margaret could still remember how good that felt. It was settled, once and for all.

Then Ernie got cancer.

Every day for the last three weeks of Ernie's life, Margaret went to sleep and woke up knowing there was a good chance she'd have to break her promise to him. She finally understood that when they'd made that pact, they didn't appreciate the level of fatigue the one doing the sending (in their case, as it turned out, Margaret) would be experiencing. She had been completely exhausted and she couldn't possibly make Ernie understand how exhausted—not that she would try to. Not that he would argue the point with her if she had. Ernie wouldn't, and that's why Margaret couldn't ask him to let her out of their bargain because she knew he would do just that without hesitating. That's the kind of guy he was.

The thing is, as he lay dying, Ernie wanted Margaret at his side twenty-four hours a day and honestly, that's where she wanted to be. With the help of friends and family, the never-ending laundry got done and the groceries got bought. But as well-meaning as those people were, they couldn't sleep for Margaret, and anyway, she didn't want to be relieved of her duties. As Ernie's caregiver all she asked was the energy to perform every caregiving task herself. It was the least she could do—Ernie was doing all the suffering. Margaret also wanted time to hold his hand, to lie in bed by his side, to whisper in his ear that he would soon be at peace.

To be perfectly honest, if Ernie hadn't died when he did, Margaret was pretty sure she couldn't have kept him at home. The hospice worker told her that yes, taking Ernie to Rockaway House was a possibility, but only if there was no one else on the waiting list who needed inpatient care.

"I don't understand. What's inpatient care?" Margaret had asked.

"Inpatient care is when someone needs continuous pain control or the symptoms require more complex attention. Otherwise, Medicare doesn't pay for someone in Ernie's condition to be in a facility like Rockaway House." Fine. Then Margaret would pay. She was pretty sure they had the money to pay.

That wasn't so much the issue as availability, the hospice aide explained. They took qualifying inpatients first. It was possible, she said, if someone had no other options, but Margaret did: a long-term care facility.

You mean a nursing home, Margaret had said with a sickening feeling of defeat.

But the conversation turned out to be a complete waste of time and mental energy. Ernie died before Margaret reached the very end of her rope. She liked to think maybe she never would have reached it.

Maybe no matter how long he'd lived, I could have done it.

Even knowing it was bad luck to rock an empty rocking chair, she often thought of how awful it would have been to leave Ernie in the care of strangers, giving him up to the place they'd envisioned when they'd made that naive promise to each other. That would have meant going home to an empty house and not being able to check on Ernie anytime she wanted to.

Quit thinking about bad stuff that either didn't happen or never will. Oh, okay, why didn't I just suggest that sooner?

Margaret looked down at Maxine, spread eagle on the cool linoleum kitchen floor. "You really are a sad thing, aren't you?" Margaret said as she gave Maxine's neck a scratch.

The past few months hadn't been all that easy for Maxine, either. While Ernie lay in his hospital bed in the living room, Maxine had kept a watchful eye from a short distance, curled up in his recliner. After Ernie passed away, that's where she stayed for weeks, refusing to be coaxed onto the bed with Margaret. At some point, Maxine gave up or moved on or forgot or got closure or something, and now she wouldn't go near the recliner. "Silly old thing." Margaret gave her an affectionate pat on the head and walked down the hall to the bedroom. Maxine stood, stretched and followed her.

A few things Margaret had picked up on today made her think it might be a good idea to share some thoughts with God. She told him about Miss Lil, not that he didn't already know about her, but Margaret had to ask: Would it be possible for Margaret to not still miss Ernie so badly—she quickly did the math in her head—in sixty-eight years like Miss Lil missed her husband? Not that Margaret would be around that long, but God knew what she meant. Or, if that's the way it had to be, would God be willing to hear from Margaret—often—because being so sad for the rest of her life seemed like a very long road ahead. She'd appreciate any help she could get and she had decided that from now on she wouldn't be afraid to ask for it. No sir, not anymore. *Amen.*

Rockaway House

Dying wasn't the only reason people came to Rockaway House. They also came to learn and they came to vent. Classes for volunteers and staff and grief support gatherings for families were held in its conference room. CCH volunteers who would be serving somewhere other than at Rockaway House came for presentations and for Margaret's favorite part of the training: "shadowing." This morning, Margaret, Amanda and Beverly were trailing along with Rose and a visiting hospice nurse, Lottie Smith.

The van door opened and they all stepped out at Rolling Hills Retirement Center. Rose and Lottie led the way and the three volunteers cautiously inhaled as they entered the long term care facility. Big relief. It was fresh smelling and bright and the first staff member they met was four-legged, a border collie who greeted them at the door, tail wagging. Amanda knelt down to meet him face-to-face as Rose and Lottie checked in at the front desk. Their small caravan traipsed down the hall to meet Rachel, who was in the final stages of ALS, Lou Gehrig's Disease.

Rachel could no longer speak and communicated with the use of an alphabet board. Rose introduced the volunteers and visited with Rachel while Lottie reviewed her medical chart and briefly examined her. As they prepared to leave, Rose asked if they could do anything for Rachel. Her only response was a crooked smile as she slowly pointed out the letters P-R-A-Y. Rose held Rachel's hands and the others bowed their heads as Rose spoke a prayer for God's peace and comfort for Rachel. Then she assured Rachel that she would continue to be in their thoughts and prayers.

While Lottie conferred inside with the Rolling Hills nurse, the four others left and waited next to the van in the late summer sunshine. Rose continued the volunteers' education. "We have a daily census of fifteen to twenty-five patients at any one time. With five patient rooms at Rockaway House, the others are in their own homes or a long-term care facility like this or in the hospital."

Amanda was the first to say what the other two were also thinking.

"That wasn't what I expected in there. That's a very nice place. I always thought—well, you know."

"It's certainly different than the nursing homes I've been in," Margaret chimed in. "When Ernie was dying I was terrified of him going to a nursing home. But he would have been fine here." Finally, she could stop rocking that empty chair.

Rose more than understood. "Because of his condition, I was able to take James to Rockaway House when I couldn't care for him at home anymore, but he and I had looked at the long-term care facilities in the area before he got bad. We knew this is where we wanted him to come—if he had to. I can tell you, Margaret, they're not all as nice as Rolling Hills, but it's a nonprofit facility with a foundation and that makes a big difference. It's expensive to provide good skilled care without charitable dollars to help, especially if they're willing to accept Medicaid patients who can't pay on their own."

Back into the van and on to Chesterton Medical Center.

Lucille was eighty-five. She'd suffered a stroke during hip replacement surgery a week earlier and never woke up. After she'd been on a respirator for two days, her family gathered to discuss Lucille's options. The doctor conceded there was virtually no chance of her arousing from this coma with functions intact. Lucille's daughter Penny finally settled the matter with this question: "If Lucille were your mother, doctor, what would you do?" He said he would hope to honor her wishes while keeping in mind his duty to help her medically, if possible.

Was it possible to help her medically, Penny asked.

No, he admitted.

Lucille's advance directives clearly stated that she wanted no life-prolonging measures. Penny laughed and said her mother had been heard to say many times over the past couple of years that her lease on life was month-to-month—she no longer bought green bananas. Twenty-four hours ago, her children and grandchildren had gathered, said their goodbyes and the respirator was removed. Lucille's breathing was now shallow and her blood pressure barely registered. Her time was short. Being moved was neither practical nor humane, so she would remain at the Chesterton Medical Center under the joint care of the hospice and hospital staffs. They were accustomed to serving side-by-side. They all worked for the same parent corporation, and as importantly, they all lived in the same community.

Lottie tended to the details of Lucille's chart. The CMC nurse assured her there were no signs that Lucille was in pain and her daughter agreed. Penny sat by, a book in her lap, watching as people moved around her mother's bed. Margaret, Amanda and Beverly stood off to the side, observing.

The duties of the visit completed, Rose and Lottie said their goodbyes, making the usual offer to do whatever they could for Penny or her mother or the family. Penny looked up, her eyes misting over as she spoke.

"You've done so much already. I don't know if you realize what it means to have Mother here, with such loving people caring for her. We could not have asked for a better passing for her." She stood and hugged Rose and Lottie.

The last stop of the afternoon was at the home of Sylvester Edmonds, a hospice patient dying of prostate cancer. Now age seventy-two, Sylvester had undergone extensive chemo and radiation and had been in remission for two years. When the cancer returned, he and his wife Dolly made the decision to enjoy what time they had left and do nothing further to treat his cancer. Sylvester was now too frail to leave the house, although he was sitting up in a chair in the living room when they arrived.

Lottie entered first. "Hello, Sylvester. It's good to see you. I want you and Teresa to meet three more CCH volunteers. This is Beverly, Amanda and

Margaret." A middle-aged woman sitting on the couch rose and shook their hands. "Sylvester, where's Dolly gotten to today?" Lottie asked as she began to make notes on her tablet computer.

Sylvester said his wife had gone to get her hair done, then to the grocery store. He and Teresa were reading the paper and were going to have a bite of lunch before his wife returned. While the others visited, Lottie was doing her medical thing, checking Sylvester's vitals and then asking him about symptoms.

Back in the van, Lottie commented that she'd be recommending more frequent visits now that Sylvester's condition was rapidly deteriorating. CCH personnel had already conducted a home evaluation, and Lottie thought it was time to have a hospital bed delivered. Sylvester and his wife were fine with the idea and had the space. CCH had also verified that Sylvester's long-term care insurance would supplement Medicare to provide nursing and home services as he and Dolly needed more help. Like most comprehensive medical centers these days, CMC had a home health care division that handled equipment and care needs.

"Tell us what Teresa is doing," Amanda asked.

Rose explained that CCH volunteers such as Teresa provide many services that Medicare doesn't cover. Sitting with a patient or fixing a light meal while the caregiver takes a break is one example. Some don't even leave the house during that time, they just use the opportunity to get laundry done or take a shower or relax, knowing their patient is safe. It's good for the patients as well because they get to see a different face and know that their loved one is having a well-deserved break.

"Family caregivers," Rose said with a sigh as she turned around and looked at the three in the back seat of the van. "Unpaid caregivers are the overlooked heart of the hospice mission. Without them, medical care in this country would not be what it is. For that matter, without them, CCH wouldn't exist."

"God bless the caregivers," Margaret said under her breath.

Caleb

When Caleb Bronson's senior year at Chesterton High School began, he attracted a lot of attention. A bald seventeen-year-old isn't something you see every day. He'd been working hard to grow some fuzz, then he had to quit school a month ago. After that it hadn't much mattered.

Rose and Margaret knocked on his door and got a "Come on in!" The six-foot teen was resting in bed, leaning on his elbow, dressed in sweatpants and a tee shirt, covers thrown aside. Tracy, Caleb's best friend—a friend who happened to be a girl, but not his girlfriend—was finishing her breakfast, a fast food egg burrito, but Rose noticed there were no signs of breakfast near Caleb.

He and Tracy looked up and smiled as Margaret and Rose entered.

"Hi, ladies!" Caleb grabbed the television remote from the bed and lowered the volume on a *Three Stooges* episode.

"Uh-oh—we're interrupting Mo, Curly and Larry. Sorry." Rose ducked down as she passed in front of the television.

Tracy laughed, "It's okay, Rose. We've seen this one about a zillion times. Hi, Margaret. How's it going?"

"Fine, Tracy. How are you two doing?" Margaret stepped forward to introduce herself to Caleb and visit while Rose freshened his untouched water pitcher, collected the trash from Tracy and discreetly left a glass of ice chips at Caleb's bedside. "Stooges fans, eh? My husband Ernie couldn't get enough of them. I think it's mostly a guy thing. What do you think, Tracy?"

Tracy grinned. "I think you're right, Margaret."

Rose finished her tasks. "No breakfast today, Caleb?"

"No. I'm still having a little trouble swallowing. I'm waiting for Dr. Bob to call in. We're gonna talk about my options." Caleb's voice was hoarse and to Rose, he seemed surprisingly delicate. Sheryl had mentioned to her just this morning that he hadn't eaten since the day before, so his appearance wasn't really unexpected, but still disappointing.

"Okay, you two. Anything at all we can get for either one of you?"

Caleb and Tracy exchanged a conspiratorial look. Caleb gave her a little nod and Tracy spoke, "We do want to talk to you about something, Rose, but we're not quite ready. In a day or so?"

"Whenever and whatever. You know that. We better let you two get back to the Stooges."

"Soitenly!" Caleb said in his best Curly impersonation, grinning and reaching for the remote.

Rose rolled the cart ahead of them; Margaret followed and closed the door as they left. They walked in silence a few steps, then Rose finally answered Margaret's unspoken question.

"Caleb has damage to his throat from radiation treatments. He's having some trouble swallowing. They're talking about maybe using a feeding tube."

Margaret stopped in her tracks. Every time she thought she understood the boundaries of hospice care, she was reminded of how little she knew. "A feeding tube? How is that possible? I thought that was one of the life-prolonging measures that isn't used in hospice. The hospice nurse spoke to Ernie and me about that not being an option." She quickly added, "Not that it mattered, of course, because Ernie didn't want force-feeding of any kind."

"We call it 'artificial nutrition'," Rose gently corrected, "because 'force' feeding would never be a part of compassionate hospice care. In this case, if Dr. Reese says tubal feeding is an option and Caleb's parents consent, we'll do it because it can provide nutrition and it might make him more comfortable. It won't be done to prolong his life—and, frankly, most likely it wouldn't anyway. It's another form of palliative care, something done to give the patient comfort. Caleb is dying of leukemia and tubal feeding won't help that. Does that make sense?"

Margaret thought for a moment, then slowly nodded. *Maybe.*

As for the next issue on her mind, she was hesitant to stick her nose where it didn't belong, but how else would she gain insights on the perspective of a young person—or any person—at the end of life? "Those two are certainly old souls," she observed. "What do you suppose they want to talk to you about?"

"It's hard to say. They're young, they have a unique take on dying. They think about it differently than the older people I've been with," Rose said.

"How so?" Margaret asked.

"They don't deny death, but they're not as eager to accept it, either. They prefer to focus on what's left of life. I don't know, it's just different." Rose's voice broke. "Sorry, but Caleb's an especially tough case for me." She took a moment to compose herself before continuing.

"Would you like to be in on whatever it is they have up their sleeve?" So many hospice volunteers—and professionals—were well-intentioned, but only a few had the passion along with the capacity to deal with the dying and all their emotionally messy issues. Rose sensed that something special in Margaret.

"Definitely. Please keep me posted."

"You bet."

No good deed goes unpunished. Pastor Matt Muller of St. Paul's Lutheran Church was doing a favor for a friend. Reverend Mike Tiffin volunteered his time as chaplain for Rockaway House whenever a patient didn't have a minister and requested spiritual support. (Rabbi Feldman tended to the Jewish patients while Father Walsh was there for the Catholics.) Reverend Tiffin was headed out of town to a Baptist conference for a few days and had asked Matt to make a visit to a member of Mike's congregation.

Would Matt have time to stop by the hospice house and see Caleb Bronson, Mike had wanted to know. His family were long-time members of

First Baptist of Chesterton. Sure, Matt said. Caleb's a great kid, Mike had assured him. Just a typical teenager who happens to have leukemia. Matt was glad to help. Consider it done.

Matt began to get a funny feeling—funny apprehensive not funny ha-ha—when, just as Matt walked into his room, Caleb pulled a list of questions from the pocket of his sweat pants.

A list. Uh-oh. God help me.

"So, how about reincarnation?" Caleb asked.

"Christians don't believe in reincarnation, Caleb."

"Not to be disrespectful, Pastor Matt, but how can you know what every single Christian believes in?"

"What I meant is that the tenets of the Christian religion do not include a belief in reincarnation. There's no biblical foundation for a belief in reincarnation." *So far, so good.*

"Okay. Well, what about God's will? Let's talk about that for a minute."

"All right."

"I'm pretty confused about this whole 'God's plan' thing. Is it God's plan that I have cancer?"

"I don't believe that it is, no. God does not make bad things happen to people, Caleb."

"We believe in prayer, right, Pastor Matt?"

"Lutherans and Baptists both believe in prayer, most certainly."

"And we believe that prayer can make good things happen, right?"

"God answers every prayer."

"Well, he doesn't seem to be answering mine." Caleb didn't sound angry or even argumentative. He was stating a fact. "Since God isn't answering my prayers to cure this cancer—and you can bet my Mom's praying even harder than me—then doesn't that mean it's his will that I have cancer? Why would God want that? I mean, he can cure people, right?"

"Yes, we believe that there are cases of divine intervention, that God has cured many people."

"Then why not me? Why am I dying at eighteen? By the way, Pastor Matt, I'm currently seventeen, but I am definitely planning to be eighteen."

Matt took a deep breath. "I don't know, Caleb. As I said, God answers every prayer, but sometimes it's difficult for us to comprehend God's plan or understand his will."

"But if God has a plan, what good does it do for us to have brains and make choices, if it's all decided ahead of time?"

"Now that's a good question, Caleb, one that's dogged man for many centuries, man's will versus God's will. You might be surprised at my answer: I don't know." Based on the conversation so far, Caleb wasn't all that surprised. He was, however, more than a little disappointed in Pastor Matt—his frown made that clear.

Matt was eager to try and regain some ground. "God gave us minds and souls, so it's up to each of us to choose between good and evil and make our own way. You remember the story of the Garden of Eden, Caleb?"

"Yeah, that didn't work out all that great for Adam and Eve."

"True, but because of that lesson we can view life as a divine balance between man's ability to learn and make Godly choices and God's willingness to assist man, according to his plan. If we have faith that God is watching over us, he'll provide for us, he'll keep us safe—even though we may not fully understand the meaning of his answer to our prayers."

"Oh, I've got a pretty good idea what his answer means for me, Pastor Matt. It means I'm not going to be around here much longer." Caleb's tone was grown up and matter-of-fact.

"Caleb, faith is believing in God's wisdom and love even when it doesn't make sense to us, even when really crummy things happen—like this cancer—to really good people—like you."

"Yeah, I know. We're all dying, right? Just some of us sooner than others?" He gave Matt a big grin. "Okay, here's one."

Matt winced.

"Can people who are dead communicate with people who're still here?"

"You mean, directly as a spirit or through a third party?"

Caleb was open to all possibilities. "Either one, both."

"The bible says we should question people who claim to communicate with the dead, that they are probably false prophets."

"But what about the people themselves, the people who died? Why can't they communicate with us? They don't go *nowhere*, do they?"

"No, certainly they don't go *nowhere*. They've gone to heaven if they were God-fearing Christians, but they're in heaven, Caleb, not floating around Earth. I guess I can't say for sure if people who have died can still communicate with us. What do you think?"

"I think maybe they can. Even if they're in heaven, they still watch over us, don't they?"

"That would be nice, wouldn't it? I just can't tell you that there's anything in the Bible that confirms that."

"What about angels?"

What is this, some twisted Baptist version of Punk'd?

"Angels exist, yes. If you're asking me if our loved ones come back as angels, I don't believe that is the case. Angels are different from departed souls."

"Is it possible to see dead people?"

"You keep asking about that, Caleb. Maybe if you tell me why, I can help. Is it something you wonder about for yourself, for once you've gone to be with God?"

Caleb could see this was going nowhere. He turned back to his list. "Never mind. Let's see."

Matt had to admit it, he was beginning to enjoy this challenge. "What else are you thinking about?"

"Is there a heaven and what's it like?"

"I'm sure you've heard Reverend Mike speak about heaven, haven't you?"

"Yeah, but I'm looking for a second opinion."

Matt pursed his lips to contain his smile.

"Well, first, you don't have to worry about whether there is one and there's absolutely no question about whether you're going there when you leave your earthly body, Caleb. Heaven is about being with God and Jesus, and it will be glorious, more glorious than I could possibly describe to you even if I had seen it with my own eyes. When Jesus wraps his arms around you, you will feel safe and loved and one with God. How does that sound?"

"That sound pretty good, actually . . . But what if you're wrong?"

"But I'm not."

"But what if you are?"

"But I'm not."

"But what if you are?"

"But. I'm. Not." Pastor Matt held up his hand, gently imploring Caleb to let him finish. "Because it's not me saying it, I'm telling you what God has revealed to us through his son, Jesus Christ. Caleb," Matt sat down on the foot of the bed and said a quick silent prayer to find the right words, "I can't begin to know what you're feeling and thinking. You have a heavy burden, but God wants to help you carry that burden. You know, Caleb, God doesn't promise smooth sailing, but he does promise a safe landing. (By the way, I wish I could take credit for that bit of wisdom but I can't.) You gotta have faith, Caleb. That's the name of the game."

Matt could see that Caleb was now studying his hands, not his list. Matt hoped to God he'd finally passed off a gem with that last one.

"Okay, I can buy that, Pastor Matt." Caleb put his hand out to shake on it. Pastor Matt asked Caleb if he'd like to pray with him before he left. Caleb told Pastor Matt not to worry, he did plenty of that on his own, but one more couldn't hurt. So they prayed. Matt prayed for Caleb's comfort and peace as he drew closer to being with God and Caleb prayed that his parents and siblings would start to understand that he wasn't going to be with them much longer.

As Matt walked to his car, he knew at least two things he hadn't known before he came to Rockaway House that day. *I see now why Mike says working here is such a blessing and boy, does he owe me big time . . .*

Margaret

Margaret realized she'd misjudged the situation. Badly.

"I think we might've been way off on the whole nursing home deal, Ernie."

Margaret was sitting up in bed, a book open in her lap. She'd had dinner and a nice long hot bath. And Maxine was settled in for the night as well, glad to warm Margaret's feet at the end of the bed, but hoping to not be disturbed again.

Margaret had the habit of reading in bed, since long before Ernie left her alone. Before he got sick, Ernie was a no television, lights off, out like a doll with rollback eyes kinda guy. He went to sleep immediately. He always claimed he didn't, but he did. Margaret had never been able to do that. She needed the radio or a book to wind down her brain before she got drowsy.

When Ernie moved into the living room to sleep in the hospital bed, Margaret was left with only the bedroom television for company. Those voices had their own addictive quality that Margaret was still trying to wean herself from. Tonight she planned to read a bit before going to sleep, but first she had a few things to get off her chest. She looked over at the picture of Ernie—the two of them, actually, it was their wedding picture—on the dresser next to the television.

"When was the last time we were in a nursing home, Ernie? With your Aunt Betty? Ernie, they've changed, thank God. I was in one today. The hospice patient was a woman with ALS like your cousin Bob. Anyway, it was very nice and didn't smell, and I think if I'd had to, I think I could have taken you there. I never really told you this, but I think we got pretty close to me falling apart. I'm hoping you would have forgiven me for that, as long as I'd taken you to Rolling Hills.

"I really like helping at Rockaway House, Ernie. I wasn't too sure at first, but I think that's just because it was something so outside my comfort zone. You know how much I like change—*not.* I'm meeting all these people who are going through what you and I went through—except they seem a lot more brave than I ever was—or am. The thing is, I'm starting to get what's going on here." Margaret stopped and took a breath. "I have to make the best of whatever life I have left, Ernie. You're gone and there's a huge hole in my heart where you used to be and I need to try and fill it.

"Please don't be hurt by this. I don't want you to think I'm happier now than I was when you were still here with me because I'm not. My best day alone could never stand up to my worst day with you by my side. I just have to figure out the person I'm supposed to be for the time I have left. That's all. I hope you understand. I don't want to be sad for the rest of my life, Ernie. I just don't. I don't think you want that for me, do you? Because I know I wouldn't want it for you."

Then Margaret cried so hard her face ached.

Miss Lil

Peggy promised her mother years ago that she'd keep an eye on Aunt Lil. It made sense for many reasons: Peggy grew up knowing Aunt Lil and spending lots of time with her; Peggy's mother Ivabelle and her big sister Lillian had always been close, at least until Ivabelle moved to St. Louis with her second husband Don, four years after Peggy's father passed away; and Peggy lived in Davenport, only forty miles from Chesterton, so it was no big deal for Peggy to check regularly on Aunt Lil. Peggy told her mom not to worry; she'd look after her sister Lillian.

One day five years ago, eighty-nine-year-old Lil called her attorney as soon as she returned from a trip to *The Marion Street Grocery*. On the way home, she'd had to pull over, park her car, get her bearings and try to remember where she lived. In a few very frightening moments, it had all come back to her, but still . . .

Was everything all right, the attorney had asked. Yes, everything was fine, Lil replied, but would he please explain to her again how that standby guardianship thing worked?

He prepared the paperwork while Lil was still compos mentis, naming Peggy as the standby guardian and conservator. Then Lil waited for the contingency to occur—in her case, the official diagnosis of Alzheimer's disease. She only had to wait six months.

A few legal formalities later and Peggy was Aunt Lil's official substitute decision-maker in all things medical and financial. Lil trusted Peggy and Peggy had willingly agreed to be her fiduciary. Lil's daughter Esther had lived her entire adult life in New Mexico and her son Richard had been career Army. She hardly knew her grandchildren, who lived everywhere but in Iowa, and she'd never even met her great-grandchildren. Practically speaking, Peggy was the only remaining family for Aunt Lil, and eventually Aunt Lil became the only family Peggy had left. They were grateful for each other.

Peggy helped Aunt Lil clean out her house and move to an assisted living apartment at Rolling Hills soon after her Alzheimer's diagnosis. In between her weekly visits, Peggy got the calls when Aunt Lil took a little spill or needed to visit the doctor. Two years after that, Peggy moved Aunt Lil into the memory unit at Rolling Hills and then into the Alzheimer's wing a year later. Less than a week ago, Peggy arranged for Aunt Lil to come to Rockaway House. Almost five years after her original diagnosis, the end was near.

Now Miss Lil was hardly eating but still willing to take an occasional sip of water. The nurse on duty, Rona, greeted Peggy when she arrived that morning, reporting to her that Miss Lil's blood pressure was beginning to drop. Peggy nodded, then said that her aunt's decline the past few years had been heartbreaking, especially because Aunt Lil had been extraordinarily healthy most of her life.

In fact, Peggy told Rona, the only exception Peggy could think of was when they discovered that Aunt Lil had a heart arrhythmia. That happened not long before the Alzheimer's diagnosis, when she was eighty-eight. Her doctor recommended that Lil have an implantable cardioverter defibrillator (ICD) surgically placed in her chest, just under the skin. The small electrical device was wired to Lil's heart, in place to deliver an electrical shock—defibrillation—if Lil suffered cardiac arrest. Peggy and Aunt Lil discussed it at the time. Lil was otherwise healthy and more than willing to get an ICD implanted. Back then, she was no in hurry to die.

That's the only time Peggy could recall Aunt Lil having a medical procedure as long as she'd known her. Looking back, Peggy had to admit that Aunt Lil probably would have decided differently about the ICD if they'd known Alzheimer's was on the horizon. But they hadn't.

Rona stopped what she was doing. While Peggy was speaking, Rona discreetly brought up Miss Lil's medical chart. As she had feared, there was no record of Miss Lil's ICD. As soon as Peggy walked away from the nurses' station, Rona picked up the phone and called Dr. Judith Gold, the physician on duty.

Peggy thought she heard voices as she opened the door to her Aunt Lil's room.

"Aunt Lil, hi. Who were you talking to?"

Lil gave Peggy a warm smile but no response. Then her brow furrowed.

"I'm Peggy."

"Of course you are. I was talking to your Uncle Leroy. He just left."

"Are you sure you weren't dreaming, Aunt Lil?"

"Yes." Peggy recognized that slightly irritated tone. Aunt Lil had seldom doubted herself, most especially over the past five years.

"As long as you're sure. How are you feeling today?" Peggy asked as she put her coat on a chair and sat down next to the bed.

"I think it's time I went home, don't you? I can't stay here forever, you know." Peggy had heard this at least a thousand times. For months after Aunt Lil moved to Rolling Hills, she had wanted to return to the big house on Meadow Lane. Apparently, now that she was at Rockaway House, she wanted to get back to Rolling Hills.

"You think so, Aunt Lil?"

I've forgotten her name again. It starts with a P. I don't want to ask her. Isn't it enough that I know my own name? What is my name? I bet she won't even notice.

"You look like your mother."

"I think you're right, Aunt Lil. When I look at pictures of Mom when she was young, I do look like her. How about a sip of water?" She offered up the glass, but Lil pushed it away. "Are you hungry? Can I get you a snack?"

"I'm not hungry, Peggy." *That's it—Peggy!* "Why doesn't someone come to take me home?"

"Maybe in a day or two, Aunt Lil. How would that be?"

"All right. Why doesn't someone come to take me home?"

"How about a cup of tea, Aunt Lil? What would you think about having a cup of tea like we used to."

"That sounds fine." *I'll drink a cup of tea with that nice girl. I think she might be my sister. Even though I'm not hungry or thirsty. I wonder if Ivabelle is coming back today.*

A few minutes later, Margaret walked in the kitchen as Peggy was searching for cups and saucers.

"Can I help you find something?"

"I think I've got it all. I'm just making a cup of tea for my aunt, Lillian Dexter. I'm her niece Peggy."

"So nice to meet you, Peggy. I'm Margaret. I'm a volunteer here. I was visiting with your aunt yesterday. Actually, I knew her from when she shopped years ago at the grocery store I worked at, but she doesn't remember me, which is understandable. Is her sister still visiting in town?"

"I beg your pardon? Her sister?" Peggy stopped her search.

"She said that her sister—Ivabelle, I think—had visited her."

"I think someone's mistaken, Margaret. Ivabelle was my mother and she passed away eight months ago, in St. Louis." There was a catch in Peggy's voice as she spoke.

"I'm so sorry. It must be your aunt's imagination. She was certainly convincing, though. She was talking about your mother wearing a turban." Peggy reached out for the back of a chair to steady herself.

"Please tell me exactly what my aunt said."

Margaret related the conversation she'd had with Lil the day before, word for word. Peggy just kept shaking her head.

"I don't understand. Two years ago when Mom got sick, she didn't want Aunt Lil to know, so we didn't tell her Mom had cancer. Aunt Lil never knew Mom lost her hair and wore a turban. I didn't tell her when Mom died because she gets so confused about who's alive and who's gone and it upsets her so when she hears about someone passing away. I don't understand."

Margaret didn't either. She was thinking maybe she shouldn't have mentioned it. "I'm sorry, Peggy, I didn't mean to upset you."

Peggy shook her head. She wasn't upset, just puzzled. These days, Aunt Lil spoke often about family members who had "gone on ahead" and how they visited her, sometimes in her dreams, sometimes while she was awake, or so she said. Aunt Lil always seemed thrilled when they stopped by. Peggy had been glad to share the joy of those appearances, even if by proxy and with some skepticism.

Just then the phone on the kitchen wall rang. An inside line, the call was from the nurses' station, Rona asking if Peggy was there. Would Margaret please tell Peggy to stay until Dr. Judy arrived? She wanted to visit with Peggy about something. Margaret said she'd let her know.

Peggy was smiling as Margaret interrupted her thoughts with the phone message. "Sure," Peggy said. "I'm on my way back up. And you didn't upset me, Margaret. That's wonderful, really wonderful news. My mom did come to see Aunt Lil. I was hoping she would. Incredible." She turned back to assembling the tea. As she was leaving, she stopped, set the tray down and gave Margaret a quick hug. "Thank you for telling me that, Margaret. Thank you very much."

"You're welcome." *I definitely want to spend more time with Miss Lil.*

Somebody screwed up. More accurately, several somebodies screwed up. It seemed so obvious, now that Dr. Judy was focusing on the issue. The admissions clerk or the triage nurse or the medical director or somebody should be verifying whether a patient has an ICD. Once a person is in hospice care, having an implanted device that's designed to jump-start the heart if it fails was—to put it mildly—contraindicated. Surely no one would deny that the heart of this ninety-four-year-old woman with congestive heart failure would soon be failing. It was idiotic to think otherwise. Who, for heaven's sake, wished her to be jolted back from eternity when that time came? They were not in the business of causing potential pain or even discomfort to their patients. ICDs and DNRs do not made good bedfellows, Dr. Judy concluded with a shake of her head.

She made a phone call and then headed to Rockaway House.

I just don't remember why I get so confused. Wait, I do remember. I remember seeing Dr. what's-his-name with what's-her-name. I remember him saying I have Alzheimer's. Like I wasn't sitting right there. What's a person supposed to think when they hear something like that? I admitted I was having problems with my memory, it was my idea to see the doctor. Don't they remember that? Maybe I've forgotten a lot, but I've never forgotten how I was at the grocery store and then how on the way home I didn't recognize anything. I've lived in this town for over seventy years. I've been in that grocery store—what's the name of it?—oh, it doesn't matter. I've got to stop trying to remember things that don't need remembering. I was in that—oh, what's the word—well, I know what I mean, I was in that place and that nice lady who always worked there, Margaret—wait just a darn minute—I do know that lady who came into the room today! But she didn't remember me. That's odd. Maybe she has Alzheimer's.

"Here we go, Aunt Lil. I even found some of those little cookies that you like to dunk." Peggy set up their tea party on the bed tray table and rolled it into place. Then she put *My Fair Lady* into the CD player and turned the volume down low.

Lil was propped up on a cloud of pillows in a pink chenille bedjacket, holding her cup of tea, served in a porcelain cup resting on the tray table. It was hard to tell where the translucent flowered cup ended and her finely veined hand began. Peggy thought back on all the tea parties she and Aunt Lil had enjoyed over her lifetime. First, it was cold apple juice in Peggy's child-sized teapot, then she graduated to hot cider, then to hot tea poured from one of Aunt Lil's vintage pots, complete with a quilted tea cozy. Peggy missed those times. And soon she'd be missing Aunt Lil, the last family member she actually knew.

There was a tap at the door and Dr. Judy walked in.

"Hello, Miss Lil. How are you today?"

"I'm not sure. How are you?"

"I'm well. But I do need to talk to Peggy about something."

First apologizing to Miss Lil that she and Peggy would have to wait a bit to finish their tea party, Dr. Judy asked Peggy to follow her into the hall. She explained that they needed to reprogram Lil's ICD as soon as possible so it wouldn't be triggered to start her heart when it failed. Peggy rushed to say she was sorry she hadn't mentioned the ICD before today. Dr. Judy interrupted her with an apology and assured Peggy it wasn't her oversight. Dr. Judy also thought—but didn't say—that thanks to this experience with Miss Lil, they wouldn't be making the same mistake with any future patients.

Peggy agreed that Aunt Lil couldn't really understand what all this was about and Dr. Judy assured Peggy that the procedure would be painless. They went back into Lil's room where they were soon joined by a young specialist from the CMC Cardiac Clinic, carrying what looked like a small laptop computer case. As she set up her equipment, Dr. Judy explained that a wand used to communicate between the ICD and the programming computer would be placed on Miss Lil's chest.

Using radio waves, the technician deactivated the ICD, leaving Aunt Lil's pacemaker still fully functional. It took only a moment. Judging from the blissfully ignorant smile on her face, Miss Lil was clueless, which was exactly what the others were hoping for.

In minutes, the technician had packed up her bag and left, crisis avoided. Dr. Judy thanked Miss Lil and Peggy, left and went directly back to CMC. She put her second call into Lauren Dunlap; this time to let her know everything was under control.

In Lil's room, Peggy smiled and refreshed her cooling tea. "Well, we didn't expect to see Dr. Judy with a magic wand, did we, Aunt Lil? Maybe I should have asked her to conjure up a husband for me while she was here."

"You'll find your true love, honey. Just as I did."

"So, Aunt Lil, speaking of Uncle Leroy, how was he when he stopped by earlier?"

Margaret

The day he retired Ernie vowed that Margaret and he would do all shopping, errand running and milling about in public anytime other than on the weekend. All the same, it was Saturday and Margaret was, as Ernie would have said, out among the working stiffs. Since Rockaway House had come into her life, Margaret didn't have a choice. *As much as we'd like to, it's just not practical to keep some promises, Ernie.*

She'd dropped off a few things at the dry cleaners. She'd stopped at the big discount store to stock up on paper items and cat litter. She'd made an obligatory visit to *Under the Covers*, the only bookstore in Chesterton. There Margaret had reminded herself that she no longer smoked (it had been just that two-day binge during senior year at Chesterton High, but that counted, right?), had only an occasional glass of wine and didn't gamble, so her only splurge/addiction/guilty pleasure was her weekly hardback book purchase at *Under the Covers*. Free Shoes!

Lisbeth and Noah, who owned the store, were so nice, always ready to help with a recommendation (or warning) about the talk show picks. And they had the absolute best coffee and cookies around. This day Lisbeth had waited on Margaret and Margaret thought she seemed unusually quiet.

There's something unique about a fall Saturday in Iowa, Margaret reflected as she made her rounds. The sun is shining, the air is crisp and half the leaves have fallen. There's a comforting familiarity about the musty scent in the air. About one o'clock in the afternoon, you notice how deserted the streets are, and you remember that a large portion of the population is either at a football game or gathered around a big-screen TV with others, watching the game they wished they were at. You're either a diehard football fan (Hawks or Clones or Panthers or Bulldogs—possibly an errant Huskers devotee) or you consider the occasion an opportunity to have some serious alone time. Ernie was the sports fanatic and Margaret wasn't.

She pulled in her driveway and it struck her for the first time that fall also implied raking. Not until this very moment had Margaret remembered that. Always glad to help drag a tarp full of leaves or point to where a shrub should be planted, that was about it for Margaret. Ernie was the yard person.

She unloaded her shopping from the car and came back outside to walk the perimeter of their property. Was there something Ernie did each fall to make sure there was a blooming spring seven months later, Margaret wondered. Was there something she should be doing now?

In the distance, she could hear a lawnmower. She could even hear the broadcast of the Iowa football game not far away. Hawkeye fans had been known to convert garages into game-watching rooms (Margaret always assumed it was at the suggestion of a wife who thought a hoseable surface just made more sense). One of her neighbors must have done that.

Margaret gazed down the street in each direction. Wilmoth Avenue wasn't much different from the Chesterton neighborhood that Margaret grew up in during the post-war Baby Boom. Technically, Margaret wasn't a Boomer since she was born one year before the official beginning of 1946, but she'd been surrounded by thirty-eight other children living in thirteen homes up and down her street. There was always a game of *Red Rover*, *King of the Mountain* (from the top of a picnic table, no less) or *Captain May I?* and always someone available to join in riding bikes, roller skating or building a snow fort. You went outside when you got up, came in occasionally to take nourishment and were expected home once the streetlights came on. Otherwise, parent-child interaction in the 1950s was kept to a minimum, to the assent of both sides of the equation.

Nowadays, young couples weren't so eager to have four or more kids. Who in their right mind ever was, Margaret had often wondered. Oh, there were children growing up on Wilmoth Avenue, just not nearly as many as during the Boom.

There's one now, Margaret noticed.

It was Lenny, the sixteen-year-old who lived three doors down. He was standing in his front yard, leaning on a rake. Margaret waved and called out, beckoning him to her yard. It took Lenny a moment to focus, then he quickly dropped his rake and stowed his ear buds in a pocket, eager for the distraction. Hadn't his mother said just the other day that they should see if Mrs. Williams needed help of any kind since Mr. Williams was gone?

Margaret looked down as Lenny made his way to her, spotting a penny on the sidewalk. *One saved is one earned.* She dropped it in her sweater pocket.

"Lenny, what are you supposed to be up to?"

"Oh, raking, I guess. Anything I can do for you, Mrs. Williams?"

"If you have a minute, I do have something I could use some help with. But I want to hire you, Lenny, no freebies."

No argument on that point.

She'd just come from *Babkas 'r Us*, next door to the bookstore and had a supply of freshly-baked cookies. How about a glass of milk, a cookie and they'd talk? Done, done and done.

Margaret wanted to know about computers, she told Lenny as soon as they were seated at her kitchen table. She wanted to surf the Web, travel the Information Superhighway, eat the whole digital enchilada. She had a feeling there was knowledge there meant for her to find, secondhand experience she could use. Ernie hadn't been a big fan of stepping outside the box, not that he'd ever discouraged Margaret, let alone held her back. Ernie had been one hundred percent supportive of anything Margaret ever wanted to do, but the remote control was as techie as he'd cared to get. Anyway, she'd never before wanted to do this. Now she did.

A dozen cookies and an hour later, Margaret and Lenny were in her car, on their way to the big electronics store in Clinton to look at laptops. Tell me again what a "router" is, Margaret said as she merged onto Highway 30.

That night, Margaret didn't have any trouble getting to sleep once she finally got to bed, once she was finally willing to shut down the new laptop and walk away. It had been a long day and the question of whether to buy a computer was now permanently settled.

Margaret and Lenny had cut a mutually advantageous deal. Lenny was her new yardman and computer tutor. She was eager to learn about the World Wide InterWeb (thinking back, Margaret figured Rose might have been making a joke when she'd used that term in reference to Mrs. Sullivan). Lenny was ready, willing and able to make money doing what he loved to do—well, not the yard work part so much—but sitting at Mrs. Williams's kitchen table, eating cookies and showing her how to surf the Web? *Sa-weet.*

"So, as maybe you saw, Ernie, I spent some money today, but I think it's going to turn out pretty cool," Margaret said, addressing their wedding photo as she climbed into bed. "I know you weren't very interested in e-mail and all that—and neither was I until now—but I just think there's a lot I can learn on the Web. I'm a click away from knowing anything I want to know about hospice work or even gardening—not that I plan to do any gardening because now I have a gardener, you know, although I do have to pay this one—or just about anything else. It's been quite a day for me, Ernie.

"Oh, I almost forgot. Yesterday, I was talking to someone who's pretty sure that her patient—it's her aunt—is being visited by her husband. He's not here anymore, either. I mean, she's widowed. You know what I mean, her husband's dead. Is there any chance you could come and visit me? I think I'd like to know that you're not far away. Just a thought. Love you."

There was one thing for sure that Margaret wanted to talk to God about tonight. She wanted to encourage God to try sending her signs, just to let her know she was on the right path and that someone agreed. She believed he could do that if he wanted to and she was open to any and all constructive nudging these days. Obviously, more the better if it came directly from God.

At the very end, she added that if the thing about Ernie visiting her was something God would rather Ernie not do, she assumed he would handle that on his end. *Amen.*

Caleb

Elise Bronson smiled and waved cheerily to her daughters as they climbed onto the school bus. Then she walked back into the house, sat down in the nearest chair and sobbed uncontrollably into her hands.

Please don't misunderstand me, God, I'm thankful for each day we've had. But I'm having trouble understanding why my seventeen-year-old son has to die before he's a man, before he falls in love, before he has a chance to live. Please, God, watch over the other three. Amen.

Elise always felt a little better and a tiny bit lighter after a good cry. She gave her face a quick splash of water in the bathroom sink and ran a comb through her hair. She was meeting her husband Jerry at Rockaway House in a few minutes. He'd be coming straight from his job at Eastern Iowa Iron Works where he'd been since six that morning.

Elise usually stayed with Caleb overnight, and then Jerry relieved her at seven a.m. She'd race back home to get the other kids ready and off to school. Caleb's best buddy, Tracy, showed up at nine o'clock and Jerry then headed to work. After school, Elise took Eli (fourteen), Sarah (nine) and Rebecca (six) to visit their big brother. Once he got off work, Jerry joined them for a few minutes and then he took the younger kids home for dinner and got them into bed. The next day it began all over again.

The routine since Caleb had gone to Rockaway House had already become habitual, and this morning Jerry was surprised to find Elise lying next to him when the alarm went off. She had to remind him of that day's agenda. The past two years had been a succession of traumatic days and today was another. The morning meeting at Rockaway House was to confer with Caleb and his hospice doctor, Dr. Robert Reese—Dr. Bob, as Caleb called him. *His hospice doctor. Maybe 'My ninety-year-old father has an appointment with his hospice doctor.' But 'My seventeen-year-old son has an appointment with his hospice doctor' just sounds wrong. Everything about this sounds wrong.*

One day almost two years ago, not long after Caleb's leukemia was diagnosed, Elise struck up a conversation with the mother of another young cancer patient at one of hundreds of clinic appointments. Elise was waiting while someone injected a cancer-killing drug of one sort or another into Caleb, no doubt using a chemical so toxic that Elise wouldn't have allowed it into her home. But, if there was the slightest chance it would help, fine, go ahead, feel free to give it to him.

Elise had asked the young woman, "Do you ever get used to this, the idea of your child having a deadly disease?" The other mother—Elise still remembered that her name was Shelley—had said "Oh yeah, you just accept it as normal after a while."

Accept it? No way. That's too much like letting the cancer be in charge. As for "normal," it might be Shelley's normal, but it isn't my normal and I refuse to let it be my family's.

From then on, it was Elise's policy to control the messages she and her family heard, as much as possible, and to never strike up a conversation while waiting for Caleb. From then on, in her ears she wore buds, even if her MP3 was turned off. On her face she wore a sorry-I'm-really-into-this-tune look, and she became expert at smiling sweetly and shrugging. She easily got away with it. Elise was a very young-looking thirty-six, more likely to be mistaken for a pediatric patient than a parent.

She vowed early on that fighting Caleb's cancer was a Bronson family mission that would be dealt with according to *their* rules, nobody else's. Caleb had been through a lot: chemotherapy, radiation and finally a stem cell transplant. Jerry and Elise insisted the whole family share these experiences as much as possible. Only Caleb suffered the pain and the hair loss and the fatigue and the nausea and more nausea, but his family shared every bit they had of the thing that was in shortest supply: time.

Now they were coming to the end of Caleb's mind-melting journey and they weren't about to desert him for even one minute. Elise made sure he was almost never alone. If she or Jerry or one of his siblings wasn't available to sit with him, his friend Tracy was.

The night before, Elise and Jerry had needed some time alone to discuss Caleb's condition and to hold each other and cry. And practically speaking, Jerry wanted to get a really early start and log in a few hours at the office before the meeting with Dr. Bob. So they had finally given in and let Caleb stay by himself, with his promise and the nursing staff's assurance that they would be called if there was the slightest concern—about anything. As far as they knew nothing out of the ordinary had happened, which was a huge relief.

Elise paused before she entered Caleb's room at Rockaway House. She caught her breath as she looked at the NPO sign on the door, "nil per os," medical shorthand for "nothing by mouth." Opening the door and finding Caleb and Jerry playing fantasy football on the laptop, Elise stopped to look at her son. Seemingly overnight, Caleb had made the turn from reed thin teenage boy to gaunt hospice patient. She kissed him on the forehead, noticing the quarter inch of stubble that was sprouting on his scalp. *He finally did it.*

Thank God, she and Jerry had discussed the crisis du jour before they went to bed the night before, because Dr. Reese walked in right behind Elise. He gave Caleb a thorough examination, then stepped back and looked at the three faces turned to him.

"As you all know, Caleb is having trouble swallowing because his esophagus is damaged from the radiation he got to treat the tumors in his sternum. I'm sorry to say, this isn't going to get any better on its own. Surgery is one possibility." At that, Caleb shook his head. "I understand, son. We can use an IV but that's of limited use for getting calories into you. However, we're pretty sure we can insert a feeding tube through your nose and into your small intestines and you can get some real nutrition. What do you think?"

Jerry and Elise both turned to Caleb. He was seventeen, so he couldn't legally consent to medical procedures, but the three had a pact that had been honored for the past two years: they made medical decisions as a team so Caleb's vote counted the same as each of his parents'.

But Caleb wasn't volunteering his opinion. He was waiting for them.

Jerry broke the silence.

"Caleb, your mother and I think you should have the feeding tube inserted. We can't have you starving. You know how cranky you get when we don't throw food into the cage." He gave his son's arm a gentle punch. At the risk of breaching the decision-making rules, Jerry had called Dr. Reese the day before. He and Elise now understood that surgically inserting a feeding tube directly into Caleb's stomach wasn't worth the risks involved with the procedure, not for such a temporary condition. Jerry didn't need to ask Dr. Bob what he meant by "temporary."

"Sure, Dad. I agree. That's fine. Let's do it." A soon as Caleb saw his mother's face relax, he knew he'd said the right thing. Elise watched Caleb's face as well, but never allowed their eyes to meet.

God forgive me, she thought. *I'm glad he agreed, because I really don't care what he thinks about this, he's having that tube put in. If there's any time to be bought, we're buying it.*

"Okay." Dr. Bob closed up his tablet. "I'd like to get you down to the clinic to do this, rather than here at Rockaway House. It won't take long. You wouldn't mind a little outing, would you, Caleb?" He patted him on the knee. Caleb shrugged but gave the doctor a small smile. "Good boy. I'll get that scheduled for later today. Mom, Dad, you'll be available?"

"Oh yes, whenever you say," Jerry quickly answered.

"Good. Any questions while I'm here?" Caleb, ever the high school student, raised his hand. "Yes, Caleb?"

"How much longer?"

Dr. Bob sat down on the bed next to Caleb. "I wish I could tell you exactly if that's what you want to know. With the feeding tube, we hope to keep you more comfortable, but your blood count still isn't good. I'm also concerned about the effects of the leukemia spreading to your chest. At some point that may give you trouble with your breathing, Caleb." From behind him, Dr. Bob heard Elise give out with a sharp little gasp.

"That doesn't sound like fun," Caleb said in sad tone.

"Caleb, you have my promise and the promise of everyone here that we will not let you get into a panic situation. I swear to you." He put his arm around the sharp-boned shoulders, now dropped. "And you know very well that your parents wouldn't ever let me break that promise, don't you?"

Caleb nodded and looked past Dr. Bob at his mother and father.

Even the bravest adults, the ones with the most faith and acceptance beyond reason were sometimes anxious at the end of life. Dr. Bob knew that. It wasn't the *if* or *when* that terrified them, it was the *how*, the unknown. Dr. Bob had started seeing Caleb even before he came to stay at Rockaway House. Since their very first meeting, Dr. Bob thought that when it came to gracefully accepting his crappy lot in life, Caleb had a more mature grasp on reality than most dying adults four times his age.

The doctor looked intently at his young patient for a moment before he rose. *So what's Caleb's unfinished business? After all he's been through, what is it he still wants to deal with?*

Dr. Bob knew that if he were lying in that bed, he wouldn't be having a feeding tube put down his gullet, he'd be letting go. Then he stopped himself in mid-thought—occasionally even the hospice doctor with a decade of experience has to remind himself that the patient is always right. *It's not for me to judge Caleb's attitude about all this. My job is to respect his wishes and keep him as comfortable as possible.* Still, Dr. Bob made a mental note to talk to Sheryl and Rose about this—*Together let's figure out how to help Caleb get done whatever it is he wants to finish.*

Caleb loved pizza, but he had never wanted to eat it three times a day. He loved his family and his friends, too, but there had been a lot of togetherness lately and his mom seemed to confuse "being alone" with "being lonely." The night before, Caleb had enjoyed a rare treat, something he hardly ever had anymore, one of many things the disease had stolen from him: time alone. He'd actually gotten the chance to think without having to share his thoughts with anyone else, not even Tracy, not even his mom.

During that long-awaited solitary evening, Caleb had talked to his grandparents, he'd talked to God and he had thought a lot of deep thoughts—deep for anyone, let alone an almost-eighteen-year-old. He was certain now what needed to happen and today he had taken the first step.

Margaret

Margaret didn't have a problem—at least not one that warranted a twelve-step program—but, no doubt about it, she was more than a little enamored with her new computer. When does a hobby become an obsession? Or a habit become an addiction? When you forget to eat dinner and miss your favorite television show and have to be reminded—not very subtly—by your feline roommate that dinner is waaaay overdue.

Lenny had shown Margaret how to turn the computer on, how to access her e-mail account, how to bring up *Google*—her first *Favorite*—and he'd shared some valuable shortcuts on the most effective ways to search.

Think of the words you'd use if you were asking someone at the library to find a book for you, he had suggested.

Brilliant. Turns out, Margaret's words were the same ones the computer whiz kids who created the websites had used as the "keywords." *Imagine me knowing the term "keyword"? Imagine them anticipating what I, Margaret Williams, of Chesterton, Iowa, the would-be visitor to their website, would be thinking? Brilliant.*

At first, Margaret had trouble taking the leap on her own. What if she hit the wrong key? You can't break it, Mrs. Williams, Lenny had assured her.

"Seriously, some of my friends are complete idiots and they haven't broken one yet. And I'm only a phone call—and three houses—away. You've got plenty of cookies, right?"

Margaret meticulously followed the notes she'd taken while sitting at Lenny's side: click *Favorites*; click *Google*; type in the search term—sorry, the keyword—click *Google Search.*

She took a deep breath and typed in the word "hospice."

Click.

Over thirty-five million results.

She quickly skimmed the top of the list. It wasn't really what Margaret was looking for. *It's probably in there somewhere, but let's try again.*

"hospice ideas"

Over five million results.

"Still too much stuff I don't want, but getting warmer."

"ideas for hospice patients"

Bingo! "Only 1.3 million hits and much closer." She giggled with excitement. She'd found a treasure trove of information and she'd done it all on her own, sitting at her kitchen table.

That's when you get hooked, she later explained to Ernie. When you go from one website to another and you just keeping find more and more cool stuff.

Lenny had wisely convinced Margaret that if she didn't get a wireless printer on the first buying trip to Clinton, she'd be back for one in a few days. She'd taken his advice. Four hours into this research, she had thirty more websites listed in her *Favorites* and a stack of stapled pages, filled with ideas that she—that all the Rockaway House volunteers—might try with their patients. More ideas than they could possibly use in a lifetime of work at Rockaway House. Or maybe not. If they had a huge menu of services and gift ideas and activities, each patient could receive customized care. Margaret's head was spinning.

Hospice professionals and volunteers across the country had come up with the most incredibly creative ways to serve patients and their families. Across the world, really. *That's what "www" stands for, silly—the World Wide Web.* Duh, as Lenny would say.

Plaster casts of a patient's hands or of them clasping the hand of a loved one
Helping a patient create an Ethical Will (the patient's beliefs and values)
Creating a patient's life story in writing or with a video
Visiting pets and resident pets at hospice facilities—cats, dogs, birds, fish
Alternative therapies, such as music therapy, pet therapy, aromatherapy, massage therapy, Reiki, healing hands, meditation and guided imagery
Ways to recognize the passing of a patient, with the lighting of a candle, special music, a handmade quilt, the ringing of a chime or a prayer circle
Special ways for the hospice provider to honor patients at the patient's own memorial service as well as remembrance gardens, wall displays and in-kind memorial gifts to the hospice facility
Ideas for gifts for hospice patients, like large print books or soothing music CDs or lotions or books of inspiration or scripture or a special pillow case or books on tape
Programs to grant final wishes to hospice patients, if possible
Volunteer projects like cooking the patient and family's favorite recipe, reading to patients, doing yard work at a patient's home or running errands for the caregiver
And on and on and on . . .

Margaret turned off the kitchen light and padded towards the bedroom, carrying a cup of tea and cookies on a tiny tray. She was bushed and her neck ached from leaning over the laptop for so long. She'd have to remember to ask Lenny about getting a computer desk—she could set it up in the extra bedroom, in front of the window so she could look out on the backyard while she worked.

Margaret gazed over at the wedding photo on the dresser.

"You can't believe how neat this is for me, Ernie. I know I was at it for a couple of hours tonight—okay, for four hours—but I got more information than I could've gotten in four weeks the old way. No, you know what? There *isn't* any old way to learn this. There is no way for me to talk to all those other volunteers all over the globe and hear about what they're doing for their patients.

"I gotta tell ya, Ernie, I know you weren't big on the Internet thing, but I could see you sitting at that computer, looking up gardening sites or playing fantasy football—whatever that is. Listen, if I can do it, you could do it. I'm surfin' like mad—a regular Annette Funicello. I wish you could see me."

Who knows? Maybe he can.

Rockaway House

Margaret wasn't usually one to draw attention to herself, certainly not intentionally. In a training session that included about ten volunteers in addition to Margaret, Amanda and Beverly, Rose asked the question, "Who knows what a Living Will is?" Of all people, these people will know the answer, Margaret had thought, and her hand went up before she realized she was the only one.

"Great, Margaret! Would you please refresh our memories?"

"I just know that Ernie—that's my late husband—and I had ours done when he got his cancer diagnosis. If I'm right, it's our instructions for how we want to be treated if we have a terminal disease, right?"

"Exactly right. And," Rose went on without a hint of recrimination, "if I may call this group 'typical' in this one sense, you are most likely part of almost seventy-five percent of American adults who either don't have a Living Will—or have one and don't have the foggiest notion what it means!" That got a guilty laugh from everyone.

Rose explained that when a patient enters hospice care with CCH, the intake nurse asks if he or she has advance directives—a Living Will and a Durable Power of Attorney for Health Care. If they don't, she helps them get the paperwork prepared. You won't need an attorney to draft these documents, Rose assured them, just good forms and a notary public.

"Knowledge leads to effective end-of-life planning. Completing those documents gives our patients a chance to talk about how they want to be treated at the end of life."

A volunteer raised his hand.

"What if the patient is already, you know, too sick to make those decisions? What then?"

"Good question. If the patient has appointed a health care proxy, we look to him or her to learn what the patient wants. If there's no proxy appointed, we talk to the family members about who Iowa law recognizes as the designated decision-maker." Rose waited a moment while her audience processed that answer.

"I hope each of you will consider your own wishes for care and let your loved ones know what you want and make sure you've signed the proper documents. That's your homework." Another group laugh, but this time heads were nodding in agreement. As always, Rose hoped their firm conviction would last at least until they got home.

"Now, who knows if hospice patients can participate in organ donation?"

Silence. Clearly, no one had considered that option. *How could that be?*

"Well, corneal donation is possible for hospice patients and even tissue and organs, depending on the cause of death. That's something else that's covered in the admissions interview with the patient and family members. Patients interested in donating need to be evaluated before they're actively dying so we can see if it's possible. If it is, we notify the organ procurement team at the time of death. For many families, it's another way for a loved one to make a difference even in dying. Any questions?"

Oh yes, there were lots of questions.

Did it cost the family anything to participate? Does organ donation mean there can't be an open casket? What if a family doesn't want organ donation, but the patient did?

This topic always created a lot of interest. The class went an extra thirty minutes while Rose answered every question. Most of the volunteers had a close family member who had been in hospice care, but none could recall hearing about organ donation during the admissions process, and most were a little sad to find out they may have missed an opportunity to participate. They all vowed to register immediately.

As Rose spoke, she jotted a reminder to herself in the margin of her class notes. What we have here is a failure to communicate, she thought. It wasn't the first time she had run into this reaction from a group of volunteers; obviously, the hospice staff needed to work on messaging. Rose would talk to Lauren about it, as soon as possible. Rose knew less than half of those present would get around to registering as donors, but those were better odds than in the general population. There were over five hundred people on transplant waiting lists in Iowa alone, so talking to volunteers about organ donation was time well spent.

The class broke up and Margaret gathered her things, wondering how she would ever keep all this information straight in her mind. Since I'm not paid, I suppose they won't expect so much from me, she thought, but I don't want to mess up the very end of someone's life by steering them wrong or being a bad listener or acting like a limp rag when they need a tower of strength. *What am I doing here?*

It was four-thirty and the volunteers were free until the bereavement support group began in an hour, the one element of volunteer education that Margaret was not looking forward to. Not at all.

Thanks but no thanks. The idea of sharing her feelings with a room full of strangers was not appealing. In fact, by repeating the phrase *Sorry, just not a good fit* she had managed to avoid getting involved in the self-help/support group movement for decades. *Not that there's anything wrong with that. It's just not for me.*

She tried to shake off the feeling of dread and think of the other participants as a well-meaning and essential part of her training, and maybe not so much as cultists on a recruitment mission.

In the kitchen, volunteers were having cups of coffee, talking about the subjects they'd just covered and checking their e-mails on their smart phones. Margaret retrieved an apple leftover from her lunch as she passed through.

She stepped into the back parking area to get some fresh air and stretch her legs, taking a bite of apple as she stopped for a moment to look around.

Between the house and the garage was parking for eight cars, with the space right in front of the elevator entrance reserved for the inevitable ambulance or hearse. Margaret took a few steps, stood in that area, closed her eyes and tried to imagine herself on a stretcher, coming in or going out. She was relieved to discover she couldn't.

The sky was cloudy, a gunmetal grey, but it was still one of the few remaining no-jacket days. Margaret meandered across the parking lot, munching on her apple. She walked toward the garage, which was as impressive as the house, with four car stalls and a second story. *Why in the world does anyone need a second story on a garage?* She stepped up on tiptoes and tried to see into the small windows of the garage doors but they were either blacked out or it was too dark inside to see a thing. Just to the left of the stalls was a passage door. Margaret peered through its glass window and saw a stairway leading to that inexplicable second floor.

If she'd thought about it, she wouldn't have done it, but without thinking, Margaret tried the doorknob. It was unlocked. The door started to open with the slightest urging and Margaret stopped to look around.

Is anyone watching? She could see the backs of the volunteers in the kitchen sunroom but no one was facing her way. Walking through the door, she quietly shut it behind her and found herself on a small landing at the bottom of the tall flight of stairs. The oak railing was smooth to Margaret's hand. The steps were painted dark green.

Without waiting to see if she would talk herself out of this mini-adventure, she started up the stairs. Half-way, Margaret stopped and looked behind to make sure she was still unobserved. *I hope no one's about to open the door, asking just who I think I am.* They weren't. She looked down. Her footsteps were leaving clear impressions in the dust on the stairs, the fine powder pushed aside in the shape of her sneakers.

Margaret kept going.

At the top of the stairs was another door, curtained with black and white gingham on the inside. There was only one way to see what was behind it. *Open it, you ninny.* Again, the knob turned easily. Again, it was unlocked.

Her courage was waning. She opened this door in slow motion, tautly posed for the inevitable surprise: a mouse, a raccoon, the boogeyman. The gap was only about six inches wide when a thought jumped into her head: what if someone's in there? Margaret gave a polite *tap tap tap* to the glass with her fingernails. No answer. She pushed the door forward but unconsciously stepped back a pace, closer to the edge of the landing and escape, reaching as far as her arm would stretch.

What lay behind the door was shrouded in darkness. The mystery would remain just that unless she opened it all the way. She couldn't seem to stop herself.

As her eyes adjusted, Margaret could see she was standing at the entrance to a room about fifteen by twenty. The overcast day peeked weakly around the edges of light-blocking curtains at the small window. Margaret looked down and saw the floor was ancient oak, varnished and waxed to a warm patina, visible in spite of the dust. Off to her left was an eat-in kitchen; an old-fashioned sink with legs, a two-burner stove, a small-scale refrigerator, all setting on a green and white linoleum floor. Where a small table and chairs might have once stood, there was an assortment of furniture, neatly and tightly packed into the small room.

When she looked back to what she supposed was the living room—now her pupils were wide open—she saw more of the same. You could hardly tell where one piece of furniture ended and the next began. She could detect the outline of a couch, chairs, cabinets, end tables, small bookshelves, a buffet, a china cabinet and a dining room table topped with a packing blanket that was topped with dining room chairs.

Just to her right there was a narrow pathway against the wall, no more than three feet wide, carved into the sea of wood and leather. She followed it. It led through an open door into another room, perhaps a bedroom, filled to the brim with even more furniture. Margaret could see headboards and footboards leaned against walls, mattresses and old-fashioned box springs set on their ends. Highboys, dressers, vanities (she counted five), side tables, a chaise lounge, and on and on, all neatly and methodically stored like the pieces of a Chinese puzzle box. Wooden crates were stacked along one wall, three high, and on top of them were lamps, mirrors and massive flowerpots, too large to be contained.

Margaret couldn't stop now. She followed the trail—another narrow lane cut along the side of the bedroom. Halfway down its length there was a break, an opening into a small bathroom. It contained a pedestal sink, a claw foot bathtub and a toilet, all set on a floor of tiny black and white hexagonal tiles. She continued a few feet past that door, following the passageway until it ended at a wall. Margaret was about to turn around and retrace her steps when a small knob caught her eye, protruding about three feet up from the floor. More like a cabinet latch than a door handle, it was hardly a secret entryway, but unadorned, not meant to call attention to itself.

She took a deep breath and slowly let it out. Just as she reached for the tiny lever, a sweet perfume wafted over her, all but making her cough. *What is that?* She stopped and stepped back a few feet, trying to sniff out the source. When she had first entered the apartment, she'd detected another smell—besides the general fustiness—a faint odor, something like disinfectant. This wasn't that, this was very different from that and definitely not faint.

Then the aroma was gone. Margaret shook her head, shrugged and put her hand back on the latch. It was only then, standing so close, that she noticed the small size and odd shape of the opening, only five feet tall but four feet wide.

Even Margaret needed to duck slightly as she entered the adjoining room and went from a living space into something entirely different. Here the floor under her feet wasn't finished; it was wide unvarnished pine planks. She stood slowly from her crouch, not sure how high the ceiling was until she looked up. It was an unfinished attic with bare rafters and trusses and the walls were the same, studs and planks with no plaster finish. But unlike the other rooms on this floor, the dormer windows weren't covered and light shown in unfettered, revealing the contents.

More of everything. Much more.

Margaret's field of vision was overwhelmed. She doubted if Walton's Furniture in downtown Chesterton had this many pieces in stock. The open area held wicker tables, chairs, settees, more beds, more dressers, more mirrors and more crates. Margaret figured this attic hovered over three of the four garage stalls. It was a vast space.

Raiders of the Lost Ark. That's what this looks like, she thought, that scene at the end where the camera spans back from rows and rows of mysterious boxes in a government warehouse. Even with the light from the windows, Margaret couldn't really make out all the contents, just the outline of furniture and boxes as far as the eye could see.

Suddenly she felt as if she was intruding. Because I am, she thought. *I have no business up here.* She stepped back through the simple opening, slowly and deliberately closing the door behind her. She stopped in the bedroom, taking it all in again, then on through to the living room.

That smell again, suddenly assaulting her nostrils. Sweet and overwhelming. Gone as quickly as it came, but not before it triggered three sneezes.

That did it. Margaret needed some fresh air. She made sure each door was closed behind her, debated whether to try to erase her footsteps from the stairs as she descended and then rejected the lame idea. She gave a quick glance at the sunroom windows in the main house to make sure there were still no onlookers, then slipped out the door back onto the driveway. She checked her watch and noticed then that she was still holding the now browning apple core in her hand. It was five-fifteen.

The kitchen crowd was breaking up when Margaret got inside. Making a quick stop in the bathroom to check for cobwebs in her hair, she freshened up a bit and got an early place in the conference room, hoping to be seated furthest from the moderator and closest to the door.

I need to stop at the grocery store on the way home. I'll make my list during the meeting. I'll just keep my mind open and my mouth shut. She took a deep breath. *Well, here goes nothing.*

Margaret thought she heard a voice. It was in her head. It was Ernie.

"That's my girl. As long as you're keeping an open mind about it, Maggie."

Oh be quiet, Ernie.

Caleb

Tracy and Caleb met in kindergarten and had been inseparable best buddies ever since. For the first week of Caleb's stay at Rockaway House, Tracy ditched school every day and thought she was getting away with it. She didn't know her parents had called Jerry and Elise and asked their permission, then notified the kids' principal that Tracy would be spending her days with Caleb, indefinitely. She didn't know until that evening when they told her she could sleep in a little later and stop running out the door in the morning, pretending to get on the school bus at seven-thirty. Tracy was glad to have one less thing to worry about.

Just a few days later, when Tracy got home late in the afternoon, she vowed that she'd eaten her last meal at Rockaway House. She'd just have to remember to have a big breakfast before she got there in the morning then she'd make some excuse and go grab a drive-through lunch somewhere. But no more eating in front of Caleb. It was too sad to see the look on his face. Never again.

That morning Caleb had asked Tracy if she thought it would work for him to chew some food, then spit it out. You can try most anything you want to, she had told him. Did he want to try that? No, he reluctantly admitted, it sounded gross.

"You know, it's funny, Trace. I don't have much of an appetite, I just miss the taste of food."

"I know, bud. I'm sorry. Ice chip?"

"Yeah, that's what I've been craving," he said sarcastically, but with a smile.

"Let's talk about something different." Tracy intentionally put some extra energy into her voice. "Shouldn't we be telling someone about our plan?"

"Who do you think's the best one? I like Margaret. I think we can trust her, don't you?"

"Agreed. Want me to go see if she's around?" Tracy stood, ready to get started.

"Yeah, let's do it." But then Caleb reached out his hand and stopped her before she left. "Trace, you won't let me look pathetic or stupid, okay?" She took his hands in hers.

"You're so freakishly smart, you couldn't look stupid if you wanted to."

"Tracy."

"I know what you mean. No, I won't. I promise." She left, returning in a moment with Margaret in tow.

"Have a seat, Margaret. We don't know if this is something we can pull off, but—"

"I'm in! What is it?" Margaret was eager to do anything she could to help these two.

"Well," Caleb began, "my birthday's this Thursday. I wanna have a birthday party, a pretty big birthday party. But not a birthday party exactly. I want to have Christmas."

It took Margaret about five seconds to catch up with them.

Before Caleb and Tracy could ask each other where she had gone, Margaret had dashed out of the room and returned in a flash with a spiral notebook in hand. She opened it, her pen poised, ready to write. "Now, Caleb, you have to tell me about Christmases with your family at home. What are some of your traditions, what do you want to include?"

He wanted a tree for sure. With lights. Oh, and once his mom knew about this, there were a few special ornaments he knew she'd want to bring from home. He wanted food at the party. Hot cider and cocoa and they probably couldn't have decorated Christmas cookies, but definitely cookies of some kind. And turkey sandwiches and black olives and cranberry sauce, the kind that comes out of the can in one big glob. Sarah and Rebecca could string popcorn and cranberries for the tree—Eli wouldn't want to do that, he'd say he was too old. No presents, nobody needed to bring any presents, but there had to be Christmas music, so could Margaret get ahold of a stereo and some CDs?

"And I don't want my mom or dad to have to do anything, okay?"

"Totally doable. Is that all for right now? Oh, who are you inviting? Do you need me to make any calls?"

"No, Tracy has the list and she's going to tell her parents and they'll let everyone know. Just some of my friends, not very many, mostly family. Tracy's mom's in charge of the food and stuff. And Dr. Golan, he was my oncologist. I'd like him to come, too. He really did try." His voice, already weakening, faded.

"Got it, boss. I just checked and we can use the living room downstairs. How's that? Tracy, you come with me and we'll bring all my Christmas decorations back from my house, it's only a few minutes away. Is it okay if we leave you alone for a bit, Caleb? Anything else?"

"No, I don't think so. No. Thanks so much, Margaret." His eyes were misty.

"You could not be more welcome, Caleb. It's my pleasure. Really." She gave his shoulder a gentle squeeze. "How about you rest for a bit while we're gone? Shall I send Sheryl in for you?"

"Sure, let's get that out of the way." Three times a day, just like regular meals—except they weren't—a nurse came and poured the high-calorie formula into Caleb's feeding tube.

"Tracy, honey, you're coming with me."

They were halfway to Margaret's house before either one spoke.

"I was already planning to talk to you about something before you came to get me, Tracy."

"Oh yeah? What about?"

"There's a new program at Rockaway House called the Jiminy Cricket Project. I don't have a lot of details quite yet about how it'll work, but it's a chance for a patient to have a special wish granted. I wanted to know if there's anything—I mean, besides this party—that Caleb would like to have. If there's any way possible to make it happen, we will."

Tracy thought for a minute. "He's trying to grow a beard because he just started getting his hair back after two years. He wanted to show some stubble before he dies. I don't think it takes much to make him happy, Margaret."

"I know. I'm sorry."

Tracy looked over as they pulled into Margaret's driveway. "He's melting, like the wicked witch, except without the wicked part."

Margaret put the car into park, turned to Tracy and waited.

"You seem like the sort of person who can keep a secret, Margaret. Are you?"

Jesus, Mary and Joseph. They didn't prepare me for this at orientation. "Yes."

"Caleb wants to go home. That's his only wish. He turns eighteen on Thursday. If his parents won't agree, he's going to trump them. Since he'll be eighteen he can make his own medical decisions. He wants to go home to die and he doesn't have much time. He needs to talk to someone—besides me—about this, Margaret. Are you that person?"

Margaret thought before she spoke. *Please help me find the right words.* "This is what I can promise you: I'll talk to Caleb, I'll figure out who we need to have join in on this, I'll check with you two first, and—only if you agree—we'll take the next step. Is that good enough?"

"Yes. Thank you. Oh, thank you." Tracy began to cry, a child's blubbering sobs, wiping her eyes with the heels of her hands.

"Honey, you just go ahead and cry. I bet you don't do that much around Caleb, do you?"

"No, I try not to, never," she choked between sobs. "I just love him so much. He's like the brother I never had. I'd just do anything for him, Margaret."

"Then that's what we shall do. Let's go get those Christmas decorations."

Lucky for Caleb and Tracy, Margaret was more than just a little OCD. The oversized green and red plastic tubs were clearly labeled and neatly stacked in the corner of Ernie and Margaret's basement: TREE DECOR. (1 of 2), TREE DECOR. (2 of 2), LIGHTS, SANTAS, GARLAND, XMAS MUSIC and XMAS MISC. Margaret didn't see how she could leave any behind and she carried them all upstairs with Tracy's help.

The seven-foot artificial Frasier fir tree, disassembled and bagged, was more than Margaret and Tracy could lug. Half of Margaret's October 2008 Social Security check had been spent on that beauty. She'd sworn to Ernie at the time that it was the last Christmas tree they'd ever own.

He couldn't say she hadn't keep her promise on that one.

Later she'd call Lance Wilson, the CCH Facilities Manager, to come and haul the tree back to Rockaway House with his pickup (and carry it into the living room). He had a big heart and, as important for Margaret today, strong arms.

The back seat of the LeSabre was bursting. So was the trunk.

There's enough stuff here to decorate three living rooms, Margaret thought proudly as she slammed the lid shut. *This'll show that smarty-pants Ernie Williams. Too much Christmas crapola, my Aunt Fanny.*

Lois

Ray Spaulding was hanging over the side yard fence, gabbing with Alma Riley, next-door neighbor to Lois and Ray for almost forty years. Alma's husband Harry had passed away five years earlier and, at ninety-one, Alma was determined to stay in the home they'd built in 1972.

Alma asked how Lois was doing and Ray told her they were waiting for a call from the doctor, to get some test results.

"How long has it been, Ray? Two years?"

"Close. Not quite twenty months. It's definitely taking its toll. Lately her legs and arms have been all swollen up. I'm not sure what that means." These neighbors had been through a lot together. Lois had jumped into the fray when Harry got cancer and now Ray found himself turning to Alma for some neighborly support.

"I pray for her every day, Ray. For both of you."

"Thank you, Alma. We accept any and all prayers on our behalf." He smiled and patted her hand.

Lois called from the back door that the doctor was on the phone. Ray gave Alma the crossed-fingers-for-good-luck sign and hurried back to the house.

"Yes, I understand. I'll talk to Ray and we'll call you back, Dr. Sims. Thanks so much for calling." Lois hung up just as Ray walked into the kitchen.

"Well? What'd he say?"

Lois took off her apron and sat down at the kitchen table. She looked up at Ray, smiled and patted the chair next to her. "Sit down, honey." Ray didn't want to sit down. After forty-two years, he often knew what Lois was going to say before she said it, sometimes even before she thought it. And right now he knew for a fact he didn't want to hear this.

He absently scratched his forehead, let out a big breath and crumpled into the chair.

"It's not good news, honey," Lois began. "My numbers are not good and Dr. Sims wants me to start having dialysis five times a week." Lois stopped. In fairness to Ray, he needed a moment to absorb that before she went on. They looked at each other. She knew she didn't really need to tell him, but she needed to say the words out loud, for both their sakes.

"It's time, Ray. It's time for me to let go. It's time for both of us to let go."

She paused while her husband—a man who always considered his options before speaking—considered his options. Over the past few months, he had watched her strength diminish, her otherwise positive attitude take a beating, her breathing become fragile while she slept.

Ray had two choices at this very moment: break down or buck up. He went with the latter.

"I'm only going to say this once, Lois, so listen very carefully, my dear one. I am with you always, here, there, wherever life takes us. I haven't been the traveler on this journey, only the companion—"

"—and I couldn't ask for a better one—"

"—so it's not for me to say when enough is enough. But it is my joy to be here with you, to make every day we have the very best it can be. I love you." Lois moved her chair right next to Ray's and they wrapped their arms securely around each either. The rest of the story wouldn't begin as long as they were holding on tight. They could both now see that the solution was simple, they just wouldn't let go.

Finally, they pulled back at the same moment, and Lois blew her nose with the handkerchief she always kept tucked up her sleeve. Ray grabbed a tissue from the kitchen counter behind him.

"I know you've been thinking about this for some time." Lois got a half smile—a sheepish half smile—as Ray spoke. "Please tell me your reasons." Ray the Journalist needed to understand the story behind her decision, why Lois was discontinuing dialysis, why she was choosing to let the disease have its way.

"Well, yes, I have been thinking about this for a while. I can put up with the inconvenience. I'm a little ashamed to even complain about that when I see some of the other folks at the clinic. Ray, some are so weak they can barely make it there, but somehow they do. You and I have had almost two good years, haven't we?"

He nodded in agreement. "I would have said almost *forty*-two good years, but yes." He smiled and gave her hand a squeeze.

"Oh you—you know what I mean. First of all, I looked some of this up on the Web—and yes, I know how to use the Web, dear. I thought this might be coming. You know, having dialysis five days a week has its own risks. And Ray, we both know I'm not getting better—that was never going to happen. I'm weaker and weaker, my joints ache, I can barely get out of bed on the good days and lately I have to be so careful of crowds, I'm practically a recluse other than going to the clinic." She paused and held his face in her hands. "Five days a week? We'd be tethered to the clinic. Between being there and my down time here, that would be our whole life. That isn't much of a life, Ray, for me or you."

Ray didn't move.

"You know that question we never asked because we never wanted to hear the answer?" Lois said gently.

"Yes."

"Well, I asked it."

"You did?"

"Yes, and it was five to seven years back when I first got sick. We're coming up on two years of this. I don't want to spend the last three to five years of my life—assuming Dr. Sims is right—going to that clinic. And I don't want you to, either." He opened his mouth to speak and she put her finger to his lips. "You don't have to say it. I know you would willingly do that for me. I don't want you to. And you know you wouldn't want me to, if roles were reversed."

He hated it when she was so logical, and so damn right.

She drew herself up in the chair and took a deep breath. "I'm not quitting this minute, but we need to make some plans. Carlene needs to be told—don't make that face, I'm not looking forward to it, either. And," she perked up, putting on a smile and taking his hands in hers, "there are some things on my Bucket List I'd like to get to. Are you game?"

"Always, Lois. Always." Ray hugged her again and held on tight.

Since his seventy-fifth birthday earlier that year, Ray had thought more and more often about how and when death would come to divide their partnership. He told himself that at his age, it was natural and not macabre to wonder how it would all play out. He'd imagined many different scenarios and he'd thought about whether Lois would be lonely or how she'd cope with the grief. Because in spite of the fact that his wife had been treated for a very serious kidney disease for almost two years, and in spite of the fact that he considered himself a reasonably intelligent guy, and in spite of all that thinking he'd done, the one scenario Ray had not considered was the possibility that Lois would go first and that he would be left alone. Now, as he held her, the realization was staring him in the face, and for the life of him, Ray could not explain how he had let that one get past him. Talk about denial.

Oh my God, it's going to be my heart that's shattered. I'm going to be the one who's paralyzed with grief. As Carlene would probably put it, This sucks. And she'd be right, anyway you look at it, this sucks.

The next thought to jump into Ray's head was, *How the hell can I possibly be thinking about myself at this moment?*

He released his embrace and took Lois's hands in his.

But Lois spoke before Ray could. "You know, honey, let's do something you've always wanted to do—and me, too—I was thinking that we should drive over to the Mississippi and get a pontoon and float on the river for a day. I'll pack a picnic."

Ray cleared his throat. "We've only been meaning to do that for about thirty years. Great idea, Lois. I'll dig out the fishing poles." He stood and headed for the garage.

Lois smiled. She was about to check the first item off her Bucket List.

Rockaway House

Healing Survivors was just one of many bereavement support groups that met at Rockaway House throughout the week. There were certainly focused groups targeting widows, widowers, children and adults who had lost one or both parents, but Healing Survivors was for whoever showed up for the meeting. Glenda Stanley, the bereavement counselor at CCH, acted as the group's facilitator. Although not everyone made it every week—and the door was always open to drop-ins—there was a core group of members who always came. Today, the newest CCH volunteers would be joining them.

Some support groups had structured programs as they worked their way through a specific grief book or guide, but Healing Survivors was purely for sharing and venting. The agenda was sometimes as simple as *Can anyone tell me where to get my car fixed—my husband always handled that?* Or as complex as *When is it okay to stop wearing your wedding ring?* For some, Healing Survivors was a place to be with empathetic people for at least one hour each week. For others, it served as their lone incentive to get out of bed and take a shower.

Glenda began the meeting by introducing the volunteers to the survivors. She reminded all the attendees of the resources available for individual counseling if anyone wanted it. If so, see her after the meeting. And, as always, she emphasized the importance of confidentiality.

Housekeeping items out of the way, the group got down to business.

An elderly man immediately spoke up. Even though there'd been absolutely no hope of a cure, he couldn't get past feeling as if he had given up on his late wife by putting her in hospice care when he did. A middle-aged woman worried because she was preoccupied with anger at the friends who had forsaken her once her husband's cancer became terminal, only to show up at his funeral, saying that they knew just how she felt. A twenty-something widow said she couldn't get her six-year-old to understand that his father was never coming back. He constantly asked when Daddy would be home, and it was driving her bonkers. A young woman wondered if others had experienced a family imploding after a parents' death. The adult siblings had fought over every single decision as her mother's life was ending and they were now feuding over the estate.

Glenda skillfully led the conversations, prompted more questions and gently invited people to participate.

First, she reminded them that hospice is not "doing nothing" or "giving up" when a cure is no longer possible. It's a philosophy of care that focuses on comfort and dignity for the person and whatever life they have left. It's often hard for a caregiver to accept helplessness where their loved one is concerned, but, Glenda assured the elderly man, compassionate hospice care at life's end is doing something—something very important. In fact, by that time, it's usually the only thing that can be done for our loved ones.

Another survivor had felt the same as the middle-aged woman until she realized that her anger toward her so-called friends was only affecting *her*—in a profoundly negative way—because those folks had moved on to some other crisis du jour. For her own sake, she focused on forgiving them and letting the anger go—along with the friendships—which weren't very meaningful to begin with, really. As far as the catch phrases people mouth in an uncomfortable death setting (and at the risk of sounding ungrateful), "I know just how you feel" usually means "Thank God I have no idea how you feel."

Glenda told the young mother about the brand new group for small children that might be of value to her son. Another survivor said she'd finally accepted that her five-year-old wasn't mature enough to get it. She'd prayed for patience and eventually he sort of grasped the concept of death—as much as anyone can—and began to work through his loss. It just took time.

As for the imploding family, half of those in the room nodded and a few even chuckled in empathy. Families were complicated and messy and there was nothing like death to re-kindle decades-old sibling rivalries. Two of the survivors invited the young woman to have a cup of coffee afterwards and they would share their own journeys and coping mechanisms with her.

The gathering lasted a little over an hour. Afterwards, many of the attendees went on to *Whole Latte' Love* to continue visiting. Margaret was headed to the front door to go home when Rose caught up with her.

"Have time for a chat, Margaret?"

"Sure, I'm just on my way to the grocery store. That can certainly wait." They each got a cup of tea and a cookie, then went to the corner table in the sunroom. They were alone.

"Well, what did you think?" Rose asked as she bit into a cookie.

"All the survivors there seemed to get a lot out of it."

"Except for you?" Rose gently prodded.

"No, I don't think it's for me." Margaret shook her head, feeling apologetic. She wasn't sure if she should share all that she was thinking, but then she decided she was more eager to settle this issue once and for all than afraid of offending Rose. "Okay, in the brochure for the support groups, it says there's a group for 'continuation of grief work.' Here's the deal, Rose: I don't want a continuation of my grief."

"That's not what it means, Mar—'

"I know what it means, Rose. I'm making a point—not very well, I'm afraid. What I'm feeling right now is the best I've felt in months. I'm actually having happy days again, I'm not crying as much, I'm starting to feel as if I have a life of my own that's still there to be lived by me. And I've just never been one to share in a group like that. I don't know, it's just not the same to talk about Ernie to someone who didn't know him. I mean, they don't share my memories, do they? I'm making my way through life. I have a faith community and good friends and family who care about me, and I'm figuring this thing out a day at a time."

Margaret would grant that she sounded like a rambling idiot but she was driven to get it all said. "The thing is, Rose, I have to do this just like every single person in that room, like Glenda said a few minutes ago: *my* way. Right now I don't want to focus on my loss, it just brings me down. If that's selfish, that's just the way it is for me right now." Margaret paused, trying to gauge Rose's reaction. "My way isn't in a group like that."

"Okay."

"Really?"

"Of course, Margaret. We're not kidding when we say we respect that each person grieves in his or her own way. We're here to help however we can, not to try to fit you into a mold. In a way, appreciating days filled with hope and joy is something you have to relearn to do after you've suffered a loss. It's part of the grief process—the good part, I think—and no way is that selfish. But you'll also come to know that staff and volunteers can experience grief from working here. I hope you'll remember that some of our bereavement resources might have value to you as a volunteer. All right?"

Margaret was so relieved.

Rose laughed out loud as she went on. "You know, I tried lots of things before I settled on volunteering for CCH. I worked at the hospital gift shop, I delivered Meals on Wheels, I read to a blind lady at Rolling Hills. I always had my hand up, but none of those situations clicked with me. When I tried Rockaway House, I knew I'd found my volunteer home. And, after four years, they asked me to come on staff. So, I admire knowing when to say 'no' to the wrong opportunity, to something that just doesn't fit. I really do, Margaret."

"Thanks, Rose. You know, when we hit our sixties, Ernie and I thought we'd figured out a few things. Now I find myself alone, only half of a couple and I have to figure it out all over again for me."

"Amen to that." Rose started to get up, ready to call it a day.

"Oh, Rose, can I talk to you for a minute about an idea I have?"

"Sure." Rose sat back down. Margaret told her about jumping onto the Information Superhighway and finding ways to help their patients. And she wanted to talk more to Rose about all that very soon, but right now Margaret needed to tell her about something that required immediate attention. Had they ever considered having a special program to grant a patient's final wish? Margaret tried to think of a couple examples. "To bring a visitor or take the patient somewhere, or—I don't know, it could be anything. Of course, it depends on us finding a way to make it happen, the wish, that is. What do you think?"

"We've done that before from time to time, but not as a special program. I think it's a wonderful idea, Margaret. Formalizing it and making everyone aware of it should increase the chances that we'll grant a wish, that's for sure."

Margaret hesitated, then took the plunge. "I thought of a name for it, if you think it works or it's okay or whatever."

"Yes?"

"The Jiminy Cricket Project. You know, he was a wise, funny little friend who went on *Pinocchio's* adventures with him. And he sang the song, '*When you wish upon a star.'* I thought that kinda fit."

Rose nodded and patted Margaret's hand. After a moment, she was able to speak again. "I think it's an incredible idea, Margaret. Why don't you put something on paper for me, and I'll take it to Lauren, so we can try to find some funds for it. But you know how tight things are."

"Yes, yes, but a patient's wish might not even cost anything. It's not always about something that costs money, is it, Rose?"

"No, no, of course not. I love it. Good work!"

That's a relief, considering I've already begun to offer the program . . .

They both stood, headed in opposite directions. Margaret's car was on the street and Rose was parked out back.

"Have a nice evening, Margaret."

"You too, Rose."

"I'll do that."

"Oh, and Rose?"

Rose turned just as she opened the back door to the parking lot. "Yes?"

"Please call me Maggie."

"I'll do that, too."

Margaret

Margaret raised herself up on one elbow, turned on the bedside lamp and looked over at the clock radio. She'd guessed wrong. From that puzzling place where one can (usually) sense the day of the week or the hour of the day, she thought it was about five a.m. If it were, Margaret could rationalize getting out of bed and starting her day exceptionally early, but she had it wrong this time. *Three-fifteen?* That hour was neither day nor night. Too early to get up, but if she went back to sleep, she'd be like *Night of the Living Dead* when the alarm went off at six.

Maybe just a little snack.

Once in the kitchen, Margaret took down the package of Mint Milanos, then stopped and put it back. She turned to Maxine, who had followed in hopes that Margaret would mistake three-fifteen a.m. for six-fifteen a.m. and feed her. "Maxine," Margaret declared, "our days of store-bought cookies are over." She took two steps to the next cupboard and lifted down her mother's oversized Jewel Tea mixing bowl, the one big enough to hold mashed potatoes, glorified rice or—in this instance—chocolate chip cookie dough.

There'd been a time when Margaret had wanted to be—and probably could have been—the Mrs. Fields of Chesterton. She baked like crazy to get the recipe just right and Ernie was more than supportive, eating all manner of test cookies until he nearly popped. A cookie needed to be chewy but have the strength of character to stand up to dunking. She finally hit the perfect combination of ingredients and methodology (to this day, she had shared the double secret recipe with only one other person). Ernie dunked, bit and gave it two thumbs up.

Margaret bugged Chester, her manager at *The Marion Street Grocery*, until he finally agreed to offer some of her cookies for sale at the store. She even got him to let her pass out sample morsels for an hour.

The first ten dozen sold in the first fifteen minutes, for a price that Margaret would never in her life have paid for a dozen of anything.

She could still hear Ernie's words when she got home that day.

"First, I'm not surprised other people think your cookies are fantastic, honey. Second, what did you expect Chester to say? Of course, he wants you to bake more. I thought you wanted to sell cookies, Miss Big Shot. That's what you wanted, right?" This was said in a very loving tone, although it was clear that Ernie was enjoying the moment perhaps more than he should.

"I don't know. I just wanted to prove I could sell cookies, which I've now done. I'm not a cookie magnate. I'm a bookkeeper."

Ernie put his head in his hands.

That had been almost twenty-five years ago.

Margaret still made cookies from time to time, but with her waistline, she simply couldn't be trusted to have that manner of temptation lying around. *Hey, wait just a minute!* Now Margaret had people to bake for, people who would welcome something homemade, people who would be glad to help her polish off a few dozen. All of that experimentation a quarter of a century earlier hadn't been for nothing.

At five-thirty a.m., Margaret packed the last cookie into the box. Now she could get a leisurely shower, stop for a chai latte' on the way and not get to Rockaway House too early.

She stretched and noticed that sometime over the past few weeks the shoulder pain she'd been having over the past few months had disappeared. Completely disappeared.

Victoria

"Stupid. Stupid. Stupid. Why did I ever take her to Rockaway House? I should have kept her here at home," Magda said aloud as she tied her shoelaces. She stood up. She sat down. She unexpectedly sobbed big, shoulder-shaking sobs. *Where is this coming from?* She grabbed a tissue, blew her nose and wiped her eyes. Magda didn't know if she wanted to quit crying or sob harder than she ever had before in her entire life.

Big breath.

Picking up her purse and the afghan she'd forgotten to send with Victoria—her favorite—Magda started to go out the door, into the garage, to get in the car, to drive to Rockaway House, to go and see Victoria.

This is absolutely exhausting.

She noticed for the first time—or had it just started—that it felt as if she was walking in a pool with water up to her thighs. What a huge effort it was just to put one foot ahead of the other.

A thought seized her. She willed herself to stop thinking it, but it wouldn't go away: she didn't want to go to Rockaway House. It made her feel disoriented and sick to her stomach to think about seeing Victoria lying in a strange bed, in a strange room. What was Magda expected to do there? There'd be a nurse to attend to Victoria, and a nurses' aide to keep things clean. They probably wouldn't even let Magda keep track of Vic's meds.

They probably have some stupid rule that won't allow that.

Where Magda wanted to go was back to bed for the rest of the morning. She hadn't gotten to sleep after calling Rockaway House at two a.m. She'd flip-flopped for a couple of hours, tried to read a book, watched a few infomercials and now it was seven a.m. Not that she wasn't used to going without sleep for a day, sometimes more, but it was different before now. For the past six months, she'd snatched bits of sleep and managed just fine because there wasn't any alternative. As her mother had repeatedly said to her, "Remember, Magda, that which does not kill us makes us stronger."

Right. Or kills you slowly, an inch at a time, so you hardly notice until it's too late, like a frog in a pot of boiling water.

And don't think for one second that Magda didn't pick up on the *you're the one who wanted this contemporary committed relationship* tone in her mother's voice.

Whatever.

It was different now that Victoria was at Rockaway House, though, wasn't it? Magda didn't really have to stay awake now, did she? But would someone at Rockaway House notice if she didn't show up this morning? Magda was Victoria's designated health care proxy. What if there was an emergency? At the very least, they would think it was odd that she'd just dumped Victoria off yesterday and didn't even show up this morning.

Wouldn't they?

If she could just nap for a couple of hours, then she was sure she'd feel like going. Anyway, what good would she be to Vic in this condition?

Magda went back into their bedroom. She took off her shoes, flopped down on the bed, threw Victoria's favorite afghan over her legs and fell asleep.

It was pitch dark in the bedroom. Magda looked over at the clock radio. *Six o'clock—a.m. or p.m.? Christ, what have I done?* She jumped up and looked out the bedroom window that faced the east. *No sunrise. It's six in the evening. I've slept all day.* She shoved her glasses on and raced to the kitchen, then punched in the number for Rockaway House.

"Rockaway House, nurses' station. Carolyn speaking."

"Uh, this is Magda Stark. I'm Victoria King's family member. I just—I don't know what happened—I just laid down for a little nap this morning and I just woke up. Is she okay? I can't believe I did this."

"Victoria's very comfortable, Magda. You must have needed that sleep. Are *you* okay?" Carolyn was speaking in a calming low tone.

"Yes, yes, I'm fine. I'm going to get a cup of coffee and then I'll be there."

"Take your time, Magda. Victoria's been asleep most of the day herself, so she'll probably be ready to wake up and visit with you when you get here. That'll work out just fine, won't it?"

"Yes. I'll see you soon."

The world hadn't stopped spinning. Victoria hadn't freaked out. *I don't think the staff at Rockaway House even noticed how undependable I am.*

Magda splashed cold water on her face, grabbed a power bar and headed for the garage. Just to be sure, she went back and double-checked the lock on the front and back doors.

Off to see Victoria. Magda smiled. She felt so much better now.

Surprised but not really. That's what Victoria said to Magda when she was first diagnosed with breast cancer. Victoria was surprised but not really. Her grandmother died of breast cancer, her mother died of breast cancer, two aunts and a great aunt all died of breast cancer.

Magda had been surprised, really. For her, the memory of that conversation was still vivid.

"You knew this was possible—probable—and you never said anything."

Victoria didn't answer. In her own defense, Victoria thought what Magda had spoken was, after all, a declarative, not an interrogatory, sentence. A few very long moments later, Magda walked out of the room and never brought it up again. Victoria wanted to, many times, to clear it all up, she really had, but it was one of those situations when she just couldn't see the point of any more dialogue on the subject. She had cancer. She would do what she needed to do to fight it. The women in her family never won the battle, but that didn't mean she wouldn't fight, even though she probably wouldn't win.

Four years before Victoria's diagnosis, about the time her mother was dying of breast cancer, the oncologist had suggested that her mother—and any other women in the family who would be willing—get tested to verify whether they carried a genetic marker for this type of breast cancer. He said there were options to consider if that turned out to be the case.

But Victoria didn't see any point in having the genetic test when her mother was already close to death and for Victoria it simply meant she might know with an eighty percent certainty what she didn't want to know at all. As far as having a voluntary prophylactic double mastectomy—that was one of the options her mother's oncologist had casually mentioned—that was out of the question. Instead, starting right then, Victoria made a disciplined commitment to lead a healthy life. She cleared out all the sugar in their house. She made sure she and Magda had only an occasional glass of wine and neither one had ever been a smoker. They both walked daily and Victoria signed them up for resistance training and yoga classes.

And a part of Victoria truly believed that she'd told Magda about her family's history with breast cancer back when it first came up. She remembered thinking about telling her; maybe she just thought she had.

Oh well, what's done is done.

It was just one of many times that Victoria decided on behalf of herself and Magda that a subject didn't merit any discussion.

I mean, it's too late to go back and change my mind, so what's there to discuss?

Magda had liked the feeling of Rockaway House from the first time she walked in. The lights and sounds were all muted and sort of out of focus to her. Even if the decor of Rockaway House was on the dreary side, that was okay with Magda because it had a reliable, settled feeling. She was enjoying a momentary obsession with the railing of the grand staircase and its comforting smoothness in her hand. She took her time climbing the two flights, looking at the magnificent 1920s wood paneling and carvings along the way, even stopping once to peer closely.

Not sure if she was supposed to check in at the nurses' station whenever she arrived, Magda stopped there just to be certain. Carolyn was still on duty. Magda introduced herself and Carolyn shook her hand and asked if Magda knew the way to Victoria's room.

"I think I remember—the one at the end of the hall?"

"That's right, down to the left. I was just in there. Victoria's wide awake and waiting for you."

"Oh, good. Thank you." Magda walked the short distance and gave a tap on the door as she opened it. Victoria was in bed, the head slightly elevated. She smiled widely.

"Hey! What'd you do all day, sleep?" She didn't reach up to embrace Magda. For weeks, any movement had caused Victoria excruciating pain.

Magda knew that so she leaned over and they gently touched cheeks, then Victoria's question finally registered with her.

"Sleep? What makes you think that?"

"I just hoped that's what you were doing. You mean you really did? You never sleep during the day."

"I know. It was weird." Magda pulled a chair up to the side of the bed and took a long look at Victoria. She looks good, Magda thought. Victoria had a sweet smile on her face, a look Magda had not seen for a long time.

She looks peaceful. "You look good, Vic. How's the pain?"

"Not bad, not bad. They whip up a mean cocktail here. I don't know what they're giving me, but it's working, so who cares? You, however, look like crap." She nodded toward a hand mirror on the tray table and Magda picked it up.

Is that really me? She looked half-crazed. In her haste to get to Rockaway House, she had left home without brushing her hair, let alone putting on any makeup, not even lipstick. *When did I last shower? Yesterday sometime?*

"Oh my God, Vic. I can't imagine what that nurse thinks of me."

Victoria softly laughed, another thing Magda had not observed for a very long time. "Carolyn? Oh, she understands. It's okay, sweetie. Let's visit for a while, then I want you to get home and have a nice long shower and go back to bed. You must be exhausted." She tenderly stroked Magda's bed head but she didn't flinch when she moved her arm, Magda noticed. "Now bring me up to date. Any messages at home?"

As previously instructed, Magda had notified everyone about Victoria's move to Rockaway House. From her pocket, Magda pulled the list she'd made at home and read the names of those who had left voice mails. A few close friends from work had already stopped by over the lunch hour that day. Victoria had been asleep, but they'd left notes for her in the guest book that Magda had put on the dresser, close to the door, as Victoria had suggested. Magda read the messages of encouragement aloud.

Magda and Victoria were both professors at Chesterton Community College. It was CCC where they'd met twenty-five years earlier. At the time, Victoria was twenty-seven and teaching English and Magda was twenty-five, teaching American History. They were co-workers, then good friends for several years. As times changed, their relationship did as well. Their public persona evolved from BFFs to roommates to joint owners of a post-war bungalow, walking distance from campus. All those years of trying so hard to be so unremarkable as a couple and it turned out no one else really cared.

In spite of Iowa being one of the first states to legalize same-sex marriage, Victoria and Magda never saw the necessity of that formality. They knew many heterosexual couples who chose to live together without the blessing of the state or church. As Victoria had put it, "We don't need all that nonsense, do we, Magda? No, I didn't think so." The time when friends asked if Victoria and Magda would tie the knot had passed along with the novelty of Iowa's status.

They built a good life together. They had their home, lovingly furnished with antiques and collectibles from weekend getaways and day trips to the plethora of B&Bs and adorable shops in the Midwest. They had friends they joined for dinner or Sunday brunch, out or at each other's homes. The Iowa winters were filled with book groups—each belonged to one of the *Under the Covers* clubs—and pasta dinners. Victoria had her pottery and journaling and Magda had her piano playing. They had yard work and flower gardening in the spring, a major vacation in the summer, and, of course, they had leaf peeping along the Mississippi in the fall.

But that was all before last January.

It was September now and it had been a long time since either one had spent an hour on a hobby or gone out of the house to socialize. Oh, there'd been no shortage of help and support, far from it. Friends organized a network of meals, so there was always something in the frig or freezer ready to be nuked. They were well meaning, but Victoria had no appetite and Magda was sick of eating healthy. *What did all the healthy living get us?* Except for that one doctor who described Victoria as one of the healthiest cancer patients he'd ever seen and Magda still shook her head at that one. *That doesn't even make sense.*

Friends had frequently offered to give Magda a break and sit with Victoria for a few hours or even a day. They were offers that Magda always refused. If Victoria was having a really bad time of it, she didn't want anyone but Magda with her. If Victoria was feeling pretty good, Magda didn't want to be gone; she wanted to be there, to enjoy that precious time with Victoria.

There really is no pleasing some people.

By May, Victoria had taken disability retirement when it became obvious that she would never again return to the classroom. In the spring, Magda juggled her own schedule, begrudgingly leaving Victoria alone while she was teaching. But anytime Magda wasn't teaching, she was at home. Students, the administration and fellow faculty members were empathetic and accommodating. Besides, there was e-mail, Skype and the good old telephone if anyone wanted to reach Magda outside of class.

They hadn't.

Magda suspected the word had gone out that she was not to be disturbed except in the case of an emergency and academic emergencies weren't all that common. A little hurt at first when she seemed to be so entirely forgettable, Magda grew to be thankful that she didn't have to worry about the needs of anyone besides Victoria. Making herself streetable to be on campus and scheduling someone to be with Victoria at the house would have been two more tasks on Magda's overwhelming list of tasks. It was way easier to just stay home.

Magda had the summer off anyway, but as the fall semester approached, it was more and more obvious that she couldn't be away from Victoria even for one course, let alone three. No one was surprised at her decision to go on official family leave, only that she had taken so long to make it.

Running out of paid leave most likely wouldn't be an issue for Magda. Except for the flu in the winter of 2006, she'd never been ill so she had heaps of personal days available. Well, she had come down with bronchitis twice in the past three months, but since she was already on leave, she didn't need to use any sick days, did she? With an antibiotic Z-pack from her doctor, Magda had managed to maintain full speed. No, between her bounty of personal days, vacation time and floating holidays, her paycheck was guaranteed as well as her position for quite some time.

"So, what about you, Vic? Were you able to get some sleep today?" Magda's question was rhetorical. She looked at Victoria and was thinking she hadn't appeared this rested for a very long time. *After just one night at Rockaway House? Seriously, it should advertise itself as a spa.*

"I did." Victoria had a dreamy look.

Probably high as a kite, Magda thought. *Hey, as long as she's not suffering like she was at home.* There, chasing Victoria's pain and comfort was a battle that Magda had fought and lost on a daily basis.

As soon as the visiting hospice nurse had suggested that good rest was one element of keeping Victoria comfortable, Magda had rented a hospital bed with a special low-pressure mattress and put it in their guest bedroom. When the hospice doctor suggested a morphine pump might aid in pain management, Magda had immediately authorized its installation. She soon learned that giving Victoria just enough meds to keep the severe pain at bay without rendering her unconscious was more luck than medical science. After a while, keeping her conscious was no longer a goal. Magda would have knocked Victoria out with a hammer if it would ease her pain, but Victoria's suffering became a beast that would not be subdued. After a while, nothing worked.

That was the point when everyone agreed that it was no longer possible to manage Victoria's pain in the home setting, even with as-needed input from the hospice doctor and daily visits from the hospice aide. Well, maybe if Magda had hired around-the-clock nursing care, but that wasn't an option, because, as Magda would later discover, Victoria had put the kibosh on that plan weeks earlier. Victoria had realized before anyone else acknowledged it that when—not *if*—the time came for her to go into residential care, she would probably not be capable of rational thinking so one day she spoke to Lottie, the hospice nurse, while Magda was out of the room.

"Can you please put me on a 'pre-waiting waiting list' for Rockaway House, if you know what I mean?" Victoria had asked. "I don't want Magda here in our home at the end, alone with a nurse and me, and I don't want to die here." End of discussion.

A week ago, Victoria had gathered her thoughts in an exceedingly rare lucid moment, accepted that her pain was very nearly unmanageable and told Magda to call Rockaway House. Tell them I'm ready to come, Victoria had said. After twenty-five years, Magda knew arguing with Victoria was a waste of time. Magda also knew at that moment that she could stop worrying about running out of paid leave.

By the time Victoria was moved to Rockaway House, there was no longer any point in asking where it hurt. The pain from the bone cancer was in a dead heat with the pain from the liver cancer. Victoria's suffering was all encompassing and unrelenting. And it hadn't gone unnoticed by the hospice team that Magda's level of anxiety and suffering was also at an all-time high.

As she looked at Victoria resting so peacefully at Rockaway House, it seemed to Magda as if some sort of miracle had occurred in the past twenty-four hours. She could hardly remember the last time she and Victoria were able to have a real conversation, never mind that Vic's half of the dialogue was now a bit off plumb. Magda made a mental note to ask the nurse what they were giving her. *I'll have what she's having. Ha.*

"Magda, can you help me go through my checklist?"

"Sure, hon." The checklist. Magda reached over to Victoria's bedside table and picked up the spiral notebook that had been all but attached to Victoria for the past five months. Just inside the cover was a folded paper, neatly titled *Victoria's Checklist.* Magda opened it.

"Do you want me to read it to you?"

"Yes, please." Victoria leaned back on the pillow, lids half closed but eyes looking up at the ceiling, ready to listen. Her slight cringe as she settled in didn't go unnoticed by Magda, but then, Magda noticed everything. The bone cancer had created the potential for a fracture or break with the slightest provocation. Even in the gentle hands of the hospice team, the move to Rockaway House could have caused injury. But, as the doctor had explained to Magda, at this stage of Victoria's disease, diagnosing whether she had been hurt would probably cause as much pain as the wound itself.

"Let's see, I'll read the things you've finished. *Legal documents* – check." When they bought their house six years earlier, Victoria directed their attorney to prepare the documents that any prudent couple needed, married or not. And nobody would ever accuse Victoria of not being prudent. Since they chose not to marry, they had to be sure to document their wishes for the other person to be an heir and a substitute decision-maker for health care and financial matters. They both knew that without those written instructions, the law would recognize primary blood and legal relationships first. And Magda was not keen to stand by helplessly as Victoria's sister stepped in to manage Victoria's health care in a crisis. No more than Victoria would tolerate being pushed aside by Magda's mother.

When the cancer came back eight months ago, Victoria double-checked the Durable Power of Attorney for Health Care giving Magda the authority to make medical decisions on her behalf. As they signed their updated Living Wills, Victoria insisted on a lengthy discussion about end-of-life care, artificial respiration, tubal feeding, all those horrible contingency plans that you prepare to address the situation you hope-to-God will never present itself.

"*Funeral arrangements* – check." Magda concentrated hard to speak the words without emotion. They had been over this in the past couple of weeks more times than she cared to recall. "Obsessive" was not an exaggeration. Victoria repeatedly asked for Magda's assurance that everything was handled. Magda was never quite sure if Victoria was being forgetful or just plain annoying.

As directed, Magda had called Mr. Forester in Victoria's presence, e-mailed the plan to him for his confirmation that all matters were covered, and then given him a deposit. Most of Chesterton's older population still practiced the "open casket visitation" concept for funerals and the Forester family was expert at that, if that's what Victoria wanted. She did not. In that case, Mr. Forester assured Magda—who then assured Victoria—they would do whatever the client wished. Victoria hadn't invited Magda to read her plan, but Magda had no doubt the instructions were crystal clear.

The wonder of the Internet. That same day, Victoria had shown Magda the selection of cremain urns she could choose from, under her *Favorites.* Magda had groaned and Victoria finally allowed that Magda was probably capable of picking something on her own when the time came. Magda really would have preferred that Victoria make the choice herself and get it over with, but that was one thing she didn't seem willing to do. "Just no Tupperware, okay?" A funny little joke from Victoria. Home parties were something for which they shared a lifelong distain. That and buffets, because anything with a sneeze guard was verboten. They thought alike on so many subjects.

Magda now whined that the whole process was creeping her out. Victoria sighed and gave her a sympathetic look. "Don't you think I know it's creepy? You'll thank me for this at some point."

I suppose that's possible, but you won't be here anymore, so probably not.

Victoria softly spoke. "I know you hate this, Mag. Let me do this for you, please. When I'm gone, I'd rather be remembered by what I did while I was here than by anything I left undone. I don't want you all upset because you have to take care of details I didn't handle. Okay?"

"Yes. Thank you, Vic. I love you."

"I love you, too, Mag. The list?" She looked up at Magda like a small child—a heavily medicated small child—and prompted Magda to continue.

"Next: *Finish journal.* I'm sorry, I don't know if you've done that or not."

"Look there." Rather than lift a hand to point, Victoria slightly nodded her head in the direction of the notebook in Magda's hand. Magda turned the pages until she got to that day's date. She didn't recognize the handwriting and she knew Victoria hadn't had the strength to write for over a week.

"Who wrote this?" Magda asked, hoping her voice didn't betray how hurt she was suddenly feeling.

"A volunteer named Amanda. I dictated it to her. She was so nice to do that for me." Just as Victoria spoke the last word, her head gently rolled to the side. She was asleep. Magda heaved a big sigh and closed the journal, stood and walked into the hallway.

In a flash her mood went from feeling pretty good about spending some quality time with Victoria, to angry at being—what? Rejected? Ignored? Taken for granted? Magda's thinking was foggy. She was a little lightheaded, but not quite dizzy. When Crystal came upon her, she was standing outside Victoria's door, her hand still on the knob.

"Hi there." The night shift nurse extended her hand. Magda looked up and extended her own by rote. "Would you like to have a cup of coffee?"

At that moment Magda could not have told you the last time anyone offered to get a cup of coffee for her—or anything else, for that matter. For some reason, Crystal's question struck Magda as funny and she started to laugh. Crystal took Magda by the crook of the elbow and led her down the hall to the upstairs solarium. This diagnosis was an easy one; it was a clear-cut case of Caregiver Meltdown.

Rockaway House

For the second time, Margaret was the most popular person at Rockaway House because for the second time, she had arrived with freshly baked cookies. Beverly said, as she dunked the Blonde Scotchie into her coffee, that the only thing missing was the smell of them baking.

"Good idea!" Margaret responded.

The next day, Margaret brought the dough instead of the cookies and filled Rockaway House with a smell that triggered memories all over the place. Amanda thought of her mother's treats each day after school. Rose remembered her granny, who taught her everything she knew about baking. Lance Wilson, who had stopped by to check on the sump pump, remembered his Aunt Winifred's incredible pies. It was the same for nearly every family member and patient who shared in the cookie fest that first morning.

So no big surprise when Rose exclaimed, as she clamped down on her third Chocolate-chocolate Chip, "Margaret, you really can't get us all hooked on your cookies, then expect us to go without if you're not here, can you?"

That was when Margaret organized the Cookie Brigade. She would have the dough on hand if others would sign up and pledge to come a bit early to bake it, only if she wasn't able to. Margaret would provide step-by-step instructions, of course. She put a sign-up sheet on the front of the frig.

By noon on the first day of posting, the sheet was blank. Rose said it was difficult to get people to volunteer—she should know—and Margaret wasn't to let it discourage her. She didn't.

An hour later a new sign-up sheet appeared. On this one, in large block letters Margaret thanked everyone for being so enthusiastic about the Cookie Brigade. Learn-and-sample classes would be held at eight o'clock on the following three mornings, for those who had (been) volunteered. That was followed with a list of assigned days, names already filled in. Margaret had borrowed the schedule from Rose. Rose read the sign, shook her head in amazement and smiled. *Thank you, sweet Jesus.*

Margaret stepped outside to have a breath of fresh air before heading upstairs to begin her daily routine. She had hoped to sit on the bench next to the hosta bed and enjoy the peace and quiet for a moment, but her reverie was soon interrupted by the sound of someone singing. At first Margaret thought it was a radio, but soon recognized that this voice was, although well-intentioned, clearly not professional.

"*Every little star above knows the one I love, Sweet Sue, just you. And the moon up high knows the reason why, Sweet Sue, it's you . . .*"

Margaret stood, paused to listen again, then followed the voice. It came from beyond the tall hedge on the south side of the lot, right in front of the garage. The closer she got, the louder it got.

"*No one else, it seems, ever shares my dreams, and without you, dear, I don't know what I'd do. In this heart of mine, you live all the time, Sweet Sue, just you.*"

As Margaret reached the hedge on the Rockaway House side, the singing stopped. It was the opening she'd hoped for.

"Hello? Over here."

The hedge parted and two garden-gloved hands framed a smiling face.

"Hi there, neighbor! Just a second." The head disappeared and Margaret could hear rustling, maybe rakes and shovels being pushed aside and then, thirty feet down the driveway at the end of the hedge, appeared the body that went with the voice. Slender with blond hair in a ponytail sticking out the back of her ball cap, muddied work shirt over capris, she was all legs and arms and energy.

"Hi, I'm Margaret Williams" she said as they shook hands.

"Hi, Margaret! I'm Suzi Roland. Oh my gosh, is that your home?" She waved in the direction of Rockaway House.

"Oh no, I just work there. That's Rockaway House, it's a residential hospice facility." As soon as she spoke the words, Margaret wished she had a better phrase at hand. It sounded so impersonal, like how the Chesterton zoning commissioner would describe 1724 Marion Street. Judging from Suzi's quizzical look, Margaret needed to clarify. "It's a house where people come to get hospice care at the end of their lives." Ah, the look of recognition appeared on Suzi's face.

"Oh my gosh, I had no idea. I've known of people who were in Rockaway House, but I didn't know it was right next door to us. We just moved in," she said, waving in the direction of her two-story. "What's it like inside? I'll show you my house if you'll show me yours!" She laughed and Margaret caught her infectious energy.

"Oh, I'd love to show you around, but let me check—it'll take me just a minute. I'll be right back." Margaret scurried into Rockaway House, found Rose heading up the staircase and asked if she could give the neighbor to the south a tour of the first floor.

"The people right next door? Absolutely! We'd love to get to know our neighbors—I knew that house had sold, but I didn't notice the new people had moved in. Great idea!"

Margaret hurried back outside and led Suzi in the front door. As she watched, Margaret thought back on her own mixed first reactions. No question, Rockaway House was a majestic home with everything on an imposing scale and, despite its wrinkles and age spots, the grande dame still made a heck of a first impression.

"Oh my, Margaret, this is spectacular. Don't you just love old houses? My husband and I've rehabbed a couple of them. But I just don't have it in me anymore, so we made sure the house next door had already been updated. Naturally, we waited until the kids were married and gone before we bought the biggest house we've ever owned! Oh goodness." Suzi oohed and aahed as she poked her head into the living room then tentatively entered. She was mesmerized by the beamed ceiling, the paneled walls and the timeworn floors.

She ran her hand tenderly across the quarter-sawn oak mantle, admired the inglenook and built-in benches and stood still for a moment in the solarium.

Suzi's husband Stephen was an architect who focused on redeveloping older neighborhoods and designing additions and remodeling projects that preserved historic character. Besides being an old hand at renovating, Suzi taught classes in interior design at the community college and she'd always been drawn to vintage homes. As for this particular one, it was love at first sight.

Suzi asked all manner of questions about the work that went on at Rockaway House. When had it become a hospice? How many patients could stay there at one time? She had noticed the big addition at the back of the house and now she wanted to know what that was all about. As they toured, Margaret retold the story of Mrs. Sullivan, as Rose had told it to her, including the history of the freight elevator. The tour ended in the kitchen where the smell of Margaret's cookies still hung in the air.

"This is a lovely space. They certainly didn't spare any money when it came to the kitchen." Suzi caught herself. She hoped that didn't sound like she thought they had failed to be so generous in the rest of the house. She looked at Margaret apologetically as they passed through the butler's pantry and into the dining room.

"It's okay, I know what you mean, Suzi. The patients and their family members are the priority, so that's where they put the money. But it doesn't seem like anyone really wants to spend any time down here except in the kitchen. And none of this area is very kid-friendly." Margaret shrugged in frustration.

There it was again.

"Do you smell that?" Margaret was on point, turning her head and once again trying to find the source of the sweet scent she had first smelled in the garage attic.

"What—oh yes, I smell it now. I recognize it, but I can't think what it is. Whatever it is, she smells good!"

Suzi stopped in the entryway, looking one last time at the staircase and French doors. "It's lovely, Margaret, really a gem. I'm so glad we met. What you're doing here is so important, so meaningful. Thank you." She gave Margaret a warm handshake, then followed that with a hug, promising to have Margaret over to her house soon, as long as Margaret could look past Suzi's loads and loads of unpacked boxes.

Suzi stopped when she got to the end of the sidewalk and looked back at Margaret, who was standing in the open door. "Hey! I think this is the beginning of a beautiful friendship!" With a giggle and a wave, she was gone.

Rose looked troubled. She joined Margaret and the other volunteers already assembled in the training room and set her class materials down. She hated it when stuff like this happened. No matter how hard they tried to educate patients and families about end-of-life issues, every once in a while there was a slipup.

"A couple of you went with me to visit Sylvester, a patient who was receiving hospice care at home." Beverly, Amanda and Margaret nodded to each other. "Yesterday evening Sylvester suffered a heart attack. Even though he had an Out-of-Hospital Do-Not-Resuscitate Order, the EMTs performed CPR on him. He's in Chesterton Medical Center now. Sadly, he's not responding and his wife will need to decide when to withdraw the respirator." Rose paused. She wasn't surprised to see the confused faces around the room. A hand shot up.

"I don't understand. If he had a DNR, why'd they revive him?"

"His wife called 911 when he started having chest pains—which of course a person would do without even thinking. But then his heart stopped on the way to the hospital—a neighbor was driving his wife separately—and in all the confusion Dolly forgot to tell the emergency workers about the DNR. Anyway, now Sylvester's wishes have been ignored and his wife has to go through the trauma of removing the life support."

"I didn't know you could do that, I mean remove the respirator once it's being used," someone asked.

"A common misunderstanding. But if you have the legal authority to start it, you have the authority to withhold or remove it."

"So what can we do to keep something like this from happening?"

"When there's a DNR or Out-of-hospital DNR, the patient should have an identifying bracelet or necklace. Sylvester had one, but he'd just had a shower and he wasn't wearing it. To answer your question, I'm not sure we can avoid situations like this every single time, but it's still tragic when it happens.

"The good news is that Sylvester's wishes were clear. Anyway, I wanted to share that with you. Remember how I said the other day that 'knowledge leads to effective end-of-life planning'? Well, now add to that, 'knowledge and *communication* lead to effective end-of-life planning.'"

Margaret remembered Sylvester very well. He was a nice man. She was glad she'd never met his wife Dolly, so she wasn't picturing her face right now. That would be too vivid. A personal sense of loss was something Margaret had hoped to avoid while spending time at Rockaway House.

She passed through the dining room on leaving a few hours later and stopped to really survey the environment. *This is drab, dreary, depressing, disappointing, dull—stop it. What would it cost to buy some decent chairs for this room, to make it a welcoming family hangout?*

Margaret would put a pencil to it when she got home. Better than that, she'd do some research on the World Wide InterWeb.

Margaret

Why is it so blasted cold in this house? Margaret put her purse down, kept her coat on, and checked the thermostat in the hall. *It's supposed to be sixty-seven in here and it's only fifty-three. This cannot be happening.* She flipped the ON/OFF/AUTO furnace fan switch. Nothing. She jimmied the thermostat lever. Nothing. *Oh great.*

Ernie had scrupulously made a list of who to call for problems concerning the roof, the car, the furnace, plumbing and electrical issues and pest eradication. (Maxine made it clear from the start of their relationship that her profile did not include "mousing.") *Smith's Plumbing and Heating* had five stars on Ernie's list. Margaret made the call.

They'd be there in an hour. At evening overtime rates, Margaret assumed as she took off her coat and donned Ernie's sweater. *Shabby it may be, but it is toasty.*

Ernie had taken seriously his responsibility as the man of the house in a very traditional manner. He'd promised Margaret that all mechanical systems were working fine. He'd assured Margaret that—barring any unforeseen circumstances—she wouldn't need to worry about such issues of any kind for a very long time. He'd sworn.

She was tired. She was hungry. She was cranky. *I'll assume this is one of those unforeseen circumstances.*

Margaret checked her e-mails while she waited for *Smith's.* Not surprising, so far only the spammers had acknowledged her existence, digitally speaking. Lenny told her it would take a while to break into the social media network. After all, her friends who were on the Internet couldn't be expected to communicate with her by e-mail if they didn't know she had e-mail. Too tired and bad-tempered to do any research on furniture, she shut the computer off again.

If she started fixing herself some dinner, that's just when the repairman would finally show up. If she snacked on what she was craving, like a cookie or chips, she'd feel better for a bit, then she'd soon be out of sorts again. As unappetizing as it sounded, she grabbed an apple and munched until the young man from *Smith's Plumbing and Heating* showed up. *Well, at least he's on time. That's something.*

Another twenty minutes and Margaret heard footsteps coming up the basement stairs. When he reached the kitchen, he wasn't smiling.

"Well, gimme the good news, Tyler."

"Well, the good news is that we won't charge you for this service call if you have us install the new blower motor. Sorry, Mrs. Williams, it's shot. Probably fifteen years old, not that it shouldn't be good for longer than that but this one wasn't," he said with a shrug. He stopped. Margaret appreciated his sensitivity, but she'd just as soon get the pain over with.

"I'm sitting down, Tyler. Lemme have it."

"Sorry, Mrs. Williams. It'll be $525, including labor. But more good news: I'm almost positive I have the one we need back at the shop, so I can run get it and have it done tonight, so you'll have heat in a couple of hours." He waited for the thumbs up.

Well, it wasn't like it was Tyler's fault, and it wasn't as if Margaret had a choice, like building a blower motor herself from parts lying around Ernie's workbench.

"Sure. Go on back and get it, Tyler. Ernie trusted you and that's good enough for me." She forced a smile as Tyler nodded and left.

Knowing she couldn't get much crankier, it was now time for those cookies.

$525? This is bad. I shouldn't have bought that computer. Margaret wondered at that moment if the whole idea had been one big mistake. *I can't afford it. And damn it, Ernie, this wasn't supposed to happen. And doesn't it just figure, all Miss Big Shot Cookie Magnate has in the cupboard is the stale store-bought variety?* She made a cup of tea and plopped down at the table to await Tyler's return.

The day's mail was stacked in front of her where she'd dropped it two frustrating hours earlier. She began to sort through the pile, hoping time might pass more quickly.

Junk, junk, junk, bill, junk, bill. What's this? Margaret recognized the return address for the attorney she and Ernie had used years ago to prepare their Wills and advance directives. She'd gotten a nice sympathy card from Ken Sylvester when Ernie passed away, and they'd had a short phone conversation a week later. He'd confirmed her understanding of the steps she needed to follow.

No need to probate Ernie's estate. There was no estate. Everything Ernie had owned, he had owned jointly with Margaret, so all of Ernie's earthly possessions were legally disposed of at the moment of his death by rights of survivorship or beneficiary. Neither one of their Wills was really relevant unless they died together; then a niece, nephew and assorted charities would have divided the bounty. That had always been their wish, but it didn't work out that way. Ken Sylvester had also mentioned that Margaret should think about having her Will redone, now that Ernie was gone.

The last thing Ken mentioned in that phone conversation was to advise Margaret to file an Affidavit of Surviving Spouse, removing Ernie's name from title on the house. She'd sent copies of the death certificate to his pension fund and let Social Security know he died (like they didn't already know). That was that.

Or so Margaret thought until she saw this envelope.

Oh great. What now?

She ripped it open.

Dear Margaret,

I hope this letter finds you doing as well as can be expected, considering your loss of Ernie.

I think you'll be surprised to learn that Ernie came to see me about a legal matter two years before his death and the time has come for me to follow his instructions.

Before his cancer diagnosis, Ernie acquired a small insurance policy, naming you as his beneficiary. I do not believe he had any reason to think he was ill at the time. He told me it was simply something he wanted to do for you. Just before he entered hospice care, he came to see me again and instructed me to handle this matter at the time of his death, which I did by filing a claim with the insurance company and submitting the required documentation.

The policy is in the amount of $5,000. An explanation in Ernie's own words is enclosed here.

Margaret looked again in the envelope and found the small handwritten note. It read:

My dear Margaret,
It's not enough money to make much of a difference in how you live. I hope we already handled that with our hard work and saving to keep you as financially comfortable as we planned. I mean for you to do something nice for yourself with this money, something special you wouldn't otherwise do.
Remember when I quit smoking in 1993? I figured at least some of the money I've been saving should go for something that would last. Here it is.
Please enjoy this, Margaret. You've earned it. I know you're going to be okay, but please remember to have some fun. I love you.

Ernie

Ken Sylvester's letter continued:

I'm afraid I have to ask you to stop by my office to sign a receipt for the insurance company before I can release the check to you, but I am usually available and hope to see you at your earliest convenience.

It has been my pleasure to serve you and Ernie and my privilege to assist Ernie with this matter. The bill for my services was paid by Ernie prior to his death.

Warmest regards,
Kenneth Sylvester

A few minutes later, Margaret was still sobbing and didn't hear when Tyler came in the open door from the garage. The poor kid didn't know what to do or say. *Five hundred dollars is lot of money to folks these days.* Maybe he could talk to Mr. Smith about a payment plan for Mrs. Williams, he thought. *Or something.* He knocked softly on the doorframe.

"Oh my, Tyler. I didn't hear you come back. I'm sorry." Margaret quickly wiped her eyes with a paper napkin she grabbed from the rooster holder on the table. She was smiling a big smile. Now Tyler really was confused. "Come on in. Don't mind me. I just got some good news from a very dear friend of mine."

"Are you sure you're okay, Mrs. Williams? I'll just get down to the basement and get out of your way or I can come back later if that'd be better but it is pretty cold in here."

"No, no, I'm fine, really. In fact, I'm going to run down to *Amore' Pizzeria* and pick up dinner for us—I bet you haven't eaten since lunch, have you? Pepperoni good? Good!" Margaret jumped up and grabbed her purse.

"No, I haven't, ma'am, but you don't need to—"

"Be right back!" She was gone. Tyler shook his head and carried his tools and parts to the basement. *Old folks. What the heck was that all about?*

Tyler was gone, the house was warming up and Maxine had gotten herself calmed down. So much banging and running up and down stairs. *And who let that strange man in our house?* What happened to the tacit agreement she and Margaret had: No more men—ever—since Ernie left and never came back. It really was too much to bear.

Margaret had calmed down as well. She was still laughing to herself about Ernie's reference to the money he'd saved from not smoking. Obviously, the computer was Free Shoes.

Your mother has never shared the Free Shoes Theory, Margaret asked Tyler. She could hardly believe it. Allow me to enlighten you, she offered as they enjoyed the thin crust pepperoni with extra cheese.

"You see, Tyler, when you find a dress—well, not a dress for you, obviously—let's say you find a great leather jacket on sale. Then, with what you've saved on the jacket, you can buy a pair of sneakers you wouldn't have otherwise bought. Free Shoes!" She threw her hands in the air, palms up. She was beaming.

Tyler felt obliged to smile back. Mrs. Williams seemed okay now, but he couldn't be sure. It hadn't been that long since he'd found her at this very table, smiling and crying at the same time. Maybe she was confused again. "But if you buy the shoes, too, Mrs. Williams, haven't you spent as much as the jacket cost before it went on sale?"

The younger generation's inability to embrace the intrinsic reward of savvy shopping is so disheartening, Margaret reflected to herself.

"That's only if you assume you wouldn't have bought the jacket anyway—which you probably would have because you love it. In which case, it's Free Shoes!" She repeated the hand gestures, which Tyler gathered were an integral part of the expression.

"Hmmm. I should get back down to the basement," he said, rising from the table, "if you're going to have heat again tonight. Thanks for the pizza, Mrs. W."

"You're welcome, Tyler."

While Tyler worked, Margaret read the letter from Ken Sylvester three more times. The cost of the computer—heck, the cost of the printer, too—was now covered. Not to mention that nasty blower motor. And maybe a couple of Barcaloungers for Rockaway House? Five thousand dollars? In Margaret's mind, the possibilities were practically endless. It might as well be five million dollars.

Now, after taking a hot shower and donning her warm robe and slippers, Margaret was walking toward the bedroom, carrying a small tray. It held a cup of tea and a chocolate chip cannoli from *Amore' Pizzeria.* They had somehow slipped into the bag along with the cheese bread and dipping sauce. Tyler was a growing boy, right? Anyway, there was cause for celebration.

She peered down to make sure she wasn't about to step on Maxine and saw something shiny on the carpet. A penny. Without thinking, she looked at the year as she picked it up. *1971.*

"The year we were married," she said aloud, smiling.

Then she froze.

She set the tray on the bedside table and went to the closet. Still in the pocket of Ernie's cardigan—her adopted house sweater—was the penny she'd found on the sidewalk last Saturday, the day she and Lenny had gone computer shopping, the day she'd taken her first steps onto the Information Superhighway.

1941. The year Ernie was born. *Wink. Wink.*

Margaret sat down on the edge of the bed and began to cry softly as she looked up at their wedding photo.

"Thank you so much, Ernie. For everything. For the surprise of the Free Shoes—I always knew you liked my theory—and for letting me know you're here with me. Sorry about being so cranky earlier. I should have known you wouldn't leave me hanging. And you're right, Ernie, I am going to be okay."

Caleb

The Christmas in September party came together just like it was meant to be. That first day, on their way back to Rockaway House, loaded down with decorations, Margaret had asked Tracy if they could make a quick stop. Tracy didn't think Caleb would mind. Margaret pulled up in front of *Babkas 'r Us.* Mr. Goldberg's goodies weren't home-baked, but they were several notches above the usual "store bought." Without question, Mr. Goldberg offered the best iced holiday cookies in a four-county area. As he was quick to explain, granted, they weren't babkas, but how he ended up making cookies was another story, for another time. He was known far and wide for his edible art, beautifully decorated for Christmas, Hanukkah, Kwanzaa, baby showers, Bar Mitzvahs, Easter, Halloween, Passover—you name it.

Margaret left Tracy in the car, appointed to guard the priceless decorations. Margaret's a sweetheart, for sure, but maybe just a little off the grid, Tracy thought. *Who in Chesterton is going to steal Christmas lights in September—or ever?*

Of course, Margaret didn't believe the decorations would be stolen, certainly not in Chesterton. The real reason she left Tracy behind was that she didn't want her to overhear the conversation with Mr. Goldberg. Margaret could see that right now Tracy's nerves were a bit too exposed for that.

Margaret told Mr. Goldberg about her volunteer position at Rockaway House and then she explained about Caleb and his party. Could Mr. Goldberg possibly bake Christmas cookies for her now, in the off-season, she wanted to know. You betcha—how many? Religious or secular? What time on Thursday did she need them? Margaret wasn't sure, but she guessed it would be an early evening party, for those who worked or were in school.

What was the total cost, she asked, because the cookies were going to be her treat, her contribution to the party.

Mr. Goldberg could not have been more insulted. How could she possibly think he would charge her? Unheard of. He wanted to honor the young man and help to support Rockaway House. He actually knew someone right now who was on the waiting list to go there. But was Margaret sure there wouldn't be a guest or two who would appreciate a good Hanukkah cookie? Maybe just a dozen or so, just to be safe?

Sure. Who wouldn't love a Hanukkah cookie?

When they got back to Rockaway House that day, Margaret and Tracy stowed the decorations in Rose's tiny office, Margaret made a call to Lance Wilson to meet in another hour to get the tree and then she went up to Caleb's room. As for Caleb's wish to go home, there was a lot Margaret wasn't too sure of, but she did know this: time was of the essence.

Caleb had so much pain in his voice, the words would hardly come. But come they did.

"I've been to a counselor, that whole bit, Margaret. My parents made sure of that. I know what I'm doing. It's not very complicated. I don't want to be sick anymore and dying is the only other option I have left. I agreed to the feeding tube because that's the one thing I can do for my folks right now, to give them what they want, just a little more time. They've sacrificed so much for me. They're just not ready, but they're never going to be, are they?"

Margaret nodded her head in agreement. *Never.*

"Don't get me wrong, I'm not just thinking of them. With this going home bit, I've thought a lot—a *lot*—about what the end's going to be like for me and I don't want to be alone. If I'm here at Rockaway House, there's a chance I will be. At home, no way. There's always a house full of people there. And even if my Mom or Dad are here with me, that means they're not with my brother and sisters at home. Or else they're all crammed in here. No thanks." They both smiled at the visual. The room just wasn't that big. "They need to be together. *We* need to be together."

"I must say, you've certainly given this some thought, Caleb. How do you plan to break it to them?"

"In a minute I'll get to that. You know, I looked up the word 'dying' on Google. Margaret, Wikipedia has over seventy words for 'death.' What's that about?"

"Hey, I just found out what Wikipedia is—don't ask me the hard questions." They both laughed. "I don't know, Caleb." Margaret shook her head as she spoke. "We spend a lot of time thinking of labels and talking *around* the things we don't want to talk *about*, I guess. What do you think it means?"

"I think we've got over seventy words, but not one of them tells me what's going to happen. What do you think happens when you die?"

Oh boy. Here we go.

"Well, I've only been outside looking in, you understand, but I can tell you that when my husband Ernie passed away, I felt a peace and a stillness around him that I have never felt before—or since. He was like you. He was very smart and when he was ready to go and be with God, he knew it was time."

"I'm not saying I haven't had a good life, because I have, Margaret, I really have, but the last two years have mostly blown. Sorry. I'm ready for a fresh start. Is it okay for me to say that?" He looked down, then he checked his tone and perked up again. "Anyway, I get to know almost exactly when I'm dying. Not everyone gets that, you know."

"What do you think about talking to Dr. Bob about this? He seems like a pretty cool guy."

"Yeah, that's kinda what I was thinking, too. And I was going to invite him to the party, anyway. Good call, Margaret. Maybe he can help me talk to my Mom and Dad after the party."

"Let me check and make sure he's available on Thursday and let's see if we can't get him here pretty soon to talk to you. Are you good with this plan?"

"Yes. Yes I am." He put his hand to his chest and tried to take a deep cleansing breath. Tracy, who had been sitting silently in the corner of the room, came to his bedside and pulled the covers up over him as he leaned back. He was fading fast.

Rona, on duty at the nurses' station, said that Dr. Reese was in the middle of rounds at the hospital and was expected at Rockaway House in about thirty minutes. She'd give him a call just to be sure. Margaret went back to Caleb's room and watched a *Three Stooges* episode with Caleb and Tracy while they waited. It was the one where the Three Stooges are in court—one of Ernie's favorites.

When Dr. Bob arrived, Tracy and Margaret offered to make themselves scarce, but Caleb wanted them to stay. Then he didn't waste any time bringing Dr. Bob up to speed.

"I don't know if you know this, Dr. Bob, but it was my idea to come here—not my parents'," Caleb said. "I thought my family could start having a normal life again sooner without me in a hospital bed in the middle of the living room. I screwed up. I wanna go home." He began to cry. Tracy put a hand on his shoulder. "Don't you see, Dr. Bob? This just isn't my life. This is somebody else's life. And no offense to anyone, but everybody here at Rockaway House is really old. I'm telling you: this isn't where I'm supposed to be. I'm sure of that."

When Caleb told his family about the party, sisters Sarah and Rebecca were wholeheartedly in favor of an early Christmas, brother Eli thought Caleb was just the most clever guy around and his mother Elise cried.

Caleb put his arm around her. "Mom, why are you bawling? It's a party!"

"Because I completely forgot what day it is, Caleb—I didn't even realize your birthday was this Thursday." Jerry Bronson couldn't help himself; he gave Elise a bear hug and had a good laugh at his wife's expense. Not that he had remembered either, but his son Caleb had a joyfulness about him that Jerry had not seen for a very long time. Jerry would take this blessing right now, right here. He was claiming it for his family.

Elise wanted to know what she could do to help. Nothing, Tracy told her. It was all arranged. She and Mr. Bronson only needed to bring the little ones to decorate in the afternoon and then show up at five o'clock on Thursday. Elise started crying again. Six-year-old Rebecca squealed that she was wearing her Christmas sweater and snow boots to the party and it occurred to no one to argue with that.

Beginning early Thursday morning, the living room of Rockaway House was dedicated to all things Christmassy. Volunteers and any staff who could get away joined Margaret and Tracy in decorating the tree and nearly every square inch of the room. Elise brought Caleb's sisters and brother straight from school, so they could string popcorn and cranberries, including Eli who scoffed at the suggestion that he might be too old for that. (Margaret had called in a couple of big favors at *The Marion Street Grocery* to get cranberries in September.)

Twinkle lights were hung from the curtain rods, artificial garlands decorated the mantle. Every horizontal surface was covered with an assortment of holiday decor from the Baby Jesus to battery-operated ho-ho-ho-ing Santas. The fireplace wasn't functional—the chimney hadn't been swept for years—but Lance rigged up an extension cord with a red light bulb and hid it safely behind some logs and greenery. For this crowd of imaginative souls, it would do just fine. Caleb sent word from upstairs that he felt well enough to join in and Tracy soon wheeled him down to watch, even if for only a few minutes. Margaret had plugged in the Christmas tunes to get everyone in the mood and as they worked, they softly sang along with Bing Crosby, Elvis and The Chipmunks.

Tracy's mother came and got help to unload a folding table for the food. She spread out a lovely green tablecloth, a huge silk poinsettia plant and Christmas plates and napkins. Santa platters awaited Mr. Goldberg's cookies.

"I always load up at the day-after sales, so I just went to the Christmas closet and there it was, just waiting for me!" she said proudly.

In short order, the living room of Rockaway House could have put Sullivan's Department Store Christmas window of 1957 to shame.

When five o'clock Thursday came, it was clear that Caleb had an eclectic group of friends for a barely eighteen-year-old. Five or six of his buddies from school showed up—the ones who still treated him like before he got sick. There was Reverend Mike and Pastor Matt—who had invited himself when Mike mentioned the party—all the on- and off-duty staff, the Rockaway House volunteers, two patients who were able to sit up for a bit and their loved ones. Bronson aunts, uncles and cousins, beloved neighbors, and Caleb's immediate family filled the room.

Once everyone was gathered—glasses full of hot cider and cocoa and little hands clutching cookies and candy canes—Tracy steered Caleb's wheelchair into the room. People hardly noticed his frailty, so mesmerized were they by the Santa hat on his head and the grin he wore, stretching from ear to ear.

Caleb said later it didn't even bother him that he couldn't eat. It was like every Christmas he'd ever known. His Mom always made the four children sit down at the table and have *something*, a roll or donut, before the Christmas morning free-for-all started. But food was always the last thing on their minds, with presents under the tree calling out to them. It had been the same at the party. Caleb was too busy having fun being with all the people he loved and who loved him to think about eating. Anyway, he could *smell* the food and it smelled just like Christmas and that was totally awesome, he said.

Nine-year-old Sarah Bronson cornered Pastor Matt and drilled him with twenty questions on where her big brother would be by the time the real Christmas came. Rebecca, six, sensed an opportunity and joined in, posing the most obvious of existential queries: There wasn't any chance that Santa would think this Christmas was the real thing and pass them over in December, was there? Reverend Mike gave Matt a little wave from across the room and ignored Matt's mouthed plea for help—it was obvious he was loving it. That happened to be the instant that Pastor Matt decided to get more involved with Rockaway House.

Dr. Reese arrived as the evening was winding down but in time to have a sandwich and cranberry sauce. Dr. Golan passed him in the entryway and advised him to have a cookie—he hadn't seen Hanukkah treats like that since childhood. In fact, he had a frosted dreidel in his pocket for the ride home. How was it no one had told him about *Babkas 'r Us* before now?

It was big fun. No one would have thought it possible for any occasion to eclipse the incredible heartbreak that brought them all together. But there was something magical about gathering for Christmas, the most anticipated holiday of the year, even in September. If you could, for the moment, suspend disbelief that there was snow outside, that Santa really would be visiting soon and that it was the season of miracles, heavy hearts could not help but be lightened.

Without being told, many of the guests knew it was probably the last time they would see Caleb, but no one let sadness mar the holiday theme. Goodbyes were enthusiastic, with hugs and kisses and many a '*Happy New Year,*' especially after Caleb's Uncle Stan pointed out that it was the natural thing to say at a Christmas party, wasn't it? Guests waited until they got outside beyond Caleb's view to cling onto each other and share tears.

On her way home after an exceptionally long day at the office, Lauren Dunlap noticed all the cars and lights at Rockaway House. She peeked inside the front door and Rose spotted her before she could duck back out. Rose took her aside and explained the occasion. Lauren couldn't speak. After giving Rose a lingering hug, she left as quickly as she came and then sat in her car for a long time before she was able to drive away.

Finally, the last guest left. A neighbor had taken Sarah, Eli and Rebecca home to Bronson's. Elise was staying with Caleb, but she and Jerry wanted to take him back upstairs together and tuck him in bed before Jerry left. Dr. Reese joined them in the corner of the living room where they were just about to send an exhausted Tracy home and wheel Caleb to the elevator.

"Elise, Jerry, there's something Caleb and I would like to talk to you about." Dr. Bob gently steered them to a couch where they could sit next to each other, then he shared Caleb's plan. It's not like Jerry and Elise were surprised. Since Caleb was a little boy, he wore his heart on his sleeve and they always knew when they were being played. Jerry had called Elise as soon as he got back to his office after the meeting with Dr. Bob earlier that week. They had both sensed it: Caleb didn't really want the feeding tube, so why did he so willingly agree? Now they knew.

Caleb let his parents hear it from Dr. Bob, then he spoke.

"I'm a man now, Mom, Dad. I'm not going to have very long to be one, but I can make my own adult decisions now and I've made this one. I want to come home." They stood and leaned over to hug their son, then together they took him upstairs for his last night at Rockaway House.

Jerry left and Elise got Caleb settled. Crystal stopped by and asked how he was feeling and if he wanted a tubal feeding before he went to sleep. No, he was fine, Caleb insisted. He was exhausted but peaceful, more peaceful than he had been for many days, maybe weeks, and the grown up young man let his mother dress him for bed.

"Ready to have some sweet dreams, son?" Elise asked as she tucked him in and sat down on the edge of the bed.

"I am, Mom. That was a great Christmas, wasn't it? Didn't Margaret do an awesome job of making it all look like home? I wanted to thank her but I didn't see her around at the end."

"She sure did, honey. We'll be sure to find her before you leave tomorrow. Now I have one more Christmas surprise for you." She reached into the tote bag she always carried and retrieved a careworn copy of *The Littlest Angel.* It had been a present to Caleb on his first birthday, not long before his second Christmas. Elise, then the same age as Caleb was now, had read it to him that Christmas Eve and every year after that, joined over time by Eli, Sarah and Rebecca.

Inside the cover was handwritten, "*To our angel baby Caleb from Mommy and Daddy.*"

"*Once upon a time—oh many, many years ago as time is calculated by men—but which was only Yesterday in the Celestial Calendar of Heaven—there was, in Paradise, a most miserable, thoroughly unhappy, and utterly dejected cherub who was known throughout Heaven as The Littlest Angel.*"

Elise looked over. Caleb was asleep.

Edward

For the family of W. Edward Everest, the day so far had been extraordinarily long and punishing.

Just as Caleb's party was winding down, Margaret spotted an ambulance passing outside the dining room windows, headed for the rear of Rockaway House. A delivery. Then she heard the familiar sound of the elevator's gears. She climbed the stairs and paused at the landing, looking up in time to see two ambulance attendants and a stretcher trail down the hall, followed by what could only be described as a gaggle of people.

In the weeks that Margaret had spent shadowing Rose, asking scores of questions and politely eavesdropping, she had picked up quite a lot. She knew that in just a few moments, the staff would need to concentrate on getting the new resident settled. If a volunteer would please acclimate family members to Rockaway House and lead them to the lounge or kitchen and out of the staff's way, Nancy the case manager and Tammy, the aide on duty, could concentrate on their work. Margaret's timing was perfect.

Seven hours earlier, Mr. Everest's adult children thought the family patriarch—they called him Big Ed—would be discharged from the hospital, finally going home after ten days in Chesterton Medical Center. They had a well-planned care strategy: the refrigerator was stocked with Big Ed's favorite foods, a daily schedule for visiting was divvied up among the family members, and a home health care worker was engaged to come to the house each morning. She'd do light housekeeping, help Big Ed with personal care and prepare the day's meals.

The wheels came off the wagon that morning just as Big Ed's daughter Holly was packing up his potted plants and the *Get Well, Grandpa!* balloon. Big Ed's heart stopped.

In the past few weeks there had been a host of health issues: the flu, followed by pneumonia, a bladder infection, intermittent chest pains and then, at ten-fifteen this morning, full cardiac arrest. It took only one jolt from the defibrillator to get Big Ed back with the living, but the prognosis was not hopeful: end-stage congestive heart failure. The recurrent infections and a long life had taken their toll, and there were no curative treatments available for this man who was one month away from his ninety-second birthday. That news wasn't totally unexpected, but shockingly at odds with everyone's expectations for the day and Big Ed's history of always bouncing back.

His children, Teddy, Roseanne and Holly, along with their spouses and the grandchildren, were filling the upstairs hallway after being gently shooed out of the patient room by Nancy. Margaret stepped up just as Tammy was heading downstairs to see if anyone could help out. She hated to do it, but she'd have to drag someone away from Caleb's party to pitch in. Margaret saved her the trip.

"Margaret, this is the Everest family. Mr. Everest is just getting settled, if you could please show them around Rockaway House."

"Good evening, folks. I'm Margaret. I'm a volunteer." Margaret extended her hand to each one. They politely introduced themselves, including the grandchildren. "I'll show you around while your father—and grandfather—gets settled in. And then you can come back up in a bit. We're headed downstairs—would anyone like to use the elevator? No? Then please follow me." From watching Rose, Margaret had learned to adopt a tone of voice that would gently guide loved ones who were often in a daze of grief and disbelief. The Everest family members were no exception. Exhausted and befuddled, they mutely followed her.

The doors into the living room were closed and Edward's family had no idea there was a party going on as they passed by on their way to the kitchen. Margaret pointed out the dining room, leaving the children there with a board game, and led the adults into the kitchen, offering coffee or a snack. They politely declined, standing awkwardly around the large table, looking down, unsure of their next move.

Margaret broke the silence. "I'm so sorry your father's not well. Has he been sick for long?" Roseanne and Holly quickly filled her in on Big Ed's recent health history, ending with that day's grueling details.

Holly's the one in charge and most likely the oldest, Margaret guessed.

"Our heads are spinning. I mean, he's almost ninety-two, but we thought he was going home today, not coming here . . . The cardiologist said he's in congestive heart failure—whatever that means." Roseanne put an arm around her sister. "Coming here was the hospital social worker's idea. Dad's own doctor said he wasn't sure it was time yet, but the social worker recommended Rockaway House and said it was really nice here and Dad's so weak, he really couldn't go home—he's pretty short of breath . . . The cardiologist signed off on this, but maybe it is too soon?" Holly voiced the doubt they were each struggling with. It was all so confusing.

Margaret remembered again the first time she and Ernie had heard the term "hospice," grappling with the implications of surrender and acceptance and—ultimately—finality. The moment was no less dicey for this family. The doctor had planted doubt in their minds, but they had decided to trust the social worker. Now came the time to second-guess their decision.

Teddy broke the silence. "Margaret, if I may ask, what is 'hospice,' anyway?"

"First, let's all sit down. Are you sure no one wants a coffee or tea?" They sat but still declined. "Well, hospice is about taking care of the patient during the last chapter of life. We'll focus on making sure your father is kept as comfortable as possible. We're here to support him and you, medically, emotionally and spiritually. Mostly, we want whatever time you have left with your dad to be as peaceful and dignified as can be. We'll do all we can to honor him and his wishes." Teddy's wife was quietly sobbing.

"What are the visiting hours here?" Teddy asked as he put his arm around her.

That answer was simple. "There aren't any. You're welcome to come anytime, 24/7. If someone wants to spend the night, each room has a single sleeper bed for you to use. And, of course, the children are welcome to visit." They all smiled with relief at Margaret's words.

"Big Ed's close to the grandchildren—he'll be glad to hear that. I think he understands what the doctor told us. He said, 'Kids, I'm almost ninety-two. It's time I joined your mother.' Understand, Margaret, Dad was living on his own, perfectly fine until a couple of weeks ago. He's always been so independent." As Holly finished speaking, it was Roseanne's turn to start crying. "Mom died ten years ago after a long battle with cancer. But I don't remember anyone suggesting hospice to us then."

"Rockaway House didn't exist yet. In fact, formal hospice care wasn't even available in Chesterton ten years ago," Margaret said.

The swinging door at the back of the kitchen opened and Tammy appeared.

"If you folks would like to go back upstairs, your father's all settled in and resting now." They rose, took a collective breath and followed Tammy and Margaret up the staircase, all except Roseanne. She volunteered to join the children in the dining room, explain what was going on and then bring them up.

Margaret waited outside Mr. Everest's room as his family and Tammy entered. Soft voices, then laughter, drifted out to the hallway. After meeting his children and hearing what Mr. Everest had said about joining his wife, Margaret could easily imagine the poignant scene inside the room.

In a few minutes, Roseanne arrived in the hallway with the grandchildren trailing along. One girl, about eight years old, had been crying, but each put on a broad grin as they squeezed into the room.

It seemed like time for Margaret to make her exit. There wasn't space for another soul in there and there wouldn't be in the hall either, once they started coming back out. Anyway, she'd get the chance to meet Mr. Everest the next morning. Margaret stopped by the nurses' station, said goodnight to Nancy and Tammy and went downstairs.

The Christmas party guests were all gone by the time Margaret walked through the first floor on her way out. It had been quite a day. Someone had taken care of the leftover food. Probably Tracy's mother, Margaret thought with a smile. In the morning, she'd recruit some helpers and tackle dismantling the Christmas decorations.

Where else would Margaret ever have met such extraordinary folks, she thought as she walked to her car. A teenage boy who is so gracefully accepting life's approaching end and a group of mature adults struggling to do the same. There were so many lessons to be learned from those who pass through these halls. What a blessing they were.

I think this is how it's supposed to be at the end of life: acceptance and grace and the chance to say peaceful goodbyes. Thank goodness Rockaway House is here.

Rockaway House

"Lauren Dunlap speaking." Not a very friendly greeting, but when the phone rings at five fifteen in the morning, it isn't usually a friend. Turns out, this time it was.

"Sorry, Lauren, but this is Kevin, Kevin Lansing."

"What's goin' on, Quincy?" Lauren had met the Clinton County Medical Examiner when she moved to Chesterton, but not through CCH. In hospice work, there weren't many opportunities to cross paths directly with the coroner. Lauren and Kevin both happened to belong to the Chesterton YMCA. Spinners. In a casual conversation, they discovered they were both in the dying business, so to speak. After that class, they had the first of many cups of coffee and had become good friends over the past two years.

"I'm at a suicide up on Division Street."

"And that has what to do with me?" Lauren turned on the light and was now sitting up in bed, taking a sip of water from the bedside bottle and putting on her glasses.

"Well, according to the daughter, who found the body, he's a patient of CCH. I thought you'd want to know."

"Oh. What's his name, Kevin?"

"Mr. Gerald Lipmann." Lauren was taking notes. "I think Judy Gold's your on-call tonight, but I thought I'd go directly to you. There's a note, Lauren."

"A note? What's it say?"

"You want me to read it to you?"

"Yes, please." She braced herself.

"Just a second, let me get outside." Lauren waited, listening to the background sounds at Kevin's location: muted voices, garbled radio transmissions, probably the police who had answered the call. "Okay, I'm alone now. Here it is: *Dear Kimberly* (that's the daughter, she's the one who found him), *I'm so sorry to do this to you. It's not like I wasn't going to leave you soon, although perhaps not quite this soon or quite as abruptly. You remember what it was like with your mother? I know you do. I refuse to do that to you, Kimberly. Or to me. I love you too much. Please don't be disappointed or angry at me. I'm ready to go. I love you.* (signed) *Dad.*" Kevin waited for Lauren to respond. "You still there?"

"Yeah. Okay. How's the daughter? It's the daughter Kimberly that's there, right?"

"Yes. She's doing well, considering."

"What was the—how'd he do it?"

"My preliminary work says the better part of a bottle of one of his prescription painkillers. I'll know more after the autopsy. I spoke to the daughter and she doesn't disagree. Says it's very possible. I don't think we're going to get any surprises on this, Lauren. Well, I thought you'd want to know ASAP."

"Yes, thank you, Kevin. Thanks. I'll see you later this week, I guess."

"Yeah, see you in class, Lauren. Hope the rest of your day goes better."

"Yeah, me too. Later." Lauren hung up the phone and sat for a moment. This was a first for her. *A patient committed suicide. Wow.* She shook off the foggy reverie and got back to business. The next few steps were largely dictated by crisis policies already in place, but Lauren had to decide in what order to make—or not make—the calls.

First to her administrative assistant, Allie Lester, who also kept a note pad by her bedside phone. Lauren asked Allie to send a mass voice mail to the leadership team. There'd be a no-excuses meeting at eight o'clock in Lauren's office and would Allie also please contact whoever was on call at CCH and get the cell phone number for Mr. Lipmann's daughter? Next, Lauren left a courtesy message on the office voice mail of Dorrie Kelly, the head of CMC public relations. It was hard to know what kind of publicity might come of this.

She then rousted the CMC corporate attorney Henry Lloyd out of bed. Lauren couldn't say she felt a bit bad about the timing of that call. Henry (not "Hank," he hated to be called "Hank") wasn't one of her favorite people. Henry said he appreciated being informed so promptly (did Lauren detect a note of sarcasm in his voice?) and said to keep him in the loop. She glossed past that, said goodbye and hung up. Not by accident, he'd already been left out of the eight o'clock meeting loop. *Oops.*

Lauren got a quick rinse in the shower, did a seven-minute hair and makeup job (a new record by three minutes) and was out the door by six a.m. She'd gladly sacrificed shower time for a drive-thru stop at *Whole Latte' Love.* The extra large dark roast—just sweetener, please—would keep Lauren fueled for awhile.

It had become their little joke every day, Lauren thanking the owner and operator of *Whole Latte' Love* for opening her shop two years earlier. Until then, Lauren couldn't get a freshly brewed cup of coffee in Chesterton until seven-thirty a.m., at the grocery store deli counter. It wasn't that she wasn't able, even willing, to make coffee at home each morning, but to have one of those coffee/chai/cocoa-by-the-cup machines would be way too accessible the rest of the time. She could just see herself pie-eyed at two a.m., the natural consequence of indulging in evening espressos and cappuccinos.

Just as Lauren pulled into the corporate parking lot, she got a text message from the on-duty nurse at Rockaway House relaying Kimberly Lipmann's cell phone number. Lauren would make that call as soon as she got to her office. There was no chance of awakening the late Gerald Lipmann's daughter.

Kimberly answered on the first ring. Lauren offered her personal and corporate condolences and asked if there was anything she could do for Kimberly.

"No. I'm just not sure what my next step is. I'm sorry, I need to run, Mr. Forester is beeping in on the other line."

The eight o'clock meeting with Lauren's leadership team was also brief. There was an established procedure for any sentinel event, such as an unexpected death or injury that wasn't related to the patient's terminal condition. Following the checklist, Lauren asked Dr. Reese, the Medical Director; Bess Goodman, the social worker; Genevieve Nillson, the intake nurse; and Delores Dean, the head visiting nurse, to review the file separately and together. Their assignment was to be sure nothing had been overlooked and to make recommendations on how the team might avoid a tragedy like this in the future, if that was possible.

Had they followed all procedures and policies? Had they missed a sign or failed to address the needs of the patient? Had they done all they could?

Lauren had barely sat down after that meeting when Henry Lloyd was back on the phone. As she punched in the line, she guessed he might have caught wind of being uninvited to the eight o'clock meeting and was feeling neglected. Lauren hoped to divert him and volunteered up front that she'd spoken to Kimberly Lipmann.

"What'd she say?" Henry demanded curtly.

"I don't know, she said something about not knowing what her next step is, I guess. Why?"

His tone was clipped. "That's code for 'I haven't had time to talk to my attorney yet.' Don't speak to her again."

"Sorry? Why wouldn't I talk to her?"

"Liability, Lauren, liability. You asked for my opinion, this is it."

No, actually, I didn't. "Well, it seems like a bit of an overreaction."

"It's the prudent way to go, believe me. I've got a call into Dorrie Kelly, so she can start some damage control."

"That really wasn't necessary, Henry. Sorry, you know what? I have a conference call I need to take. I'll talk to you later."

"Fine. Keep me in the loop."

Right, when donkeys fly past this third story window.

Lauren called Dorrie, who thanked her for the heads up phone message earlier that morning. Dorrie had already talked to a reporter at *The Bee.* They were running a story on Mr. Lipmann's passing—he was well known in the surrounding farm community—but they considered the suicide nothing more than his tragic cause of death.

Yes, Dorrie said, she'd also gotten a message from Henry Lloyd.

What did Dorrie think, Lauren wanted to know.

I think he's a jackass, just like you do, Lauren, Dorrie said without a hint of sarcasm. She told Lauren not to worry about it, though, she had enough on her plate.

Then Kimberly Lipmann was back on Lauren's phone. She was calling to apologize for cutting Lauren off so abruptly. She wondered, could she stop by the CCH offices for just a minute?

"I'm sorry, Kimberly. I've been advised by our corporate attorney that it may not be prudent for us to speak any further at this time." Lauren got a bad taste in her mouth as the words came out.

"Really? Oh. I guess I don't know how to respond to that. Thanks for your support, I guess." Kimberly hung up with a soft click.

Lauren slowly laid the phone back down. She had never felt so ashamed in her entire life.

Lois

At the risk of sounding like she was tooting her own horn, Lois Spaulding didn't see how her husband Ray would manage without her. It wasn't that her skills were irreplaceable, just not by Ray. Lois had spent her working years as the office manager in an accounting firm in Chesterton. It was her typing speed of seventy-eight words per minute that got her the entry-level job, not her bachelor's degree in 19th and 20th century English literature. But it was her skills as a flawless organizer and a quick study number-cruncher that ultimately put her in charge of the firm's day-to-day operations. She'd kept it running smoothly for over thirty years. As for her higher education, she'd met Ray at an Iowa State Teachers College alumni event in 1968, so it was four years well spent, anyway you looked at it.

Lois was at the kitchen table, paying bills and sorting papers. Her mind was preoccupied with another matter, now pushed to the top of the list by The Big Decision. Lois retired when Ray retired, but she had continued to use her organizational skills at home, keeping everything shipshape. Ray would soon be managing the business side of the household and Lois knew that to avoid any major calamities, drastic measures needed to be implemented.

Since the day they'd met, Lois truly believed—and had told Ray to his face countless times—that he was the smartest man she'd ever known. His head already filled with mountains of knowledge, he perpetually sought ways to add to it. However, when it came to money and details, not so much. When Ray walked in the kitchen, Lois was wondering if her plan—whether any plan—had a chance of working.

"What's cookin', good lookin'?"

"Just checking our paperwork and figuring out what needs to be done."

Ray pulled out a chair and sat down. "You know, I've been thinking about it and maybe—just maybe—after forty plus years, it might be my turn to manage the household. Can you show me how it's done?"

Lois gave Ray a doubtful look but, having few viable options, took a chance and slowly slid the oversized three-ring binder across the table.

"What the hell is this?"

"I beg your pardon?"

"Sorry. What the divil is this, Mrs. Magullicuddy?"

"That, Ray, is the Big Blue Book. It holds all the secrets of this house and of our lives." Her tone was somber. "You guard it with your life."

Ray playfully pushed it back at Lois. "Oh no, that sounds like way too much responsibility for me."

Lois wasn't laughing. And if these forty years had taught Ray nothing else, he usually knew when to hold and when to fold. Not always, but this time for sure. He pulled the notebook back and flipped open the cover. "May I just predict that teaching me to be responsible around here will be the hardest part of this whole process?" At this, they both laughed.

So the lesson began. Lois had equipped The Big Blue Notebook with plastic sleeves, each one holding a piece of their paperwork puzzle. From insurance policies to bank accounts, car titles to the house deed, passports to copies of their credit cards. And then there was the last page, entitled "Wills." Ray glanced through the papers, waited a moment, then looked up.

"So what now, boss?"

"First, I've put all of our regular bills on automatic payment, so you won't need to write monthly checks for them. Then I'm going to show you how to access the bank accounts online, so you can check the activity and balances. (I'll write all this down for you.) You shouldn't need to keep the paper checkbook up to date, just keep a cushion in the account. Our retirement and Social Security checks are deposited automatically. That totals—" Suddenly she stopped. Ray waited.

"What is it, honey?"

"I just realized, my checks will stop soon." It was one thing to make a detailed plan concerning her affairs, post-death, it was another to have the Social Security Administration in on it. "Oh well, we've never spent what we make anyway, so you'll be fine." She dismissed the issue. He took her hand.

"Let's do whatever makes you feel better about this, Lois. I promise not to screw this up—too much. How about this: I know the kids at the bank. I can ask them if I get in a jam, right?" Lois was visibly relieved. It was a strategy, sort of. At least Ray knew where to go for help.

In the week since Lois had made the decision to stop dialysis, she had checked two items off her Bucket List and five items off her to-do list. The Big Blue Notebook was one more. A remaining to-do: she still needed to share the decision with her doctor.

Lois had seen Dr. Sims for several periodic checkups, but this was the first time she and Ray had been seated together in his office since that haunting day, twenty months earlier. Right away, Ray thought the young doctor seemed, well, more kind, softer around the edges.

True, as a nephrologist, Dr. Sims had lost more patients to death than many of his peers in the wellness business. "Statistically, one of every four dialysis patients will choose to discontinue treatment, Lois," was his response to her news. Even in his short career, several of his patients had already done so. Ray was surprised to hear him say that but Lois wasn't; she'd read all about it on the Internet.

Dr. Sims understood the difficulty and complexity of the situation, for everyone concerned, he said. He asked enough questions to assure himself that Lois and Ray were making an informed decision, and then he said he hoped and prayed that with research, he'd have more to offer to his patients in the future. He was so very sorry it hadn't come in time for Lois. Lois heard his voice break a little when he said that.

Dr. Sims didn't argue or try to dissuade them, but he did recommend that Lois begin dialysis five times a week until she believed her affairs were in order and she was ready to stop. Ray and Lois appreciated his advice. They'd keep that in mind.

When they were almost finished, Dr. Sims came around from behind his desk and sat on its edge, close to Lois. He looked at each of them and then asked if they understood what the end might be like. Had they considered hospice care? Ray looked at Lois and spoke first.

"We hadn't really thought about that, doctor."

Lois cleared her throat.

"Actually, I have thought about it. I'd like to go to Rockaway House when I get closer to the end. Our daughter Carlene will be here soon, and I don't want her and Ray to have to take care of me at home." Ray stared at Lois in disbelief. There had been no talk of this between them, none whatsoever. "I'm sorry, honey, you probably think I'm ambushing you, but, Ray, Dr. Sims, I don't want to die at home."

Dr. Sims was listening intently. Most patients voiced a wish to stay in familiar surroundings, although few managed to do so. But not Lois Spaulding. It didn't surprise him that she already had a practical plan to do exactly as she intended.

As long as neither Ray nor Dr. Sims was responding, Lois went on.

"Our home is full of happy memories for me, for us, Ray. I don't want dying to be the last thing I do there. And that's not a memory I want to leave behind for you, either, Ray. So, doctor, who do I see to get signed up for Rockaway House?"

Dr. Sims would start the paperwork and CCH would contact Lois to talk about care options and timing issues. He emphasized that it was probably best to get on the waiting list because once Lois stopped dialysis, she might have weeks, but perhaps only days.

When their meeting was over, Lois thanked Dr. Sims and gave him a hug. He held on for an extra moment. He shook Ray's hand warmly, grasping his forearm with his other hand.

Ray and Lois were quiet as they left the office. Ray wasn't about to argue with Lois about this new momentous decision she had made—without any input from him—but only because he'd promised to respect her wishes. But somebody had to say something, didn't they? "Well," he observed lightheartedly as they approached their car, "I guess Dr. Sims took my speech to heart. He's had quite a little attitude adjustment since last year."

Lois just smiled. She hadn't mentioned it to Ray six months earlier when she met a young woman in the waiting room of the dialysis clinic. After all, there was patient confidentiality to consider. Renee, thirty-one, had recently developed end-stage kidney disease as the result of diabetes. Married with two small children, she told Lois that the biggest annoyance—as she termed it—of dialysis was that she'd missed several of her children's school programs because she just didn't have the energy to attend. But she'd been quick to say she was grateful that dialysis was even an option for her because it was the only one she had.

Lois clearly remembered Renee adding that she really felt quite blessed. She has a family member who's a kidney specialist, her twin brother Randy Sims.

On to the next item on her to-do list. Between the brochure the hospice nurse gave to Lois and the information she'd found on her own, Lois had identified the legal matters that needed attention. She'd been to the clinic that morning for a treatment and took a nap as soon as she got home. Now she and Ray were enjoying a late lunch. Lois set her fork down and looked over at him.

"Remember you said you'd do whatever I wanted?"

"I don't remember saying that." Never hurts to try a little humor, to test the waters. Lois went on exactly as if she hadn't even heard him. Good, at least that hasn't changed, Ray thought with some relief.

"Here's what I'd like to do today. I'd like to get all the nasty, unpleasant stuff out of the way. Then we can move on and not have to think about it anymore. Okay?"

"Okay, boss. Like what?"

She put her hand on his as she said this, "I want to talk about my end-of-life wishes, so you're clear on what I want to happen—and not happen."

Lois got a quick shower while Ray did up the dishes, then they met back in the kitchen. Lois had already gotten an advance directive form for them to complete and she opened Ray's copy in front of him and read aloud from hers.

Ray looked at his wife and shook his head. "How do you do this? How do you talk so calmly about dying, honey? You seem so peaceful, so comfortable with this all."

"I shriek like a banshee whenever you're not around," she said simply. Her face didn't betray her and she wasn't saying anything more; he had no idea whether or not she was kidding. "Let's just do this, okay?" She gave his hand a pat. "We don't need to change our Wills. You get all my riches. Since they both say that if the other one is gone, Carlene gets everything, you don't need to change your Will later on unless you plan to cut her out—only kidding. We already have Durable Powers of Attorney for Financial Matters, so you can sign anything for me until I pass. All that's left is this one form, so let's get it over with."

Together, they worked through the health care advance directive, including their wishes for end-of-life treatment and the appointment of a substitute decision-maker. They discussed the possible scenarios for a terminal or irreversible condition, then they each marked whether they wanted a respirator or a feeding tube and whether to have the doctor issue a Do-Not-Resuscitate Order. Once or twice, Ray gave Lois a questioning look—he wasn't quite sure he agreed with her decision. She'd been expecting that.

"Think of it this way, Ray: Whether or not we agree with it, it's our duty to carry out the other one's wishes—if we say we'll be the proxy. No more. No less. That takes away the guilt because you're not the decision-maker. You're just there to make sure the other one's wishes are respected."

Ray smiled and nodded, but he was certain these situations were a lot easier to consider when they were still on paper, not actually happening.

They named each other as proxy and each made Carlene an alternate.

"Just one more thing." Lois resolutely closed the form. "We need to talk to Carlene as soon as she gets here, so there won't be any confusion later."

Carlene. Her name remained on the to-do list—the biggest item, actually. They hadn't yet called and told her of Lois's decision. Carlene would be pretty darn surprised when she heard that her mother was discontinuing dialysis, since she didn't know Lois had started it in the first place. Many an evening over the past two years had been spent thoughtfully debating that strategy. Lois had never wanted Carlene to rush home or for every phone conversation to have a nameless veil hanging over it because she thought her mother was in a constant state of dying.

How many times had Lois or Ray said to the other one, "What if we *don't* tell her and she finds out later that we kept her in the dark?" They'd played all the what-ifs, but the most vexing was "Just exactly how annoyed will she be?" Looking back now, thoughtfully and with 20/20 hindsight, they had absolutely no idea whether they'd miscalculated.

"Did we make a mistake by not telling her when it all started?" Lois wondered aloud.

"I don't know. But if we did, it's too late for a do over, isn't it? Let's just take it from here, honey. What's the worst that can happen? **Dad Disappoints Daughter—Again**? Film at eleven." Lois laughed and gave him a peck on the cheek.

"Let's call her. I miss our little girl."

As soon as they figured out how to work the speakerphone, Ray took a deep breath and dialed the number at Carlene's apartment. It was six o'clock in California. They figured she'd be home and she was. Ray and Carlene got greetings out of the way and then Ray told her he was very sorry, but they had some sad news to give to her. Her mother's kidney condition had gotten quite a bit worse. They had tried dialysis but it wasn't working. They were sorry to be telling her this on the phone, but the disease was terminal now. They'd like Carlene to come home as soon as she could arrange it.

In the past, they'd always handed the phone back and forth when they called Carlene. This time, Lois wasn't saying anything for fear of breaking down and Ray did all the talking. They'd settled on that before they made the call.

Carlene listened mutely.

When he finished speaking, Ray waited for her to respond.

One could never be entirely sure how Carlene would react. But make no mistake, they had said to each other before making the call, there would definitely be a reaction.

"Carlene, honey? Are you still there?"

"Yes, Dad. Let me figure it out and I'll call you back."

She hung up.

Ray's first thought: God willing, that was the worse phone call I'll ever have to make. Then he looked at Lois and put his arm around her as she began to cry. Being a wordsmith, Ray really hated it when he had none to contribute, but there was no point in blubbering well-meaning platitudes and getting their hopes up, he reasoned, in case Carlene ultimately decided to stay away. Ray had anticipated very little of what was happening to his family these days, so anything was possible, he supposed.

It was difficult to know what to think. Of all the potential outcomes, they hadn't expected silence, not from Carlene. Now Lois couldn't be sure she'd ever see her daughter again.

"See it and be it." Isn't that what Carlene had taught them? Lois consciously pushed aside all the disturbing scenarios and decided to focus instead on wondering exactly when Carlene would arrive. She resolutely pulled out her list and diverted her mind by sorting through storage closets and dressers. She was making a record of special items to be given to nieces and cousins—and Carlene, too, of course. They were things that had belonged to Lois's parents and grandparents and nothing that Ray was interested in keeping. For Lois, they were treasures that needed to stay in the family.

She had been at it for about two hours when the phone rang. Ray called out that he'd catch it in the kitchen and Lois could hear his muffled voice.

In a few moments, he stood at the door of the guest bedroom.

"Who was that?"

"Carlene."

"What did she say?"

"She gets into Chicago at noon tomorrow. She'll rent a car and she'll be here about three o'clock."

"Does she want you to wire some traveling money?"

"She didn't mention that."

"Oh my. I better clean up this mess. We need to get her room ready, Ray. Carlene's coming home."

"Yes, batten down the hatches, as they say. **Unexpected Storm Front Moving In**."

"Oh, Ray."

Lois reached in the pocket of her apron and retrieved her little spiral pad, the to-do list. She made a note: she'd call the dialysis clinic as soon as she'd seen Carlene with her own two eyes.

Edward

When Ernie first died, Margaret couldn't get enough sleep. Twelve, even thirteen hours a day wasn't unusual. Then about a month after he passed away, Margaret couldn't sleep worth a darn. She either woke at three in the morning and was up for a couple of hours, then woke again like a zombie with the alarm at seven, or she chose to ignore the alarm, which blew the morning and turned the following night's routine on its head.

There was a third possibility and that had been last night's sleep pattern. Margaret was wide-awake at five o'clock this morning. Might as well get up, she thought, since she wanted to be at Rockaway House by seven-thirty. She'd make some coffee, maybe some quick muffins, leisurely read the paper and have some overdue one-on-one time with Maxine. Not a bad way to start the day.

The kitchen radio was tuned to KCTN, the 1,000 watt station that broadcast from the top floor of *Hotel Chesterton*, the tallest building in town. Margaret didn't really care for its talk radio format during the day, but it carried local news first thing in the morning and late afternoon. Everyone said it filled the gaps nicely between editions of *The Bee*. As if there was so much happening in Chesterton that one dare not wait even twenty-four hours for the next installment.

While she skimmed *The Bee*, Margaret listened to the radio announcer drone through the funeral notices, including one for a Mr. Gerald Lipmann, services pending.

I don't know a soul in the funeral notices or the obits. It's a good morning.

Margaret wasn't the only one whose day had begun needlessly early. Rose had fallen asleep in front of the television during an eight-thirty sitcom the evening before. For Rose, once she had eight hours in, she was done sleeping. Period. Unfortunately, that was at four-thirty this morning. Like Margaret, she tried to make the best of it. She got up, had breakfast, changed the bedding, put in a load of laundry and took the paper to Rockaway House to read with a cup of strong coffee. Lord, did she ever love that coffee brewing pod contraption they'd had installed a couple of months ago. *Fresh-brewed, any flavor, any strength. Bring it on.*

Rose was so absorbed in reading *The Bee* that Margaret's appearance in the kitchen armed with cookie dough didn't even register. Head buried in the paper, Rose was talking to herself. "Oh my. This is not good."

"What's that, Rose?" Margaret stopped and peered over her shoulder. The headline was on the front page, but well below the fold. FORMER CO-OP EXEC DIES. Margaret saw, but hadn't bothered to read, the story. She didn't know any co-op executives, current or former.

"It's one of our patients, being served at home, a Mr. Lipmann. I never met him, but I remember his name on the visiting nurse list."

"What happened?"

"He committed suicide. And the article makes a point of saying that he was in hospice care with CCH." Rose read the excerpt out loud, "'*Authorities declined to say if there was a link between the suicide and Mr. Lipmann's medical condition.*' Well, that's idiotic. Of course there was."

"That's a shame. Do they have a picture of him?" Margaret asked. Rose shook her head. "I don't recognize his name, but I thought I might know him, you know, if he worked here in Chesterton," Margaret said. So many nameless faces had passed through the grocery store over the years.

"Says here he worked for the grain co-op out on the edge of town before he retired. Well," Rose said as she folded the paper, "I don't think any of my volunteers had been to see him. He wasn't on continuous care yet, just routine home care when he died."

Margaret went back to begin her baking. She spoke without turning around.

"Did James ever talk to you about suicide?"

"No . . . Did Ernie?"

"Once, but it was a long time before he got sick, nothing to do with him. The subject came up because we knew someone who died that way. We swore we could never do that to the other one. But I guess when a person makes that decision, they're not really in their right mind, are they?"

"I don't know. I wouldn't think so."

"That's the thing about dealing with dying, it's never the same for any two people, is it? I guess while you're still able to do it—commit suicide, that is—you're not ready to go. Then, once you're ready to call it, that's at least partly because you're helpless, which means most likely you can't pull it off on your own. It's a Catch-22. But what about the people who help a loved one commit suicide, you know, assisted-suicide? I mean, if the only way a person can die is to have someone help them, that's really euthanasia, isn't it? Can you imagine asking someone you love to help you do that and just leave them to face the music?"

"Well, physician-assisted suicide is legal in four states, I believe—so far. It's hard to wrap your head around, isn't it? I would never have asked James to be involved with that—even if it were legal here. I don't think he would have ever asked me either."

"We never really know until it's us, though, do we, Rose?"

"True. Never say never. And I'm pretty sure you and I aren't going to get this topic all untangled on our own." Rose stood, revived by the coffee and ready to start her day. "When will those cookies be done, Margaret? I might have to wander back down here."

"About twenty minutes. I'll put together a basket for you to take upstairs."

"I'll see you in twenty. And if you have a few minutes then, there's something I need to talk to you about." With that, Rose was out the door and on her way upstairs.

Cookie sheet posed in mid-air, Margaret immediately racked her brain. She'd picked right up on the "need" to talk to you, not "want" to talk to you. *Does that mean it's something unpleasant?* What had she done or omitted to do in the past couple of days, Margaret asked herself. She hoped it wasn't that whole grief support group thing again. She thought that was settled; Rose had seemed to respect Margaret's opinion. Maybe Margaret had inadvertently said something that hurt someone's feelings or made someone uncomfortable. She was extra careful to not talk about politics or give her opinion on religious matters, but sometimes people were super sensitive, especially during an end-of-life crisis. She more than understood that.

Margaret Elizabeth Williams, you stop it. This time she didn't need to wait for Ernie, it was her own voice she heard. She recalled a practice she'd recently read about in an article on grief, even though it sounded like something off a *Hang In There!* poster featuring a dangling kitten. "*When sad or bad thoughts come into your head, you get to decide whether they stay.*" Actually, Margaret had tried it the day before when she woke up in a bad mood, a really nasty temperament. She was amazed to find it actually worked. By the time her feet hit the floor, she was at least open to the possibility of having a good day.

Now alone in the Rockaway House kitchen, Margaret took a deep breath and tried to focus on the task at hand. *I need to concentrate on these cookies before I set off the smoke alarms. Then I need to sit down and eat a couple, hot off the rack, with a big glass of milk.* She set the oven to preheat and was getting the cookie sheets out when the back door into the kitchen swung open. There stood Holly Everest Lang.

"Well, good morning, Holly. How is your—" Margaret stopped mid-sentence. Something was very wrong. Holly's eyes were puffy, her complexion was blotchy and she wasn't quite focused on Margaret or her greeting.

"Dad died this morning." Holly remained standing just inside the kitchen door. Margaret's thought process was paralyzed for a moment, then it was her experience as a friend rather than her training as a hospice volunteer that kicked in.

Holly looked unsteady as a range of emotions raced across her face, each one instantly leaving its mark.

"You have a seat, Holly." *Get her off her feet before gravity does.* "I am so very sorry. What happened?"

Holly shook her head as she sat down. "I don't understand . . . He was fine when we left last evening . . . His vitals were good, he was laughing and making jokes with the grandkids—then out of the blue they called at five this morning and said he was having a lot of trouble breathing and I rushed here. I called Teddy and Roseanne on the way and Larry and I raced like hell to get here, and when I got here, he was already gone . . . Dad was gone . . . How did this happen?" She looked up at Margaret. "We shouldn't have taken him out of the hospital, Margaret, we should have made them keep him in CCU."

Somewhere in the midst of this manic stream, Holly's tone went from distraught to defiant. She looked up at Margaret, waiting for an answer or an argument or an explanation. Margaret slowly sat down next to her, carefully choosing her words.

"Holly, I am so sorry. Have you had a chance to talk to the doctor?" Based on the little she'd known about Mr. Everest's condition, Margaret could guess what had happened, but she knew better than to offer her opinion. She also knew it didn't really matter. What was missing here was not information. What was missing was Holly's father and a sense of reality.

"He's on his way, I think." Suddenly Holly stood back up, refocused. "I came down to get some coffee. I need some coffee."

"I'll be glad to get that for you, Holly. Why don't you sit back down?" Margaret grasped for something normal to talk about, something to ground them both. "I was just getting ready to bake some cookies. I bake every morning I'm here—just to make the house smell good." She grabbed the box of tissues that was always on the kitchen table and handed one to Holly, who blew her nose and wiped her eyes.

"His own doctor told us yesterday that Dad had weeks, maybe even months. Why didn't someone warn us of this? I would have stayed with him last night if I'd had any idea this could happen." She was beyond comforting, but Margaret still felt she should offer a few words.

"Holly, I can't explain why your father died so quickly after coming here, but I do know it's not unusual for patients to pass away while loved ones are away or out of the room."

Holly's head jerked up. "But why? Why would they do that?"

"I don't know for sure, but I hadn't anymore than left the room to take a quick shower and my husband Ernie passed away. If I'd thought for one second that could happen I would never have left—I'd been at his bedside for hours without a break. But after awhile, I decided it was Ernie's choice to die when he did. I think our loved ones have more control over that than we give them credit for." Holly was listening intently, her gaze locked on Margaret. "And I think sometimes they want to spare us that final moment of letting go. I don't know, Holly, maybe your dad wanted to go out on his own terms, you know, at the top of his game. You all seemed to be having such a wonderful visit when I left yesterday."

A smile slowly appeared on Holly's face.

"We did have a nice evening," she allowed. "He loved Chinese food, so we ordered in and we all got to eat there in the room with him and we watched *The Big Bang Theory* together—he loved that goofy show. Did you know he was a physics professor at the University of Iowa? He was very peaceful when we said goodnight . . . He was such a wonderful dad." The tears began anew. Margaret knew there were no more words to be said.

Holly's was a standard-issue broken heart, nothing to be done but wait for the passage of time. They sat in silence for a few minutes.

"Is there anything I can do for you or for your family?"

"No, thank you, Margaret. You've been so kind. No, we're just spending some time with Dad right now. They said we could stay as long as we want. We decided not to have the kids come over—they're so young—but everyone else is up there with Dad. That's okay, isn't it?"

She was the alpha sibling, all right. The one who makes the decisions, keeps everyone on schedule and ensures that all steps are taken and in the proper order.

"Stay as long as you wish, Holly. It's important to spend this time with your Dad—and with each other. We'll call the funeral home when you're ready and not a minute before." Some of the redness in Holly's face had calmed, and she looked like she could breathe easily again, ready to rejoin her family. "How about you take a cup of coffee now? I'll bring some cookies up in a few minutes." Holly took a deep cleansing breath and then hugged Margaret as soon as she was standing.

"Maybe it turned out like it was supposed to—I'm glad we're here. I hate to think of going through all this at the hospital. Dad might have been all alone last night—when it happened . . . Anyway, I'm sure they'd have kicked us all out by now. Thank you, Margaret."

"You're welcome, Holly. Again, I am so sorry for your loss. Please let us know if there is anything you need." Holly left with a lidded go-cup.

Margaret turned immediately to the task at hand. *I need to bake cookies. There are folks upstairs who need to eat a snack and this house needs to smell like there's going to be a tomorrow—it needs to smell like home.* Margaret opened *The Bee* to read the entire story about Mr. Lipmann as the room filled with the intoxicating aroma of White Chocolate Macadamia Nut Sparklers.

Margaret heard Rose's familiar whistle out in the hall, drifting down the grand staircase. Had it already been twenty minutes? The approaching sit-down had floated out of Margaret's mind, what with the unexpected appearance of Holly, the cookie baking and the story about Mr. Lipmann.

How very sad. Margaret couldn't begin to understand it all, but the article did say that Mrs. Lipmann had passed away in 2003. When Margaret and Ernie discussed suicide and were so sure of themselves, she'd had Ernie and he'd had her. It was hard to say what might have happened under different circumstances.

She picked up the newspaper and refolded it, the same way it was delivered. She always did that, put things back exactly as she found them. She waited for Rose to appear, her hands folded on the tabletop, her foot tapping.

"Can we talk for a minute, Margaret—Maggie? Let's go into the dining room. I don't think anyone's around." Margaret followed Rose without comment. They sat at a table with chairs that were one notch above the kind you'd find folded and leaning against the wall of a church basement.

"I've been watching you in action, Maggie. I hope you enjoy your time here as much as you seem to." Margaret was thinking that Rose's face looked hopeful, even positive. *A good sign.*

"Oh definitely. It's different than I expected, but I don't think I could have imagined the way it really is here at Rockaway House."

"I'm glad to hear you say that, because I think I've figured out what needs to happen next, what would be the best thing for you."

Oh no. Here we go.

"Would you like to know what it is?"

"Sorry, I thought I'd answered you. Yes, of course."

"I'm creating a new position for you, Maggie, a sort of concierge, a go-to person for special requests, things that patients or their family members want. You have a real gift for getting people to talk and you have a lot of initiative and imagination. And you're a natural leader. That's a great combination for me—for us. What do you think?"

"Are you sure you know what you're doing?"

Rose laughed. "Yes, I'm positive. Look what you've already done."

Like what? Margaret's stumped look signaled Rose to elaborate.

"You've organized the Cookie Brigade, as you call it, you put Caleb's Christmas party together, you've got us thinking outside the box and that's making us all better at what we do. And I wondered if you'd consider being here Monday through Friday—even just a few hours each day? I mean, it would make it all work much smoother if you came every day. As you've seen, things can change pretty quickly around here. What do you think, Maggie?"

Margaret was speechless, her face slowly breaking into a grin. "I thought maybe you were going to fire me."

Rose laughed out loud. "It's not really possible to fire a volunteer, although I did have one lady that had to be gently coaxed out the door. Well, are you game for it?"

"I am absolutely game for it. Thank you so much." No one was more surprised than Margaret when she began to choke up. Rose thought she knew what was behind that and she laid her hand on Margaret's.

"I know. Sometimes it seems like after you lose your best friend in the whole world, life won't ever hold wonderful surprises again. But it really can."

Margaret nodded.

"Hey, I promised that basket of cookies to the folks upstairs. I better get going!"

Rose left Margaret sitting in the dining room, lost in thought.

I've got to find the right time to ask Rose about having a resident cat at Rockaway House. Too soon?

Caleb

Margaret's throat was all tight and achy. She wished she knew how to go about making those muscles relax. Her voice cracked as she greeted Rona at the nurses' station and it was no more reliable when she got to Caleb's room a moment later. Eight-thirty a.m. the day after the Christmas party and time to say goodbye. Caleb was sitting on the edge of the bed. His mother had gone to pick up his father, and they'd be back any minute. CCH's home health care division was on the way to deliver a hospital bed and the visiting nurse would be there later to administer his last tubal feedings. The tube was scheduled to be removed the following morning. Everyone had agreed.

"Well, Caleb. You put on a heck of a party last night." Margaret pulled a chair up to his bedside.

"Yeah, it was somethin' else, wasn't it? Afterwards, Dr. Bob and me had to have one of those 'Now listen to us, you two' talks with Mom and Dad, but it wasn't too bad. I think they kinda already knew." His breathing was even more ragged, just since the night before. Margaret thought he looked tired but content, almost blissful.

"What do you think happens to my Facebook account or my e-mail once I'm gone, Margaret?" he asked abruptly.

"I'm afraid I'm not the right person to ask, Caleb. I'm a pretty recent convert to the Internet."

"I think it's like when you talk to God. Do you pray, Margaret?"

"Oh yes."

"You don't actually hear God's voice, do you? But it's not like that means he doesn't hear you or your question bounces back to you like an echo. I've been thinking that if my Facebook account or my e-mail account is closed when I'm gone, then when someone sends something over to me, it'll bounce back to them. At least I think it will. That would be weird for them, wouldn't it? I wouldn't want that to happen to my friends and family. I had better have Tracy keep them open when I'm gone. So I guess that's handled."

"Now you have a plan. I've always been big on having a plan."

Caleb went on. "I used to worry 'cause I never got the chance to get really good at something, like sports, or writing—I think I'd have liked to be a writer—but I'm okay with all that. I've tried, ever since the leukemia came back, to just be the best at whatever I was able to be right then—I mean *now*. You know what I mean?"

Margaret was hesitant, even a little ashamed, to admit that she truly did understand—but for the very first time in her sixty-seven years. "I'm a work in progress, Caleb. I'm just starting to get what you've already figured out. Every day is full of lessons and chances to grow and do our best. The secret is to remember to notice that. You're way ahead of me, buddy, and you're doing a great job of it, if you ask me." She smiled, working hard to keep her voice steady, to keep her lip from trembling.

Caleb had hoped to have a moment with Margaret before his parents got back. Now was his chance, his last chance.

"Can I tell you something, Margaret?"

"Yes, of course."

"I saw my grandparents a week ago."

"I'm glad. Do they live here in town?"

"Not exactly. Actually, Gramps died when I was eight—I just kinda remember him. Grams died two years ago." His brow furrowed as he looked intently at Margaret, awaiting her reaction. "You know what I'm saying?"

"I'm not sure, but I'm listening."

"Well, I was getting a little shut-eye and I heard someone in the room and I thought maybe Tracy had gotten here or you or Sheryl or someone, but when I opened my eyes, no one was there. And then I felt a hand on my arm and I looked to my left—right where you're sitting—and there they were. Just as big as life. And my Grams—" Caleb stopped speaking. He half stifled a sob, then went on, choking on the words, his voice little more than a whisper. "She was right there, right there. I coulda reached out and touched her. And I said 'Grams! What are you guys doin' here?' You think I'm nuts, Margaret?"

"Hardly. Go on."

"And Grams said 'We'll see you soon, sweet boy.'" He looked down at his hands. "She always called me that. I was the first grandchild and they kinda spoiled me, I think. Anyway, they both smiled at me—Gramps wasn't much of a talker—and then they just sort of faded away." His head came back up.

He was looking into Margaret's eyes, beyond her eyes, really. Margaret was crying. She gathered her strength and her thoughts before she spoke. "Your grandparents must love you very much, Caleb. That had to be reassuring to see them."

He sighed, obviously pleased by her response. "It was, it really was. I'm looking forward to seeing them again . . . soon . . . Thanks for not thinking I'm nuts." Margaret smiled and nodded. "I think I'd like to rest now, Margaret. Tracy'll be here any minute to take some of my stuff and I want to be awake then."

"Of course you do. Anything I can get for you?"

"Just turn on the CD player, please." She pushed the button. *The Nutcracker Suite* began to play. "We always went to that. My mom took us every year at Christmas." Margaret stood, taking a breath and preparing to leave. She wanted to hug him but stopped herself; he looked as if he might break. But that didn't worry Caleb, he reached his arms out to her, more like a small child than a newly-minted adult. She held on until he started to let go, after a long moment.

He looked up as she hesitated at the door.

"I'm glad I got to know you, Margaret. Oh, and thanks for all your help with the party—it was the best."

She nodded. He laid down, his eyes closed and Margaret softly stepped out.

No one but Caleb knew that he had really hoped to die on a Sunday morning. He thought it seemed more holy and maybe gave him a leg up on the afterlife with so many people already in church, because some of them might even be praying for him at exactly the right moment.

And so he did just that, not long after he got back home.

As Caleb had hoped and expected, the house he returned to was full of bustling life. The second day there was a parade of family and friends, a soft murmur of life continuing around him in the living room. Quiet conversations, children playing board games, occasional laughter, with the Hawkeyes providing muted background noise. Someone was always at Caleb's side, holding his hand, stroking his arm, watching him as he took it all in, a smile on his face.

The following morning Elise was cooking a big Sunday meal for those planning to stop by, although it would be a smaller group today, their closest friends and immediate family. Tracy had been there all night, sleeping on the couch, and had just run home to freshen up. Jerry was getting ready to take the little ones to church. Elise peeked in at Caleb in the living room, alone for a brief time during the mad rush for showers. She sat on the chair placed right next to his bed and picked up her oldest son's limp hand, taking it in hers.

"Mom, where's Dad?" As Caleb whispered the words, Elise knew it was more than idle curiosity. She stood and smiled down at Caleb, then dashed up to their bedroom, catching Jerry just as he finished dressing.

"Honey, come now."

They hurried back to their son's side. Caleb smiled apologetically and whispered that he wanted his sisters and brother there, too. Elise waited with him while Jerry ran back upstairs, calmly told Eli, Sarah and Rebecca what was happening and brought them back down with him, holding hands in a line. Jerry and Elise had talked to them many times about the moment when they would say goodbye to Caleb and wish him well on his journey to heaven. They were as prepared as any three young children could be.

They stood together in a family circle, each one touching a part of Caleb, his foot or arm or hand or cheek.

"I love you guys. Thanks for everything. I'm gonna be fine, I see Gramps and Grams. Honestly, Mom, Dad, I do, I see them. Tell Trace I'll see her later and tell her I said thanks for everything. I gotta go."

They remained huddled at his bedside, sobbing and hugging and praying for a long time. Then Elise wrenched herself from the group, went to the tote bag by the front door, got baby Caleb's copy of *The Littlest Angel* and read it aloud one more time, to all their children.

Lois

Putting a hard date on Carlene's arrival kicked everything into first gear. Lois wanted time as a family—every possible minute—once Carlene got there and the way Lois looked at it, since they didn't know how long Carlene would be able to stay, it made sense to immediately stop dialysis. Ray wasn't so sure that was best but it was a trade off, wasn't it? If Lois continued the treatments, hoping to feel better, the clinic visits and daily fatigue would steal away precious family time.

Dr. Sims had been straight with them. He had taken Lois's hand and said not to tell anyone, but doctors aren't quite as wise as they let on. He'd be guessing to say how long she would live once she stopped dialysis. And if she continued it three times a week, he couldn't promise that she'd feel even half as well as if she came five days a week.

Now a week had already gone by. During the first days after her decision, Lois thought obsessively about the sadness of the loss, hers and everyone else's. Then she decided she simply didn't have time to waste on grief. There was too much to do and the hands on the clock seemed to leap when she looked away for just a moment. Then with all she still wanted to accomplish, she thought maybe she'd jumped the gun; maybe she should keep on with the dialysis. She could always quit another day, right? Then she realized she wouldn't have the energy or time to do much of anything if she was still in treatment. She always came back to her original decision, to quit now.

And she was certain—well, fairly certain—that would also be best for Ray and Carlene in the end. If at all possible, Lois wanted Carlene to be in Chesterton with her father when she lost her mother. It was obvious to Lois: if she stuck around too long—past the time Carlene could spare for her visit home—it could really mess things up. It was settled. Lois would stop in the clinic soon after Carlene arrived and say her goodbyes to the staff, who had become dear friends.

It was a process. Letting go was a process. Lois prayed on it, and then she knew she was doing the right thing, quitting right away.

Whenever Ray was gone out of the house for a bit, Lois took the opportunity to grieve a little, to have a teeny tiny pity party. I can handle this grief in small doses, she told herself. *That will have to do because that's all I have time for.*

Her mini-meltdowns always began with a prayer, asking God to grant her peace and grace. Then she let the tears fall, tried to sob just as hard as she possibly could and finished by splashing cold water on her face before Ray returned. Ray's routine was about the same, only he was usually sitting in his car in the parking lot of *Rex's Drugstore* or *The Marion Street Grocery* or *Globe Dry Cleaning*. Lois and Ray had an unspoken agreement to handle it this way for now. For now, this was best.

The previous Wednesday they had invited their very closest friends and a few nearby family members for dinner. Ray grilled marinated pork chops, Lois made a couple of salads and the company brought appetizers and desserts. Some guessed that the occasion was more than just social, others were caught completely off guard when Lois and Ray told them—after the chops and before dessert—why they had been gathered. Some just couldn't understand the decision; others told their spouses on the way home that they would do exactly what Lois was doing under the same circumstances. At least they thought they would.

Lois was relieved to have the burden of the announcement out of the way and saddened anew to witness their friends' reactions. There were tears, lots of hugs and offers of support and continuing prayers. These were the people Lois knew would never say, "Let us know if we can do anything, Ray." No, they would just show up with food or sneak over to mow the lawn or shovel the snow or have Ray over for breakfast, lunch or dinner. All three, if they thought he needed it.

Now Ray and Lois were focusing on the coming arrival of Carlene.

Except for the addition of Lois's trusty Singer sewing machine on a card table in the corner, Carlene's bedroom looked the same as the day she'd left for California nineteen years earlier. At one time, Ray and Lois had considered turning it into a den for TV watching, but then what would they use the living room for? Ray had read about "man caves" when they first became popular. Lois observed under her breath that she couldn't grasp why the male of the species was always so eager to mimic their Neanderthal ancestors. So much for the man cave idea.

The room had remained unchanged and was now a freeze-frame tribute to the life of a teenager in the 1980s and early 1990s.

The walls were decorated with movie posters for *Dirty Dancing* and *Sixteen Candles*. Nearly twenty years earlier, Carlene had set off to make a fresh start in California and in her Chesterton closet her acid-washed jeans, leg warmers and a denim overcoat still hung. Carlene went Valley Girl long before she got to California. She had been the first in her group of friends to discover yogurt and granola, the first to respond to Reaganism with an eye-roll and a "what-ev-er" and the first to use "impact" as a verb.

While Lois gave the room a quick dusting, she could still hear the sassy response she'd gotten when she had suggested that Carlene might stick around and attend Iowa State or the University of Iowa after high school.

"As if, Moth-er. Gag me with a spoon. Iowa is like totally bogus."

Ray glanced over as he ran the vacuum cleaner, saw Lois's smile and thought how grateful he was that Carlene was on the way home. He had missed that little stinker—a lot.

The bed now had fresh linens, the guest bathroom was clean and everything was aired out. Lois and Ray made a mammoth trip to *The Marion Street Grocery*. They needed to stock up on the fresh vegetables and fruit that

Carlene would demand. For Lois, who had followed a restricted diet while on dialysis, it was time to enjoy some of her own favorites. If not now, when? Ray joined in the spirit, loading up on comfort foods for himself, foregoing all guilt as he piled high the ice cream and pizza makings.

"I feel like a naughty kid!" Lois giggled as they put the groceries away at home.

"Then our work here is done!" Ray proclaimed, giving her a quick kiss.

Everything was readied for the prodigal daughter, short of slaughtering the fatted calf, and tofurkey would hardly be the same. Lois was irritated at herself for being so organized, now all they had to do was sit and wait for hours. Ray read a book while Lois sorted some old photos and thought the hands on the clock would never move.

Ray made two cups of tea and they went out to the back deck, enjoying the last of the Indian summer sunshine and killing time. Lois looked out over their yard and admired the visual reward from decades of landscaping and tweaking. Each year they had committed to finish a project or add a feature, no matter how small. Four months ago, it had been the wooden glider facing the flower beds. They sat in it now, side-by-side, an Irish blanket over their laps. Lois would miss all of this. Or maybe she wouldn't.

Impatient, with nothing special to do for the moment, Lois thought it might be a good time for Ray and her to talk about his future, the one without her in it.

"Ray, we need to talk about your future."

"Okay . . . "

"Have you thought about whether you'll remarry?" *Lois, Lois, Lois.* Ray had suspected this question was lurking, just beneath the surface. It had been only a matter of time. He put his mug down, shaking his head and smiling.

"To be perfectly honest, honey, it hasn't been a priority for me."

"Well, I really think you should."

"Okay. Did you have someone in mind?"

"No, that should be your choice."

"Fair enough. Well, understand I'm just spitballing here, but I've always been fond of Alma."

"She's a lovely woman and a dear friend, Ray, but she's ninety-one."

"What's your point? Afraid I won't be able to keep up with her?"

"Ray."

"Lois."

It was a standoff, and for a moment Ray thought what life with Alma might be like. She was a sweet lady—the sweetest—but . . . He looked at Lois and immediately felt bad for almost laughing out loud, because Lois seemed so incredibly deadpan serious about it all. Ray could see she just wanted some assurance that he wouldn't be lonely, that he'd be taken care of when she was no longer around to see to it. She probably wanted him to be happy, like the two of them had been. That wasn't going to happen.

"Honey, I get it. You think I'll forget to eat or I'll go out in the winter without a coat. That's certainly a possibility. And I could tell you that I'll keep an open mind to the idea of getting married again. But right now my heart is broken and I can't consider life without you and I sure as hell can't imagine putting myself in the position to ever feel like this again. So, there ya are."

When you're right, you're right, Lois thought.

"I can accept that." She stood up, leaned over and planted a kiss on the top of his head. "So, I guess Alma's on her own." She went inside to make sure everything was ready for Carlene. Ray smiled and could not, for all the world, imagine life without Lois.

For some reason, Lois and Ray always pictured Carlene differently than she really was. In their minds' eyes, they saw a refugee from Woodstock, a calf-length peasant skirt, tie-dyed tee shirt, Janis Joplin hair, Sylvia Plath cheerfulness, perhaps a flower behind one ear. Every time they reunited with their daughter, they had to readjust their thinking. She usually wore stylish slacks and sweaters and her hair was in a shoulder length pageboy. When they really thought about it, she'd worn her hair like that for years. When they really thought about it, there was very little about Carlene that was how they remembered her.

The morning after her arrival, as they ate breakfast, Ray and Lois revisited the evening before. In the kitchen, just down the hall from Carlene's room, their voices were hushed, just like thirty-five years earlier.

Lois had been worried that maybe they wouldn't get on once Carlene arrived home. They had simply not spent much time together as adults and, in some ways, the two of them were strangers to Carlene and she to them. But Lois had smiled as she lay in bed the night before. They had all gotten on just fine.

"You know, Ray, last night was like a dream. Carlene's just something, isn't she?" Ray had to agree. Funny how memories of battling with Carlene the Obstinate had quickly receded and were almost forgotten.

The evening had turned out perfectly unscripted. The first thing Carlene wanted to know was if they could please go to *Amore' Pizzeria* for dinner like when she was growing up, pre-vegan. It sounded like a wonderful idea to Ray and Lois. They couldn't remember when they'd last been there, but for sure it had been almost two years ago.

Before dinner, they each enjoyed a glass of wine and Lois wanted to hear what Carlene had been up to. Oh no, Carlene said, first she wanted to hear all about the Christmas cruise. Ray and Lois looked at each other and smiled and Ray said that it was—in a word—unreal (literally true). Now, tell us about your life, Carlene, Ray had encouraged her.

It was hectic; business at the shop was good with a fair amount of Internet sales as well. There was always an evening reception or a weekend event to attend and many places to be. Lois and Ray were so pleased that

Carlene had lots of friends. Was there anyone special? Ray was picturing the boobly-dooblies that Carlene had coupled with in high school. He hoped that prototype had gone the way of her tie-dyed tee shirts.

Carlene blew past the question. Everyone was in such good spirits, Ray and Lois didn't seem to even notice. With each tidbit of information Carlene shared, her parents were more delighted, and Carlene didn't see any point in clarifying that the receptions and events weren't social, they were trade gatherings and health fairs, all part of networking and building her business. And make no doubt about it, business was very good, she said. She worked seven days a week. You couldn't very well not be open on Sundays if you wanted the Millennials, her target market of twenty- and thirty-somethings. That was the day they did their errands and stocked up on healthy snacks and herbal supplements for the coming week. She had an assistant, Rainbow, now working full-time. In fact, Rainbow was running the shop while Carlene was in Chesterton.

They talked and laughed and laughed and talked. Carlene didn't volunteer how long she'd be in Chesterton and Lois and Ray didn't ask.

Finally, seizing on a momentary lull in the conversation, Carlene took a big gulp of wine and looked from one to the other.

"How long have you been sick, Mom?" Carlene had never before been around anyone who was dying. She hadn't known what to expect and she'd dreaded what she would find when she arrived and they opened the door. But she thought her mother looked good; tired, maybe, her eyes weren't quite as bright as Carlene remembered, but not bad.

"A couple of years, honey. Blame me. Your father wanted to tell you, but—I just—it was selfish on my part. It was so much easier for me if I stayed healthy in your mind, more like you remembered me. Does that make sense?"

Actually, Carlene thought to herself, that approach makes more sense than you could possibly know. She nodded.

"I did a little research on the plane, and I respect your decision, Mom, I really do, but couldn't you continue dialysis, just to make you feel better, you know, in the meantime?"

Lois was touched. "Well, it's funny how it works out, Carlene. It's called palliative care when you do something just for the comfort, not to try to cure the disease, or even to treat it. And here's the thing: since it's kidney disease that's killing me, Medicare won't pay for dialysis once I'm in hospice care because that would be treating my disease." She gave Carlene a moment to take that in. "Now, if I had cancer and my kidneys failed, I could probably have dialysis, no problem." She and Ray were miles ahead of their daughter in figuring it all out and Lois smiled sympathetically at Carlene.

"If money's a problem, I'll pay for it, Mom. I can afford it."

Lois looked across at Ray. He got the message—it was time for the tag-team approach.

"Honey, Medicare coverage isn't the issue, really. It's more an issue of palliative care versus life-prolonging care. Once your mother decided to go into hospice that means she doesn't want to do anything to treat her illness or to simply prolong her life." He paused to gauge Carlene's reaction. "We know this is difficult to understand, we really do."

Lois took a breath and spoke again. "You see, honey, I don't want to just keep going and that's what dialysis would do, just keep me going, like an Energizer bunny, running out of juice."

"So you stop the treatment and then you stop eating and drinking and you . . . " Carlene couldn't bring herself to finish the sentence.

"That's pretty much it." Lois reached out and put her hand on Carlene's as she spoke. "But the important thing is that it's on my terms as much as possible. I didn't choose to have kidney disease, but I can choose whether or not to treat it and how I spend whatever time I have left. It wasn't an easy decision—we don't want you to think it was."

Some things about Carlene had not changed. She was in her consideration mode. Taking in information, weighing options. No different from when she was seventeen, Ray thought. No different from her father, Lois thought. They waited for the inevitable signs. After a few moments, Carlene pursed her lips, took a deep breath and spoke.

"So, what now, Mom? Is there anything special you want to do while I'm here?"

"I'm doing it right now." Lois's voice broke.

"Me, too." Ray chimed in.

"Me, three." Carlene smiled at her parents. *When did they get so old? When did I?* She really was glad to be home.

All in all, it was a most enjoyable evening, one that far exceeded everyone's expectations. On the way to dinner and again on the way home, Lois and Ray pointed out the many changes in Chesterton. To Carlene, it didn't look as if there'd been a single one, which was more than a little comforting.

While Ray washed up the breakfast dishes, Lois dressed and then stepped quietly to Carlene's bedroom. She just hated to disturb her, but she could hardly wait for Carlene to wake up. Lois tapped softly and opened the door. Carlene was fully dressed, sitting on her bed, sorting through a carton of papers.

"You're up?"

"Oh sure. I'm used to getting up at the crack of dawn. I walk a couple of miles each morning before I open the shop. Mother, I can't believe all this stuff is still here. This place is like a frigging museum."

Lois sat down on the other side of the bed and reached into the box. She'd had no reason to go through Carlene's things and never had. "What is all this?" she asked.

"Every card and letter that you and Daddy ever gave me."

Lois's hand went to her mouth.

"Hey! I even found a five-dollar bill in a birthday card! Can you imagine me letting that slip by?"

"Not really. May I see?" Carlene handed Lois a pile of envelopes. Lois turned one over; it was addressed to Carlene in Ray's handwriting. "What's this?"

"That's one of Daddy's letters to me. You know, the ones he wrote every year on my birthday." Carlene continued to leaf through the pile until she noticed the palpable silence. She looked up. "Mom?"

Lois was reading one of Ray's letters, tears running down her cheeks.

"Oh, Mom. I'm sorry."

"No, no, I'm fine, I just didn't know—how is it I don't know about these?"

"I don't know. I guess I thought you did." Carlene shrugged, picked up another envelope from the pile and pulled out the single folded sheet of paper. "*Dear Carlene, I can hardly believe you are ten years old. A decade. 3,650 days, 87,600 hours, 5,256,000 minutes. Time will go faster for you now, so remember to be a little girl for as long as you possibly can. And remember that Mommy and I are so proud of you. Love, Daddy.*" It was tough, but Carlene got through it without breaking down. "I wish I'd had this box with me in California. There were a few times I could've used these." She looked over at her mother. Lois had pulled the ubiquitous hankie from her sleeve and was wiping her eyes.

"I'm so glad you're here, Carlene." Her hug reached across the bed.

"Me too, Mom."

Ray arrived at the bedroom door. "Well good morning! Have you eaten, Carlene? I think we've got something you'll like."

"No, and I'll tell you what sounds good, Dad. You still make that French toast with whipped cream and strawberries and chocolate sauce? And maybe some bacon?"

Lois and Ray looked at each other and burst out laughing.

Edward

Everyone was peaceful but totally exhausted and everyone was ready for Big Ed's journey to continue. Around ten o'clock that morning, the Everest children and in-laws looked at each other and without a word agreed that it was time for Mr. Forester to take their father's body away.

As soon as Edward had died, the night nurse and her assistant, Crystal and Trish, began preparing Edward and his room for the family's arrival. All the medical equipment and medications were removed, Dr. Reese was notified and Edward was readied. With Big Ed's hands folded on top of the Wedding Ring patterned quilt, Teddy commented when he arrived that his dad looked just as Teddy frequently found him, fast sleep in his recliner, planted in front of a Chicago Cubs afternoon game. Most especially since Big Ed's pipe was resting in his grip.

The previous evening, while they waited for dinner to be delivered, Roseanne had made a quick run to the family home, not far from Rockaway House. She returned with her father's robe and slippers, Bible, Glenn Miller CD, and the quilt their mother had made for him—for them—for their golden wedding anniversary in 2001, just two years before she died. Roseanne also brought Big Ed's pipe—but no tobacco. (Back at the hospital, Edward had agreed without protest to give up his after-dinner pipe. He figured it wouldn't be for all that long.) The quilt had covered Edward and his wife, and then Edward, every night for the past eleven years. It was a fixture of Edward's life that he was glad to have nearby at Rockaway House. It covered him now as his children sat circling the bed trying to imagine life without their father. A scented candle burned on the dresser and *In the Mood* was playing softly in the background.

The end for Edward had been brief, once it began in earnest. When Trish stopped by his room at four forty-five a.m. to check vitals, Edward was wide-awake. He smiled as she entered, but as soon as he tried to speak, he struggled to get breath. Trish pushed the button to let Crystal know and Crystal called his daughter Holly, then joined Trish at Edward's side. The head of his bed was already raised to help with his breathing, but they tried adding a pillow behind his back. Crystal was prepared to medicate him for anxiety or pain if need be, but when she offered, Edward shook his head and smiled, in an accepting, knowing way. They remained with him, holding his hands, speaking softly and calmly to him.

What they knew—but Edward's children did not know until they told them—was that Crystal and Trish and Edward had spoken earlier about how his end might come and Edward was ready, as ready as anyone could be.

At the end of the evening spent with his children, their spouses and his grandkids, Edward kissed each one, saying he loved them and saying goodbye, knowing the odds were good that this—or some day in the very near future—would be their last time together on this earth. As he often had in the past few years, he considered the grief that was to follow. He more than knew what it meant to be heartbroken by death and he felt bad, knowing what was in store for his survivors. He'd buried his parents, followed by his two brothers, a sister and his wife, and—at almost ninety-two years of age—friends too numerous to recall.

On the other hand, even if he'd tried, he couldn't have explained to them how much he was looking forward to reuniting with those he had lost. Not that he was in a hurry exactly, but he'd accomplished all he wanted to. It was time. Only a few weeks earlier, he'd confided to Frank McCarthy, his good buddy and former office mate of over fifty years, "You know, old friend, I can count more people I love on the Other Side than here—that's a milestone of some sort!" They both laughed. They knew exactly what that milestone was marking: steps further from this life and closer to the afterlife.

The family had left for the night and Trish was busying herself with end-of-day details in Edward's room. As his nickname implied, Big Ed was plainspoken and didn't mince words. "So, young lady, what is The End going to look like for me with this bad ticker I've got?" No longer surprised by patients' questions, Trish pulled a chair up close to Edward's bed.

"Well, Mr. Everest, it's hard to say exactly. It could mean that your heart stops suddenly or that you may even pass away in your sleep. I know you had an episode of cardiac arrest this morning. Do you remember what that was like?"

Edward thought for a moment. "Well, I was sitting in the chair while my daughter packed up my things, then I felt a helluva pain in my chest, and the next thing I knew, I woke up flat on the bed with a whole lot of people looking down at me." He smiled warmly at Trish. "To be honest, I would have been fine with going right then, but I'm glad poor Holly didn't have to be there for that."

"And it might happen that way, Mr. Everest, except now you have a DNR, a Do-Not-Resuscitate Order, from Dr. Reese, so we won't try to revive you. You understand that, right?"

Edward thought he did but he wanted no stone left unturned. "I told the kids once I turned ninety that I didn't want any of that CPR nonsense, but I didn't know until the cardiologist told me yesterday that apparently my word isn't good enough." He laughed at how silly it seemed.

Crystal, passing by the room, noticed Trish sitting at Mr. Everest's bedside and stopped, leaning against the doorframe. She'd come on duty at nine o'clock and the needs of others had kept her running. She welcomed the chance to get to know their newest patient.

"How are you doing, Mr. Everest? That's quite a family you have."

"I'm doing fine, thank you, but I take very little credit for my kids turning out so well—my late wife Irene deserves that."

Trish continued her thought. "You know, Mr. Everest, I've met a lot of patients who don't really understand how DNRs work. It's true, you can tell your family that you don't want to be revived, but unless there's a written DNR order from a doctor, medical personnel have to try to bring you back. If you start having trouble breathing, there are some things we can do to help you with that, so you'll let us know, okay? In fact, would you like to try some oxygen while you sleep?"

Edward thought for a moment. "Sure, let's give it a try. But you know, Trish, I've been very blessed. Sick hardly a day in my life 'til the past few weeks. If I have to struggle a little at the end, I'm all right with that. You met my kids and grandkids—am I a lucky man, or what?" His smile could not have been bigger.

"Indeed you are, Mr. Everest." Because of Edward's congestive heart failure, Dr. Reese had left a standing order for oxygen, so Crystal went to get a small portable tank, then she helped Mr. Everest don the plastic tube that reached into his nostrils. "So, did I answer your question?"

"You did, Trish. We'll just see what happens. I trust in God—he's always done right by me."

"And I'm guessing you've done right by him as well." Trish gave his arm a pat and turned off the ceiling light. "Good night, Mr. Everest. Sleep well."

"Good night, girls. Thank you."

So, as the end came for W. Edward Everest, Crystal and Trish stayed at his side, talking to him, offering the comfort of their presence but knowing that medically, there was nothing more to be done. His breathing soon became less labored and more shallow. In a matter of minutes, he took one large breath and closed his eyes. He was gone. Less than ten minutes later, Holly and Larry Lang rang the bell at the front door of Rockaway House.

Before they left at the end of their shift, Trish and Crystal shared the details of Edward's final hours with the family members. Since then, the siblings and their spouses had been huddled around their father's body. They reminisced about their parents, crying, laughing, commiserating, praying and planning his memorial. For the first time ever, Big Ed was not inserting his animated comments into their conversation, but not to worry, their father had already made his wishes clear. There was to be no viewing of his body, no organ music and definitely no solemnity.

"It's been just twenty-four hours since Dad's heart stopped yesterday morning. Who could have imagined all this in one day?" Holly said.

Roseanne's husband, Bob, spoke up. "You know, I was just thinking how great it is that we put on that party for Big Ed's ninetieth birthday. Or should I say, it's a good thing *Big Ed* put on that party?" Thinking back, they all laughed. Big Ed had announced two months before his birthday that just in case they were planning a surprise celebration, he would indeed be having a celebration but without the surprise part—he wanted in on the planning. He soon had them madly researching addresses for every person he had worked with at the university, the neighbors, friends from church, all the civic organizations he and their mother had served, his favorite checker at the grocery store, and please not to forget the mailman.

As he put it one day while Holly toiled over the invitation list, "It's simple, honey. I'd much rather be around for all the accolades, so just invite every person you think would attend my funeral. You know how I love a good party!" He and his late wife had been famous hosts, inventing most any excuse to gather friends and family, whether a holiday, a sporting event or a month with an "r" in it.

That birthday party, not quite two years ago, had been a memorable occasion indeed, held at the family home. Holly finally agreed to hire a caterer to handle the food and drinks at her father's insistence that he wanted her—all of his family—by his side, sharing in the celebration of his ninety years of joyous living.

Such a party! Riotous laughter, all of Big Ed's favorite songs ("Has there been any music since Glenn Miller?"), fantastic food, fellowship and fun. One unforgettable day. Among a litany of toasts and well-wishes, there was a tear-jerking moment when the best man from Edward's wedding fifty-nine years earlier, Irving Brinkman (also age ninety), had offered a toast to his longtime friend and to their brides, now both passed. Not a dry eye in the place.

"Dad knew what he was doing, didn't he?" Roseanne looked down at her father admiringly. "What a great idea to host his memorial while he was still around to enjoy it. Then yesterday he made sure we knew that he was ready to go when his time came, that he didn't want any more heroics."

They each looked upon Big Ed for the last time, with gratitude and love. Always so proud of the way their father had lived, they could now appreciate how graciously he had approached his life's end as well.

Teddy stood, ready to leave. "So, pull out that invitation list, Holly, and let's do it again."

Everyone nodded in agreement. There were few things Big Ed loved more than a good party.

Margaret

The holiest of all holidays are those kept by ourselves in silence and apart; the secret anniversaries of the heart. Margaret had recently come across that quotation from Henry Wadsworth Longfellow. *Amen, Henry.* Today marked six months since Ernie's death. Tick-tock, another month.

What is this compulsion to recognize the anniversary of a tragic event? To Margaret it felt like making an appointment to feel sad, or, in the case of Ernie's death, sadder. Five times—once each month since Ernie had died—she had made a plan to definitely feel bad on those particular days, a disturbing thought in itself. Today she considered going to the cemetery and maybe sticking in a few more flowers. No, probably not a good idea this late in the year, and it had been so dry. Anyway, as she admitted for the first time, going to the place where Ernie's body was resting for eternity didn't comfort her. In fact—and nobody else knew this—the last time she went there, she'd gotten really angry with Ernie for leaving her behind. *Never forget, grief doesn't have to make sense.* She'd had to apologize to him when she got home, for what she'd said—out loud, no less—standing at his grave.

A visit to the cemetery was consoling for many people—Margaret appreciated that, she really did, and that was fine for them—but not for her. She didn't need or want to go there to be close to Ernie or even to focus her thinking on Ernie. Most especially not today.

"If I want to be reminded of you, I just look around, Ernie. It seems like you're still here—you're everywhere. In the closet, in that recliner or in the kitchen cupboard." *Or, I can always just smell your sweater.*

On the other hand, to not recognize the significance of the day seemed disrespectful, even soulless. Just the other day, Rose had confided to Margaret that she'd totally missed an anniversary of James's death, and it had been a big one—seven years. But after beating herself up for a few days, she got to thinking that it might even be seen as a good thing. She wasn't quite so obsessed with James's death; she was thinking more these days about his life.

As if, Margaret had thought with envy.

Couldn't any one of these anniversaries be celebratory? Please? A recognition of Ernie's life, of their life together? That's it, she'd call their niece Robin. Robin and Ernie had been close. She'd meant the world to him and he'd been her absolute most favorite uncle—Robin had said many times how thankful she was that she'd had him in her life. Margaret would call Robin, and they'd have a laugh about something funny Uncle Ernie had once done or said.

Robin was glad to hear from her. Aunt Margaret had been on Robin's mind more than usual lately and they immediately made a date for lunch the following Saturday. Robin knew from her aunt's voice that something wasn't right—beyond the obvious. When she asked, Margaret said it was because the day marked six months since Uncle Ernie's death.

Clearly, Robin suggested, her Aunt Margaret needed an ELC.

"Okay, Robin, I give. What's an ELC?"

"An Emergency Laugh Cue, Aunt Margaret. You think of something ahead of time that always makes you laugh—without fail. Then you have an ELC to go to when you're feeling blue or just need a giggle. Surely, you can come up with something, Aunt Margaret. I've got faith in you."

Margaret could always count on Robin. She hung up feeling better, even smiling. Robin had reminded Margaret how Uncle Ernie would always ask if Robin had seen the prior week's Iowa State Cyclones football game; then he'd give her a highlights recap without waiting for her answer. When he finished, Robin would give him a peck on the cheek and say, "Don't you remember, Uncle Ernie? I went to U of I—I'm a Hawkeyes fan." And Ernie would always smile and say, "I know, honey, but there's eternal hope for redemption."

That phone call to Robin had been a step in the right direction for Margaret. She always felt a little better after talking to Robin. Sometimes that's all it took, just a break in the silence, just a friendly voice, talking to someone who knew the person you missed. They probably didn't miss the person as much as you did, but they missed him and, most importantly, they knew him.

Now, for an ELC. Let's see. Actually, Margaret didn't have to think all that hard or long. She was remembering the wedding of a friend years—decades—ago. Let's just say there'd been quite a bit of drinking at the reception. One of the guests, another friend, was wearing a dress with ties in the back. Unbeknownst to her, another friend ("friend" was a term thrown around very loosely in the 1970s), tied her sash to the folding chair she was sitting on. As soon as someone asked her to dance, she was off to center stage, undeterred by the clattering metal chair that followed close behind. She boogied on, mindlessly hauling that personal anchor.

That story had never failed to make Margaret laugh out loud anytime she'd been reminded of it over the past forty years. Now she had her ELC.

'A work in progress,' that's what I told Caleb Bronson. A work in progress.

Rockaway House

Lauren Dunlap stared out the window. From her office, she could see Marion Street; it ran downhill to the north. Craning her neck, she could just make out the tiled roofline of Rockaway House. She loved that place and she didn't get there often enough. As a matter of fact, she wished she was there right now.

She gazed at the picture of Helen Sullivan on the wall across from her desk. Lauren found it stored in a closet soon after she came to work at Chesterton Community Hospice. When Mrs. Sullivan passed away, the family gave the portrait to the hospital, assuming someone would want to honor Helen's years of service on the Chesterton Medical Center Board of Directors. Without a doubt they did, but both Sullivans were already looking down from the walls of the corporate office lobby and the board room. That's how this surplus image of Helen got passed on to CCH, tucked away until Lauren came across it.

When she accepted the job at CCH, Lauren was living in Davenport managing a group of neighborhood clinics for a national conglomerate throughout Eastern Iowa and Western Illinois. The company aspired to provide cradle-to-grave services with a long-term strategic plan that included hospice and home health care divisions. Lauren had been tapped as the one to lead those missions when the time came. Her career path was clear.

Then in 2005, Lauren met Helen Sullivan.

Serving together on the program committee of a health care trade organization, the two women immediately hit it off. Helen saw in Lauren Dunlap the executive she herself might have been in another era and the qualities that she most valued and admired: integrity and compassion. Lauren was drawn to Helen Sullivan's no-nonsense take-charge attitude and sense of civic leadership. They grew as professional and personal friends until Helen's death in 2008.

In 2010, even though Helen had already been gone for two years, she played a significant role in Lauren's decision to apply for the job with CCH. Looking now at Helen's portrait, Lauren thought of how Mr. Sullivan's struggles at life's end had inspired Helen to pioneer hospice care in the area and Helen's passion had inspired Lauren. It was the first time in a very long time that Lauren had thought about the jigsaw puzzle of life events that she'd been drawn into, the "God winks" that had caused her to be standing in this office on this day.

She took a deep breath, sat down at her desk and dialed Henry Lloyd. With a grimace, she told him she'd conveyed his message to Kimberly Lipmann. Henry said he was pleased that Lauren had followed his instructions.

That did it.

"I'm sure you are. Say, Henry, do you happen to have a copy of our mission statement handy there?"

"Uh, no, not at my fingertips."

"Well, it so happens I do. Here's what it says: '*Chesterton Community Hospice is a not-for-profit organization dedicated to providing compassionate palliative, emotional and spiritual care to patients with a terminal or irreversible condition—*" Lauren thought she heard Henry Lloyd start to speak. "Please don't interrupt me, Henry." She continued to read the mission statement. "'*–as they approach the end of their lives and to provide their loved ones with compassionate support during and after this final journey.*' And that's exactly what I intend to do. I'll let you know how my meeting with Kimberly goes, *Hank*." The way she said his name sounded a lot like a cat bringing up a hair ball. She hung up before he could sputter a response. In less than three seconds, her direct line rang. *Bite me, Hank.* Lauren let it go to voice mail.

Then she called Kimberly Lipmann. First, she thanked Kimberly for taking the call and asked if she would please meet Lauren for a cup of coffee. Kimberly hesitated. Finally, saying she had some errands to run, she agreed to come to Lauren's office in two hours, since she'd already be in the area.

Lauren looked at Helen's smiling face. She buzzed Allie and asked her to order a sandwich for her—Lauren was staying in over lunch. She needed to think about the mission here at Chesterton Community Hospice and her role in keeping it alive, she needed to think about her dear friend Helen and all Helen had stood for and she needed to think about the upcoming meeting with Kimberly Lipmann. She had a lot of thinking to do.

"To be honest, no, I still don't understand why you wouldn't talk to me earlier today. I can only guess that the attorney who advised you about that has never lost a loved one to a long, drawn out, dreadful death. Am I right?" Kimberly Lipmann was sitting in front of Lauren's desk. Lauren was in front of her desk, too, seated not far from Kimberly. In spite of everything, Kimberly had a slight, knowing smile as she spoke. Actually, Lauren couldn't be sure; it might be amusement or even loathing.

"I can't say whether he has any personal experience as a survivor, although I see now that's something I should have asked." Lauren paused and gathered her strength. "But following someone else's bad advice is no excuse for bad behavior. I hope you will accept my apology for my hurtful words to you, personally, as well as in my role as executive director of this hospice. We failed you when you needed us most."

Kimberly looked grateful but unwavering. "As far as my father's death is concerned, I came to tell you that I don't think it would have mattered what you all did. My father was going to kill himself regardless." She paused for a moment, and then moved forward to the edge of her chair, resting her hand lightly on Lauren's desk. "Did you know my father left a suicide note?"

Lauren nodded.

"Did you know that it was dated March 4th, 2012?" Kimberly let her words sink in. "Yes, Lauren, that means he made the decision to do this about a week after his doctor said his cancer was incurable, last spring. As I've now discovered, he's been putting his affairs in order since then. My father was very independent, Lauren. His opinions about most everything were unshakeable." She smiled, then went on. "He loved my mother very much and he was her caregiver while she fought and then died of cancer nine years ago. I don't know if you have any personal experience as a caregiver, Lauren, but it's not a memory that fades. Ever. He had no intention of putting me through what he endured. I respect and love him for that."

Kimberly slid back into her chair. Her shoulders dropped and the look on her face went from steadfast to resigned. "I don't agree with my father's decision, Lauren. I'd like him to still be here. I would have liked the chance to take care of him." Again, that little smile. "But I'm not the one with cancer. I'm just the self-centered orphan—what do I know? It's not me facing helplessness and incontinence and pain—at least not right now." She slowly rose from her chair and extended her hand. Lauren quickly stood as she grasped it, holding on for a long moment as their eyes met.

"My father received excellent attention from your staff. There wasn't anything more anyone could have done. Tell your attorney he has nothing to fear from me. I just wanted to let you know that." Kimberly started toward the door, then stopped and turned to face Lauren. "You seem like a decent, kind person, Lauren. You might want to think about firing that little pisher of an attorney and hiring one who doesn't have a corporate wallet where his heart should be." She opened the door and was about to walk out when Lauren responded.

"Point taken. Kimberly, again, I am so very sorry for your loss. Please accept my pledge that we are here for you if there is anything we can do. There are no words to say how much it means that you agreed to see me. It was incredibly generous of you. Thank you so much for doing so."

"You're welcome." And Kimberly was gone, closing the door behind her.

Lauren sat back down. She picked up her iPhone and fired off a text to Henry Lloyd.

Relax. Kimberly Lipmann isn't suing us.
You and I need to talk.
I'll be expecting you momentarily.

Lauren looked once again at Helen's smiling face. Then she rolled her eyes and spoke aloud, "I know. I know. I lost my way. I'll do better, Helen. I promise."

By the end of the following day, the nicest thing Lauren could think to say about it was that it was finally over. *Following on the heels of yesterday, enough already.*

It began with the front page story in *The Bee*, which certainly couldn't be labeled damaging, but the mention of hospice involvement with Mr. Lipmann had caused a certain buzz in town. Lauren overhead a few tidbits at the coffee shop this morning and Allie reported similar chatter in her rounds. People were, well, confused. They were sad for Mr. Lipmann and his daughter and they wanted to make sense of it all. Did hospice play a role somehow? If so, what was it?

Lauren spoke again to Dorrie in Public Relations. Dorrie continued to believe there was no crisis to respond to or damage to control. The less said, the better, she advised, in respect for the family, if for no other reason.

Just as they were hanging up, Lauren told Dorrie that after her meeting with Kimberly Lipmann the day before, Lauren had given the heave ho to the ever-aggravating Henry Lloyd, dismissing him as counsel to CCH. Lauren liked and trusted Dorrie so it was unfortunate that she didn't have the power to fire Henry outright—he was employed by CMC. Dorrie would still have contact with "Hank" from time to time.

"Oh," Lauren remembered to tell Dorrie, "make sure to call him by that nickname." Dorrie laughed and said she appreciated the reminder.

Then, when Lauren was sure the day couldn't get any more intense, her direct line rang. The caller ID indicated Cissy Peters, a long-time hospice board member, currently the chairperson. She came to hospice service after years of volunteering in the Chesterton hospital, where she'd already been involved with dying patients. When Helen Sullivan organized the formal hospice program, Cissy made that the focus of her work. For Lauren, Cissy was often a pain in the neck, but her motives were pure and she was a tireless advocate for their mission.

Lauren didn't even consider letting Cissy's call go to voice mail. *Fasten your seat belt.*

Cissy's purpose was clear from her first words. They had all read the article in this morning's *Bee,* and Cissy was calling an emergency meeting of the Board. She had taken the liberty of contacting the other directors, and it so happened they were all available this afternoon at three o'clock, and nothing in her tone indicated that was open to discussion. Would Lauren please have Allie make the confirming calls and they would all see Lauren at three?

Lauren hung up the phone and held her aching head in her hands, considering the two hours she had in which to prepare. She already had a suspicion of what the board's agenda would be. She had heard things, rumblings about closing Rockaway House.

Lovely concept, Mrs. Sullivan was an angel, incredible legacy, yada yada yada. But Rockaway House served very few patients and financially, it was a big fat loser. Medicare didn't pay enough to provide adequate care for hospice patients and competition for the charitable dollars they needed to supplement Medicare and insurance payments was challenging at best. Even though forty-four percent of all deaths in America occur under hospice care, public awareness of its true nature was murky. People don't know or care anything about a mission that focuses on dying until they have a loved one who is dying.

As Lauren had told her board members countless times—not to put too fine a point on it, but—most donations are of the memorial type, i.e., they came *after* a death, not *before.* And because bureaucrats are as clueless as the general public—probably more—hospice doesn't fare well when it comes to health care reforms, so that threat is ever present. For good measure, Lauren didn't have to be told that no hospice wished to be associated with the concept of suicide.

Lauren could presume that the agenda of the board's emergency meeting was almost certainly bleak.

She was frustrated. She'd been on the job for two years, and it had taken most of that time to clean up after the neglect of her predecessor, a nice, well-meaning man who was totally lacking in vision, leadership and competence. For the first few years of CCH's existence, all energy and resources had been focused on facilities, infrastructure and gathering gifted support staff. Then Helen Sullivan got sick and passed away in 2008 and, without her Iron Lady leadership, things at CCH quickly went downhill. Lauren had finally gotten a solid grip on what changes needed to be made and how to best safeguard the mission of CCH and assure its survival for the next generation.

And now this.

Lauren served at the will of the Board. Many an executive director of many an organization had been fired for situations less extreme than the negative perception of Mr. Lipmann's death. Sometimes the fortuitous timing of an unfortunate—in this case, tragic—event gave management the excuse they'd been hoping for.

Looking out her window, Lauren's gaze was unfocused as she recalled one of countless conversations with Helen Sullivan. They were enjoying brunch at Helen's house not long before Helen's health so dramatically declined. Actually, Lauren remembered as she thought back on that day, it was their last social time together.

Lauren was complaining—okay, bitching—about her job in Davenport, how unfulfilling it was to manage neighborhood clinics, spending her days swamped with the minutiae of health care administration.

Out of the blue, Helen had said, "Today I'm going to meet someone who will change my life in a most remarkable manner."

"Are you psychic now, Helen?" Lauren had asked as she kept eating her quiche.

"No, why?"

"How do you know that's going to happen today?"

"Because it happens to me every day. Sometimes the change is big, sometimes small. I might step back to let someone get ahead of me in the grocery store checkout line and then, two hours later, I'm not in the wrong place at the wrong time because I'm seven minutes behind where I would have otherwise been. Or maybe that seven minute delay allows me to witness a sunset I would have otherwise missed. See?"

"The whole space/time continuum deal?" Lauren had said. Looking back, she realized her tone could have been taken as mocking.

In a pensive voice, Helen had replied, "I don't know if that's it. I don't know."

A few weeks after that brunch, when Helen began to suffer a series of little strokes, Lauren thought back—as you do when you wonder if you missed a symptom—and wrote the conversation off to the start of her friend's circulation problems. Now she was rethinking that notion. But she still felt the same pang of guilt she'd had since then for taking so lightly something her friend had taken so seriously.

She raised her head and her gaze met Helen's, looking back from the wall. Lauren felt the slightest regret for hanging that picture in her office, giving Helen carte blanche to observe Lauren's every misstep and every up and down.

Okay, let's start over, Helen, she thought. *Who have I met that might change my life—and how?*

Cissy gaveled the meeting to order at exactly three o'clock. She made a few introductory remarks for the record, officially acknowledging the death of Mr. Lipmann. Then she turned to Lauren, who stood at the head of the table, and gave her the nod to begin.

"Sadly, it is the suicide of our patient Gerald Lipmann that brings us together here today. I have some brutal facts to share with you. The second highest rate of suicide in the United States is among the demographic group most likely to need and use our services: those 85 years and older. It's also worth noting that for those who choose physician-assisted suicide where it is legal in America, the number one reason to do so is the loss of autonomy. We've gotten pretty good at pain control—which, by the way, is the *sixth* reason on the list—but we haven't quite figured out how to make some people believe that having others care for you and about you at life's end is not something to be avoided—at any cost.

"We have an obligation to consider the mental health of our patients and to address those needs when we become aware of them. To that end, we are reviewing this case in detail and our policies in general to make whatever adjustments are appropriate going forward. To be honest, I'm not even sure if what was lacking for Mr. Lipmann and others like him comes under the category of mental health or spirituality or maybe even a sense of community. And sadly, we won't be able to help every single patient with every single issue. We just won't. But we're going to use any and all resources we can get our hands on to figure this out, on that you have my pledge.

"The suicide of someone in our care may well add to the confusion that already exists in the minds of the public about our mission here at Chesterton Community Hospice and the practices that we do and do not subscribe to. And make no mistake, folks are confused.

"Some people believe that allowing a person to refuse food and hydration is assisting suicide. It is not.

"Some people believe that giving a person sufficient pain control—pain control that may unintentionally hasten death—is assisting suicide or euthanasia. It is not.

"Some people believe that withholding or withdrawing nutrition from a person who is no longer able to make his or her wishes known is euthanasia. It is not. A person may have a religious objection to that—and, if they do, we will always respect the beliefs of our patients and their caregivers.

"Of course, we all know that we do not have legalized physician-assisted suicide in Iowa. But if we ever do, it will not alter our mission here at CCH. Our role is to care when cure is no longer an option. We acknowledge dying, but we do not welcome death nor do we cause it to happen."

Lauren paused and took a sip of water.

"This tragedy has brought to our attention that we need to do a much better job of educating the members of this community. That will also be addressed, post haste.

"The cause of a patient's death—in Mr. Lipmann's case, suicide—also does not alter our mission. I have personally reached out and offered our bereavement support to Mr. Lipmann's daughter." She paused again. "I have one more thing to say on this matter."

And then Lauren looked directly at each person seated at the table, one after another, and acknowledged aloud that at one point in reacting to this crisis she had disregarded the true mission of Chesterton Community Hospice. She had failed Mr. Lipmann's daughter by being more concerned about possible liability than about the duty to address the needs of a patient's family. Lauren had allowed the corporate attorney to deflect her attention from its right and true focus. That would not happen again. To that end, she told the directors, she had informed the Chesterton Medical Center administrator that she was terminating Henry Lloyd as counsel to the hospice.

"I'll be looking for outside representation, probably someone from a local firm, and I'm seeking a candidate who appreciates that the mission of Chesterton Community Hospice is founded in compassion, not profits."

She gazed out at her board of directors for a moment, meeting each set of eyes again, then sat down. Cissy rose and was the first to respond.

"I believe I can speak for the board when I say that your willingness to accept responsibility for the issue with Mr. Lipmann's daughter speaks to your character and your leadership." She paused. "Lauren, we had a special meeting by conference call earlier today before you and I spoke on the phone."

Here we go. Cue the drum roll. Where's my blindfold?

"Without the need for any further discussion at this meeting, we wanted to give you our unanimous vote of support."

Lauren cocked her head slightly as the words sunk in. Then she stood back up. "I want to thank you, thank you all for that, and," she paused to give her board members a big smile, "as long as we're gathered here together, I'd like to speak to you about a few other matters."

Lauren leaned back in her chair. After the board meeting, she'd talked to Glenda Stanley about starting another bereavement group, this one for survivors of suicide in the community, whether or not CCH was involved in the person's life. Then she pulled Rose Sears and Dorrie Kelly into the phone call. Lauren wanted the four of them to meet ASAP. They were going to ramp up community education and develop a meaningful public relations campaign for Chesterton Community Hospice. The other three began to brainstorm ideas during the call and they scheduled a meeting for the following week.

Just one more task and then Lauren could call it a day and glad of it. She wrote a quick e-mail to Allie, who had left an hour earlier at five o'clock. Lauren needed her calendar cleared on the following Monday afternoon. She would be attending the memorial service at Forester's Funeral Home for someone who had changed her life that day in a most remarkable manner, someone who had unknowingly bequeathed to Chesterton Community Hospice a deep and lasting legacy. Mr. Gerald Lipmann.

Lois

Time warp. Here I am, standing in the kitchen on Merklin Way, washing plates. What next? Getting grounded? Carlene finished loading the supper dishes into the dishwasher, wiped off the counters and went into the living room. Ray had run to the grocery store for more provisions. It was now indisputable that Carlene had taken a major tumble off the vegan wagon, at least for the duration of this visit. Ray was delighted to have his junk food partner back—the one from so many years ago.

Lois was relaxing in Ray's recliner, watching *Downton Abbey*. Carlene sat down on the couch and started to speak. Without taking her eyes off the screen, Lois interrupted her.

"Honey, can you hold that thought for just a few more minutes? This is almost over." Carlene was taken aback for a moment, then shrugged, settled in and picked up a three-ring notebook that was lying on the coffee table. Opening its cover, she recognized her mother's handwriting, the last entry on the page:

> Carlene has come home. We are a family again. How good she looks, how glad we are to have her with us. We had the most wonderful time at Amore' Pizzeria last night. For the past couple of years, I have not let myself dwell on things foregone—I didn't realize how much I had missed Carlene—and pizza!
> There is so much I want to share with her while she is here. I feel well right now and I'm anxious to have this time with her and Ray before I start feeling not so well.
> I have so very much to be thankful for. Thank you, God.
> Thank you thank you thank you.

What is this? Carlene was stumped. She waited impatiently while the television show wrapped up then spoke as soon as the credits began to roll.

"Mom, you keep a diary?" Lois looked at Carlene. Her brow furrowed and then came a look of recognition as she saw what Carlene had been reading.

"Oh, my journal. I forgot I left that out. It's nothing."

"Nice try, Mom. You're busted. A journal?"

"Well, if you must know, yes, I've kept a journal for my entire adult life."

"No shit?"

"Carlene."

"Okay, yeah, yeah. Can I read it?"

"Oh, I don't know," Lois said hesitantly. *Why am I hesitating?*

"Why write it if no one ever gets to read it? At least tell me about it."

"I started it when I was in college. It just got to be a habit. I suppose I did intend for you to see it one day. All right. Go get up in the closet in our room. There's a box up on the shelf. Please bring it here."

Lois didn't know Carlene could move that fast—she was back in a flash. Lois put the recliner in the upright position, with the carton on her lap.

"Most of what's in it is just day-to-day stuff. Not very interesting." She was digging through the contents of the box. "Here it is." Lois pulled out a notebook. This particular one had a label stuck on the front reading "1975." Carlene peered over the edge of the carton—it was filled with similar three-ring binders. She grabbed the footstool, plopped on it right next to Lois's chair and Lois handed the notebook to her. Without a word, Carlene flipped pages purposefully, then stopped and began to read aloud.

Tuesday, May 13, 1975
I can't believe the day has finally come. I had my first labor pain this morning at 6:00 a.m. Ray and I are heading to the hospital. I've never seen Ray so nervous. It's hard to say which one of us is more excited.
I need to go now. More later.

Thursday, May 15, 1975
Missed a couple of days but it couldn't be helped—I forgot to take this journal with me to the hospital.
Carlene has come home. We are so glad to have her here. We are a family. How beautiful she is, how glad we are to have her with us. Carlene Marie Spaulding. Carlene for my mother Charlotte, and Marie for Ray's mother Mary. She has lots of hair and the biggest brown eyes I've ever seen.
We are so thankful to have gotten this amazing gift. Ray can't wait to teach her how to fish and I can't wait to show her how to watch her daddy clean fish and how to be happy. Right now I feel like Ray and I are experts at that: we could not possibly be happier.
I hear Carlene calling. Gotta go.

"That's amazing, Mom. Did you hear what you said? You wrote almost exactly the same words last night as in 1975. What are the chances?"

Lois smiled down at her. "The chances are pretty good since I feel the same now as then. Sorry for making you wait for *Downton Abbey* to finish but I just love that series. Your dad thinks it's a chick show, so I have him record it for me. Do you watch it?"

"No, I don't watch much television. I do think it's interesting that you choose to spend your time doing that. No offense, Mom."

"None taken. What should I be doing? Life is made up of many, many small events, Carlene. Of course, I know I'm getting close to the end of my life but right now it's still going on, even if it's been shortened for me. There's really no reason for that to decrease the value of each moment. Quite the contrary, that should *increase* it." She stopped to study Carlene's face. It was taut with concentration and her eyes were shiny with emotion.

"Go on."

"All right. Consider a person who has an enormous accomplishment to her credit, something big like the cure for cancer. Do you really think it's possible to live like that, in that one magnificent moment all the time? It's not. What about all the other days of her life, all the ordinary days she spent with her children or doing what was necessary to get ready for the big event to happen—are those days less important because they don't get the headline or the promotion or the medal?" Lois paused to rest.

Carlene broke the serious tone of the moment and smiled at her mother. "That's some pretty deep stuff, Mom."

"Not really, honey. Here's the abbreviated version: I don't want to get so busy dying that I don't take time to live." She put the lid on the box and handed it to Carlene. "You're welcome to read any and all of my journals. There's nothing there I wouldn't want you to see, and I suppose I've always known that someday you would. Who knows? Maybe there's something in there you can use in your own life."

Carlene took the box from her mother, setting it aside.

"Thanks, Mom. I'd like that. Now, how's your Bucket List coming?"

"It's pretty short, to be honest. Your dad and I went over to the Mississippi one day last week and rented a pontoon."

"Was that fun?"

"Your dad loved it. I think peeing over the side of the boat was the highpoint for him. It was fine, but I would just as soon have spent the day sitting on the glider with him out on the deck. Other than that and you coming home, my list is pretty short."

"So, what would you like to do tomorrow?"

"What kind of herbs do you carry in your store?"

"What? What do you mean?"

"Oh, I don't know. I just thought I heard that maybe, you know, in California you can sell, you know, marijuana."

"I'm sorry?"

"I've always thought I'd like to try it sometime. Have you?"

"Have I what?"

"Smoked marijuana."

"This is making me uncomfortable."

"It is? Why? I just thought it might be something I'd like to try before I die. I mean, your Dad and I sort of missed out on the '70s. We were busy raising you."

Carlene could hardly speak for laughing. "Let me get this straight. You are laying a guilt trip on me for cramping your style by being born in 1975 in the hopes that I'll drive into Chi Town and score some weed for you, Mom?"

From the kitchen came the sound of a slamming door and "Who wants a hot fudge brownie sundae?"

"Oh—oh, there's your father coming in the door. Don't say anything about this, honey."

Carlene welcomed the opportunity to jump up and help Ray with the groceries. "Don't worry, Mom. Tick-a-lock."

Lois couldn't imagine having had a better time. The next day, she and Carlene spent the morning sorting through family heirlooms as Lois told her the story of each piece. There was the coal miner's lamp worn by Lois's grandfather and the bible that belonged to her great-grandfather. It didn't have much practical use for her—it was in Swedish—but Lois told Carlene that it had always been inspiring to hold it, knowing that her great-grandfather's hands had done the same one hundred fifty years before. And she cherished it because it was among the very few possessions her ancestors had chosen to bring with them when they left their home behind.

Embroidery and crocheting done by Lois's grandmother were handed off to Carlene. There wasn't much modern use for doilies and such, but Carlene made a fuss over them and that pleased Lois. She gave Carlene the gingham aprons her grandmother had cross-stitched and Carlene knew a lady who she bet could make them into toss pillows for her. That way she would get to look at them every day.

"If that's okay with you, Mom?"

Lois thought that was a grand idea. The only joy she'd gotten from them all these years was in looking forward to giving them to Carlene.

During a simple lunch at home, Carlene suggested they go out to dinner that evening—her treat. In that case, Lois wanted to take a nap. While she slept, Ray and Carlene sat on the glider sipping iced tea. Ray asked Carlene if she'd noticed her mother's color. Carlene said no, she hadn't noticed—when really she had. They sat in silence for a long time, gazes forward, pretending to watch an ambitious squirrel intent on burying a meal for months down the road. *Lucky little bugger.*

Dinnertime came but then Lois wasn't up to going out, so Carlene went and picked up Chinese food. Lois had avoided it for almost two years because of the sodium. She ate very little but kept saying how much she enjoyed knowing she could have it if she wanted to.

Ray tucked her into bed early and then joined Carlene at the kitchen table for a cup of tea.

"Your mom just asked me to call Rockaway House tomorrow morning, Carlene. I think she might be right. No, I know she's right."

"Don't you think the two of us can take care of her here, Dad?"

"I think we can, but that's not what she wants." He told Carlene about her mother's pre-emptive strike at the doctor's office when she announced her plan to go to Rockaway House. "I gotta tell you, Carlene, at the time I was very upset with your mom. But after we got home, we talked about it and I think I understand now. Your mother reminded me—can't you just hear her?—that she's the only one who's dying right now, so this is hers to do in her way. I've tried to be a good partner for her on this journey, but she's right, at the very end of the road, she'll be alone, so she gets to decide how she prepares for that."

"What's this Rockaway House place like?"

"I've never been there, but you know your mother, she did her research and got recommendations from a couple of her friends. It's what she wants."

Carlene thought for a moment before she spoke. "Did you know it would be this fast, Daddy?"

"No. No one could tell us for sure." He paused. There was a question he had been putting off since Carlene's arrival two days earlier. Now he would ask it quickly, just get it out. "Will you be able to stay for a few more days, Carlene?"

"I'll be here as long as you want me to be. Is that okay?"

"Of course it's okay. It's more than okay." He sat down, dropping his head, holding on tight to it with both hands. Carlene could see his shoulders shaking as he sobbed and she put her hand gently on his back. She'd never before seen her father cry.

"We'll take care of Mom together, Dad. Let's get her moved to where they can make sure she's comfortable. Then we can all concentrate on spending the rest of our time together."

Carlene expressed it perfectly, Ray thought. Going forward, that's just how he would think of this. Not as if they were taking Lois somewhere to die, but that they'd all have a better chance of spending meaningful time together if she were at Rockaway House.

Ray was thinking ahead to his breakfast in the morning with Lois. He was looking forward to telling her that their daughter had stepped up to bat and turned out to be quite the source of comfort in this crisis.

He and Lois would be sharing breakfast for the very last time.

Ray gave Carlene a goodnight hug and went to be with his wife.

He and Lois would be sharing a bed for the very last time.

Miss Lil

One of the children must have left the television on. Oh, look, it's Andy Griffith. Andy and Barney are singing a song. What is that? I know that song. It's 'The Little Brown Church in the Vale.' I know this story. Mr. Tucker came into town and he's all worked up and then he meets Andy and Barney and Aint Bee and sees how peaceful life can be. But I didn't watch that episode with Richard and Esther, they'd already gone off to school by the '60s.

Is it the 1960s?

How did it get to be the '60s? Where did the time go? Now Esther and Richie are away at college. I miss them. When they were little we'd go the park and they'd play on that old fire engine that was there. And we used to read books and sing songs and we'd memorize poems and little things to recite. What was that poem? I learned it when I was little and I never forgot it and I made Esther learn it. What was it? Something about a turkey on a hill. It seems like they were babies not so long ago.

And it'll be Halloween soon and we'll have trick or treat and I'll make costumes for Esther and Richie and they'll go door to door. I'll have Esther memorize that poem for her trick. Now, what was it? Something about a turkey on a hill.

Miss Lil was singing as Margaret walked into her room, but Margaret didn't recognize the song. "*Macavity's a mystery cat, he's called the Hidden Paw . . .* " It sounded like gibberish to Margaret. Well, Miss Lil was certainly entitled to that.

Margaret did a bit of tidying up in the room and then picked up the little book from the bedside table.

"Would you like me to read some more, Miss Lil?" Lil nodded. Margaret offered her a sip of water before she began. Lil politely shook her head.

"*Just a month from this day, on September 20, 1850, I shall be sitting in this chair, in this study, at ten o'clock at night, longing to die, weary of incessant insight and foresight, without delusions and without hope. Just as I am watching a tongue of blue flame rising in the fire, and my lamp is burning low—*"

Lil's soft voice interrupted Margaret. "Did you forget that you know me? I used to trade at *The Marion Street Grocery*."

Margaret's jaw dropped.

"Actually, I did remember that but—I wasn't sure you remembered me. I sure do remember you from the grocery store, Miss Lil. It's been quite a few years since you shopped there . . . "

"Has it? Are you sure? A little earlier I thought this was the 1960s, but I'm not sure now. Is it the 1960s?"

"No, no, it's not the 1960s."

"You believe in heaven, don't you?"

Margaret thought for a moment before she answered. "Yes, I believe in heaven. I'm not sure I can say what exactly happens when we die, though. What do you think?"

"First, I'll see stars. There will be stars and moons and suns and clouds and it will be, well, it'll be just overwhelming. But in a good way. And I think I'll see all the people who have gone on ahead. And I hope I get to see Misty, the little dog I had when I was little. Papa didn't want us to keep her, but Aunt Sylvia said 'Burt, they've given up enough,' so we got to keep her." More today than yesterday, Margaret noticed Lil needed to catch her breath after a long monologue. Lil gazed off in the distance and Margaret waited a moment before speaking.

"Miss Lil, we have something here at Rockaway House called the Jiminy Cricket Project. We try our best to grant a wish for a patient. I wondered if there's anything special we can do for you?"

Lil's forehead wrinkled as she thought for a moment.

"Like in Pinocchio?"

"Actually, yes, the same Jiminy Cricket as in Pinocchio."

"Then there is, actually."

"What is that?"

"I'd like to see my children again."

Oh great, now what? Break the news to Miss Lil that her children are no longer living? Try a fake out or stall?

"Miss Lil, I believe you told me that Esther and Richard have passed away, that they've gone on ahead." She laid her hand lightly on Miss Lil's arm. Miss Lil looked over at Margaret, puzzled at first, then her face relaxed as it came back to her.

"Oh, that's right. If you can't grant my wish, it's okay. I'll see them again soon enough."

"I believe you're right, Miss Lil."

"Can I have another wish?"

Margaret laughed. "You sure can. What would that be?"

"I'd like to feel the sunshine on my face."

There were two patient rooms at Rockaway House with doors leading to second story decks. Miss Lil was in one of them but there was no way she was strong enough to be taken outside, even in a wheelchair. Anyway, Rose said that no one was to be on the decks—the railings were original to the house and not up to code for height.

This Jiminy Cricket thing wasn't working out as Margaret had hoped. She looked over at Lil, regretting that she'd ever gotten her hopes up. Just then she saw Lil turn her head and look over at the window where the noon sun was peaking in—and it would be blinding if not for the lowered shade.

"I'll be right back, Miss Lil." Margaret disappeared and returned in a moment along with Sheryl. Together they moved some small pieces of furniture out of the way and rolled Miss Lil's bed a few feet closer to the window. Margaret raised the shade with a "Ta da!" and the sun instantly streamed across Miss Lil's face. At first she squinted, then she closed her eyes and smiled as she felt the warm rays on her skin. Margaret and Sheryl left her to nap.

Here's hoping that every wish is as simple to grant as Miss Lil's, Margaret was thinking.

Lil opened her eyes as she heard Margaret softly close the door. She looked over in the corner of the room and smiled a big smile.

Of course you can do this, Esther. First listen to Mama, then you try it. "The Owl and the Pussy-cat went to sea in a beautiful pea green boat. They took some honey, and plenty of money, wrapped up in a five-pound note. The Owl looked up to the stars above, and sang to a small guitar, 'O lovely Pussy! O Pussy my love, What a beautiful Pussy you are, You are, You are! What a beautiful Pussy you are!'"

Why doesn't someone come to take me home?

Rockaway House

Peanut Butter was the subject of the day's baking lesson. Margaret could only hope that at eight a.m. her students would be ready—and that Margaret the Teacher would appear.

Not to worry, the members of that morning's Cookie Brigade were waiting when Margaret arrived. Leonard was a retired high school teacher whose wife had passed away in hospice care two years earlier. He was bored. Apparently, there was a limit to the number of birdhouses that neighbors, friends and family were willing to accept, and Leonard had no idea how perilously close he had come to a birdhouse-building intervention.

Ben was a Chesterton firefighter who worked a three days on/four days off schedule and wanted something meaningful to do in his spare time. Contrary to common belief, not all firefighters can cook. Ben had managed to dodge that duty for twenty-five years.

Two more people I would never have met if not for Rockaway House, Margaret thought as the three of them enjoyed a cup of coffee. The first batch of cookies was baking and then *Ding!*—it was done. She gave them each a gold star for class participation and sent them upstairs with a basket of freshly baked comfort food.

If need be, Margaret could make these cookies in her sleep. She planned her day as she rotely baked the rest of the dough. She'd been thinking that Suzi Roland seemed to be a high energy idea person, and Margaret had a question for her when they met for coffee a bit later: *How do you buy a whole bunch of furniture without any money?* Ernie's insurance policy was a Godsend, but Margaret had done some snooping at Walton's furniture store on the way home yesterday. God—and Ernie—were sending her only about a third of the way to where she needed to be.

Margaret had approached Rose about the chances of getting funds to "refresh" the first floor. Rose might still be laughing. No, that was not going to happen, she had guaranteed Margaret. As they say in the corporate world: not on the radar.

Margaret had briefly considered the possibility of getting in-kind donations but then she met Mr. Walton who ran Walton's Furniture and she could be wrong, but he didn't seem like the sort who would willingly part with any of his inventory for no money—even for a very worthy cause. Margaret mined her limited experience with fundraising. Forget bake sales, bike-a-thons and raffles. That's penny ante stuff, she thought. *I'm thinking on a much grander scale.*

The grandfather clock in the Rockaway House dining room, a bequest from a patient's estate, softly chimed. Nine-thirty. Margaret grabbed her purse. She was fresh out of ideas but she had a hunch she was about to visit someone who still had plenty. Margaret was headed for coffee with the charming resource who had dropped into her life in such a timely manner.

Suzi called out for Margaret to come in the front screen door as soon as she knocked. She certainly didn't exaggerate, Margaret thought as she stood in the entryway. There were boxes everywhere, except for one room to Margaret's right. Suzi appeared, gave Margaret a quick hug and then followed Margaret's gaze. "Oh that room? I learned the hard way: always get the kitchen unpacked and one other room—immediately. Then you have a place to eat, have a cup of coffee and flop down. Anyway, Stephen doesn't get quite so crazy about the mess if we have somewhere for a cocktail when he gets home from work. It's so good to see you, Margaret!" Suzi took Margaret's arm, steering her down the main hall and into the kitchen.

"Now, this is a kitchen!" Margaret admired the gourmet cook's delight of granite, white cupboards and checkerboard tile floor, all overlooking a beautifully landscaped backyard through eight-foot windows.

"It is gorgeous, isn't it? And the best part is, I didn't have to create it." Suzi poured Margaret a cup of coffee and Margaret uncovered the plate of cookies she had brought along. Taking one, Suzi settled in a chair. "I can't stop thinking about Rockaway House. It's so lovely, so much character, so much history. Do you know much about the original owners?"

"Nothing really, not before Mrs. Sullivan found the house." Margaret looked around Suzi's kitchen and eating area, impeccably decorated, tastefully filled with antiques and accessories. "Your home is absolutely beautiful, Suzi, unpacked or not. You do your own decorating, don't you?"

Suzi smiled proudly. "I do, but I have a bit of an advantage."

"What's that?"

"I have a degree in interior design. I teach it over at Chesterton C.C.," she said matter-of-factly.

"Interior design? So you know about furniture and what it costs? Hmmm. You know, you got me thinking the other day. I need to find a way to make that first floor more welcoming for our patients' families."

"Well, since you brought it up, it is rather, well—"

"Depressing?"

"Okay, 'depressing' works. I'd be glad to help you if I can, Margaret. What kind of budget do you have?"

"The kind that's all zeros. There's no money. I have a bit from—just some special money I have—but I need fundraising and donation ideas." She waited.

Suzi thought for a moment, calling on the bounty of experience she'd had helping nonprofits raise money for charity. Before teaching, when she'd had her own decorating business, she'd been constantly pulled into donating "opportunities" as well as doing her own share of putting the squeeze on others over the years.

"Let me give it some thought. I'd love to work on Rockaway House—it'd be a joy to help that beautiful home get a bit of a facelift," Suzi said.

"In the meantime, can I see this beautiful home?"

"If you can look past the boxes and boxes and boxes. What's with all the things people have? We're in our late fifties—aren't we supposed to be downsizing? No, no, not Stephen and I—instead we upsize to a house big enough to hold all our stuff. I think we might be borderline hoarders."

It was almost noon by the time Margaret returned to Rockaway House from Suzi's. She was heading up the stairs to check in when Rose nearly mowed her over coming down.

"Whoa, where's the fire? Before you go, Rose, do you know anything about the people who owned Rockaway House before CCH bought it?"

"Sorry, late for a meeting, as usual," Rose said as she put on her sweater while juggling a tote bag, a purse and a cookie. Margaret relieved her of the tote. "No, I don't know a thing about them. Why?"

"Well," Margaret looked sheepishly at Rose, "I was sort of snooping around the property the other day. Have you ever been up in the garage attic?"

"I didn't even know there was a garage attic."

"Well, there is and it's full of furniture. And I was just thinking—"

"Anything we can use here in the house? Anything would be an improvement." Rose rolled her eyes. "Give Lance Wilson over at corporate a call. You know Lance, right? He'll know what to do. Sorry, gotta run!"

After Margaret reminded him, Lance did recall the garage attic, but he'd never been in it, he'd never had a reason to be. He asked if Margaret needed some help with something and she laughed and said not right now, but he should be careful about making open-ended offers like that.

What Margaret did need was to eat lunch and take a few minutes to think before she headed back upstairs to visit with patients. To escape the buzz of activity in the kitchen, she retreated to the dining room, certain she would be alone with her thoughts. She sat at one of the wobbly tables and unconsciously munched on her sandwich and chips.

What are the chances, she thought, that I would meet a person who knows something about old houses and furnishings just when I need someone who knows something about old houses and furnishings? *I guess Mrs. Sullivan would call that a God wink.* Until now, Margaret couldn't say for sure that she believed in such things, but maybe, maybe. She brushed the crumbs off her shirt, tossed her trash away and wondered if Suzi was still at home.

She was, and welcomed Margaret's reappearance as an excuse to abandon the unboxing she had vowed to definitely get to that day. Would Suzi take a look at some furniture for her, Margaret asked. Maybe she could help her figure out if it would work in Rockaway House? Lead the way, Suzi said.

At the top of the garage attic stairs, Margaret turned just before opening the door. "I gotta warn you, it's dark and dirty in here." Not a problem. Suzi was up for any adventure that didn't involve unpacking. Stephen would have to understand, which Suzi was sure he would because it was for a good cause, right?

The two women were huddled shoulder-to-shoulder in the small open space just inside the apartment door. In a moment, their eyes adjusted to the dim light and without a word, Suzi stepped past Margaret and followed a narrow opening to the far wall. She pulled back the makeshift curtain that covered the single window in the living room.

Margaret heard Suzi gasp as the room flooded with light. Suzi's hand was at her mouth, her eyes were wide.

"What's wrong?" Margaret said.

It took a moment for Suzi to respond. "What is all this?" She whisked passed Margaret and was examining random pieces. Slowly at first, leaning over to look at the legs, the upholstery and the undersides of the small items, then her movements began to quicken and her head rapidly turned as her gaze darted from one side of the room to the other. She shot in the direction of the bedroom and Margaret hustled to keep up with her long strides.

"What do you think? Can we use any of this stuff?" Margaret asked hopefully.

Suzi stopped at the bedroom doorway as if she'd hit a wall and Margaret nearly ran into her backside. Before Suzi could answer her question, Margaret remembered.

"Oh, there's some more." She wriggled past Suzi and continued through the bedroom to the *Alice In Wonderland* door. She opened it and with a flourish, invited Suzi to enter. Suzi rushed toward Margaret, bending down as she passed her.

"You cannot be serious."

"What? What is it?" Margaret followed her through the door, giving Suzi a gentle push ahead when she stopped again in a few steps.

As soon as they were both standing inside the unfinished space, Suzi spun around and took Margaret by the shoulders. She looked and sounded very serious. "You won't be able to use this furniture in Rockaway House, Margaret."

"Really?" Margaret's heart fell. That's why it had all seemed too good to be true—it was. Suzi, the expert, had appeared serendipitously in Margaret's life for the sole purpose of confirming that fear. *Some God wink this turned out to be.* Margaret glanced around, hoping to find a chair or stool where she could sit down. Then she heard Suzi laughing.

"What? What?" Margaret spun around.

"Maggie Maggie Maggie!" Suzi started jumping up and down, doing some version of the Snoopy dance. "Wait—wait—I'll show you!" She stopped, looked around frantically and went to a spot in the attic that was brightly lit by the midday sun. She pulled a dining chair away from the cluster of furniture and turned it over. "It is! Oh my gosh, Maggie! This is Stickley—look!"

"Look at what?" Suzi brought the chair to Margaret and pointed to a small metal plaque on the underside of the chair's seat. Margaret shrugged. "Sorry, I don't get it."

Suzi began to speak in a staccato tone at high volume. "It's Stickley, Margaret! Stickley! This is, well, it's a gold mine is what it is. It's very collectible. I have a friend who—wait a minute." She pulled her cell phone from the pocket of her capris and punched in a number. "Bruce? Suz here. What are you doing right now, never mind, I don't care what you're doing. Drop it and get over to—" She stopped and turned to Margaret. "What's the address of Rockaway House?"

"Uh, 1724, 1724 Marion Street."

"1724 Marion Street. You know, that gorgeous two-story right next to our house . . . No, no, the new house. I'm in the back of the property, above the garage—you're not even going to believe this . . . No, but I'll give you one hint: Roycroft . . . That's right! Get over here—now!" She gave the phone's screen a satisfied poke with her index finger, hanging up.

Margaret was flummoxed. "Suzi, what are you—"

Suzi's response was a whoop of excitement as she all but dove into the furniture, managing to be frenzied and gentle at the same time. Like a mother lifting a car off an injured child, Suzi's adrenaline had kicked in and she was moving chairs, bookshelves and lamps, quickly looking at each underside before carefully putting it back. Margaret watched in confusion.

"I don't understand. What's a Roycroft?"

Suzi materialized back at Margaret's side. "You, my friend, have uncovered King Tut's Tomb of arts and crafts furnishings. This is Stickley and Roycroft furniture. The bad news is that you can't use it in Rockaway House."

"That's what you said, but why not?" Margaret was still trying to catch up.

"Because the good news is it's much too valuable! Unless I'm very mistaken, this stuff is worth boocoo money. But you can sell it! This furniture has been untouched for—how many years, do we know, oh, it doesn't matter—in this little museum of an attic. It's in perfect condition—well, except for the dust." She ran her finger across the top of a table. "Who in the world owned this house originally, Margaret?"

"I don't know. Suzi, I still don't understand."

"My friend Bruce'll be here in a second and he can give us a better idea. He's on his way—" They heard a car door slam below in the parking area. Suzi retraced their steps back to the landing. "He certainly didn't waste any time." Sticking her head through the doorway, she called down the stairs, "Bruce! Up here! Wait until you see this! You are going to completely vapor lock!"

Bruce took the steps two at a time, having practically no idea why he'd been summoned, but judging from the tone of Suzi's voice on the phone and the look on her face now, he trusted that something exceptional had already happened or was about to.

Suzi made quick introductions. Margaret was slowly coming around, and Suzi was getting even more excited watching Bruce take it all in just as she had a few minutes earlier. Mimicking Suzi's reaction, Bruce went from the first room to the kitchen then into the bedroom—pausing to poke his head into the vintage bathroom—without saying a word. Then Suzi led him into the *pièce de résistance*, the attic warehouse space.

Margaret stayed back. She waited and, sure enough, his reaction was slightly lower pitched but, in essence, an echo of Suzi's.

"Suzanne Roland! Where are we? Is this heaven?" he shrieked.

"No, it's Chesterton, Iowa!"

The two of them squealed like teenagers.

In the following weeks, when Margaret thought back on those days when she first discovered the contents of the attic and what it all meant, Margaret thought in terms of her favorite ride at the amusement park, the roller coaster.

The climb to the top is excruciatingly slow. You wonder if you'll ever get there. You sit at the crest. It's probably only a few seconds but it seems so much longer. Then it's down, down, down. Faster and faster, your stomach lurches in a sickening, exhilarating way, and you think you're probably going to be all right, but for a moment—a deliciously scary moment—you're not entirely sure.

That first afternoon when Margaret showed Suzi—and then Suzi showed Bruce—what she'd found was the last tranquil time the three of them had together. It was the crest of the hill.

Bruce had raced to his car—nearly tumbling down the bottom half of the stairs—and retrieved a notebook. Suzi and Margaret left him in the attic space making a crude inventory of the furniture, just a rough list of items by category. And, of course, he was taking pictures with his cell phone like a fiend. He planned to e-mail the photos to his address book of dealers and customers—he was jotting more names in the margins of the inventory as quickly as they popped into his head.

Meanwhile, Suzi and Margaret were looking over the crates and boxes that outlined each room. Suzi was like a little kid on Christmas Eve.

"Let's pick one at random and see what's in it!"

And why not? That's what this was most like: a child's fantasy, an embarrassment of riches.

Margaret and Suzi both sensed that they shouldn't open just any box, because this wasn't just an attic of furniture and household items. It was more like a shrine to the people who had left it behind. These were things, but somehow they seemed as alive as the people whose world they had once adorned. Something momentous had happened long ago, and Margaret and

Suzi knew in their hearts it was not something good. People don't walk away from a house full of beautiful furniture unless their world has been turned upside down.

Their attention was drawn this way and that, overwhelmed by the mountains of cartons and crates they had to choose from. Out of all these boxes, there was a particular box, the one Suzi and Margaret were meant to open first, and they only had to figure out which one it was.

They spied it at the exact same moment.

Up over Margaret's head but eye level for Suzi, it was smaller than most of the others and Suzi easily lifted it down from its perch atop a crate. It was a hatbox, a lady's hatbox. Without speaking, they nodded in agreement and she and Margaret took it to the kitchen, away from Bruce's whistling and occasional hoots that bounced off the rafters.

Finding a table with four chairs upended on its top, Suzi and Margaret each picked one up and set it on the linoleum in the narrow walkway. Stored upside down for a very long time, the seats were spotless. Margaret folded back the dusty packing blanket that protected the table, revealing a white enamel top decorated with a red art deco border. Suzi slowly placed the hatbox on the table between the two of them.

She looked over at Margaret. Margaret blinked and held her breath as Suzi carefully lifted the lid. They expected to find a hat and were eager to imagine the face it had once framed, each thinking maybe they might even take turns trying it on. There was no hat. Instead, the box held what looked like the contents of a lady's dressing table. It was obvious: someone had frantically swept a hand across its surface, catching the miscellaneous items in this time capsule just as the movers were about to carry the vanity away.

Suzi gingerly pulled out a tin of talcum powder (Cashmere Bouquet), tortoise shell hair combs, a leather manicure case (monogrammed MPM) and a small pewter picture frame containing the black and white photo of a handsome man. There was a silver-backed comb, brush and mirror set. The silver plate was worn off each piece where a hand had gripped it, thousands of times. And then never again.

Margaret took her turn and retrieved a Max Factor lipstick, a jar of Lady Esther "Four Purpose Cream" and a flowered handkerchief. Then, on the bottom of the box Margaret felt a small square glass bottle with a stopper. She grasped it tight to make sure it remained intact. Once her hand was outside the box, she opened her palm. Removing the glass top, she tentatively took a whiff.

"That's the smell," she said in a whisper.

"Here, let me see." Suzi took it from Margaret, waved it under her nose, then replaced the stopper and turned the bottle over, revealing its label. *Chanel No. 5*. "That's it! How could I have not remembered it? My grandmother always wore it—well, on very special occasions. Say, if we didn't already know this family had money, we do now. You're right, that's what we smelled in Rockaway House the other day. How odd." She looked over at Margaret.

"Don't even say it. I just got chills."

"Okay, I won't say it but we both know what you're thinking, Margaret."

"Me? Yeah, I'm thinking this is giving me the heebie jeebies."

"Hey, you don't suppose—" Suzi's thought was interrupted by Bruce fairly leaping into their space, making them both jump.

"Have you ever? This is completely over the top! What've you two got there?" He stopped and peered at the hatbox and its scattered contents.

Margaret and Suzi looked at each other and shrugged. They didn't know how to answer that question, they really didn't.

"Did that belong to the lady of the house? By the way, who is the lady of the house? Where in the world did all this stuff come from?" Bruce picked up the manicure set and studied the monogram for a moment.

"We don't know," Suzi said.

"But I'm going to find out," Margaret pledged. Standing, she looked at her watch. "I need to get back inside. They probably think I've deserted the ship. I have to make some calls. I have to tell my supervisor and—I don't know what I have to do first." She threw up her hands. Suzi stood as well and went nose-to-nose with Bruce.

"Well? What do you think, Auction Boy?"

"I think I must be dreaming. There are pieces here that belong in a museum—honestly. I need to do a lot of research and get some pictures taken and get an accurate inventory. Help me, here. I don't even know who the owner of this is—I mean, the owner *now*." Margaret quickly explained to Bruce what Rockaway House was and why she had asked Suzi to look at the stuff in the attic in the first place.

"My dear," he said to Margaret, "I think you'll definitely be able to buy some knickknacks for that house when you sell all this. This 'stuff in the attic' is conservatively worth a quarter of a million and that's without opening one crate and who knows what's in them. Margaret, honey, you look like you need to sit down." Bruce was right, Margaret was feeling woozy. "And before you make any other calls, you better call your security company and get this place locked up—tell em' to do extra drive-bys. I know it's Chesterton, but I also know of some thieves who would travel a good distance to get their mitts on this *stuff*."

Margaret took a few cleansing breaths. She thought back to when she'd suggested an adult education class called *Breathing 101* to Ernie. She remembered exactly what he'd said: "Hey, good news! I don't need a class—I already know how to breathe!" Just for crackin' wise, she'd made him go with her.

What was it we learned? Seven quick breaths in through the nostrils, hold for seven, exhale for seven—

"Earth to Margaret. Girlfriend, are you all right?" Bruce was holding her hand, giving it a gentle slap. Margaret laughed.

"Oh, I'm fine. This is really incredible, isn't it?" She stood again. "I know who to call and I need to get to that, *right now*. Let's keep this between the three of us until I can let the people at CCH know and get the garage secured. Back here tomorrow at eight a.m.? Does that work for you two?"

"In the vault, baby, and I'll make it work!" Bruce agreed enthusiastically.

"You bet!" Suzi seconded. "I've gotta get home and make some notes—I have an idea for us, but I don't want to say it until I figure some stuff out." Hugs were shared all around and Suzi and Bruce went on down the stairs. Margaret hesitated for a minute. Carefully putting the items back into the hatbox, she decided to take it with her to show Rose. Once she stepped back into the world outside this attic, Margaret needed something tangible to hold onto, something to prove that this was all real. She whispered a prayer, *Thank you, thank you, thank you, Amen,* and carefully shut the two doors behind her.

Making a mental list as she walked across the parking lot, Margaret knew there was Rose and Lance to tell, who would need to contact their boss, Lauren Dunlap. Margaret hadn't met her, but she'd heard she was a handful. Other than that, Margaret was clueless on the next move to be made. She knew who to tell, she just wasn't sure what to tell them.

Even with the visual aids, it was hard to explain it all to Rose, who kept repeating, "Are you sure he said a quarter million?" Finally, in exasperation, Margaret took Rose's hand and led her through the kitchen, out the door, across the driveway and up the stairs. Rose stared, she gasped, and then she agreed, Lance Wilson was the guy to call next—that was for sure. Rose would call Lauren Dunlap and let her know what was going on. Knowing Lauren, Rose said, she would want details, lots of them. No question about it, Margaret would need to go and meet with the executive director, Rose added.

"I'm not so sure about that, Rose."

"Margaret," Rose paused and made eye contact with her, smiling, "you've stumbled upon what may determine—what *will* determine—the future of Rockaway House. Please accept that sometimes a really good thing happens. It's okay to take credit when you're the one who makes it happen."

Elation, gratitude, shock, adrenaline. Margaret thought either her heart or her head was going to burst. She nodded mutely. "I'll call Lance and have him arrange for the security. You're going to call Lauren?"

"You got it. Oh, and I'd say you've jumped into your new job with both feet, Maggie."

Lance was as shocked and excited as Margaret when she told him the estimated value of what she'd found. He'd get *Ace Security* on the phone as soon as they hung up. And until a full-fledged system was installed, he'd put his own hospital security men on hourly checks and didn't Margaret agree that he should call the property insurance agent and get a rider for additional coverage in the meantime, until they knew more? God forbid there was a tornado tonight, he chuckled. Margaret said yes, yes, that's an excellent idea, grateful that someone was thinking straight.

It was four-thirty. Margaret felt like she'd been pulled through a knothole. Not that she was complaining, because the reason was breathtaking—in every sense of that word—but this day had been filled to the very brim. She climbed in her car, started the engine and was pulling out of the driveway about to take a right for home when she was overtaken by an irresistible impulse and turned left instead.

The sign on the door of *The Chesterton Bee* said *Hours: M-F 8:00-4:00.* Margaret peeked in the window, smiled and waved to the woman at the counter who was sorting mail. As Margaret had hoped, she unlocked the door.

Once inside, Margaret introduced herself to Lynda Wyatt, receptionist, weekly columnist (*What's the Buzz?*) and *Chesterton Bee* archivist and historian. Margaret explained her connection to Rockaway House on Marion Street. Could Lynda help her research who the previous owners had been?

The Bee doesn't have those type of records, Lynda told her. Margaret shrugged, smiled and turned to leave.

Coincidentally though, Lynda's voice stopped Margaret in her tracks, she had grown up near Marion Street a couple of blocks from Number 1724. If Margaret had a minute, Lynda would pull up the Clinton County Recorder's website and find out what's what. Lynda had always loved that house. She'd walked past it every day on her way to school, starting in the fall of 1970.

Of course you did, but it's no coincidence, I'll just tell you that, sister.

Margaret waited.

In a few minutes Lynda stepped back to the counter with a printed readout of the Clinton County Recorder's title history for 1724 Marion Street, Chesterton, Iowa. She pointed to each entry as she explained the records to Margaret.

"The Chesterton Medical Center Corporation bought the property in 2004—I guess you knew that—from the Estate of Clarence Harris. He and his wife Laura bought the house in 1944 from—and it looks like these are the people who built the house in 1922—Daniel Patrick Murphy and his wife, May Powell Murphy." Lynda stepped back, pleased with her efficient detective work.

May Powell Murphy. Monogram: MPM.

Bingo.

Margaret

Maybe if she cleaned out a drawer or closet each evening, it wouldn't seem so overwhelming. *Sure, instead of seeming overwhelming, it would seem oh so never-ending.*

The discovery at Rockaway House found Margaret elated and disturbed at the same time. True, it probably meant financial security for Rockaway House, but she sensed something more to do with the abandoned property, something troubling. And finding all those things in the attic garage had brought the issue of Ernie's earthly possessions to the front of Margaret's mind. That was disquieting in its own way.

For a month after Ernie died, Margaret hadn't changed their sheets. To be perfectly honest, they weren't changed for close to two months because Ernie spent the last three weeks of his life in a hospital bed in the living room. Margaret could hardly believe it herself. She'd never told another soul, not that anyone who knew Margaret would believe that she could do such a thing, little Miss Daily-Change-the-Pillowslips-and-Weekly-Change-the-Sheets. Like the aura of his sad sweater, she just hadn't been ready to surrender the scent of Ernie that lingered on the bedding.

You can close your eyes and see a place or a person or an event in the theater of your mind, right? The same with sounds. Margaret could transport herself to childhood, to her teen years, to her wedding, even to the day of Ernie's funeral by simply hearing a tune from one of those times. She could close her eyes and see the people and each place, the foreground to the musical background.

For Margaret, aromas were even more potent memory triggers than sights or sounds. A familiar scent gave a distinctive tug on the brain—on the heart, really—as if a memory was tagging along with the smell, peeking around its shoulder, waiting to see if you would recognize it before it stepped into full view.

But the thing about a song was, if you wanted to use it to trigger a memory, you could play a CD over and over and over. God knows, Margaret had been guilty of that. And she'd just recently stopped kicking herself in the butt for not having Ernie record their phone machine message. If only he had, she could hear his cheerful hello now, whenever she wanted to. One of the prices she'd paid for being such a control freak.

As for recalling a smell, well, you could duplicate some, like baking cookies or a fall day—or *Chanel No. 5*. As for the unique ones—the most important ones—like Ernie's sweater, good luck. You couldn't just pull up an aroma from your memory bank, at least Margaret couldn't.

Margaret wasn't stupid. She knew that when the last thing that smelled like Ernie was gone, the memories that surrounded it might be gone forevermore, too. At the very least, they were much less retrievable, which amounted to the same thing.

Yup, there was something to be said for holding onto stuff.

Where was Ernie right about now, Margaret suddenly wondered. Was he doing good works from afar—something more meaningful than just leaving shiny pennies laying around? Leaning back on a cloud, his hands clasped behind his head, the same pose he had struck on the hammock between yard projects? Or was he already back on earth, a little baby—or a cat, if he had anything to say about it?

Margaret wasn't exactly sure where she stood on the specifics of the afterlife. Without getting all balled up in the how, where and when, her thinking always ended in the same place: *Does it really matter?* No doubt the details would concern her when her own time came, when she thought she was closer to the possibility of Ernie and her being together again, but for now, the only relevance from her perspective was that wherever Ernie is, it's not here.

It was stating the obvious to say that things had changed since Ernie died. Obviously, she was no longer married, she now lived alone and she cooked for one, when she cooked. It was a lot deeper than that. *Everything* was different. Dinner out. Holidays. Sleeping. Not sleeping. Breakfast on Sunday morning. Yard work (hey, watching someone do something was doing something). Emptying the dishwasher. Laundry. Shopping.

Shopping was a perfect example. Margaret had usually gone alone when Ernie was alive, but now Ernie wasn't here to share the pride of a successful bargain hunt when she got home. That made the shopping part different as well as the getting home part. *Everything.*

Margaret longed to measure progress of some kind. Had she officially moved past "anger" and on to "acceptance"? There were times when she felt like she'd slipped back into "denial." How was that even possible, so many months after Ernie's death? Ernie was gone, no argument there. And yet, just the other morning, when she first woke up, she'd had to remember all over again how Ernie got cancer, had months of chemo, endured a lot of pain and then died. How was that possible, to have forgotten all of that just because she'd been asleep for a few hours? More and more it seemed to Margaret that when it came to grief, what's possible is whatever is. *Brilliant.*

Her life was different now, but different wasn't always better, so did *different* count as *progress*? Margaret liked it best when there was a clear strategy and it was being followed and she couldn't say if that was happening or not. Ernie dying, her working at Rockaway House, finding the Murphys' furniture. Was each thing a small part of a huge plan or just a series of random events? If it was a plan, it certainly wasn't Margaret's plan, but it would be a small measure of comfort to know that *someone* was overseeing this cosmic drama.

A few pieces did seem to be falling into place.

Margaret bought the computer, then she got that check from Ernie and then Rose pegged her to be a problem-solver for patients and their families. If Rose had noticed Margaret putting into practice some of those ideas from the

Internet, then one thing did seem to be leading to another. Then there were the pennies. She could definitely use some more of those. Margaret wanted to think she was making some headway. She wasn't in the same place as back on September 3, that was for sure, and maybe she was being greedy to ask for more right now. It was hard to know.

She looked around and realized she'd been standing at the closet door for who knows how long, lost in this meandering stream of consciousness. *So, what about clearing out some of Ernie's things?*

She shut the closet door.

Nope. Not today. This isn't an evening for sorting. This is an evening for making an early night of it. Pardon me while I slip back to Denial for a bit.

Forty-five minutes later, just before she went to sleep, she remembered she had a few items to be addressed with God. The usual blessings for those she loved and who loved her, then a special word on behalf of Lillian Dexter. It was clear Miss Lil was ready to meet her maker and to be reunited with her husband. That had gotten Margaret to thinking.

She asked God to help her understand why she'd been left behind and Ernie got to go ahead. And if she wasn't meant to understand, then would God please grant her some acceptance. The Murphys were making her think about all manner of legacy-type issues because it seemed—and Margaret allowed she might be all wrong about this because she was sure about very little these days—that whatever had gone terribly wrong in the Murphys' home back then was somehow linked to things going incredibly right in the here and now. And, if that were true, did that mean it might be decades before Ernie's death made some sort of sense to somebody? Because Margaret doubted very much if she'd still be around to share in that enlightened moment. *Just saying. Amen.*

Noah

Even after his death, the welfare of Edward Everest and his family remained a priority for the staff at Rockaway House. Because he died in hospice care, the legal procedure was to contact Dr. Reese, then the medical examiner, and then Forester Funeral Home. No need to dial 911, because the coroner would accept the hospice nurse and doctor's certification as to cause of death. No need for an inquest or investigation of any kind.

Those calls were made soon after Edward passed at five a.m., and all the paperwork was completed before Crystal got off duty at seven. The next shift of workers made sure the Everest children were comfortable and encouraged them to spend whatever time they wanted with Big Ed. By eleven o'clock the Everest family, Big Ed and Mr. Forester had all bid farewell to Rockaway House.

As soon as Edward's room was vacated, the transition crew from the corporate offices arrived. They thoroughly cleaned and prepared the room, down to the freshly made bed, and let the nursing staff know it was ready for the next resident.

By then, the CCH admissions clerk, Genevieve Nillson, had already called Rolling Hills Retirement Center, where the person next on the waiting list for Rockaway House, fifty-nine-year-old Noah Smythe, was living. The social worker at Rolling Hills said they'd arrange for Mr. Smythe to be transported to Rockaway House later that day. She said he'd be pleased to hear he was that much closer to where he wanted to be.

Noah had been at Rolling Hills for only five weeks. Looking back, it was hard to believe, but ten days before moving there, he was still working full-time at *Under the Covers*, where he'd been employed since one month after his thirtieth birthday.

Noah had always believed he'd make his living in the company of books, but his career didn't begin quite as he had hoped. The only available job when he graduated from Iowa State University in 1978 with a master's degree in library science was at the Chesterton Public Library. Noah didn't have unrealistic expectations about his chosen profession, and he was ready and willing to start at the bottom. He just hadn't anticipated being stuck there for quite so long.

The joy of working in an atmosphere of books and no longer being in college were enough to sustain Noah for quite a while. Then the promise of advancement ("as soon as [fill in the name] retires, you're next in line") placated him a bit longer. But after spending forty hours a week for over five years reshelving books because people were too ill-mannered to put them back where they came from (*after reading one paragraph and deciding it wasn't a good fit, I suppose*), Noah was losing his passion for the written word. He had never imagined that was even possible.

Heaven knows Noah had tried to make the best of the situation over the years. To his way of thinking, there was obvious growth potential in treating the library as a business and its patrons as customers. He proposed a children's corner with story times, guest author readings and a self-service coffee bar with a donation cup to defray costs. He envisioned a book festival on a spring afternoon. Neighborhood residents could sell refreshments and used books in the library parking lot while authors made presentations inside. Once he even brought up the possibility of organizing book groups, making multiple copies available to borrow along with discussion guides.

His suggestions to the head librarian, Miss (not Ms.) Rhoades, were summarily dismissed, time after time. Miss Rhoades was, if nothing else, consistent in her response to Noah's suggestions: "Well, I can certainly take a look at that."

But she never did.

Noah's decision to avoid pushing back at Miss Rhoades came more from a lack of alternatives than a lack of courage. That, and having once met the trustees of the library board, Noah knew they were no more keen on modernization than Miss Rhoades. It hardly made sense for Noah to post a challenge without a fallback position. And that's where he believed himself to be trapped until one day in 1983.

A library patron approached Noah—standing on a rolling stool, reshelving Moby Dick for the gajillionth time (*What exactly do they imagine it is about?*)—and asked if she could bother him for a moment.

The wiry redhead with freckles, her tortoise shell glasses slipping down her nose, asked if Noah had read the most recent book by Peter Lovesey. No one had ever before asked Noah for his opinion on any book in the entire library, which was certainly the waste of a valuable resource, considering Noah had read thousands of them.

He quickly stepped down from the stool. Noah's one-hundred-sixty pound, six-foot pencil frame still towered over the tiny woman. He asked enthusiastically if she was familiar with Arthur Conan Doyle or Agatha Christie. That led them to discuss contemporary versus classic mysteries. That led the young woman to ask if Noah would possibly be interested in coming to work at the bookstore she was about to open, without knowing one single detail about this nice-looking man. And that led Noah to say yes, without knowing one single detail about the job offer he had just accepted.

Noah gave Miss Rhoades a two-week notice and was thrilled when she rejected his courtesy and told him to leave immediately. He began working at *Under the Covers* the next day, and consulted on every decision concerning the environment and inventory of Chesterton's newest business.

The day Rolling Hills Retirement Center got the call for Noah to come to Rockaway House, he would have celebrated his twenty-ninth anniversary at the store. That is, he would have if he weren't so busy dying.

The owner of the bookstore, Lisbeth Jones, was thirty-three when she hired Noah in 1983. She'd also known her entire life that she would someday make her living around books, but Lisbeth was lucky enough to skip the whole Miss (not Ms.) Rhoades/public library chapter. She began her career as the administrative assistant to the superintendant of the Chesterton Consolidated School District.

One Saturday as Lisbeth drove back home from *Waldenbooks* in Clinton, it had occurred to her that she couldn't possibly be the only person in Chesterton who would appreciate having a bookstore closer at hand. She did the research. Many paperbacks were being sold out of *Rex's Drugstore* on Main Street, as well as at *Holly's Sundries*, from behind the rack of pantyhose. That's all Lisbeth needed to know. She would have to steer the frustrated book lovers to the door of her bookstore and she knew in her heart she could do that. She just had to.

Even while Lisbeth was showing Noah the empty space on Main Street—the future home of *Under the Covers*—the brainstorming began in earnest. Noah suggested bookshelves on rollers so large spaces could be easily carved out for in-store events—that would allow browsing customers to see and hear what was going on and would encourage them to participate. Lisbeth would talk to her friends throughout the school district and organize field trips to teach children how a book went from being an idea to being on the bookstore shelf. He thought background music would foster leisurely shopping, and she chimed in that a mix of classical and jazz music would minimize offending anyone's tastes for too long. He agreed. She smiled.

Over the years, the partnership of Lisbeth and Noah built a thriving business. Early on there were some lean times, but at the end of each month when the accounts were settled and Lisbeth was able to pay Noah and herself, she always said she never once regretted being an entrepreneur. Meeting Noah that day in the library was possibly—no, it was—the luckiest day of her business life, no question.

Noah developed a following of customers who considered his opinion indispensable. *Have you read this one yet? Do you think I'll like it? Don't you think it's insulting when authors write just to satisfy a publisher's contract?* Lisbeth thought Noah's idea to organize book groups was beyond clever. They asked a regular customer what she thought of the notion and before they knew what was happening, there were ten themed clubs meeting throughout the month. The temptation was overwhelming and Lisbeth and Noah each joined two groups, covering for the other during those meetings. Noah chose one that read biographies and another that focused on poetry. Lisbeth was fond of mysteries—ever since that fortuitous day in the Chesterton Library—with historical novels as her second choice.

As time went on, Noah and Lisbeth readily embraced new technology for inventory control and accounting and a simple website. With the advent of e-books, rather than fear the competition, they recognized an opportunity to guide their customers down new paths to reading. Naturally, some of their clientele were aging, so Noah helped them appreciate the advantages digital books held for adjustable font sizes and even audio options. So what if they were using an electronic reader and ordering e-books online? Those folks still bought print books for their grandchildren when they came in for their monthly book groups. This bookstore would be about people and relationships, Noah and Lisbeth wholeheartedly agreed. Book sales would naturally follow.

The issue of p-books versus e-books took care of itself when it came to the store's book groups. By an informal poll of the members, it was decreed that since Lisbeth and Noah provided the meeting place at no charge, only print books ordered from *Under the Covers* would be used by book club members. So there.

Soon Noah suggested that for a small fee he and Lisbeth would offer to place e-book orders on behalf of customers, a huge relief for those who had received the gift of an electronic reader from well-meaning family members, patrons who didn't even own a computer. They became even more loyal to *Under the Covers* and would never consider ordering a print book from an online vendor—even if they had the means or the slightest clue how to do so.

Thanks to Noah's ideas and Lisbeth's community network, the children's book corner and reading hour, the self-service coffee bar (without the donation cup and with freshly-baked cookies from the bakery right next door), the author events and the annual book festival all came to fruition. *Under the Covers* traditions became Chesterton traditions.

Then, of course, there was the private side. Lisbeth couldn't count the number of people who had said at one time or another, *Do you think there could ever be anything between you and Noah?*—or something to that effect. Best friends, they shared a thousand bits of gossip and jokes and always looked out for the other when a cold or the flu hit. Lisbeth thought Noah was hilarious. Noah thought Lisbeth was incredibly bright. They developed a serious weakness for babkas and neither one ever forgot a birthday, celebrating hers with chocolate, his in lemon. Noah was an only child whose parents had long since passed. Lisbeth's minute family was a brother who lived in Boston. There were plenty of invitations to holiday dinners for both and sometimes they ended up at the same home, often not. They each had a nice apartment, a haven to which they were glad to retreat at the end of the day, alone with a cup of tea or a glass of wine and a new release or an old favorite volume.

So no, there wasn't any reason or desire to mess with things as they stood.

Fifty-nine and sixty-two years old, respectively, neither Noah nor Lisbeth ever thought about retirement. Lisbeth had made Noah an official partner in the business twenty-eight years earlier, monthly earnings from the store were dependably ample and life had a reliable and most agreeable cadence.

Until the morning of February 5, 2012.

Rockaway House

Suzi's husband Stephen would be at a conference in Chicago for the next three days. As he pulled out of the driveway the morning before, Suzi's parting words to him had been a sworn oath to make some headway on the unpacking while he was gone.

"Well, that's not gonna happen!" she said aloud as she finished her third cup of coffee, sitting in her sun-drenched kitchen, making notes on a legal pad. The discovery of the Murphy booty was one of those "unforeseen circumstances" that one cannot be expected to plan for. *When something like this comes along—and incredibly miraculous things like this come along so seldom—you simply have to go with the flow.* That's what Suzi had always believed and this was no time to go off course, philosophically speaking. Anyway, she had already figured that they—she and Stephen except he didn't know it yet—would be hosting a wine and cheese party in the not too distant future. The house would have to be organized in time for that, wouldn't it? It would all get done. Somehow, things always got done. Besides, Stephen was a big-hearted guy and he would f-l-i-p once he got a chance to step inside Rockaway House. He loved old homes and all their trimmings even more than Suzi did.

Margaret arrived at Rockaway House especially early that morning. It was easy to wake up, considering she'd barely slept all night. Like Suzi, she'd been making notes of the ideas and questions whirling through her brain. There were no cookie protégés today, so at seven-thirty, Margaret was alone in the Rockaway House kitchen. As she baked Peanut Butter Chocolate Explosions, she reviewed the mental checklist she'd compiled between two and five a.m. that morning.

At eight o'clock Lance Wilson was meeting the owner of *Ace Security* at Rockaway House. The timing worked out fine, Margaret thought, for Lance to meet Suzi and Bruce as well. Lance didn't yet know it, but he was an integral part of the project.

Project? That was Rose's word, not Margaret's. *What project? Now Rose has me calling it that.* They had a boatload of furniture. They needed money. They had to figure out how to convert the former into the latter.

How would they go about selling this house full of antique furniture? They certainly couldn't invite throngs of strangers to traipse around the property to browse, could they? Not to mention letting the whole world in on the secret of the treasure that was stashed on site. It would have to be moved somewhere else for sale, wouldn't it?

What about pricing it all? At three this morning, Margaret had done a little checking (the Internet never sleeps) and discovered that Bruce not only had a successful interior design firm, he was also a certified antique appraiser with over ten thousand Google results on his name—quite impressive. Margaret would let Bruce worry about the pricing.

Speaking of Bruce, did they need to pay him or would he donate his time or what?

So much to think about. If Margaret didn't stay on top of the situation, she would end up completely overwhelmed by all the unanswered questions. *Up to my earlobes in alligators*, Ernie used to say.

Margaret Elizabeth Williams. Snap out of it. Do you think that God or the Universe or whatever benevolent force brought this blessing would leave you hanging? Seriously, get a grip. This is all going to work out as it's meant to. Just take a deep breath and be thankful for the angels like Suzi and Bruce and Lance who have already come into your life. Seven quick breaths in through the nostrils, hold for seven, exhale for seven . . .

Margaret looked up at the sound of the swinging door. Rose had arrived, beaming.

"Did you sleep at all I didn't I still can't believe it did that happen or did I dream it?" She gave Margaret an impulsive hug. "I talked to Lauren Dunlap she wants an update as soon as possible I gotta say she is *very* excited about this I mean *really* excited."

Margaret had never met Lauren Dunlap. She didn't know how to take that news.

"You may want to make that next cup decaf, Rose."

Rose nodded rapidly in agreement.

In the back door came Lance, shaking his head.

"I just went up there and saw it. Margaret, Margaret, Margaret. What have you done?" He was beaming. "I think our world just got rocked, ladies."

At eight o'clock Rose and Margaret went to join Bruce and Suzi, already serving sentry duty outside the garage door. Standing shoulder-to-shoulder, it was hard to say if they were guarding it or holding a spot to be the first up to the vault.

Handshakes and friendly hugs all around, then Suzi spoke. "I was thinking we could go next door to my house. We can talk there without disturbing anyone." They all agreed. Margaret motioned Lance over for introductions and to let him know they were headed to Rolands'. He promised to join them as soon as he gave *Ace Security* their marching orders. He was hoping the smoke and burglar alarm systems could be installed in the garage yet that day. Just as she was walking away, he pulled Margaret aside.

"You get to choose the codes. I need a four-digit number and I need a security word. If the central station gets an alarm signal, they'll call us to verify whether it's a true emergency." Margaret had to think for only a second.

"For the number, let's use '1922.' For the word, let's use 'Murphy.'"

"Perfect. See you next door in a little while."

As they walked in side by side, Suzi stopped Margaret and asked if she would object to Suzi getting them started this first time. Between her business, charity events, church committees, alumni clubs—you name it—she'd run about a thousand meetings but she was not about to step on the toes of her new best friend.

No objection from me, Margaret assured her, relieved.

Oh, Margaret added as they joined the other two, a family named Murphy was probably the original owner of the furniture. She didn't have the whole story yet, but Lynda Wyatt at *The Bee* was on it, so you can bet they'd know soon enough, she assured Suzi. Margaret had tempted Lynda by hinting that there was a big surprise in store for the whole Chesterton community. She'd told Lynda she couldn't say what, first she needed to learn all she could about the Murphys. That had done it. Lynda was on it like Banacek.

With everyone circling Suzi's kitchen table, armed with coffee, Margaret's cookies and pads and pens, Suzi charged ahead.

"First we need to set our objectives. To raise money and awareness, right?"

All heads nodded.

"Then I think I've got the way to do it. We'll have a decorators' show home. I've seen the first floor of Rockaway House, and we're talking paint, paper, window treatments and rugs. It doesn't need rehabilitation, it needs redecorating. The kitchen's been updated, so that saving's huge and we'll get all the labor and materials donated. Now, I'm assuming that all the goodies in the garage were once in the house, so we furnish the show home with all that furniture—this is the scathingly brilliant part—then we sell the furniture at an auction, maybe a silent auction, during the fundraiser. We charge admission, with a high-price ticket for the first night.

"We'll make oodles and kaboodles of money that you can use to buy the furnishings you really need for the house. And I'm guessing you'll have quite a bit left over, to boot. Maybe even enough for an endowment."

Rose was the only one there who was paid to keep her head when all about her were on the verge of hysteria. "I hate to be a wet blanket, but how do you see this happening over there when we have patients and their family members to consider?"

"I thought of that, Rose," Suzi answered. "First, that house is solid, so I don't think sound will be a problem during the project—it's just painting and papering and cleaning, the floors don't even need to be refinished. The event itself is just people walking through, it's not like it's a Delta Tau Chi house party. It wouldn't be any more disruptive than having a class in your conference room is now."

That made sense and, if there was any way at all, Rose wanted to agree.

Margaret trusted Suzi implicitly even though she didn't totally get the "show home" concept and understood practically none of the details that would be involved in making it happen. Still, she already knew it would be spectacular. All she could think was that thirty minutes earlier, she didn't see how any of this could possibly work out and now there really was a "project."

Having done all the due diligence she thought necessary, Rose was now fantasizing about all the activities that could be part of the show home event. The first floor of the four-stall garage was ideal for exhibit booths about the hospice mission and volunteering, maybe demonstrations of some of the alternative therapies she hoped to introduce and some old-fashioned games for the children. The possibilities were endless. Maybe they'd even have that Annual Remembrance Day they always talked about but never seemed to get off the ground.

Bruce hadn't gotten much sleep the night before either but he was still three steps ahead of Suzi. No two-bit silent auction, no way. Bruce was thinking *online bidding*. Overnight he'd been researching how to reach the collectors of high-end mission/arts & crafts/prairie style furnishings. There was no shortage of buyers in the five-state area: Chicago, Minneapolis, Des Moines, Omaha and Kansas City. Of course, there'd be a lot more bidders if it was a nationwide or international auction event, he mused.

Each one was engrossed in his or her thoughts. Suzi couldn't stand it.

"Well? What do you think? Somebody say something!"

They all burst out laughing, squealing and putting voices to ideas and slapping backs and talking over each other. Suzi gaveled them back to order with her empty coffee mug.

"I know this is very ambitious, but I really think we should try to make it happen this year. If we don't, we have to move the furniture twice—it can't stay out there in the attic much longer—we're on borrowed time now. And in this economy I worry about the market for collectibles like those. As we all know, the Iowa winter can start as early as November, so we have to consider the threat of bad weather. Seriously, this is a *lot* to accomplish. Are we all in?"

Rose could answer Suzi's question on behalf of Chesterton Community Hospice.

"I had a very interesting conversation with Executive Director Lauren Dunlap late yesterday afternoon. I told her what Margaret found and the potential value. I told her I didn't know exactly how it would happen, but that it looked like Rockaway House and our mission to help our patients and their families and our community will be financially secure for quite a while. When I told her I was coming to meet with you all this morning, she gave me a message to pass on. These were her words: 'Let's make this happen.' So, yes, Suzi, we're all in."

Recently, Rose had been careful to not let on to anyone how threatened the future of Rockaway House was, but she suspected Margaret had her ear to the pump handle and staff members and other volunteers had already heard things that maybe they shouldn't. Everyone associated with Rockaway House was justifiably fearful that Helen Sullivan's dream might be allowed to perish. For those now gathered around Suzi's kitchen table, Rose's words put a face back on who and what was at stake. And now, for the first time since Margaret's incredible discovery, they truly appreciated the magnitude of what had suddenly become possible and of how lives would be touched, in a most remarkable manner.

Margaret's sniffling was the first to be heard. Soon the table was surrounded with blubberers. Enter Lance.

"Hey, I knocked but no one answered, so I thought I'd—" He stopped at the kitchen door, mid-sentence. They each looked up, tear-stained faces, all smiles. "Well, if you aren't a bunch of bewildered looking folks!"

As Suzi passed around the box of tissues, Lance reported that *Ace Security* hoped to have the system up and running by day's end. Coincidentally, the owner's mother-in-law had passed away in hospice care three years ago. Margaret smiled. *Coincidence, my Aunt Fanny.* The other committee members excitedly reported to Lance that he was going to be a very busy guy for the next couple of months. They laid out their plan—as much as they knew so far. Lance immediately volunteered friends in the trades who he was sure would donate their painting, wallpapering and carpentry talents.

As soon as Suzi had a better idea of what the renovation was going to look like, her interior design class at the community college would be getting their homework assignment. Being part of a project like this was a once-in-a-lifetime opportunity for students who aspire to be decorators when they grow up, and Suzi was eager to get them involved. A real win-win.

Rose jumped on that one. She was thinking about family members who often asked about having wireless Internet at Rockaway House. They never complained, of course, but it would make visiting loved ones so much more convenient. Naturally, there had never been any money for it—until now. Rose wondered if Suzi's students could help design a computer lounge for adults and children—they seemed perfectly suited for that. And, speaking in her role as volunteer coordinator, Rose added that their involvement would give her a chance to talk to them about the mission of hospice. Young people were a demographic cohort she was eager to recruit.

Before anyone asked, Bruce announced that all of his efforts would be his contribution to the future of Rockaway House. He would prepare the catalog (maybe some of Suzi's students could provide some brawn to move furniture and help him with photography?), coordinate the online bidding, and in a day or so he'd have a slew of names to add to Suzi's massive mailing list.

Suzi offered to host a V.I.P. wine and cheese party for major donors, maybe the evening before the public was allowed inside Rockaway House. It would be an easy walk over for a preview tour. But—and she was just thinking out loud, so bear with her—maybe they also needed to have a kick-off event right away. Would Lauren Dunlap be willing to give Suzi the list of existing CCH and CMC donors and stakeholders, she asked Rose. The guests at the unveiling party would be the first in the know, so it really would get the network churning, secure some seed donations of money and materials, and—most importantly—"It's all about the buzz! What we need here is some shameless self-promotion!"

What they also needed was a working name for the event, and soon after, the first meeting of *The (Secret) Rockaway House Heritage Show Home and Auction* was adjourned. Code name: *The Auction.* Margaret and Rose headed back to Rockaway House.

"You know, Maggie," Rose said, putting an arm around Margaret and steering her into the tiny room that served as her office, "there's only one person who has what it takes to sell this idea to Lauren Dunlap and the board. Only one person who has the passion, the creativity and the contagious excitement to 'make this happen'."

Margaret was getting a sick feeling in her stomach. She began to shake her head and wave her hand in front of her face. *No no no no no.*

"Oh yes, it's you."

Rose invited Margaret to have a seat. She was going to prepare her, as much as was humanly possible, for her first meeting with Lauren Dunlap.

Margaret

Rose was not taking a chance on Margaret skipping or chickening out. She made the call to Lauren Dunlap while Margaret still sat in the tiny makeshift office. In no time, the face-to-face between Margaret and the CCH executive director had been scheduled for early the next morning. Margaret pleaded to take Suzi along. If Lauren asked Margaret a question about the show home she couldn't answer, it might blow her credibility. Knowing that they had to first sell Lauren on the idea, so she could sell the board on the idea, Rose agreed. Heck yes, pull out all the stops. Margaret made a quick call to Suzi and of course she'd go with her. In fact, if Suzi could just find the right box, she'd bring along some budget information from another show home her sorority had done years ago as a fundraiser. Or had she finally thrown that out? Oh well, she'd look for it anyway.

The following day, Margaret was leaving for the meeting with Lauren, just about to open the door to the garage, when the phone rang. She hesitated and then went back in the kitchen to answer it.

"Margaret, it's Suz. Big trouble here. I'm in an awful mess. Some idiot hooked up my washing machine all wrong and it's flooded most of my laundry room and kitchen. Stephen's out of town, remember? I've got to stay here. The appliance man—the idiot—is on his way along with the insurance adjuster and the cleanup crew. But you'll be fine."

Margaret froze. *You cannot be serious.*

"No, listen, I'll just call and reschedule the meeting. You can make it by tomorrow or the next day, can't you, Suzi?"

"Margaret, listen to me. Every day is precious for this to work. You know everything I know. If Lauren has a question about the show home that you can't answer, just write it down and tell her you'll get back to her toot sweet. That always works. I know you can do this, Maggie."

Suzi heard Margaret sigh. "Oh all right, I'll go, all by myself, alone. Will you be home so I can call you right after?"

"Trust me, I'm not going anywhere. Just come over when you're done—I'll find a dry spot for us." She laughed.

Well, Margaret thought, if Suzi can still see humor sitting in her flooded house, I can certainly do this. *I'm sure I can do this. God help me to do this.*

Runs a tight ship. A bit hard to read. Probably good-hearted deep-down, but sometimes tricky to take. A tough nut to crack. That's how Rose had described Lauren Dunlap during her prep session with Margaret. In the evening after their meeting, Margaret had thought a lot about Rose's comments. Rose worked for Lauren, right? But Margaret didn't. She didn't really work for anyone, she was there by choice. She thought maybe Rose's perspective as an employee was a little warped, a bit cynical?

Margaret decided to forget about Rose's warnings and take Lauren Dunlap as she found her. That way of thinking had worked for Margaret for the better part of sixty-seven years. Why not now? She pushed on with cautious optimism. *Or is this cockeyed optimism? Because that's really more foolishness than optimism. Stop it, Margaret.*

Very little that Rose said had prepared Margaret for what was to follow as she entered the executive director's office at CCH headquarters. A diminutive woman waited behind a massive desk, watching as Margaret walked in the door. Lauren Dunlap was slight and barely five foot four. Her face, pale with a blush like a china doll, broke into a wide smile as she greeted Margaret. That's when Margaret recognized her.

"Hello, you must be Margaret. I'm Lauren Dunlap. So nice to meet you." She put her hand out and gave Margaret a shake, then didn't let go. "You look so familiar to me. Did you work somewhere before Rockaway House?"

"Yes, *The Marion Street Grocery*, Lauren." It had come to Margaret just as she took Lauren's hand that they had met before—many times. True, Margaret had been the store's bookkeeper, but at *The Marion Street Grocery*, you wore many hats. Margaret had worked at the customer service desk, run a cash register on occasion and, as in the case of Lauren Dunlap, had served and shared a cup of coffee with many a customer in the store's deli.

"Oh my gosh! *The Marion Street Grocery*—of course! I started driving through *Whole Latte' Love* a while back—it seems I'm always in such a hurry in the mornings anymore—but I've thought about you so many times, Margaret."

Margaret sat down and told Lauren about being close to retirement when Ernie got sick and that was that. Ernie had died and she'd started volunteering at Rockaway House. And now here she was, sitting in Lauren's office.

"I'm so sorry to hear of your husband's death, Margaret. So you are the 'Margaret' that Rose was talking about. Could this town get any smaller?" Lauren looked toward the door. "Wasn't someone else going to join us?"

"My friend Suzi Roland had an emergency this morning and couldn't come at the last minute. But if you have any questions about our idea—the project—that I can't answer, I'll get the answer from Suzi and get back to you."

"We'll be fine, I'm sure. So," Lauren said as she folded her hands on the desk in front of her, "I understand you made quite a discovery two days ago. Tell me about it."

As her story unfolded, Margaret became more and more animated. By the time she got to the part about the scheme for the show home fundraiser, she had scooched to the edge of her chair. She ended with Suzi's words about how quickly this all needed to happen.

"Whoa, Margaret! I guess I can see why Rose sent you. Let's be practical, 'cause that's what I'm paid for—I'm the designated buzz kill. What about the patients' comfort and care during this process?"

Margaret was ready. She reminded Lauren about the Christmas in September party they'd had for Caleb Bronson. In fact, hadn't she heard that Lauren had popped in that evening? The show home wouldn't be any more disruptive than that was. And, of course, folks working on the show home would understand what this is really all about: the patients and their loved ones.

"Let's say, for sake of discussion, that I'm sold on this idea. I'm not saying I absolutely am, but let's just say I am. Unfortunately, this is not solely my call to make. We've never taken on anything of this magnitude before at CCH, so someone has to convince my board of directors. How do you intend to convince *them*?"

Me? I thought that was your job. I'm pretty sure Rose said that's your job.

"Hmmm. Well, the people on your board are all familiar with Rockaway House, right?"

"They certainly care about it, but I'm not sure all of them have ever even visited Rockaway House. Why do you ask?"

Then Margaret heard someone say that the board should meet at Rockaway House to see it first-hand, have a tour and then she'd explain to them all about the fundraiser. *Who said that? Oh my God, that was me.*

"That's a splendid idea, Margaret. I'll call the chairperson." As Margaret sat by, paralyzed and mute, Lauren dialed the speakerphone. Cissy Peters answered. Lauren gave Cissy a brief synopsis of what was going on, just enough to peak her curiosity. Margaret listened with fascination as Lauren used just the right inflection with the terms she skillfully sprinkled in the conversation: "financial stability," "jewel in the crown of CCH," "endowment," "amazing windfall," yada yada yada.

By the time Lauren hung up, the availability of the conference room at Rockaway House had been verified with Rose and the emergency board meeting was scheduled.

"So," Lauren said as she sat back, "I hope you'll be ready for them day after tomorrow, Margaret. They're very engaged and committed and they'll want to know—first and foremost—that the patients and their families will be respected. And they'll want to know how much money you think the show home will raise. Which is a very good question. How much will the show home raise?"

Margaret was caught off guard, but not for long.

"Well, Bruce—he's the antique furniture expert—says at least $250,000, and he hasn't really had a chance to inspect all of the furniture or any of the small things. Suzi Roland thinks we can get all the labor and materials donated for the redecorating and for the party, so I guess $250,000, at least."

I'm throwing these figures around like I know what I'm talking about and she hasn't kicked me out of her office—yet. This is surreal.

Lauren whistled. "That would keep Rockaway House open for a very long time and give us a perfect opportunity to increase community awareness about the great job you're all doing."

"Yes, public awareness is certainly one of our goals," Margaret nodded as she parroted Suzi's words from the day before. *Whoever said the secret is to surround yourself with smart people certainly knew what she was talking about.* "I didn't know anything about hospice until Ernie—that's my husband—needed it. As I'm sure you know, Lauren, that's where most of our volunteers and supporters come from right now—they're survivors."

Lauren's mind was drifting as Margaret spoke. This conversation had shaken loose another story of survivorship for Lauren, a memory that was never far from her mind. She was debating whether to share it with Margaret. Then she recalled the countless cups of coffee they'd had together at *The Marion Street Grocery*, talking about everything and nothing for a few minutes once or twice a week. She sat up straight.

"I'm a survivor of sorts myself, Margaret. Twelve years ago, my brother was dying of cancer in a hospital in another town. At the time, our family didn't know anything about hospice or what it could do for him at the end of his life, and no one there told us—looking back, I'm not sure they knew any more than we did. It wasn't the peaceful end of life we would have chosen for my brother. It was a horrifying experience for us, his family." She stopped and took a deep breath.

"Then, in 2005 I met someone whose husband died in hospice care. Up until then, I didn't know one thing about hospice. I learned what she was able to do for him at the end of his life and then for many others. Then I knew how different it could have been for my brother Wes." Lauren paused again. "I didn't know the end of life could be so peaceful and so dignified until I met her and she taught me about hospice." Margaret turned in her chair to see where Lauren was pointing. It was the portrait of Helen Sullivan.

"You mean Helen Sullivan? That's her, that's Helen Sullivan?" Margaret stood and stepped up close, studying the serene face. "I wish I'd gotten to meet her."

"I wish you had, too, Margaret. She was my friend and an amazing woman."

"Is that why you took this job, Lauren?"

She nodded.

Margaret remembered what so many of their coffee chats had centered around, when Lauren still had time to stop at *The Marion Street Grocery* in the mornings. Lauren had usually done the talking while Margaret did the listening. "What do you suppose Mrs. Sullivan would think of all the issues you have to deal with, how hard it is to stay focused on the real work of caring for the sick and dying, Lauren?"

"You mean what would Helen do if she was still here?"

"Yes."

Lauren smiled. "I think she'd appreciate the treasure you found at Rockaway House for what it is: an incredible blessing and a true God wink. I think Helen would say, 'Let's make this happen, Margaret!' And I think she'd be right."

Margaret was grinning and shaking her head in disbelief as she drove away from the medical center corporate offices. She had made a quick call to Suzi from the parking ramp and told her she was pretty sure the meeting had been a success. Now Margaret was headed to Suzi's house.

If anyone had told Margaret six months ago that she'd be meeting with the head of the Chesterton Community Hospice to convince her to proceed with what Suzi called "mid-six figures" and what Margaret called a "colossal" fundraising project, Margaret would have fallen down laughing. This time six months ago, she was probably putting in a load of laundry, trying to get Ernie to eat a bite of breakfast and wondering how she would ever find the strength to give him the care he deserved. This time six months ago, she wasn't capable of picturing a future beyond the edges of the pool in which she was drowning.

Whoever said God doesn't have a sense of humor doesn't know her very well.

Victoria

Ordinarily, Magda didn't follow someone just because they said "Follow me," but she was tired of driving the bus. She was tired of taking charge. She was tired of being the only one in the room who wasn't medicated far beyond good sense. She was just plain tired.

She mutely trailed behind Crystal into the upstairs solarium. Crystal handed Magda a steaming cup of coffee and got herself one as well. She sat down across from Magda, looking at her drawn face and vacant demeanor before she spoke.

"So, Magda, how are you?"

"I was just thinking that Victoria seems to be doing so much better, maybe she sort of jumped the gun and came here too soon. Maybe I should take her back home. She worries about me being able to handle it all, but I think maybe I just needed a little break for a day or two."

"Have you been Victoria's primary caregiver since she got sick?"

"Oh, yes. We have lots of friends, but it's just the two of us at home. It was just me, mostly. Well, the visiting hospice folks, of course, but mostly me."

"How long has Victoria been really ill?"

"She's been bedbound for about six months."

"How have you been feeling, Magda?"

"Me? Oh, I don't know. A little tired, I guess. Okay, mostly. I haven't really thought about it I guess."

"I'm sure you haven't, but you can now, you can think about yourself for a change. It's okay to let others help you with caregiving, Magda. It really is." Crystal stopped. As she paused, Magda's head tipped down and her shoulders moved with a slight shudder. Crystal put her hand on Magda's arm. "Sometimes our role as caregiver changes. Physical care and medical care are only part of what Victoria needs right now, Magda. That's what we're here for, so you're free to spend whatever time you two still have together concentrating on Victoria's other needs, on what you *both* need now, like friendship, love, handholding, a chance to say 'I love you' and 'goodbye.' That's all you have to be in charge of now."

Crystal bent close to hear Magda's response, barely a whisper.

"I'm just so tired. And so angry. I don't understand why I'm so angry."

"It could be the fatigue and it could be the frustration of your loved one having cancer. Cancer doesn't have a conscience, Magda, and that can be pretty frustrating in itself. It just happens and we don't usually get to know why."

"But I do know why." Magda raised her head and looked directly at Crystal. "Victoria could have prevented this. She refused to find out if she had a gene for breast cancer when she had the chance. Then she got breast cancer four years ago. I think she could have prevented this."

Crystal knew a decisive moment when she saw one. Her input on this might affect how Magda viewed Victoria's death now and for the rest of her life.

"Magda, I've seen many people die, and I can only think of one or two where you could say for sure why that condition or disease happened to that person. You might be right about Victoria's decision, but maybe you want to ask yourself whether dwelling on that serves any purpose for you? Just as we each have the right to manage our treatment at the end of life, we each have the right to make decisions about our health care and about all sorts of lifestyle choices throughout our lives. Each person is on his or her own journey." Crystal paused for a moment. "I'd hate to see you hold onto these feelings at the expense of making the most of the time you still have with Victoria."

"But I wanted to talk to her about all this and I never got the chance." Magda sounded like a petulant child. Crystal saw in Magda what she often saw in caregivers: like the little kid at the mall, so tired that the only emotional option left is a meltdown.

"Magda, when was the last time you got a day off, a day to yourself?"

Magda laughed a little, then wiped her eyes on the tissue that Crystal offered to her before answering. "I didn't want Victoria to come here, Crystal. I know I couldn't do it at home anymore but, still, she made all the arrangements. Our friends offered to sit with her sometimes, but Victoria didn't like that. I think she was embarrassed to have our friends see her so helpless—and I understand that, I really do—but that left me to handle everything. And then when she said she wanted to come here, she didn't even ask me what I thought—I wanted to keep her at home. I mean, I wanted to let her have her way about this, but, you know, I just couldn't do it anymore. But I really wanted to."

Crystal doubted if Magda had any idea how befuddled her reasoning sounded. "I wonder if one of our caregiver support groups might have helped you, Magda. It still might."

"I heard about them, but I couldn't come because I couldn't leave Victoria alone." She looked so sad, so frustrated and so defeated.

Crystal drew herself up and took Magda's hands in hers. "Now, I want you to listen to me, Magda. I believe that being a caregiver is a blessing, to know that you have made a real difference in another person's life. It's also okay for you to give yourself a break. We were called in while we could do the most good for Victoria and for you. Too many people wait until it's so near to the end that most of the advantages of hospice care are lost and it's just too late.

"You two did it right, you really did. You had us help you at home, and then—and it doesn't matter whose idea it was—Victoria came here when the time was right."

"Victoria definitely gets the credit for that," Magda quickly allowed. "She took care of that. She took care of most details for us."

"The important thing is, it got done. You've been her advocate, Magda, and that was key to Victoria getting the right care. Everyone needs a strong advocate."

Me strong?

But never mind that distraction, Magda's needle was stuck on the one pressing, persistent issue for her. "I put off saying what I wanted to tell Victoria. I wanted to talk to her before it was too late. Now it's probably too late."

"She may not seem fully engaged at times, but that doesn't mean she doesn't hear and understand what you're saying." Crystal let Magda ponder this for a moment. "Sometimes the end of life is a time to forgive or to ask for forgiveness. You and Victoria love each other. It sounds like you've had a wonderful life together. Only you can decide if you want to share these thoughts with her, but if you do, now is the time."

Magda stood, fortified by the brief period of rest and validation and knowing what to do next. She gave Crystal a hug and went back to Victoria's room. Victoria was softly snoring. Magda sat down on the bedside chair and took Victoria's hand.

"I have something I want to say to you, Vic." Magda took a big breath and went on, speaking softly but confidently. "I've been really angry with you for almost four years because you didn't get that DNA test when you had the chance to find out if you were going to get breast cancer, even though you knew you could do that. And you never told me and you should have told me, Vic. You could have gotten the mastectomy and maybe not gotten cancer at all. You know I would have stood by you if you'd done that, don't you?

"You don't have liver cancer, Victoria. You have breast cancer in the liver. Now I get that and that's why I'm so mad—maybe you could have avoided this all if you'd had that test and had the surgery. If you hadn't gotten breast cancer, you wouldn't be dying now. Right? You made this decision without me and you shouldn't have done that." Magda stopped speaking and began to cry, laying her head down on Victoria's bed. Having a crying jag—twice in one day, no less—was a first for Magda for longer than she could remember. She just hadn't had the time. And if she had, what would the point have been?

After a few minutes, Magda sat up. She shook her head as if throwing off a bad dream, sat up even straighter and took a deep breath. The heavy hand that had been on her shoulder for years had lightened its grip.

"I forgive you, Victoria. I wish things had been different, but I forgive you."

Magda blew her nose and as she turned to toss the tissue away, her glance fell on Victoria's journal. She opened it to the entry that had been neatly written by Amanda, the entry Magda hadn't gotten to read earlier:

Very soon I won't be here anymore. I'm looking back at my life and wondering which parts I would change if I could.
I would never change having Magda in my life, that's for sure. We have had such a life together, a wonderful life together.
One thing I probably would change is that I'm sorry that I've been such a burden on her. I don't know if I did the right thing by not having that genetic test back when my mother was dying. At the time, I really thought it was the right decision. Now I'm not so sure, I haven't been sure for a long time.
I have tried to not live in regret, especially since I got sick again. What good is that, to live in regret? And time was so precious for us. If I made a big mistake and messed up Magda's life, I truly am sorry. As I look back, I did the best with what I knew at the time. I've tried hard to forgive myself. I know Magda's been angry with me about this and I hope she can forgive me one day.
My dear Magda: Thank you for being my friend, my lover, and, most of all, for taking such good care of me. Except for all this awful cancer stuff, we had the best time, didn't we?
You know I love you, now and forever.

Magda set her purse down on the kitchen table and took off her jacket. She looked up at the clock. Nine-thirty and she was starving. She opened the freezer, put a package labeled "Vegetable Lasagna for 2" into the microwave and checked the phone machine for messages.

One was from a friend; two were from Victoria's sisters who lived in Oregon and Florida. Victoria had asked them to please come while she was still able to enjoy their visit, but not after she was too far gone. They'd been in Chesterton for a long weekend two months earlier. Now they called daily to check on her.

There was a message from Magda's mother asking how they were doing. Magda had meant to return yesterday's call today, but time had gotten away from her.

She wandered into the living room while she waited for the casserole to heat. There sat the baby grand piano. Most days Magda simply didn't possess the necessary energy or concentration and the poor thing hadn't been played for ages. Victoria had often asked Magda to play—she wasn't musical herself and she loved to listen—but over the past few months, Magda always begged off. It wasn't that she didn't want to perform for Victoria, it was just that, well, it was hard to explain.

Suddenly Magda realized that the thing she wanted most in the world was a shower. She headed into the master suite, stripped off her clothes and stood under the hot spray for a long time, letting the water relax her while she tried to wash away days, months, maybe even years of anger.

Refreshed, she slipped into sweats and went back into the kitchen. Her lasagna was ready and still hot. Magda gobbled it down, then sat back and looked up at the bulletin board. She spotted the reminder for her annual mammogram. The notice had been ignored since it arrived in April and the appointment should have been scheduled for May. Magda took the postcard down and laid it on the table under the pepper shaker, a reminder to make that call the next day.

What now? She wasn't exactly wired, but after her day-long nap, she wasn't expecting sleep to come very soon; that would probably happen about the time she needed to get up the next morning.

Magda walked back to the bathroom and found the bottle of sleeping pills. They'd been prescribed months earlier for Victoria when she was having trouble getting good rest, when a sleeping pill had been enough to help. Magda took one out and filled a glass with water. Just as she was about to pop the pill into her mouth, she stopped and set the glass and capsule on the counter.

She went back to the living room, sat down at the piano and began to play Victoria's favorite song, the one she always requested, *Clair de Lune.* When she finished, Magda pulled out all her favorite sheet music. She played without a break until a quarter past midnight and then she went to bed and went sound to sleep.

Rockaway House

All in all, not a bad morning for Margaret. It turned out the executive director of CCH wasn't any sort of a mean-spirited corporate hack. Margaret had probably inferred that, because Rose would never have used those words, but at any rate, Rose had it all wrong. Lauren was a survivor, someone with a personal tie to hospice just like most of the volunteers and a good number of the staff. Just like Rose and Margaret. Maybe, Margaret thought as she drove back to Rockaway House and Suzi's, someone should think about moving the administrative offices closer to the heart of the hospice program, "the jewel in the crown" as she had overheard Lauren so adroitly put it to Cissy Peters.

While the appliance man, insurance adjuster and cleaning crew were doing their respective things, Suzi had managed to locate the box with all her fundraising files. It contained the budget details for the show home of 2005, held at the birthplace of the first Chesterton mayor, a Victorian behemoth with decades of deferred maintenance—the house, not the mayor, Suzi was quick to point out. As for condition, there was no comparison to Rockaway House, so they could disregard all those rehab expenses, but the rest of the information was invaluable. Suzi promised to have a detailed outline ready for Margaret to share with the CCH board in two days. And *The (Secret) Rockaway House Heritage Show Home and Auction Committee* could definitely use the other materials to guide its work.

As she sat in Suzi's living room, giving her a blow-by-blow recap of the meeting with Lauren, Margaret's cell phone rang. It was Lynda Wyatt at *The Bee*. If Margaret had a few minutes, Lynda had some juicy info to share with her. Margaret was on her way.

Purposefully guarding the privacy of Margaret's project as well as her own behind, Lynda led Margaret to the back room of *The Bee*'s offices as soon as she arrived. Lynda had spent the better part of the past two days conducting clandestine research, convincing herself that nearly every life event held the potential for a great news story. That's what her old boss Ray Spaulding taught her. There was absolutely no doubt in Lynda's mind that there was an exceptional human interest feature buried in the history of Rockaway House, and if the current editor questioned her activities, that was Lynda's story and she was sticking to it.

She sat Margaret at the large table and plopped down next to her.

"Iowa's number one in the nation for something, Margaret. Guess what it is."

Number of pigs? Acres of corn? "I don't know. Do I wanna know?"

"Oh yes. Give up? Iowa's number one for counting its residents." Lynda took Margaret's blank look as license to continue. "The federal government does a census—it's required in the U.S. Constitution. The first one was 1840, and they did it—still do it—every ten years. But starting in 1852, Iowa decided to do some off-year counting of its own." Lynda was getting very excited while Margaret was getting very confused.

"Okay . . . "

"They did that again in 1854, 1856, 1885, 1895—we've had our own censuses more often than any other state—1905, 1915 and *1925*!" With that, Lynda slapped her hand down on the table in triumph. "You know, *1925*! Three years after the Murphys bought Rockaway House? Don't you get it?"

"Apparently not."

"The 1925 Iowa Census is one-of-a-kind—it's the census by which all future censuses were measured. I not only found out who was living in the house, I *will* find out who the Murphys' parents were, where they were born, where they were married. Heck, I can tell you what church they attended. I'll find out where the Murphys—well, probably just Mr. Murphy—worked and if they had a mortgage on the house. And if their parents lived in Iowa, I can find out the same for them—oh, I already said that. Anyway, this is huge!"

Margaret was starting to understand. "All that from one form?"

"If it's filled out, which they're sometimes not. So far, this one's looking good. Like, once I know Mr. and Mrs. Murphy's parents' names and where they were born and married, then—if the parents were in Iowa in 1925—I can do the same for them. I can see where *their* parents were born and married, and on and on and on. It's like a genealogical scavenger hunt—each clue leads you to the next one."

Margaret took a big breath and let it out. "Wow. It's a good thing you don't have anything else to do all day, Lynda." They both laughed.

"As far as I'm concerned, right now I don't. I'd say this is one of the most important stories I've ever researched, Margaret." Lynda had stopped smiling. She hesitated, then went on. "I don't know what you're up to, Margaret—although I wish I did and I'm sure you'll share that when you think the time is right—but there is something extraordinary about that house, there always has been. I've wondered about it my whole life, and now I'm finally going to find out."

The nudge about what Lynda was hoping to learn from Margaret hadn't gone unnoticed. Margaret nodded, accepting the terms of their silent bargain. "So, what do you know so far?"

"Okay, so, I pulled it up at the library, but there's always somebody hanging over your shoulder to use the one computer with the online genealogy database. I can't stand to have that nasty head librarian breathing down my neck. God, isn't she *ever* going to retire? I'm headed over to the Clinton County Historical Society to look at microfiche, so I can take my time and see the whole form. But I already know that in 1925 there was a daughter Annabelle, age two, and a female named Bridget Quinn, age twenty-two, living with Daniel and May Murphy. The "Relationship" is blank for Bridget Quinn, so I'm not sure who she was. Maybe an aunt or something? Oh, and I know the Murphys didn't have a mortgage."

"Isn't that unusual for back then?"

"I don't know—I'll research that question some other day."

"What else?"

"That's it so far. I'm headed over to Clinton right after lunch. I'll call you when I know more."

Margaret returned to Rockaway House. By the time she got there, she was having that roller coaster feeling again. She was at the crest of the hill and she was dreading what the rest of the ride might bring. And she couldn't wait to find out.

Lynda called Margaret again about two o'clock. The trip to Clinton had been very productive. Could Margaret stop by that afternoon? Did Lynda want Margaret to pick up a coffee for her on the way?

Fifteen minutes later, Lynda pointed to the census forms as she recited the new details for Margaret. She now had the names of Mr. and Mrs. Murphys' parents. (Yes, May Murphy's middle name of Powell was her maiden name). And Bridget Quinn? Lynda was almost positive she was the Murphys' housekeeper because even though "Relationship" was left blank, the form showed her "Engaged in Domestic and Personal Services" and that she'd been in the United States for only seven years. It didn't seem very likely that a member of this family would be working as a servant in someone else's house, so Lynda guessed the blank under "Relationship" was just an oversight.

"I saw that Mr. Murphy worked in the 'Trade and Transportation' industry, so I pulled the Chicago & North Western archive records while I was over there—you knew it was a big deal railroad in Clinton back then, right? Right. I found out he went from being chief clerk to the assistant superintendant in 1920 to trainmaster by 1929. The Chicago & North Western went bankrupt in 1935—the 1930's were brutal for the railroad industry. There's tons of info on that, too, by the way. But the C&NW survived and in 1937, Mr. Murphy was named superintendant. A pretty important dude for the times.

"And check this out: Daniel Murphy's father-in-law was Thomas Powell, which just happens to also be the name of the superintendant that Daniel Murphy was the assistant to, when he was the assistant. I think he married the boss's daughter." Lynda looked at Margaret, raising an eyebrow. These were the sort of innuendos that turned facts into a great story for Lynda, and they made the researching a lot more fun, too.

"Everyone in the family seems to be native Iowans except Mr. and Mrs. Powell, May Murphy's folks. They were married in Rockaway, New Jersey." Lynda paused for a moment to breathe.

Rockaway? Whoa. Margaret realized she was holding her own breath and remembered to exhale.

"Now, fast forward to the next federal census, 1930. That year's form isn't as detailed as Iowa's 1925 census, so the information's not as extensive, but there's been lots of changes at the Murphys'. By April 1, 1930, they've had another baby girl, Lauralee, and now we know that Bridget Quinn was born in Ireland, but—this is weird—'Relationship' is still blank, so she's our mystery woman."

Lynda pulled out another photocopy, the 1940 census form for 1724 Marion Street. Ten years later, all the 1930 household members were present with two more additions: another daughter, Elizabeth, and a son, Danny.

Goodness, five women in one house? That explains all the dressing tables, Margaret thought. She shook her head. "I think you've missed your calling, Lynda, you should have been a detective."

"I've always loved the investigative part of being a journalist—not that I get very many chances to practice that here in Chesterton. Now I'm going to start looking at old newsprint—I figure that's the only way to know the full story." She stopped. She had a hopeful look, like maybe Margaret might be having an urge to spill—or at least hint—why she wanted this information so badly in the first place.

Not quite yet.

"I wish I could," Margaret answered the unspoken question. "But I promise to give you an exclusive scoop when the time is right, how's that?"

"It's a deal. So, *The Bee* is digitally archived from 1877 to 1929 and then since 1985, so I can search names in those years, but, obviously, the years we need to search aren't, you know, digitized, so I'm going to have to look at microfiche. My poor eyes. Oh, and I've already searched the death records for Clinton County and I haven't found anything for Daniel or May Murphy, so they didn't die here. Probably died wherever they went to when they sold the house in 1944. That piece of the puzzle I haven't found yet—but I will!"

All Margaret could think about as she drove back to Rockaway House were the words of Alice, in Wonderland: "*Curiouser and curiouser.*"

Margaret

Margaret couldn't wait to get home and tell Ernie about her day.

It began with a very interesting patient. At Rockaway House, the first order of business each morning is to make the rounds of every room, freshen flowers, generally tidy up and, most importantly, start each patient's day with one smile and two ears. Since moving into the position of volunteer coordinator, Rose had sorely missed one-on-one time with the patients, so on that day she relieved the volunteer on duty and invited Margaret to come along.

Meet one Isobel Baines. If there was a tornado and a grade school art class collided with a party supply store, Isobel's room was the morning after. Margaret's gaze darted to each wall, nearly every square inch adorned with cards, streamers, the sagging remains of helium balloons, banners and handmade construction paper decor, obviously the work of artists still learning to stay inside the lines. The hodgepodge mural was a holiday timeline: Thanksgiving turkeys, Christmas Santas, Easter eggs and bunnies, Fourth of July firecrackers, even a Baby Jesus and three wise men. The 1958 Connie Francis hit, *Who's Sorry Now?* softly drifted from the clock radio.

"Good morning, Isobel," Rose greeted the tiny woman who was lying in the bed, reclining. Her face lit up. Her wild bed-head of silver white hair was eye-catching, but it was the frames of her glasses that drew Margaret's gaze away from the walls. "Oh, I see you found your specs," Rose said. She picked up a vase of flowers from the dresser, and took it into the bathroom to change the water.

"I did, indeed, and it's a good thing, too. I can't see with 'em and I'm practically blind without 'em! Hello—I'm Isobel." She reached out a small pale hand with bright red nails.

"Margaret, this is Isobel Baines. Isobel, this is Margaret. She's a volunteer." Rose came back into the room and busied herself poking at what was left of the floral arrangement.

"Glad to meet you, Miss Baines. Your glasses are quite amazing." Margaret wished she had the nerve to wear such things. Leopard print glasses and a lime-green flowered robe.

"Nifty, eh? I like 'em and what the heck—it's a bit late for me to worry about fashion. And I'm not a 'Miss'—I'm a 'near-miss'." Margaret glanced over to Rose for clarification but got only the glimpse of a smile as Rose quickly averted her eyes.

"Isobel, you'll have to explain yourself to Margaret."

"Well, it's this way, Margaret. My life is a series of almost tragedies, close calls—you know, near misses. There was the time I fell off the roof of the barn and landed in a pile of hay. Then I stepped on a nail and got blood poisoning but survived. Then my car got rear-ended by a semi—that was a bad one—but I walked away without a scratch." Her sweeping arm took in the room's walls. "And here I am: eleven months in hospice care, beating the odds and still dodging the Grim Reaper. Do you think you'll ever get rid of me, Rose?" Rose stopped her bustling and sat down on the bed, putting her hand on Isobel's.

"I think it will be a very sad morning when I don't have you to start my day, Isobel, that's what I think." They shared a look and a quiet moment. "In the meantime, what's on your agenda for today?" Rose stood and picked up yesterday's newspaper from Isobel's bedside table, replacing it with that morning's edition of *The Bee.*

"Oh, the usual. Need to work on the obit, re-do the Will." Isobel gave Margaret a wink and a smile. "I like to keep my family on their toes. Rose, did I tell you that Rhonda's coming in later today?"

"She is? Well, I hope you girls'll have a nice visit." Rose stopped at Isobel's bedside. "Maybe you'd like to share some of your writing with Margaret later?"

Isobel nodded as she picked up the newspaper and pulled a notebook and pen from a bedside drawer. "Stop by if you have time, Margaret. I'll tell you all about my little venture."

"I'd like that, Isobel. It was nice meeting you. Is there anything we can get for you before we go?"

"Just shut the door as you leave, please. Other than that, not a thing. You two have a great day." She took up her paper and dismissed them with a smile.

Rose closed the door and looked at Margaret, waiting for her to speak.

"Eleven months? I thought six months was the limit for hospice care."

Rose answered in a low tone as they continued down the hall. "There isn't really a limit, per se, it's just that initially to qualify, a hospice patient is certified to have six months or less to live. They start with two ninety-day certification periods, then it's month-to-month—unlimited—after that. The patient can be re-certified indefinitely, which is the case with Isobel. She's eighty-two and has end-stage congestive heart failure. That's especially tough to predict. She'll be in our care as long as she needs to be.

"We were serving her at home until a few weeks ago. Then she ended up on a respirator and she came here from the hospital."

"A respirator? How can that be?" Margaret said. "I thought hospice meant no longer trying to keep the patient alive." *Here we go again.*

"Isobel went into the hospital with pneumonia and then needed the ventilator to help her breathe. I'm told she asked for it and she knew it was possible that she wouldn't be able to breathe on her own again at some point. It turns out that she just needed the help for a day or so, so it didn't affect her hospice certification. It's a little confusing, I know, but since she's dying of heart failure—not pneumonia—she can still receive medical care for that. If she hadn't wanted to be treated for the pneumonia, then they wouldn't have treated her." They were working their way down the hall as Rose spoke.

"When Isobel came here, she brought all the decorations her granddaughters have made for her. She told me those are the ones she's gotten since she entered hospice care so they have a special significance for her." They were outside the next patient's door. Rose paused before they entered.

"Sometimes it's hard to apply black and white rules for hospice care, Maggie. Every patient is different, every medical crisis is a judgment call. Trust me, one day, it'll click and you'll see the big picture. Let's keep going here and get these morning rounds done, then you should go back and talk to Isobel when you get the time. She's a very interesting person."

Isobel

The puzzling furniture, the decorators' show home, the unraveling Murphy family history. It was all so inspiring and breathtaking and totally exhausting. Right after lunch, Rose was thinking that Margaret could use a little break and found her making a pot of coffee in the upstairs solarium.

"Maggie, why not go down to the kitchen, get a drink for yourself and Isobel—she likes Diet Coke—come on back up and have a nice chat." Margaret liked that idea. In a few minutes, she was knocking on Isobel's door.

Isobel got right to the point. From her perspective, there was no time to waste. "Do you read obituaries, Margaret?"

"Sure. To be honest, Isobel, anymore, it's the main reason I subscribe to *The Chesterton Bee*. How about you?"

"Oh yes. Actually, I *study* obituaries. I've been working on mine for some time now and I try to keep up with the latest trends. Here, have a look." She handed a legal pad to Margaret, filled with handwritten script. Two sentences into it, Margaret was pursing her lips, working hard to maintain a straight face.

Isobel Ruby Baines
1931 - 2012
Isobel Baines leaped into the arms of Jesus today at ____ a.m./p.m. And was she ever ready to go! Isobel is survived by her daughters Rhonda Baines of West Palm Beach, Florida and Jeanne Evans (husband Chuck) and grandchildren Isobel and Lucy Evans, the lights of her life.
Isobel was divorced by that low-down dirty dog husband of hers, Stanley Baines, in 1975. She raised her daughters on her own, doing the best she could, working as the activity director for The Sunshine Retirement Village here in Chesterton until she couldn't take it anymore (because of her health, not the people there, who were really lovely folks).
Her favorite pastime was being with her family, especially her grandchildren, and going to the racetrack once in a while. She never bet more than she could afford to lose and she usually won!
Isobel was cremated and she asked that her friends and family gather to remember the good times and to scatter her ashes over the lake at Redwood Park, where she spent many happy hours, picnicking with her daughters when they were little.

> And she wants to thank all the wonderful people at Chesterton Hospice who came to be friends and family when it took her so long to die.
> Instead of wasting good money on flowers, Isobel would prefer that any memorials be made to Rockaway House or the Chesterton Animal Shelter.

"Well. I must say it looks like you've covered the key parts of your life. Are you satisfied with it?" Margaret handed the paper back to Isobel. Isobel studied Margaret's face intently, cocking her head to one side.

"Too much? I don't want to embarrass my family."

"Which part do you think might be too much, Isobel?"

"Oh, that stuff about my ex-husband Stanley. Everyone knows he was a dirty dog, but maybe I shouldn't spell it out like that." Indecision crossed Isobel's face.

"Here's what I think, Isobel," Margaret said gently, "imagine it's twenty years from now and your granddaughters are looking through all the wonderful photos they have of you, and they're thinking of the special times they spent with you and they come across your obituary. If it were me, I'd want my obituary to be nothing but a ray of pure sunshine in that scrapbook. That's a memory that will last a very long time. But maybe that's just me."

Isobel's face screwed up tight as she seriously considered Margaret's comment. "You're right," she finally allowed.

Just then the door opened without a knock and a young woman entered. With a face that was unmistakably Isobel minus forty years, Margaret knew it had to be one of Isobel's daughters.

"Hey, Mom. Hi, I'm Jeanne Evans." She extended her hand, shifting the tote bag on her right arm over to her left.

"Hello, Jeanne. I'm Margaret Williams. So nice to meet you. I understand your daughters are responsible for decorating your mother's room?" She waved her hand in the direction of the wall art.

"They are indeed. The three of them insisted that this all needed to come along when Mom moved in here. Sorry the girls aren't with me, Mom. I decided to let them stay in after-school care today."

Margaret started for the door. "I'll leave you two to have a visit."

"No, no, I just stopped by for a minute before I go and get the girls. I don't need to interrupt what you two were working on." Isobel lifted her face to receive a peck on the check from Jeanne.

"Then I'll come back in a few minutes, how's that? Jeanne, so nice to meet you."

"You too, Margaret."

Jeanne worked from home as a graphic designer. It gave her more time with her daughters, Isobel, five, and Lucy, three. And for the past few months, it had meant more time with her mother. Jeanne brought Isobel up to date on the girls' activities: Lucy's most recent cute little trick and young Isobel's academic progress. They shared a can of pop and some dry-roasted nuts—Isobel's favorite—from Jeanne's bag.

"Do you know what time Rhonda's getting here?" Isobel suddenly asked. If she had noticed the inevitable drop of Jeanne's shoulders at the mention of her sister, Isobel ignored it.

"Yes, Mom. I think she e-mailed she'd be here sometime after four o'clock." They visited for a few more minutes, and Jeanne rose from her chair just as there was a tap at the door.

"Yes?" Margaret poked her head through the opening. "Come on in, Margaret, I was just going. Perfect timing." Jeanne gave her mother a quick kiss and hug and scooted out the door. Margaret took her place at Isobel's bedside.

"Would you like to work on that obit some more, Isobel?"

"Oh yes, I do want to make a couple of changes. It'll just take a sec." Margaret handed Isobel her pad and pen. Isobel edited, then looked over at Margaret. "Have you thought about what you'd put in *your* obituary, Margaret?"

Margaret paused before answering. Seven months ago she would have said 'no' without hesitating. Then six months ago, she wrote her first obituary: Ernie's. She hadn't realized until then what a weighty job it would be. Considering the momentous event at hand, what was too important to be left out and which facts were no longer relevant?

"Not so much mine, but I had to think pretty hard when I wrote my husband's obituary a few months ago."

"I'm so sorry. It's not easy, is it?" Margaret didn't know if Isobel was referring to Ernie's obit or Ernie's death, but she figured her comment applied either way.

"No, it isn't. May I?" Seeing that Isobel was done, she reached out and Isobel handed her the newest version of her obituary.

"I'm not crazy about this whole third person bit, but I suppose it would sound weird to have it begin 'Dear friends,' wouldn't it?" Isobel looked hopefully at Margaret, clearly waiting for Margaret to disagree and give her permission to do just that.

"That's hard to say, Isobel. I think you should do whatever pleases you—it is your obituary, after all."

"I took the part out about my ex-husband and tried to make it sound all more, you know, *upbeat.* I thought about what you said and I agree, Margaret, better to keep out the negative bits. I mean, I should think about the girls and how it might make them feel sometime in the future, like you said. It's hard to know what to leave in. When you think about it, isn't life just the space between *'Isn't she the most beautiful baby ever?'* and *'Don't she look natch'l?'*"

Margaret laughed aloud, nodding. "Let's see here." She read the amended copy.

> Isobel Ruby Baines
> 1931 – 2012 (assuming I finally die this year)
> ~~Isobel Baines leaped into the arms of Jesus today at ____ a.m./p.m. And was she ever ready to go!~~ Isobel Baines, born March 31, 1930, passed away at Rockaway House on ________. Isobel is survived by her daughters Rhonda Baines of West Palm Beach, Florida and Jeanne Evans (husband Chuck) and grandchildren Isobel and Lucy Evans, the lights of her life.
> ~~Isobel was divorced by that low-down dirty dog husband of hers, Stanley Baines, in 1975.~~ She ~~raised her daughters on her own, doing the best she could, working~~ worked as the activity director for The Sunshine Retirement Village here in Chesterton ~~until she couldn't take it anymore (because of her health, not the people there,~~ who were really lovely folks~~)~~.
> Her favorite pastime was being with her family, especially her grandchildren. ~~and going to the racetrack once in a while. She never bet more than she could afford to lose and she usually won!~~
> Isobel was cremated and she asked that her friends and family gather to remember the good times and to scatter her ashes over the lake at Redwood Park, where she spent many happy hours, picnicking with her daughters when they were little.
> And she wants to thank all the wonderful people at Chesterton Hospice who came to be friends and family. ~~when it took her so long to die. Instead of wasting good money on flowers,~~ Isobel would prefer that any memorials be made to Rockaway House or the Chesterton Animal Shelter.

"Very nice, Isobel. Are you pleased with this final version?"

"Oh, this isn't the final version, it's not nearly the final version. I figure as long as I'm still around, I might as well keep tinkering with it. But I appreciate your input, Margaret, I really do. If I pass away today, I'm good with it, but I don't plan to do that, so I'd like to add something more, maybe some advice about how to live a good life. But I'm not quite sure how to put it. Any suggestions?"

"I'm not much for coming up with my own inspiring words, Isobel, but I've always enjoyed the wisdom of others. Do you happen to have any favorite quotations you'd like to include?" Isobel put the pen down and adjusted her oxygen tube.

"Maybe I do, now you mention that. I used to have a book of quotes. I wish I had that here with me."

"I think I saw a Bartlett's downstairs in the bookshelves, Isobel. Be right back." Margaret quickly retrieved the heavy volume and then found Isobel dozing when she returned, the legal pad about to slide onto the floor. Putting it on the bedside table, Margaret tiptoed out.

When Jeanne arrived with young Isobel and Lucy, her mother was still sleeping. Recently, that was the case more often than not. A child-sized table and two chairs were in the corner for the frequent small visitors. Jeanne got the girls settled and they sat quietly, having a snack. Jeanne began to meticulously fold a sheet of construction paper as Isobel and Lucy looked on.

"Is it an airplane?" Young Isobel whispered to her mother.

"No, not an airplane."

"I know! I know!" Lucy excitedly jumped up in her chair.

"Be quiet, Lucy. Can't you see that Nana's napping? Anyway, you don't either know what it is."

"I do! I do!" Lucy lowered her voice but not her level of excitement. "It's an airplane!"

"Mommy just said it isn't. You're not even listening."

Jeanne slowly shook her head, continuing to fold. They watched, mesmerized by their mother's precise movements. Folding. Turning. Folding.

Suddenly the door burst open. "My little petunias!"

"Aunt Rhonda!" The girls ran into her arms as Jeanne watched. She'd learned long ago there was no point in trying to quell this excited reaction. Her mother would not be far behind.

"Mom!" Rhonda ignored her mother's closed eyes, leaned over the bed railing and planted a big smooch on Isobel's cheek.

"Rhonda, you're here!" Jarred awake, Isobel pulled herself up slightly in the bed. Her mother's demeanor brightened considerably when Rhonda was around, Jeanne always noted.

Rhonda's gaze immediately went to the legal pad at her mother's side.

"Working on the old obit, eh? And how is your Last Will and Testament Version 8.0 coming along? Still love the decor, Mom." Jeanne was never sure if Rhonda's snarky comments came from a sense of humor or a sense of irritation.

"Of course. I only get one chance to get them right, dontchaknow? Sit down, let me look at you." Isobel patted the bed next to her and smiled at her oldest daughter.

The polar opposite of her sister, Rhonda was a ball of nervous energy. A smile was pasted on her face, but deep down she was tetchy, always tetchy. Her hair was flawlessly coifed, her nails manicured and painted an elegant beige, all packaged in a perfectly tailored off-white pants suit. The look was completed with a designer tote.

Jeanne got a smirk on her face and shook her head. *Who else but my sister travels in off-white?* "Nice outfit, sis. How was the flight?"

Rhonda turned as if noticing Jeanne for the first time. "Fine. What are you doing there? Origami?"

"No, not origami. Actually, I was just showing the girls how to make something in anticipation of your visit." She jumped up from the small chair. "A cootie-catcher! Hey, look, girls, I got one!"

Rhonda was not amused.

"You are such an infant, Jeanne."

"Oh yeah? Well, I'm rubber and you're glue. Everything you say bounces off me and sticks to you." The girls loved to watch the childish sibling behavior that emerged as soon as Aunt Rhonda arrived. Then they pulled their mother back to the table to help them make their own cootie catchers as Isobel looked on, beaming at her small family.

Rhonda suddenly rose. "Jeanne, help me bring in some things from the car."

Jeanne hated this part, the part when Rhonda took her aside to give her opinion on how their mother looked, to get an update on her condition and to explain why she wished she could, but she wouldn't be able to stay in town very long.

Out the door they went, leaving the girls to finish decorating their cootie-catchers and then demonstrate them on Grandma, a willing subject.

"She looks like hell. What's the deal?" Rhonda demanded as soon as they closed the door.

"Let's have this conversation outside, Rhonda," Jeanne whispered. She led the way in silence to Rhonda's rental car, parked smack in the center of the Rockaway House parking lot. "What's the deal, Rhonda? Mom's dying, that's the deal."

"Well I know that, smart ass. I just mean, this is the third time I've been here in the past two months. What's the doctor say?"

He says 'How can you stand your sister Rhonda?' Jeanne took a big breath. "He says she's getting weaker each day and it's just a matter of time."

"And what's with that stupid obituary and Will nonsense of hers? It's not like she has anything to leave to anyone."

Jeanne silently mouthed a prayer before she responded. *God, give me strength.* "I don't know what to tell you, Rhonda. Working on them gives her some satisfaction and she's happy right now, so what's the harm? And, if it makes you feel better, she is making some progress: she isn't able to get out of bed anymore."

Jeanne's sarcasm was wasted on Rhonda as she plowed past the remark. "The problem, dear sister," she said in a most perturbed voice, "is that the real estate market has finally picked up, I'm swamped with business and here I am in God's back half acre, wasting my time again. And I can only stay a couple days before I need to get home."

Gee, never thought you'd say that. Jeanne tried the car door. It was locked, of course. *Locking a car in Chesterton? Puleez.*

"Unlock the car, Rhonda, I want to get back upstairs." They retrieved the packages and returned to their mother's room in silence. As always, there were presents for everyone. Isobel watched as the others opened theirs.

"This reminds me of Christmas mornings when you two were little," she said wistfully, looking at Jeanne. She smiled back at her mother, then stood.

"Girls, let's go see if there's any cookies in the kitchen." It hadn't taken long for little Isobel and Lucy to find Margaret's treats on their first visit weeks earlier. "You two have a nice chat." Jeanne took Lucy and Isobel each by the hand and started for the door.

Their grandmother had had enough. "Why don't you all go along? I'll see you tomorrow afternoon for a tea party. I love you all very much."

Each one came in turn to Isobel's side, gave her a hug and a kiss and a goodbye. Rhonda was the first one out the door, looking peeved. *Is my mother so loopy that she thinks I still live here in town, that I didn't just make this trip all the way from Florida, for God's sake?*

Jeanne was thinking she was grateful that her mother told them to leave if she didn't really feel up to having visitors, but her parting words meant that Jeanne would have Rhonda underfoot—*all to herself* while the girls were in school—until they returned the following afternoon. *Oh wonderful. Maybe I should declare an early snow day.*

Once they were gone, Isobel relished the quiet. This day had been all she could have asked for. She'd worked on her obit and, with Margaret's help, made some real progress. She'd gotten to see her oldest daughter—all the way from Florida—she'd spent time with Jeanne and the grandbabies, and was now wearing the tastefully muted pink bed jacket that Rhonda had brought to her (by Isobel's count, that made seven of them).

Isobel thought about all that was going to be happening very soon and she almost had the energy to get excited. At least she could smile. She realized that for the moment, except that she was dog tired, she didn't believe she had one single thing to complain about.

Noah

Lisbeth loved holidays. Each was another opportunity to create imaginative window dressings at *Under the Covers.* She relished meandering through their shop, plucking relevant classics and new releases, novels and nonfiction from the shelves, hoping to cast her promotional net as widely as possible. In anticipation of Valentine's Day, she had even thrown in a book on home repair. Its cover was bright red, in keeping with the color theme, and—who knows—it just might be the perfect gift from a frustrated wife to a husband who needed some direction.

On the morning of February 5th, Noah stepped back to admire the completed display in their front window. Lisbeth had chosen the books and it was Noah's task to arrange them among the red fabric, vintage valentines and decorations that Lisbeth found at the flea market last year. Finished, Noah returned to unpacking a newly arrived box of bestsellers when a stabbing pain in his head took him to his knees. Lisbeth ran to his side. The pain was gone as quickly as it came and, in a moment, Noah stood, brushing away Lisbeth's concerns. But Lisbeth refused to let it pass, called her own doctor and scheduled Noah for a checkup the following week.

There was another incident after that first one, two days before the doctor's appointment, but that one lasted for over an hour and Noah was at home alone when it happened. The pain was so unbearable that he relented and called Lisbeth. She came immediately, took one look at him and summoned an ambulance. Noah didn't protest. By that time, he would have agreed to call anyone who might possibly stop the pain, which they did at the hospital with a shot of morphine, followed by a second shot.

A week later, Noah was glad to have Lisbeth with him to review the MRI results with the oncologist. When Lisbeth had asked if he wanted her there, Noah said that sounded like a good idea because, without really thinking about it, he had assumed Lisbeth would be with him. He'd been picturing her at his side.

Noah liked the oncologist. He was a man who made every word count.

"Grade IV Glioblastoma multiforme brain tumor."

That explained the pain.

Afterwards, Lisbeth drove Noah back to his apartment and made them each a cup of tea. Their friend Molly began as a loyal customer years before but now pitched in for holiday sales and the rare occasion when both Noah and Lisbeth needed to be gone from *Under the Covers.* She was watching the store that morning.

"I know what you're going to say, Lisbeth, and I made up my mind before we went today."

"Made up your mind about what, Noah? How, may I ask, did you make up your mind about something when you didn't even know what the doctor would say?"

"Actually, I did. Do you think I didn't do my own research ahead of time?" He stopped to smile at the person in the world who knew him best. "There were only two possibilities, Lisbeth, bad news and worse news. I got the latter. You heard him. Surgery is not an option, and I'm not interested in having chemo and radiation turn me into a human glow fish. So, there you are." He didn't sound bitter or sad or even resigned. Noah sounded like he always sounded, practical and uncomplicated.

Lisbeth fixed spaghetti for them that Sunday evening and over dinner they devised The Plan. Noah insisted they write it all down. Did Lisbeth want him to sign it, to show that he agreed, in case there was a misunderstanding or memory lapse of any kind later on? No, that would not be necessary.

Noah would continue to work as long as possible. They both thought it best that he not be left alone in the store. He made Lisbeth swear that if he started to display any other symptoms and didn't mention it himself, she must tell him. He refused to be an object of pity or ridicule or, worse yet, risk making customers feel uneasy in any way. Besides, hadn't they always promised they would be there to wipe the drool from the other's chin as time marched on? Tag, it's your turn, Noah teased. Lisbeth, who always laughed at Noah's jokes, didn't laugh.

The first phase of The Plan was in place for six months. Far from making anyone uncomfortable, as each customer learned of Noah's cancer, the proof of friendships nurtured over the years was displayed in abundance. Offers to help at the store, now or in the future, flooded in. Not meaning to pry, but were there any financial issues because those could be addressed as well? No, Lisbeth assured each well-meaning person, there were no such concerns, but she and Noah were both grateful for their support and friendship.

Over time, Noah became easily distracted, sometimes confused. He started having trouble reading and understanding price tags on the merchandise, so Lisbeth made sure that either she or Molly was always available to ring up sales.

Phase Two of The Plan went into effect when it was obvious that Noah could no longer live alone. He lost his eyesight seven months from the day of his diagnosis.

"It could be worse, Lis. I read about a condition called 'word blindness' where you can see the words but you can't understand them. Now I don't have to worry about getting that. That sounds horrible—wouldn't that be worse?" Lisbeth squeezed his hand. For that one moment, she was thankful he couldn't see her, that he couldn't see her lips trembling.

Much earlier, during Phase One, Lisbeth and Noah had explored potential living arrangements after he rejected her instinctive offer to have him move in with her. It wasn't practical for Lisbeth to be his caregiver and manage the store on her own, Noah insisted. They chose Rockaway House on a recommendation from Molly, whose father had been there two years earlier. After being evaluated and certified as hospice-worthy, Noah's name was put on the waiting list. In the meantime, he would go to the skilled nursing wing of Rolling Hills Retirement Center.

Noah asked Lisbeth to pull a collection of audio books by some of his favorite authors from the shelves of *Under the Covers*. He'd never been a fan of anything other than holding a big heavy book in his hands, but now that he was fully retired, he observed, he could catch up on his reading.

On the day Noah came from Rolling Hills, he was sitting in a chair as the nurses' aide Patsy settled his few possessions in his Rockaway House room. On the bedside table was a book with the audio version right next to it. She made sure the CD player was within reach, so Noah could easily access it and then she picked up the small volume.

"This looks interesting, Noah. Dylan Thomas? I've never read him. What kind of books does he write?"

"Oh, prose and poetry. He's a favorite of mine, Patsy. I first read him when I was about your age. Mid-twenties?"

"Yup, I'm twenty-seven. I understand you own the bookstore downtown, is that right?"

A smile immediately came to Noah's lips. "Yes, I do. My partner Lisbeth Jones and I own it. Have you been in? I'm sorry I can't see your face or I'm sure I would know you."

"I have, actually. I drop in to get a book for my children for every holiday, their birthdays, you know, Christmas. They always get books—whether they want them or not!" She laughed as she finished her tasks and then sat on the edge of the bed.

"That was never a problem for me. I've loved words and books since I was little. My father was a lexicographer."

"Oh gosh, what is that?"

"He wrote definitions for the Funk & Wagnall's Dictionary."

"Really? You know, I never thought about someone sitting down to do that—it seems like one of those things that just happens on its own, like it's always been there."

"That's where my name came from. I'm named after Noah Webster, as in Webster's Dictionary."

"That's totally cool. I'm named after my mother's manicurist. But she does always have beautiful nails!" They laughed together. "I'd like to read more myself, but I don't seem to have much time for it these days with a six-year-old and a three-year-old."

"I should think not. I'm afraid I didn't have a mother like you, Patsy. I didn't have brothers and sisters and, well, my mother had mental health issues, so she wasn't around as much as I would have liked. Books became my friends at a early age."

"That must have been difficult for a little boy, Noah."

"My father and I shared the love of books and words so that became a way for us to communicate, something for us to talk about. I never thought of my life as difficult. If I was unhappy, I just opened another book and found a story to get lost in and make me feel better. I came to love books *because* of the childhood I had. You see, I was—I still am—a nerd." Patsy giggled softly, and Noah smiled in her direction at the sound. "I really didn't mind being a nerd. Thanks to books, I found a lot of other nerds to hang out with—and they're the best people in the world."

"Don't I know it, my husband's a bit of a geek, too. In fact, I always liked the nerdy boys, they just seemed nicer. So how did you come to own *Under the Covers* with Lisbeth?"

Noah told Patsy about working at the Chesterton Library and how Lisbeth stopped in one day, doing research for the bookstore she was about to open. He told Patsy how he and Lisbeth had started the book festival and the children's story hour and his pride and joy, the monthly book groups.

"You know, my mother would say that was no accident, you meeting Miss Jones. That was serendipity," Patsy said.

"Maybe you're right, because Lisbeth has turned out to be my best friend in the whole world . . . " He drifted away for a moment and Patsy watched closely, making sure he was all right. Then Noah raised his head. The moment, whatever it was, had passed. "Did my Word-A-Day calendar get unpacked? Do you see it anywhere, Peggy?"

Patsy ignored Noah's misstep on her name and glanced around. "Yes, here it is. Do you want me to read today's word?"

"Yes, please."

"*marsupial: any of an order (Marsupialia) of mammals comprising kangaroos, wombats, bandicoots, opossums, and related animals that do not develop a true placenta and that usually have a pouch on the abdomen of the female which covers the teats and serves to carry the young.* I'd say that's too much information!" Patsy laughed. Noah got a quizzical look on his face.

"Would you mind reading that again, Patsy? I've forgotten the word." His voice was soft. He spoke very slowly. Maybe he's hoping the word will come back to him before he finishes his sentence, Patsy wondered.

"Sure, no problem." And so she did, and he laughed along with her this time. "We got a bonus word too, 'bandicoots'—that's a good one!"

A head poked in the door of Noah's room. "Accepting visitors?"

Noah immediately recognized the voice of a good friend, a neighbor from the apartment building. Fritz had been checking for the mail and watching over Noah's seven-year-old cat since the move to Rolling Hills. "Come in, Fritz. Fritz, this is Patsy. We're just going over the word for the day. It's 'bandicoots.' How's Hermione?"

"She's fine, Noah. When I get to your apartment, she's always sitting right there, looking at the door. Once I go in to feed her, she leads me on a tour of the place. I think she's looking for you, Noah."

Noah didn't answer for a moment. Fritz grimaced, afraid his comment might have upset Noah, but Noah composed himself, then spoke sternly. "Well, she should miss me, the little beggar. I certainly miss her."

"Hermione sounds like my Maxine." No one had noticed Margaret hanging at the door, waiting for a pause in the conversation. She stepped forward, reaching out to gently touch Noah's sleeve. "Noah, I'm Margaret, a volunteer here at Rockaway House." He slowly raised his hand for her to shake.

"Nice to meet you, Margaret. Hermione is my capricious feline. She had to stay behind when I left home."

"Uh-oh. I've got one of those, too. Noah, we've actually met before—coming to your store has become a weekly habit for me. I wanted to thank you for helping me spoil myself."

"I'm sorry I didn't recognize you, Margaret, but your voice does sound familiar to me. And thank you for your business."

"You're very welcome, Noah. I won't stay, I just wanted to stop in and introduce myself. I'll leave you to your visitor." Margaret ducked back out and made a beeline for the nurses' station.

There was only one way to keep all the book groups straight and that was to name each for the day it met. Noah's favorite group, *Second Thursday Club*, had four original members and two newbies who had belonged for only five years. One of the members phoned ahead to Rockaway House and asked if they could possibly gather while Noah was staying there. It didn't have to be on a Thursday, they assured the nice lady named Margaret who took the call. They would make themselves available on any day or time that Noah felt up to it. Margaret said she would make it work.

Now she just had to figure out how to do that.

Rose was one hundred percent on board to have Noah's book group visit. It was just the sort of thing they wanted Rockaway House to facilitate: making patients feel they were still involved in life—however defined by each individual.

Margaret wondered if Noah was up to leaving his room to join his friends. Nancy, the nurse on duty that day, assured her that Noah would be fine as long as he travelled by wheelchair. Scoping out gathering areas on the first floor, Margaret could see that the solarium didn't have the necessary furniture and the sunroom off the kitchen wasn't really private. She also realized just how well the Christmas decorations for Caleb had hidden a multitude of sins; the dining room and living room were once again dark and depressing. With a smile, she reminded herself that at least there was now hope that the ghastly conditions weren't permanent.

For an evening meeting, there would be few other visitors to disturb, so Margaret checked with Nancy about using the cheery and comfortable upstairs solarium. Nancy agreed and everyone was eager to hold the first gathering that night. Margaret arranged the furniture to allow access for Noah's wheelchair and made sure there was plenty of coffee and ample tea supplies in the solarium cupboard. She replenished the basket of cookies.

Once the group gathered, Carolyn, the evening nurses' assistant, brought Noah to join his long-time friends. It was the poetry group, his favorite. All chatter suspended when he appeared at the doorway. Some out of respect and some because they were seeing Noah for the first time in nearly a month. The Noah in their minds hadn't gotten frail and thinner—this one had.

"You can't stop talking—that's the only way I'll know who's here." The awkward silence was broken and everyone laughed and rose to give Noah a hug, a handshake or to speak a word of greeting. Then Carolyn left, telling them she'd be just down the hall if the group needed anything.

It got quiet again. Finally Ronnie spoke. "So, Noah, how are you?"

"Well, a lot like the boy who said he preferred radio to television because the scenery was better. You'd be surprised what you see when you're blind."

Silence.

"You know, I take that back about radio versus television: you folks were a lot more entertaining when I could see you." At that, someone convulsively sputtered. "That's the spirit, Sally. That's Sally, right?"

Thanks to Noah, they realized right then that in spite of his appearance or the circumstances, nothing had really changed. He was still Noah, their treasured friend and literary guide. The book discussion began with that month's selection from the Library of Congress's list of *88 Books that Shaped America*, Walt Whitman's *Leaves of Grass.* They quickly fell into the comfortable patter they had practiced for years.

While Noah's book group was meeting, Lauren Dunlap was in her CCH office, looking at an e-mail from Rose, copied to Sheryl Dawes, a case manager at Rockaway House. Lauren's old friend, Margaret, was requesting permission for a patient's pet cat to visit him at Rockaway House. Rose's question for Lauren: *Was there any policy prohibiting that?*

Lauren rubbed her temples and took a swig of lukewarm coffee. This had been a long day, including budget meetings with the CMC administration. As always, the mandate from the higher-ups at Chesterton Medical Center was to figure out how to provide more hospice services with fewer funds, thank you very much. There were the usual veiled threats that it might be time for a quantitative review of the viability of providing inpatient hospice care (read: *Do we really need Rockaway House?*).

Lauren spent her time at CCH trying to maintain the level of compassionate and competent hospice care that Helen Sullivan had envisioned, while keeping at bay the corporate dogs who thought of CMC's hospice division as simply another potential profit center. It was torturous. At least she could see the prospect of salvation on the horizon, The Rockaway House show home and auction. *If only.*

She hadn't even had a chance to sit down with her boss at CMC and make them aware of the miracle that she hoped was about to happen, thanks to Margaret's discovery, but that was somewhat intentional on Lauren's part. This "secret" was already too widely known. In the fantasies Lauren had been enjoying for the past twenty-four hours, her CCH board approved the show home and she was imagining all the good works they would do with the money raised by the auction. The members of her board were decent folks, every one of them. She was sure they'd favor the idea—she'd know tomorrow afternoon. As for the CMC bigwigs, let them learn about it at the Rolands' launch party along with everyone else. What a great *neener-neener* for her own loyal board members.

Yes, there was hope, real hope for the future of CCH and its mission.

She looked again at the e-mail from Rose and hit Reply.

Rose,
Margaret raises an interesting question. I am not aware of any policy that would prohibit a cat from visiting one of our patients and I know of no reason why there should be such a policy (I assume Kitty will be in a carrier anytime outside the patient's room).
Please thank Margaret for a marvelous idea and let me know how it goes.
Lauren

She hit Send.

Margaret

The Hidden Treasure of Rockaway House. It's like being in the middle of a Nancy Drew book, Margaret thought. Growing up, she'd been a big fan of the girl detective. Of course, Margaret knew it was Helen Sullivan who most closely resembled the Renaissance woman Nancy Drew, not her. Nonetheless, Margaret felt a part of the Murphys' story as it peeled like the multi-layered plot of a whodunit, complete with a mystery woman, maybe a little palace intrigue and certainly the hint of romance.

The presentation before the Chesterton Community Hospice Board of Directors was the following afternoon. Logically, Margaret knew they'd be nice people like the ones she'd come to know at the grocery store, small town folks just like her, goodhearted and well-intentioned. Sadly, logic couldn't hold a candle to her escalating stage fright. She had the perfect visual for how she felt: there was a piano suspended by a fraying rope—right over her head. In her heart, Margaret knew having a plan was key to relieving a good deal of the stress. Now all she had to do was have a plan.

It had taken a bit of patience, a bit of panic and a bit of prayer, then it came to her. The piano was replaced with a brightly lit bulb and Margaret headed for bed.

She was still sitting up, absently petting Maxine with one hand, putting her glasses on the bedside table and then setting the alarm clock with the other. Time for a quick chat at Ernie.

"Remember that young lady who used to come into the store, Ernie, and I'd have coffee with her once in a while? Well, it turns out now she's the boss lady for the hospice! Can you believe it? I had no idea. She's very sharp. And she lost a brother to cancer, I didn't know anything about that before . . . Anyway, I met her yesterday and told her all about the furniture in the garage.

"You know that money you left for me? I finally got away from Rockaway House early enough to pick the check up from Ken Sylvester and put it in the bank. I'll tell you, that really was fun. Oh yeah, and on the way home, just to celebrate my good luck in having you for a husband, I drove through *Whole Latte' Love* and got myself one of those chai latte's and I told Liz—you know, the girl who works the window—that I'd pay for the people behind me in line, too. *That* really was fun. Big philanthropist, me.

"You know, it looks like I won't really need to use any of that money for Rockaway House furniture—the stuff I found in the garage will take care of all that—but I do want to do something special there with some of it, I just haven't decided what yet. You're so funny—you knew what a kick I'd get out of this, didn't you? I love you, Ernie. I miss you, I really do."

She turned out the light, lying down and reaching over to give Maxine a quick pat on the head.

Margaret kept her conversation brief this night. She thought God would understand. She just wanted to say *Thank you. That's all, just thank you. Amen.*

Rockaway House

Margaret moved the coffee carafe an inch to the left. *No, it's better back where it was. I should have brought fresh flowers. No, that would look like sucking up.*

It was two forty-five. Lauren Dunlap had already arrived, ready to greet and direct the board members to the conference room. Rose, all a twitter, was making a last minute scan of the second floor. Suzi would be there in a minute to answer any questions about the show home logistics after the meeting. Everyone had agreed—everyone but Margaret—that Margaret was unquestionably The Chosen One to make the presentation.

Make a presentation? I don't make presentations. I listen to presentations. And I'm not even all that good at listening to them. But, as Suzi, Rose and Lauren had coached her, speaking to the board wasn't complicated. Share your passion for the project and make the directors want to be a part of it, they had told her. As for details, fuggedaboutit. Once the directors saw what this would mean for the patients, the families and the community of Chesterton, they wouldn't care how it happened—they'd only want to know how to be part of it.

Lauren had implied her consent although she hadn't voiced a firm commitment to the project. As Margaret understood these things, Lauren got her orders from the board, not vice versa—but Margaret was pretty sure that Lauren wanted it to happen almost as much as Margaret did. Margaret didn't know it, but as soon as she'd left Lauren's office after their first meeting, Lauren had immediately called the CMC Legal Department and asked for anyone—other than Henry Lloyd—to do a little research for her. An associate raced to the records archive and dug up the original contract for the purchase of Rockaway House by CMC in 2004. An hour later, she called and assured Lauren that its language was very specific: the sale included any and all personal property located in the house or garage. Until that moment, Lauren had envisioned some heir of the previous owner coming forward from out of nowhere to claim the newly-discovered treasure, so that was one hurdle out of the way—legally speaking, they were good to go. And Lauren definitely wanted it to go.

It was two fifty-two. Margaret stood alone in the conference room, her heart and mind racing, her breathing slightly hyper. *Seven quick breaths in through the nostrils, hold for seven, exhale for seven . . .*

At three o'clock, everyone was seated. Only eight of the board members were available to attend on such short notice, but Chair Cissy Peters had proxies for the other four. Suzi, Rose and Margaret sat along the edge of the room. Cissy called the meeting to order, then turned it over to Lauren, who introduced Margaret.

The previous evening, Margaret had tried to prepare as best she could. Public speaking wasn't something she enjoyed. Well, actually she couldn't say that for sure—since she had never done any before today—but she certainly didn't enjoy anticipating it, she now knew that for certain. There had been more unsolicited but appreciated advice from Suzi and Lauren before Margaret had gone home that day: don't talk longer than fifteen minutes. At minute sixteen, board members start nodding off and that would not be good.

Say it all in fifteen minutes? That didn't sound like enough time. Margaret would need a list. The evening before, Maxine had stretched out on the desk as Margaret thoughtfully composed her goals for the board members: *Goal #1. Understand the importance of Rockaway House. Goal #2. Understand the importance of the show home. Goal #3. Trust we will respect patients and family members.*

What is it people always say? Picture the audience naked? That doesn't help. Imagine yourself in the audience? You mean naked? This is really not helping.

"Maxine, pretend you don't know anything about Rockaway House or what it does—that should be easy for you. Come to think of it, that would have been easy for me not too long ago. I'd never been there myself."

That's when it came to her. The veil lifted and Margaret knew exactly what to say and do.

But that was the evening before. Now it was showtime.

Margaret slowly stood and cleared her throat.

Share your passion for the project and make the directors want to be a part of it.

"First, welcome and thank you for your service and all you do to make what we do here possible. If I may ask, for how many of you—that is—is this your first visit to Rockaway House?" Hesitant at first, then as others fessed up—even at the risk of being viewed as slackers—seven hands were raised. Only Cissy Peters had visited Rockaway House before that day.

"I have a confession to make." Margaret paused, counting one, two, three to herself. Then she raised her own hand. "Two months ago, I hadn't either." She let that sink in.

First, she told them how the death of a loved one—that would be Ernie—had brought her to Rockaway House, like most volunteers. Then she told of finding the Murphy family's furniture, while she was snooping in the garage attic. That made the board members laugh, and Margaret offered them a tour of the amazing treasures after the meeting. Heads nodded.

Margaret briefly spoke of how the show home and auction would work to raise money for the renovations and new furniture at Rockaway House and fund patient services for a long time. Things were still all a bit iffy, but the organizers had talked about a Wifi lounge and conversation areas in the living room and solarium. If anyone wanted more details, Margaret had an estimated budget handout for them and Suzi, who most of them already knew, was there to answer questions.

Margaret finished her background comments in less than five minutes.

One thing she'd had no doubt about the evening before was that the next important element of her presentation had to be Caleb Bronson. Caleb's story showed most clearly what was at stake, how personal the care at Rockaway

House is and that making end-of-life wishes come true can only happen if this place and its family of staff and volunteers are allowed to continue.

Her fifteen minutes was up and by then nearly everyone was wiping away a tear. Margaret turned to Lauren and Cissy and offered up Rose to lead a tour of the second floor where the patients lived and died and where the family members currently spent most of their time. One patient room happened to be vacant that afternoon, so they'd be able to see that as well. As Margaret had carefully instructed her earlier, on their return Rose was to bring the directors down the back stairs into the kitchen, through the dining room and into the entryway.

While Rose and Lauren led the Board upstairs, with Suzi's help Margaret put the next phase of her scheme into motion.

A few minutes later, they were positioned in the living room, Margaret with her ear pressed against the inside of the closed French doors and Suzi twenty feet away, waiting for the high sign from Margaret. Margaret was listening intently for the predetermined code phrase from the entryway, which was supposed to be something about the welfare of the patients and family members and how they would never allow them to be disturbed.

Suddenly, Margaret realized she hadn't fully worked this all out—there was no way she would be able to hear Rose speaking as she approached the living room doors. Beginning to panic, Margaret pushed aside the curtain on the door ever so slightly and peeked out—she could see that Rose was halfway through the dining room, headed her way with the group of visitors trailing along. She could see Rose's lips moving.

Close enough. Here goes nothing, Margaret thought. She opened the French doors into the entryway and the boom of the finale to Tchaikovsky's *1812 Overture*—complete with cannon fire—blasted the startled board members. Lauren, bringing up the rear of their group, was shaking her head, trying not to laugh out loud. Margaret subjected the board members to no more than five seconds of the high decibel music and then she gave Suzi the signal to mute the stereo in the living room.

The silence was deafening. The board members looked at each other, open-mouthed. Margaret smiled sweetly. "We've been playing that magnificent music—don't you just love Tchaikovsky?—since you went upstairs. Could anyone hear it before I opened these doors?" They looked at each other, shook their heads and began to laugh.

"This house is very well built, folks. And there is nothing that could get us to sacrifice our patients' comfort. You may have noticed upstairs that all the patients' rooms were closed for that little demonstration. Oh," Margaret waved in the direction of the living room and dining room, "I hope you'll take a moment to appreciate the lovely decor of this floor as it looks right now. Although, like our family members, you will not want to linger—except in the kitchen, of course." They laughed some more.

Then Lauren led them all back into the conference room and addressed them for less than a minute. She recommended approval of the project, promising to personally oversee it and to keep them informed with regular updates. Then she nodded to Cissy.

Cissy called for the question. "All in favor of putting on the Rockaway House show home as soon as possible indicate by saying 'aye.' Any opposed? The motion is unanimously carried."

A board member raised her hand. She introduced herself as Doris Walton, and she wanted to know if they would be allowed to volunteer for the project and who should she talk to about an in-kind donation? Her son ran their family business, Walton's Furniture, and he didn't know it yet, but he would be helping them buy all the new furnishings for Rockaway House at wholesale. Suzi had known Mrs. Walton's son, Christopher, since grade school and she lowered her head to hide a smirk. Really, she'd give anything to see the face of that tight-fisted mama's boy when Doris broke the news to him. Lauren thanked Doris and assured everyone there would be ample opportunities for donations of all kinds.

Cissy closed by asking them to keep the project on the QT for a few days. Within the week, they'd each receive an invitation to the exclusive launch event at Suzi and Stephen Rolands', right next door. The formal announcement of the show home would be made then and wouldn't they be the cool ones, in-the-know all this time and not letting on to anyone?

Lauren was leading the group out to the garage to view the attic and Suzi was joining them, but first she stopped to share a quick high-five with Margaret and Rose. "Outstanding, Maggie! We did it!" she whispered. "Fasten your seat belts, ladies, now the fun begins!"

Rose turned to Margaret. "And nice touch, baking those cinnamon rolls while they were here. That kitchen smelled like heaven!"

Margaret had a blank look. "I have no idea what—what cinnamon rolls?"

"We came down the back stairs and I thought the smell would knock us down. C'mere." Rose led the way back to the kitchen. There was not a whiff of cinnamon rolls. There were no cinnamon rolls.

Curiouser and curiouser.

Lois

Go figure. Just when you were good and ready for disappointment, all geared up to have your worst fears confirmed, it didn't happen. When they left Lois at Rockaway House the day before, Ray didn't say anything to Carlene, but at the time he really thought that morning's breakfast had been the last for Lois and him. But when he stepped into her room the following day, he was greeted by a wife who seemed almost like her old self again, or at least the Lois of a few weeks earlier.

"I thought you'd be bringing breakfast to me, Ray Spaulding," she chided him as he came in the door. Lois was sitting up in bed, wearing the floral nightgown that Carlene had bought for her the previous afternoon.

"Well, well! If I'd known you'd be so chipper, I certainly would have." Ray went to Lois's side and sat on the edge of the bed so he could give her a morning kiss and slow hug. "If you've got twenty minutes, I'll be right back with it." He looked so encouraged, Lois couldn't refuse his offer. He dashed out the door, but took time to stop at the nurses' station where Rona was on duty.

"Excuse me. I'm Ray, Lois Spaulding's husband."

Rona smiled and reached over the counter to shake Ray's hand. "What can we do for you, Ray?"

"I was wondering, I just stopped in to see my wife and she seems so much better than yesterday. I'm amazed."

"She is doing better this morning. We gave her a diuretic last night. That got rid of some of the excess fluids, which is making it easier for her all around. Sometimes a patient's condition improves when they come here just because they're so relieved to take the burden from their loved ones. You know, when someone is determined to come here, as your wife was, it can be a huge relief once they get here and they know there won't be a medical crisis at home." She paused a moment while Ray considered this. Rona wasn't sure—she thought Ray might be second-guessing the decision to bring Lois to Rockaway House when they did. "You should certainly enjoy this improvement in how Lois is feeling, but I think she was right when she decided it was time to come here, Ray."

So there was the good news and the bad news. Rona waited as Ray took it all in.

"You're right, let's make the most of it. I'm running home to get her some breakfast."

"You do that, but when you have the time, let us know what food you'd like to have here for her, and we'll certainly make every effort to get it for you."

"That would be great." He wanted to hurry home and get back while Lois was still up for it. Last night as he lay in bed, alone for the first time in forty-two years, Ray had resigned himself to no more special breakfasts. He wasn't about to squander this unexpected blessing.

The food, carefully wrapped in foil, was cold by the time Ray got back to Rockaway House and Lois hadn't regained her appetite overnight, but eating had little to do with their familiar ritual. This morning, they dispensed with reading *The Bee* and visited about how Lois was feeling and what they thought of Rockaway House. They both agreed it was the best place ever. Wasn't the staff amazing? This whole setup was just what the three of them needed.

Ray and Lois were both eager to exchange their impressions of Carlene and talk about what a wonderful time they were all having, which was a very peculiar thing to feel and say, considering the circumstances. Still, it was all so much better than Lois or Ray had dared hope for.

There was a knock at the door just as Ray was packing up the tray and dishes. Rona had left a note for Margaret about the special food request and she was there to follow up.

"Hi, I'm Margaret. I understand we need to get you two some breakfast supplies?"

Lois and Ray looked at each other. "It would be great if I didn't need to bring it from home—it got cold by the time I got here," Ray said, thinking he was getting special treatment and feeling a little guilty.

"If you'll come with me for a few minutes, I'll show you what we have for you down in the kitchen. Can I steal him away from you for just a bit, Mrs. Spaulding?"

"Certainly, Margaret. And please call me Lois."

"And please call me Ray."

"Lois and Ray it is. Be right back." Margaret led the way to the kitchen area, pointing out features of Rockaway House as they went. Ray and Carlene had gotten the usual tour the night before but, mixed in with the drama of bringing Lois to Rockaway House, that was a blur and Ray was glad for the refresher.

When Rona came to her with the Spauldings' breakfast needs, Margaret had immediately thought of the solution. She led Ray to the butler's pantry between the dining room and the kitchen.

"Here's a cupboard for you to store your special tray and dishes, Ray. I'll be glad to arrange for the food items you want. Just make a list for me. I'll put a toaster here for you and there's a microwave there in the kitchen. The coffee and tea maker is always on with plenty of pods to choose from. What else can I do for you and Lois?"

It was too much for Ray. While he'd showered, shaved and dressed an hour earlier, his heart was heavy, preparing for one of the worst mornings of his life. It had turned out so differently, in a good way, but it was like being in an emotional slingshot. He pulled a handkerchief from his pocket, removed his glasses and wiped his eyes.

"I'm sorry. My wife was so frail when we left her here yesterday, I didn't know what to expect this morning. This is not what I thought this morning would hold for us. It's very kind of you to do this for me, for us. I'm just so glad that Lois came here."

Margaret smiled warmly and gave Ray a moment to compose himself. "That's why we're here, Ray, to do what we can to be of service to you and Lois. Leave that list for me today, and I'll see that your breakfast foods are here by tomorrow morning." She handed him pen and paper.

Ray wrote down a few items and left it on the kitchen table for Margaret. He quickly washed up the plates and cups and squirreled them away with the wood inlay tray, a wedding gift from friends of Ray's parents in 1970. Lois and Ray had used it every day since then.

When he'd returned to the house to fix their breakfast, Ray hadn't wanted to disturb Carlene, who was still sleeping. But now that Margaret had figured everything out, Ray could calm down and he wasn't nearly as frantic. So before going back into Lois's room, he stopped in the hallway and called home on his cell phone. Carlene was up by then, having a bowl of cereal. He told her how well her mother looked. He asked her to please hurry.

"What's *The Secret*, anyway?" Lois was propped up in bed, Carlene was sitting in the mid-morning sunshine near the window. At their insistence, Ray had left to meet his coffee group downtown.

Carlene was confused. "Who's got a secret?"

"Not *a* secret, *The* Secret. You know, the book, the DVD. That has to have begun in California."

"Oh, *that* Secret. It's more a philosophy than a secret. It's the belief that you can affect the Universe around you, what happens to you, by repeating positive affirmations and by being grateful for what the Universe wants to bring your way. I believe in it."

"Really? Tell me why." This sort of thing fascinated Lois. Ray called it *woo-woo stuff and nonsense*, which was amusing to Lois since she'd watched Ray follow and practice these same principles his entire adult life. Of course, Ray Spaulding would never recognize or acknowledge Norman Vincent Peale's *The Power of Positive Thinking* as the retro version of new age stuff and nonsense.

"Well, not long after I got the idea to open the store," Carlene recalled, "I started using affirmation cards—index cards with statements of what I'm grateful for—each morning. Sure enough, not a month later, I came across the empty storefront, then I met my banker at a neighborhood function within a few days. Don't laugh, Mom, it's real."

"I'm not laughing, believe me. I always hoped you'd find your passion and what you truly want and need in California. Have you?" Lois debated whether to go on, then thought, *If not now, wh*en? "You always seemed so angry with us, Carlene. And so unhappy."

"I wasn't angry exactly, Mom, although it probably came off like that. I was afraid. And I still am. That's probably why I seem to be angry." She held up her hand to stop Lois's rebuttal before it began. "I know it doesn't make sense, Mom. Emotions seldom do. And it doesn't have anything to do with you and Dad, so don't worry. I've spent thousands of hours in therapy going down that rabbit hole and it's not you."

"That's a relief." Lois smiled at Carlene. "What are you afraid of, honey?"

"To be honest, I don't know. I guess I always think things'll be perfect and happy and wonderful when—I don't know—fill in the blank: when I move to California, when I get my herbology degree, when I open my own store, when it's a success."

"And?"

"Every one of those things has happened and I'm still in therapy. It seems like it's always the next thing that needs to happen. That sounds selfish, doesn't it? I have a great job and a nice little apartment. But, you know what, Mom—and this will blow you away—I'm more peaceful, happy, I guess, now, being here for just three days than I have been for years. Which makes absolutely no sense, considering what prompted this trip."

Lois smiled and laid her head back on the pillow. "Then I can check another item off my Bucket List."

Carlene stood, came to sit on the edge of the bed and took her mother's hand. She was skeptical but she was grinning. "What? Me living in Chesterton?"

"Only if that would make you happy. What I meant was you choosing to be happy, whatever that means for you, Carlene."

"That's great Mom. Assuming you're right, a minor hitch is that my life happens to be located in California, not here."

"True, but who's in charge of where you live, honey? When you talk about the power of positive thinking, you must never discount the power of negative thinking. You are what you think about, you know."

"Oh yeah? When'd you get so enlightened?"

"Sometime in the past couple of weeks to be honest. Timing's everything, isn't it?" Lois smiled and looked pretty proud of herself. Carlene laughed and gave her mother a hug.

Just then Trish peeked around the door jam. "How does a nice sponge bath and back rub sound, Lois?"

"That sounds wonderful. I think I'll have a little nap afterwards, Carlene. Why don't you go relax for a bit, and when you come back, I'll be all freshened up and rarin' to go."

"That's a deal, Mom. I'll be just down the hall." Carlene gave Lois a quick kiss, grabbed her bag of tricks and headed for the sunroom.

Margaret

"I've got mail!"

Margaret clicked and there it was, her first message—from someone other than a foreigner who needed help accessing his inheritance. Her attorney, Ken Sylvester, had sent it. When Margaret stopped by to get the insurance check she'd told Ken about buying the computer and until just now she'd forgotten that Ken had asked for her e-mail address. In his short note, he congratulated her on getting online and said, again, how he hoped she would enjoy the special gift that Ernie had left for her.

"He's a nice guy, Maxine. How sweet of him to send this." As soon as she figured out the whole Reply thing, she'd reply. That was another item on her expanding to-do list. Margaret didn't even have time to look for any more hospice ideas right now. She already had a pile of materials she'd printed out and one of these days—soon—she'd get it organized and make copies for Rose. Heaven knows Rose didn't have time to do such a thing herself and Margaret knew she'd be grateful for the help. Margaret was growing accustomed to the idea of being indispensible to others and this whole feeling useful thing was definitely good.

Margaret sat on the edge of the bed and looked over at their wedding picture. She was planning to tell Ernie about her meeting with the board of directors, how well it had gone, how she'd been inspired by having known Caleb and being able to share his story.

Without warning, a wave of profound sadness washed over her. It was a palpable ache somewhere in her middle, where Margaret imagined her solar plexus to be.

She voiced her frustration aloud, "Where did this come from?" She hated it when this happened. Out of nowhere, right in the middle of a good day—right in the middle of a good thought for God's sake—some unknown something inside her determined that she needed a dose of grief.

There's no way the human brain will ever be capable of understanding how the human brain works.

She hung her head and let it happen. *This has to be a chemical thing. I swear to God, I did not feel this sad a minute ago—I didn't feel sad at all!* Margaret practiced her deep breathing, willing herself to relax. She'd have a good cry if it was in her. It wasn't. This was a fit of grief, not to be confused with weepiness, which she also knew well.

After a few minutes, it receded. Closing her eyes, in her mind she could actually see the wave washing back out to sea.

Good riddance.

"Remember when you quit smoking, Ernie? I know you do. Well, losing you isn't like that. When you quit smoking—at least it's what you told me—you want a cigarette less and less over time. Time lessens the craving. This isn't like that. This is more like thirst. If you don't have water, you don't get less thirsty over time, you get more thirsty. Is it possible that the sadness of losing you won't get smaller, Ernie—that it might even get greater as time goes by? Please say that isn't true."

Maybe that's the way it is. I don't know.

Margaret turned out the light. She wasn't feeling especially creative. She recited the *Lord's Prayer* and tried her hardest to think peaceful thoughts.

Miss Lil

By the time Lillian Dexter had her thirty-second birthday, she had personally encountered more sudden, unexpected deaths than most people of any age. At eight, her mother, in childbirth; at twenty-six, her husband, a casualty of war; at thirty-two, her father, a massive heart attack. As she looked back on those deaths—which she had done countless times throughout her life—she reflected that sudden death is a ruthless heartbreaker for the survivors. When you really thought about it, though—which she had also done countless times throughout her life—probably not a bad way to go for the one who dies. In the twilight of her years, Lil's theory was confirmed as she watched peers linger, trapped in plodding, drawn out dying trajectories. She saw the wake of sorrow it left for all concerned. *No thanks. Not for me.*

Lil made up her mind. Suicide was out of the question and she couldn't control whether she had a sudden—hopefully, painless—death, but she could insist there be no pointless lollygagging. So, ten years ago she'd had her attorney, Cameron Lane Sr., draft a Living Will and Durable Power of Attorney for Health Care, custom made for her. Would niece Peggy be willing to stand up to anyone who tried to keep her Aunt Lil around past her "Use by" date? Peggy said she would. Lil appointed Peggy as her proxy decision-maker.

Peggy was present when Lil signed the documents—Lil made sure of that. She read each aloud to Peggy, her attorney and his secretary, the notary public. Lil didn't want any dispute later about what she had meant or what she did or didn't understand. Five years after that was when Lil added the standby guardianship, right after the whole getting lost on the way home from the grocery store incident. That's when Peggy agreed to serve as Lil's guardian and conservator, if necessary.

No loose ends, that's what Lil believed in. No loose ends. She knew what she stood for and how she wanted to be remembered and that had not changed. Even now, in spite of the Alzheimer's, that had not changed.

For the first few days at Rockaway House, Lil pushed her food around the plate, hoping to make it look as if she'd eaten some of it. Then she politely refused every other meal, claiming she was still full from the last. Then she simply refused to eat. The hospice volunteer who was trying to assist Miss Lil with her breakfast wasn't exactly sure what to do, so she went to Rona, the nurse on duty. Rona said she'd speak to Lil and her niece Peggy.

Peggy didn't hesitate in her response. "My aunt's wishes are very clear, Rona. She does not want artificial nutrition or hydration. Since she has Alzheimer's, if there's a question about her ability to manage her own care, I'm here as her proxy to see that her wishes are carried out." Peggy had been well schooled by Aunt Lil, but she put a call into Cameron Lane, Jr. to verify the legal grounds, just to make sure. Cameron confirmed Peggy's understanding.

Rona didn't argue. Why would she? She knew the law as well and when it came to life-prolonging measures, hospice care was on the side of the patient—always. She remembered only three times when the corporate attorney for Chesterton Community Hospice had been called in on the question of a patient's rights. All three instances involved siblings at loggerheads with staff: those who were not willing to honor the wishes of the patient versus those who were, respectively.

Two of those conflicts had arisen more from ignorance than moral conviction. As the staff had patiently explained to the family members, in our culture we equate food with nurturing, but when a person is actively dying, food and water can actually cause discomfort. The patients' loved ones were surprised to learn there's very little evidence that forced or artificial feeding prolongs life. Once they truly understood the role of hospice—which is *not* to kill the patient—they no longer argued. They acceded to the wishes of the person who was doing the dying.

The third case was a bit different. It involved family members who were conflicted on religious grounds. Were nutrition and hydration life-prolonging measures (the legal position) or humane and moral treatment (their church's attitude)? Luckily, before it became a battle royale, everyone agreed that since the patient had made his wishes clear and there was no question about him being terminal, the argument was moot—legally and religiously.

In any case, Rona understood and respected Lil's right to refuse food. Everyone agreed she was to be kept as comfortable as possible and that any anxiety would be addressed by the doctors. The mission of the staff and volunteers of Rockaway House was to provide Lil with a respectful, dignified and pain-free death, as much as was humanly possible.

As Rona and Peggy agreed on the plan for Lil's care, Lil lay nearby, mutely listening. *Good, that loose end is handled.*

Someone's out in the hall.

"Hello? Who's there?" Lil called out.

A young woman peeked tentatively in Lil's door.

"Hi. Were you speaking to me?"

"I was. Come in, come in!" The young woman did as charged. "Do you live in this house?"

"Uh, no, my mother lives—is staying here. Is there something you need? Can I call the nurse for you?"

"Oh my no, I don't need a nurse. I was just watching *Andy Griffith* and thinking about my children. Do you have children?"

"No, no, I'm not married, no, I don't have children. Yet."

"Come in and visit, won't you?" Not sure why that seemed like a good idea, the visitor accepted the invitation, entered and sat on the chair closest to the bed. Lil got right down to business. "I need to go home. Can you help me with that?"

"I'm sorry. I don't think I can."

"Well, I don't know why someone doesn't come to take me home. I want to see it."

"I know how you feel. I'm just visiting here, too. I'm planning to be around for a while, but I miss my home, too."

"We're always planning, aren't we? We actually think we're in charge of our lives, don't we? We're not, really. A person could make herself crazy trying to predict what's gonna happen next in life. I'm ninety-four years old. My plans have gotten upset lots of times, I can tell you. Lots of surprises."

"Like what, for instance?"

"Like my husband went off to war and never came back. He just never came back. I got letters from him for months after he died. It was like he was writing to me from heaven."

"I'm so sorry."

"Thank you, but there's no need for you to be. I don't think you had anything to do with it, did you?"

"Well, no. What war was he killed in?"

"World War II. We thought it was the war to end all wars. That's another surprise and now we're friends with the country that killed my Leroy. People forget, but I never forgot. I never could forgive them. He was a very sweet young man and he didn't do anything to deserve to die, did he?"

"It sounds like he was a hero."

"Yes, that's right. He was a hero. He got some medals. I can't remember what for, but I know he did his best . . . I never got married again. I never wanted to get married again. I don't think I was supposed to be married again to anyone else. Are you married?"

"No, no I'm not."

"You should think about getting married. Leroy and I were only married for five years, but it was quite extraordinary. You should think about getting married. Do you know how I met my husband?"

"No, but I'd like to hear."

Lil told her visitor about growing up in Chicago and about performing with the Chicago Symphony when she was only nine years old. She spoke wistfully about playing the violin with Isaac Stern. Later, Lil had wanted to be a teacher, so she went to Iowa State Teachers College in Cedar Falls and got a job in Chesterton when she graduated.

"Papa wanted me to play violin in the orchestra, but I didn't want to do that. I wanted to teach little children to love music so that's what I did."

On a Sunday afternoon, Lil was walking down Marion Street, before the war, before any of that awful business. She and her friends used to stroll down the boulevard on Sunday afternoons. They called on folks and had a cup of tea or a glass of lemonade on the front porches. Lil always wore white gloves.

Lil dropped her hankie. She knew she had, but she pretended she didn't and a young man came up and tapped her on the shoulder and said, "I think you dropped this, miss." She looked at him and she knew, she knew right then that he was the man she would marry, the only man she would ever love.

"Sometimes it happens like that. Sometimes life just surprises us like that." Lil's eyelids began to droop a bit. Her visitor stood.

"I think I might be keeping you from a nap. It was nice meeting you. My name's Carlene."

"My name is Lillian. You should think about getting married, Carlene." Lil took Carlene's hand in hers, holding on firmly.

"I'll certainly give that some thought, Lillian. You take care." And Carlene left with a smile on her face, which she had not had when she entered the room.

Rose approached Peggy on the second day of Lil's stay and told her about the service they could provide in case Peggy wasn't available to be with her aunt all the time. In four-hour shifts hospice volunteers would sit with Miss Lil to make sure she wasn't alone at the time of death.

"It's entirely up to the family or patient if they'd like us to do this. We had one lady who woke up to find the volunteer at her bedside and yelled 'Who the hell are you?' Scared the bejesus out of both of them. Of course, that's not in line with the goals of the program," Rose said to Peggy with a roll of her eyes. In spite of that ringing endorsement, Peggy declined the offer.

"After all we've been to each other, I know she would be there for me. I figure my duties don't end until Aunt Lil's safely on the other side." Peggy was taking family leave from her teaching job, and she'd be with Aunt Lil now until the end, sleeping each night on the fold out bed in Aunt Lil's room at Rockaway House. Unspoken was Peggy's added hope that she could witness another of Aunt Lil's visits from family members who no longer lived "around here." She decided against sharing that with Rose.

It was Aunt Lil who had introduced Peggy to music. Together they'd attended nearly every musical production in the Quad Cities and even travelled to Lil's hometown of Chicago for major shows. Lil had taken those opportunities to show Peggy where her Great Uncle Burt's violin shop had been and the house where Lil grew up. Peggy had made sure Aunt Lil's CD collection came with her to Rockaway House.

Peggy was listening to *The Music Man* and reading a book when Margaret stopped by the room.

"How's Miss Lil doing today, Peggy?"

"Hi, Margaret. She's resting peacefully. She spoke to me a little while ago, but mostly she's resting."

By the third day of not eating, the change in Miss Lil's appearance was noticeable. She was no longer taking liquids except for a wetted sponge to keep her mouth and lips moist. If Peggy asked about pain, Lil still responded by slowly shaking her head, but she was restfully sleeping most of the time except for an occasional twitch or minor spasm.

I'm not really asleep, but I'm too tired to visit, even with you, sweet Peggy. What a treasure you've been to me. Do I hear Margaret from the grocery store? Is that Margaret?

"Would you like to go downstairs for a coffee break, Peggy? I'll be glad to sit with Miss Lil while you're gone." Peggy stood and stretched.

Well thank goodness. Peggy shouldn't be sitting here at my death bed for hours and hours. Good thinking, Margaret.

"I'll take you up on that, I need the stretch. I won't be long, Aunt Lil. Margaret, would you mind putting another CD in the player?" Peggy gave Lil a pat on the hand and left. Margaret pulled the next CD from the pile, loaded it and hit play. She took Peggy's chair next to the bed.

"I've been thinking a lot about what we talked about the other day, Miss Lil, about you missing your husband. I bet you're looking forward to seeing him again. I know I'm looking forward to seeing my Ernie one day."

That reunion can't come too soon for me, Margaret.

Margaret stood to freshen the water in a vase of flowers. Her mind was wandering. *What if the show home idea doesn't work out? What if we don't make enough money to save Rockaway House? What if the patients end up being disturbed by the renova—"*

"Something's gonna happen—all will be revealed."

Margaret nearly dropped the vase.

"Did—what did you say, Miss Lil?"

"Everything will work out just fine." Lil hadn't even opened her eyes and Margaret wasn't absolutely sure she hadn't imagined the words. As she leaned close to check, Lil's eyes were still shut and her chest barely moved with each breath.

Here she was, hoping for wisdom from a dying lady, a lady with Alzheimer's, no less. Well, Margaret thought to herself, Miss Lil has made more sense in the past few days than a lot of other folks I know. Margaret felt better. *Don't ask me why I'm putting so much store in these gems from a ninety-four-year-old Alzheimer's patient or why they make so much sense to me, but you better believe they do.*

She moistened Lil's lips with petroleum jelly and gave her a tender arm massage with lightly scented lotion. She thought she saw Lil get a little smile on her face as Margaret gently touched her.

Now this feels good. I miss being touched. I miss my babies and my husband. I've had a good life. I tried to make a good job of my life and of raising my children and being a good friend. I'm ready to go now. And I can't see any reason to hang around here, making Peggy spend anymore of her precious life here. Wherever "here" is. What is a Rockaway House, anyway?

I am so tired. I don't think I've ever been this tired in my whole ninety-four years. I'll think about not being tired. I'll think about being young and playing with Ivabelle, when Mama was still alive, before Tom was born. There's Ivabelle—and there's Tom. Oh my, oh my. Mama . . . Papa . . . Leroy . . . Misty . . . Esther . . . Richard . . . Look at all those stars. Oh my, oh my.

Lil opened her eyes and smiled just as Peggy walked back in the room.

"Goodbye, Peggy dear. I'm going home now." Her eyes closed but the smile remained.

It was September 20, 2012 and the soundtrack from *Wizard of Oz* was playing in the background:

Somewhere over the rainbow, way up high
There's a land that I heard of once in a lullaby.
Somewhere over the rainbow,
Skies are blue and the dreams that you dare to dream
Really do come true.

Isobel

In 2004, as Helen Sullivan oversaw the renovation of Rockaway House, she cherished the practical and spiritual significance of the kitchen, but she got just as excited about the upstairs solarium. With windows on the southeast corner of the house, it got full sun in the morning and even on a cloudy day, it was cheery. Family members needed such a place to rest.

The young attorney looked at his watch. He had time. Now, with a few minutes before his appointment, he might as well have a comfy seat and do a little business.

The firm of *Lane, Roderick, Brown, and Lane* had first been retained by Isobel Baines decades before, in the matter of *Baines vs. Baines.* Back then, she was represented by Cameron Lane II's father, Cameron Lane Sr.

Stanley was a party boy when Isobel married him and, as Isobel came to recognize, didn't have the sense that God gave a goose. After Rhonda and then Jeanne arrived, Isobel tired of the evenings and weekends with a husband unwilling to fulfill his role as a parent or even as a spouse. So the first time Miss Slotkin—his secretary and so much more—called for him outside work hours, Isobel gave Stanley two choices and five minutes to choose: marriage or not. Stanley went with *not.* He went on to marry Miss Slotkin and have two more children before she became his second ex-wife. But before all that nonsense, Cameron Lane Sr. got the little house and a decent amount of child support for Isobel. Those monthly checks turned out to be the extent of Stanley's involvement in the lives of Rhonda and Jeanne, which was fine by everyone concerned.

Throughout the years, when Isobel needed the services of an attorney, Mr. Lane was who she called. The first time was a year after the divorce when she had a Will drawn up saying that if anything happened to Isobel, her cousin Emma would get custody of the girls. The second time was six years ago when she sold her house and moved into the Sunshine Retirement Village. The cash proceeds from the house provided nicely for Isobel's little apartment and meals in the dining room. Not long after close of Isobel's escrow, Cameron Lane Sr. retired and now his son Cameron II was handling this final matter for Isobel: her Last Will and Testament.

Word processing and the laptop computer were invented with Mrs. Baines in mind, Cameron thought with a smile. He sat in the solarium, reviewing his notes before going to her room. His presence had been commanded no less than four times in the past six weeks, each occasion to "tweak" the Will as Isobel liked to say. The first version left all assets equally to Rhonda and Jeanne. Three weeks later, Isobel wanted to add a small bequest to the local animal shelter. Ten days after that, right after one of Rhonda's flyovers, Isobel called Cameron II back again.

Cameron remembered that conversation only too well. As soon as he arrived, he noticed how distressed Mrs. Baines looked and she didn't hesitate a moment to share why.

"As it turns out," she said, "there's no reason to include Rhonda."

"Are you sure you want to remove your daughter from your Will, Mrs. Baines?"

"Yes, I'm sure. Actually, she suggested it."

"Oh?" That didn't sound right, from what Cameron knew of Rhonda.

"I heard Rhonda say to Jeanne—I guess she thought I was asleep—'I don't know why she keeps messing with her Will. I don't want or need any of her money and you and I both know she hasn't got diddly to leave to us. Who is she trying to fool, anyway?'" It was clear to Cameron that Isobel had played that conversation over in her mind many times. "I don't even know what 'diddly' means, Cameron, and I know that was not a nice thing to say."

Cameron hesitated before responding.

"I'm sure she didn't mean it in a disrespectful way, but if you'd like to remove Rhonda from the Will we can certainly do that." Truth be told, Cameron had met Rhonda just once and thought she was an especially unpleasant piece of work, so he didn't feel obligated to argue otherwise. *The client is almost always right.* And if he ever needed to swear whether Mrs. Baines was competent by any standard, he could and would. She was free to change her Will every day if she had a mind to and he would be pleased to help make that happen.

Soon after, he presented the newly amended Will to Isobel, gathered two witnesses from among the staff, notarized the signatures and went on his way. That was ten days ago and Isobel's most recent call had come earlier that very morning.

"Can you be here pretty soon, Cameron? I have one more change to make," Isobel said.

Cameron was more concerned about the sound of her voice than what Mrs. Baines was saying. A lot of the air had gone out of her balloon. Even with her cheerful tone still intact, her voice was undeniably weaker. "Of course, Mrs. Baines. How about later this morning?"

"I'll see you then. If I'm napping, please wake me."

"Will do. Take care, I'll see you in a bit." So here he was, intent on his computer screen, refreshing his memory of the most recent documents and speculating on what Mrs. Baines was about to share with him.

"Kitten video or angry birds?"

A bit startled, Cameron looked up into the biggest brown eyes he'd ever seen. The young lady wasn't tall, maybe five foot five. She had a sleek pageboy haircut. Without the smiling face it framed, Cameron thought, you might say the style seemed in the wrong decade, more the '40s than the New Millennium. But those eyes and the healthy glow to that flawless skin. *Wow.*

"Neither one. Not guilty. Just reviewing some paperwork. Which one is your favorite?" She took a chair across from Cameron, setting an overstuffed tote bag at her feet.

"Oh, I'm a sucker for a talking kitten anytime or, even better, one in a glass vase—have you seen that?"

"Can't say that I have. I'm Cameron Lane." He extended his hand.

"Nice to meet you, Cameron. I'm Carlene."

Cameron glanced at his watch and stood, truly regretting that he was expected elsewhere. *Maybe Mrs. Baines is napping? No, better go.*

"Well, I'm off to see my client. Nice meeting you."

"Client? Doctors have patients, so I'm guessing you're an attorney?"

"Yes, actually. How about you?"

"Nope, not an attorney. An herbologist."

"Okay . . . I wish I had time to learn more about being a herbologist—or even to find out what it is—but I really have to go." He flashed his best boyish grin.

"Maybe another time."

"I'd like that." He backed awkwardly from the lounge and slowly went down the hall to Isobel's room, unconsciously smiling. *Well, that was a pleasant little surprise.*

Tapping on Isobel's door, Cameron let himself in. She was awake, eyes wide open. "Hello, Mrs. Baines. Good to see you." Putting his portable wireless printer on the dresser, he pulled a chair close to her bed and opened his laptop. He noticed the oxygen tube, an addition since his last visit. Isobel took a moment to gather her strength before speaking.

"Cameron, you're a good boy for getting here so soon. Here's the new plan: I want my Will to say that there'll be a charity, a—what's the word?"

"A trust?"

"Yes, a trust. It's for three things: to take care of women whose husbands desert them. It's to provide scholarships for the women and for their children and for housing and such. And it's also for people who are in nursing homes and don't have family to provide for them. Are you getting this down?" Cameron's head was spinning as quickly as his fingers were flying.

"Yes ma'am."

"Cameron, look behind you. You see that sign hanging on the inside of the door?"

"Yes ma'am."

"Hang it on the outside and shut the door, would you please?"

Cameron rose, got the *Do Not Disturb* sign and did as Isobel asked.

"Now, where was I? Oh, and it's also for animals, the ones that people abandon. That's all."

Maybe her oxygen needs to be turned up a notch. Cameron was familiar with the approximate size of Isobel's estate, and he couldn't see how it would support philanthropy of this scope. *Well, let's see where this is going.*

"All right, Mrs. Baines. So, did you have someone in mind to act as the trustee, the one who makes the decisions?"

"Oh yes, my daughter Jeanne. She knows all about how to put things together, and she can figure out how to raise even more money to keep it all going." Isobel paused. "I was going to just leave the money to the girls, then I—well, you know all about that—then it seemed better to have it all go to a trust. I don't want to make problems between Rhonda and Jeanne—they do a fine job of that on their own." Clearly, Mrs. Baines had put a lot of thought into this. Cameron stopped typing for a moment and looked over at his client. He wasn't exactly sure how to proceed. He'd better call his dad.

In 1975, Rhonda Baines was eight, Jeanne Baines was three, and their mother, Isobel, was forty-two. She was working as an aide to the activities staff at the Sunshine Retirement Village. Facing her inevitable future as a single mother of two little girls with dread and dismay, the last thing she could bear was unemployment. As her marriage imploded, Isobel was trying very hard to keep it together at work. She put on a happy face every day, but there is only so much a smile can hide.

Her boss, Mary Jo Nelson, took her aside and asked if everything was all right at home—Isobel seemed distracted and not herself. Isobel confessed that Stanley had moved out and she didn't expect—and wasn't hoping for—a reconciliation. Mary Jo, motivated to help her employee and friend, made an introductory call to one of her husband's golfing buddies, the young attorney, Cameron Lane Sr. As Isobel would readily tell you, thanks in large part to his counsel and advocacy, life for Isobel and Rhonda and Jeanne was stabilized.

Isobel paid for Cameron Sr.'s representation on the installment plan, twenty dollars a month for thirty months. And with every check she wrote, she was reminded of God's grace in bringing Cameron Lane Sr. her way just when she needed him.

Over the years, Isobel had little call for an attorney herself, but she worked in a place (God's waiting room) crammed with folks who needed all variety of legal services: guardianships and conservatorships, estate plans, powers of attorney for health care and financial matters or even just handholding through the Medicaid or Medicare labyrinth. Isobel didn't have to think twice: there was only one lawyer she knew for a fact would do his very best and that was Cameron Lane Sr. *He'll treat you with respect and integrity.* You can trust him, she'd say. *He's a very good man.* Those who Isobel did not directly refer came to Cameron because they knew someone who knew that nice lady at the Sunshine Retirement Village. Sooner or later, the children of those clients called Cameron when they needed an attorney, and they told two friends and they told two friends and so on . . .

Isobel's straightforward loyalty was ultimately the cornerstone in the foundation of Cameron Sr.'s very successful estate and probate practice. Years earlier, Cameron Sr. stopped trying to quantify the numbers, but as a small token of his gratitude, not a Christmas went by without a huge delivery to the Sunshine Retirement Village from *Babkas 'r Us*, courtesy of attorney Cameron Lane Sr. Only he and the administrator knew that he also underwrote the Christmas dinner there, upgrading the residents and their guests to turkey and all the trimmings, complete with a gift at each place setting. And it was always a mystery how every resident got a present to open on birthdays, even if they had no family to speak of.

Of course, Cameron's primary way of thanking Isobel for her allegiance was to make sure he did the best job possible as he handled each legal matter for those she entrusted to his care. And he'd made it clear to Cameron II as soon as he joined the practice—and many times since, in no uncertain terms—that Isobel Baines was a long-time and valued friend of the firm and was to be given all due reverence.

Cameron II didn't need to be reminded. Over the past few weeks, his own affection for Isobel had grown. That was the problem. What exactly was his obligation now? Did he have a duty as her attorney to explain that her meager estate couldn't possibly accomplish what she was dreaming of? Did his role as her counsel extend to breaking the heart of someone who he now counted as a dear—although perhaps slightly delusional—friend?

"I believe I understand what you want, Mrs. Baines. I'll need to do some work on this at the office, though. Can I come back tomorrow morning with the new version?" Cameron was young but not naive. With a client who was already in hospice care and visibly failing, it was best not to dally.

"In the morning? That's fine, Cameron. I'll make sure I'm here." Isobel's smile told him her sense of humor was intact.

"Of course you will," he smiled back. "Is there anything I can get for you before I leave?"

He waited. Isobel had a quizzical look on her face. He could all but hear the wheels turning. She was obviously pondering something.

"There is another item we need to talk about, Cameron. Can you keep a secret?"

"Yes ma'am."

"Well, here's the deal."

When Isobel stopped speaking sometime later, Cameron looked at her in disbelief. Then he nodded, opened the door and removed the sign just as Jeanne arrived. She was on the way to the grocery store and stopped by to check in. These days, it seemed prudent to verify her mother's condition before her two little girls arrived.

"Hey, Jeanne. Good to see you." Cameron extended his hand.

"Uh-oh, looks like Mom's messin' with her Will again." She gave Cameron a wink and her mother a peck on the cheek.

"She is indeed. And I need to get to work on it, so I'll see you tomorrow, Mrs. Baines. About one o'clock?"

"See you then, Cameron. And say hello to your father when you talk to him next."

"Yes, ma'am, I will and I can tell you he always asks after you. You're one of his very favorite people." Isobel smiled back. As many times as Dad has thanked her, she still has no idea what she did for him, Cameron thought.

Jeanne took the seat Cameron had vacated and Isobel told her about the charitable trust she was creating and the work it would accomplish. Jeanne didn't know what to think or say.

"That sounds pretty ambitious, Mom. I'm not sure I really have time to be in charge of something as involved as that, with the girls and my own work." She didn't want to burst her mother's bubble or make false promises. Isobel quickly waved away Jeanne's objections.

"Oh, honey, you can quit your regular job. This'll be a full-time deal and I made sure Cameron is providing for the salary you deserve in all that paperwork. But enough of that, how are you?"

"I'm good, Mom. How about you?"

"The next time Rhonda gets on your nerves, remember what the dormouse said, Jeanne, 'Keep your head'."

"Seriously, Mom? You're quoting Jefferson Airplane to me?"

"Hey, in the 1960s I was only in my thirties—I was still a hip chick!"

"Except the dormouse didn't say 'Keep your head', Mom. He said 'Feed your head'."

"Okay, then feed your head."

"What does that mean?" Jeanne began to giggle.

"I'm not sure. I think maybe it means to keep an open mind. Or, knowing life in the '60s, it might mean absolutely nothing!" They were having a good ole laugh when Margaret tapped on the door and stuck her head in.

"Sorry to interrupt. I just wanted to check and see if you still need any help with your project, Isobel."

"I do feel up to that, Margaret. Jeanne, honey, why don't you run on home and I'll just see you later today?"

Jeanne stood to leave. "Just one word of caution, Margaret: she's in rare form today." She gave her mother a quick hug and left. Isobel let her head fall back on her pillow. The day had already been exhausting and it wasn't even noon yet.

Whatever might be on Isobel's agenda, Margaret was looking forward to sharing it and spending time with her. With each new day at Rockaway House, Margaret was discovering more about the patients, her role in their lives and vice versa. Isobel Baines most especially fascinated Margaret. Delightful and unexpected revelations emerged during each visit. Her attitude, her philosophy and her continuing eagerness to learn, even in this final chapter of her life, were inspiring.

But Margaret was just one of many who would be amazed by Isobel Baines over the next few weeks.

Margaret

That made three. Three of the patients Margaret had been closely involved with had died. In Margaret's mind, her life was most certainly better for having known them, but she couldn't keep from asking herself: Were their deaths better for having known her?

She was thinking about all she exchanged with patients as they approached the end of life together—the witness and the travelers. Measuring the impact of her involvement from the perspective of the patient, Margaret observed it was the littlest things that seemed to make a difference. Like organizing breakfast supplies for the Spauldings. Like assisting Isobel with her obituary. Like planning an early Christmas for Caleb. From Margaret's viewpoint, each little kindness she extended had lifted her own heart, had focused her on something other than her grief and loss, and had been another tiny piece of the puzzle. She also granted that fully grasping the impact of all this cosmic interaction wasn't always possible; you just had to believe it existed and watch for the signs. Like that little prediction from Miss Lil the day she passed. That was the part they couldn't teach in volunteer orientation. You had to be there.

And then there was the really big thing that Margaret had stumbled upon: the Murphys and the treasure they'd left behind. It might make a difference in many lives for a very long time, long after Margaret was long gone.

The butterfly effect.

Margaret took a deep breath. She was too tired for such introspective notions. *The Auction* was proceeding, everyone had assigned duties, it was all coming together and Margaret was on total and complete sensory overload, on all fronts. What she'd really welcome would be some busy work to take her mind off such things.

Maybe, she thought, she could do some of that sorting she kept meaning to get to. That was certainly mindless.

Or maybe I should go shopping?

She went ahead and opened a drawer. There were Ernie's tee shirts, the ones that had seen better days. Ernie always argued that they were still good for puttering around the house or doing yard work or detailing the cars. Naturally, that relaxed attitude had frequently led to, "You're not going out in that, are you? You look like a hobo," as soon as Ernie had announced a trip beyond the homestead.

Margaret would listen to Ernie rail on about how his shirt was much nicer than what most guys wore, how this was Saturday in Chesterton for the love of God, and it was just the hardware store or gas station or car wash. Who would see him? Who would care?

Once he paused long enough to notice that Margaret wasn't arguing back, he stopped. She'd smile, look at him and say, "Ernie, you know that line you're not supposed to cross? Look behind you." He'd change the tee shirt, give her a quick peck on the cheek and head out. Those were the little bits of life with Ernie that she missed most of all.

Better keep these. Who knows? She might want to do some yard work herself one of these days. Probably not, but it could happen.

Next drawer, Ernie's sweaters. That green cardigan he'd had for more years than Margaret could remember because he'd actually had it when they met. A couple of nice sweater vests Ernie wore when a sport coat was a notch too high for the Chesterton dress code. The maroon argyle that Margaret had given him for Christmas two years ago. She'd forgotten about it. Now she knew why—she hadn't seen it since. He'd never worn it, not once. Had he not liked it and just didn't want to hurt her feelings? What good had that done? Did he think he couldn't tell her that? He could have exchanged it for something he wanted, she wouldn't have cared. Instead, it lay in the drawer, worn by no one. *What a waste.*

"That's enough. I'm not doing this. Not tonight." She shut the drawer and looked at her watch. Six-thirty. *Good.* It was the one evening a week that *Under the Covers* was open until eight o'clock.

Ninety minutes later and Margaret had enjoyed a good cup of coffee, two of Mr. Goldberg's cookies, a nice visit with Molly and left with the newest Patricia Cornwell mystery. It was dark as she pulled into the garage. *Days are getting shorter. No, that's not right—hours of sunlight are getting fewer. Every day has just as many hours to be filled, you idiot. A few months ago, I would have dreaded that. Now I can't imagine how I'll get everything done. What do you think about that?*

Margaret walked into the kitchen, noticed that her cell phone—still lying on the counter—was turned off. She plugged it into the charger anyway. Margaret wasn't especially good about using that piece of technology. Sometimes she forgot to take it with her and when she did remember, she sometimes forgot to turn it on. Never mind about checking for voice mails because they'd had that feature de-activated five years earlier when she and Ernie first got their phones. Weren't they meant just for emergencies? Voice mail was one more thing for Margaret to forget to check, which would mean that somebody's feelings would get hurt if their call went unreturned. The phone machine was enough responsibility.

That's why Lynda Wyatt hadn't been able to reach Margaret that afternoon, that's why she'd left a message on the machine at Margaret's home and that's why its light was blinking now.

"Margaret, Lynda Wyatt, here. You know, *The Bee*. If you have a minute to stop by in the morning, I'll be here at eight o'clock. I've got some more to share with you. Well, okay, see you in the morning—I hope."

Lynda sounds funny, Margaret thought. *Funny strange, not funny ha-ha. Hmmm.* As if Lynda was about to reveal the next chapter of *The Hidden Treasure of Rockaway House.*

I do love a good mystery.

Rockaway House

Lynda Wyatt could hardly stand it. She'd already had three cups of coffee while she waited for Margaret to show up or call. Barely resisting the urge to call again to make sure Margaret got the first message, Lynda didn't have to suffer for long. At ten after eight, she spotted the Buick LeSabre pulling up in front of *The Bee.*

It didn't go unnoticed by Margaret that Lynda wasn't smiling as she opened the front door for her.

"I'll be in the back for a few minutes, Jeff," Lynda called out to her coworker as she steered Margaret to the small conference room. Jeff recognized Margaret and racked his brain, trying to remember from where.

Lynda slid an oversized manila portfolio across to Margaret. Reaching over the table, she spread out a yellowed copy of *The Bee*, dated September 3, 1943. Pointing to an article on Page 4, she handed Margaret a magnifying glass. Lynda impatiently tapped her fingers on the tabletop while Margaret read the headline, "*Rebekah Lodge Initiation.*" Margaret peered closely at the photo of two beautiful young women, each holding an oversized bouquet, each wearing a long white dress with a ceremonial sash around their shoulders. The caption under the photo read, "*Miss Annabelle Murphy and Mrs. Helen Sullivan née O'Neill, pictured at their initiation as officers of Chesterton Rebekah No. 137.*"

Margaret shrugged. "What's a Chesterton Rebekah No. 137?"

"The Rebekah Lodge is the women's counterpart to the Odd Fellows Lodge. Fraternal organizations. I'm guessing these young ladies' fathers were Odd Fellows. Remember, Annabelle is the eldest of the Murphys' daughters? But look, that young woman with her is Mrs. Sullivan, the lady who started Rockaway House. She was friends with one of the Murphy girls. Don't you think that's a weird coincidence?"

I passed thinking these coincidences are weird—or that they're coincidences—quite a ways back down the road. Maybe by 2004, the elderly Helen Sullivan had forgotten that she'd known the original owners of the house, Margaret speculated. Or maybe she'd never visited Annabelle Murphy at home. "That's certainly interesting." Margaret waited. She knew Lynda hadn't summoned her for that tidbit.

"I found something else, Margaret." Lynda's eyes were shining.

"Lynda? What is it?" Margaret was starting to feel anxious and she didn't even know why. Lynda's only response was to open a second folder, revealing another edition of *The Bee*, this one dated Tuesday, April 18, 1944. Lynda pointed hesitantly at a story on the bottom half of the front page.

Tears were about to spill over for Lynda, her eyes locked with Margaret's. In her heart, Margaret knew she did not want to read that story and she intentionally stalled, clearing her throat, buying a few more seconds.

Just then Margaret's cell phone rang, making them both start. She pulled it out of her purse, grateful for the distraction and saw Suzi's number on the Caller ID.

"Suzi?"

"Hi. Can you get right over to the garage?"

"Is it something that can wait? I'm at the newspaper office—can you come here? I think there's something here you need to see—something Lynda found."

"And you need to see what I found."

It was one of those times when Margaret was grateful that it took less than ten minutes to get anywhere in Chesterton. That was long enough for Margaret to read the small story in *The Bee* and then finally share with Lynda the discovery that had prompted this quest in the first place. Just as Margaret finished, Suzi appeared in the office doorway, ushered back by Jeff, who knew Suzi and was by then half crazy wondering what the heck Lynda Wyatt was up to.

Suzi walked in and slapped a small leather-bound book on the table. Her face was somber, and then she saw that Margaret's and Lynda's were as well.

Margaret found her voice. "Do you two know each other?"

"Hi, Lynda, good to see you."

"Hey, Suzi."

Suzi pulled out a chair and sat down and then laid her hand on top of the small volume she had brought with her. "This is the diary of a fourteen-year-old girl named Elizabeth, one of the Murphy children, I'm guessing. It was in one of the attic boxes. The first entry is January 1, 1944. The last entry is April 12, 1944."

That did it. Margaret and Lynda both started to cry. But Suzi still wasn't sure they knew what she knew. Margaret grabbed a tissue from her pocket and dabbed her eyes with one hand. With the other, she slid the April 18, 1944 newspaper in front of Suzi and pointed to the story. Then Suzi was sure.

All three of them now knew why the garage attic at Rockaway House was full of furniture.

The Murphys

On the morning of May 3, 1938, Daniel Patrick Murphy gazed out the window of his office overlooking the yards of the Chicago and North Western Railway in Clinton, Iowa. He was waiting—impatiently—for his secretary Miss McGarvey to announce a call from his wife May. At the same time Daniel had left for the office that morning, May had left for an appointment with Dr. Burroughs, their family physician. As the superintendent of the railroad company's Iowa division, Daniel held a position of considerable authority. But that authority did not extend to giving himself the morning off to accompany his wife to the doctor.

May had confided two days earlier that Daniel was not to get his hopes up, but she thought she might be expecting. It was an unanticipated prospect. Daniel and May had been married for nearly seventeen years. Their first daughter, Annabelle, was born in 1922, in their first year of marriage, just after they moved into their new home. The plan, when they built the oversized two-story, was to fill it with the running feet and rowdy laughter of many children.

It was four years after Annabelle that Lauralee came along and another four years later Elizabeth was born. Daniel's daughters were a blessing for which he thanked God on a daily basis and he could not imagine their home any way other than filled with the delightful and trying temperaments of these four remarkable females, including his wife. Well, five, if you counted Mrs. Quinn, the prodigious housekeeper and cook, and there was no doubt Mrs. Quinn counted. But Daniel had always hoped for a son.

Each and every morning for twelve years, as Daniel rode the interurban railroad from Chesterton to Clinton through a fifteen-mile patch of farmland, he had stared out the rail car window and imagined a small boy bobbing up and down on the leather seat next to him. The youngster was excited to be riding along, anxious to trail his father through the yards and roundhouse. There he'd see firsthand all the jobs Daniel had held over the past two decades as he advanced from yard laborer to corporate executive.

Not long after Elizabeth celebrated her fourth birthday, Daniel quit daydreaming. For the four years since then, he had read *The Chesterton Bee* every day during the thirty-minute train ride.

The morning of May 3, 1938, however, was different. That morning Daniel left the newspaper lying on the seat, unread. He even absentmindedly abandoned it when he stepped off the train at the Clinton station. That morning Daniel was thinking once again about that little boy. Of course, it might be another girl—and that would be a blessing—but it might be a boy, mightn't it?

And so it was. Daniel James Murphy Jr. was born on December 5, 1938, a tike blessed with five mothers. For May Murphy, Mrs. Quinn and his three sisters, Danny was a well-behaved, enchanting little boy—in spite of their full-time doting and spoiling. For Daniel Murphy Sr., Danny was the walking, talking fulfillment of those twelve years of daydreams.

Danny first visited the rail yards at three years of age. On his fourth birthday, the railroad workers held a party for Danny just inside the roundhouse. He greeted each one of his father's twenty-seven employees by name. When he turned five, Danny asked Mrs. Quinn to please start rousing him at 6:30 a.m. to join his father for breakfast before he left to catch the train. On any given weekday, Danny was the third person out of bed in the Murphy household. After a few days, he didn't even need to be beckoned; he appeared at Mrs. Quinn's elbow Monday through Friday, just as she dropped the eggs into the bacon grease.

His mother told Danny it was important for a boy to spend time alone with his father and May took the opportunity to sleep in for a few extra minutes. Mrs. Quinn told Danny that a man needed a good breakfast or Lord knows he'd be no good to anyone the rest of the day. Every morning, she lovingly prepared fried eggs, crisp bacon, cinnamon rolls and fresh-squeezed orange juice that the two men of the house dutifully ate.

It was six forty-five a.m. on the Monday after Easter by the time Mrs. Quinn realized that five-year-old Danny hadn't yet appeared. Mr. Murphy quickly finished his breakfast and told her that she needn't interrupt her work, he would run up and say goodbye to the sleepyhead before he walked to the station.

Daniel sat on the edge of Danny's bed and leaned over to kiss his son good morning and goodbye. He smelled the urine and sour sweat even before he noticed the droplets on Danny's upper lip. Putting his hand on Danny's burning forehead, he softly called his son's name. The whispered response was spoken into Danny's pillow—he couldn't turn his head to look up at his father.

The next few hours were a flurry of panic. First, Daniel instinctively carried his son into the bathroom and put him into a cool bath. Then he called out for Mrs. Quinn to phone Dr. Burroughs and have him come immediately to the house. That alarm woke his wife and daughters. The entire family pressed into the bathroom, able to do little but pray and whisper words of comfort to Danny. He was oblivious.

In a matter of minutes, the doctor arrived.

Dr. Burroughs had practiced medicine for thirty years, the past six in Chesterton. Prior to that, he had lived in the country of his birth, Canada. On April 11, 1944, the polio epidemic nightmare was still in the future tense for the United States. But in 1937, Ontario was the location of Canada's largest epidemic of infantile paralysis and Dr. Burroughs had been an active witness to its devastation. Danny's arms, his left more so than his right, were limp, his breathing was labored and when able to speak, he complained of a headache.

Dr. Burroughs needed no more than a cursory examination to make his diagnosis.

With a calm and authoritative voice, Dr. Burroughs told Mrs. Quinn and May to gently prepare Danny to be taken to the hospital in Clinton. He phoned a peer in Chicago and requisitioned an iron lung. Then he instructed Daniel to call the C&NW offices to organize a train to bring the life-saving equipment to Clinton as quickly as possible.

It was the midst of World War II. Besides the endless communal sacrifices and public reminders, hardly a family in Chesterton had not, in some way, been touched directly by the war. One would think that might have rendered folks accustomed to devastating misfortune and less emotionally vulnerable. Instead, Danny's critical illness seemed even more grievous. Hadn't the justification for all the suffering and dying been to make the world a safer place for the children? It wasn't working. At Mr. Murphy's office, the word of Danny's illness burned through the corporate personnel and then on to the yards and throughout town. Thoughts and prayers went forward. Men openly wept.

But by noon the following day, Danny was stable, breathing with the help of the iron lung. He lay inside the six-foot tube, a rubber ring around his neck creating an airtight seal. An electric motor pulled oxygen in and out of his lungs by changing the pressure inside the tank. Dr. Burroughs, who knew only too well the workings of the massive machine, patiently shared his expertise with the nurses. As much because of its menacing and incessant whine as of the terrifying health crisis it foreshadowed, they were nearly overcome with apprehension.

Mrs. Murphy came home briefly that day, for the first time in twenty-four hours, to collect some personal items and then return to the hospital. She gathered the family and Mrs. Quinn around the dining room table. She had two announcements to make.

May had recently read about a mother in Buffalo, New York who was kept from seeing her polio-stricken child once he was hospitalized. He died alone. Neither one of those options was acceptable to May. Because of the nerve-racking appearance and sound of the iron lung, Danny was in a private room, now also outfitted with an additional bed. Mrs. Murphy would be staying at the hospital indefinitely.

Second, she would not take a chance that one of their daughters would get sick. The family was moving to her parents' home for the time being. She had already called her mother and father, Edwina and Thomas Powell. They had plenty of room. They would re-open the wing that had been shuttered when May and her younger sister moved out to start their own families.

Mrs. Murphy then drilled Mrs. Quinn and Mr. Thornton, the gardener and caretaker, on their next steps. Every piece of furniture was to be moved to the garage attic. Washable items were to be thoroughly cleaned with disinfectant, boxed up and taken to the attic as well. Burn anything that cannot be scrubbed, May ordered. Yes, she said sadly, that includes all of Danny's toys and stuffed animals, even his beloved Teddy. Any articles which they did not believe to be absolutely hygienic were to be disposed of. Period. Then the interior of the house was to be scoured from top to bottom with carbolic acid. If a stronger disinfectant could be found, use it.

Absolutely no one but Mrs. Quinn and Mr. Thornton, and perhaps Patricia, the day maid, were to be allowed back in the house. Fearing transmission of the disease in both directions, Mrs. Murphy said she had no intention of further endangering either their daughters or someone else's children.

Shouldn't the missus be concerned about her own health, Mrs. Quinn timidly asked. Mrs. Murphy dismissed the question with the shake of her head.

Mr. Powell arranged for a car and driver to be at his daughter's disposal, twenty-four hours a day. May returned to the hospital.

On April 13, 1944, Daniel and the girls moved to the Powells' house with few possessions and without protest. Mrs. Powell was eager to help however possible and May put her mother in charge of contacting Lauralee and Elizabeth's teachers. They would be receiving lessons at home until it was safe for them to be around other children. Until then, they were housebound—another nonnegotiable issue. Annabelle, in her senior year at Clarke College in Dubuque, was at home for Easter break when Danny took sick. She announced she absolutely would not return to classes until Danny was well and home again. Daniel and May did not argue with their eldest daughter. They had raised her to be a compassionate and strong-minded young woman and she was. Truthfully, all three girls were relieved to stay close to family, sheltered by their grandparents and huddled together as they fretted over their little brother's condition.

The National Foundation for Infantile Paralysis had issued a Bulletin, Publication No. 51, filled with speculative—and grossly inaccurate—theories on how the poliovirus was transmitted. The flyer found its way into Daniel's hands, and he and May began to agonize over their decision a year earlier to have Danny's tonsils removed. Had that somehow weakened him or increased his chances of infection? It wasn't as if the surgery had been an emergency—it could easily have been put off for a year or two. Then Daniel, after days of anguish, confessed to May his suspicion that he was responsible. Hadn't he recently returned from a trip to Canada on railroad business, even bringing back souvenirs for Danny and the girls? Perhaps he had somehow unleashed this curse upon his innocent family.

May looked at her tortured husband, went to the nurses' desk in the hallway and asked that Dr. Burroughs be summoned to Danny's room.

There was no reason to think the operation in 1943 or Daniel's travels were the source of this disease, Dr. Burroughs assured them. Most likely, they would never know how Danny came to be infected. It was best to not focus on that and instead use one's energy to keep the family together and everyone working toward the day when Danny would return home, safe and sound. Daniel and May were visibly relieved.

Mrs. Quinn wasn't just the Murphys' housekeeper. She had been a member of the family since not long after the newlyweds, May and Daniel, moved into the house on Marion Street.

May and Daniel first met in the summer of 1920, when he was invited to Sunday dinner at the home of his C&NW supervisor, Thomas Powell. On the day Daniel became trainmaster of the Clinton terminal, Thomas confided to his wife Edwina that he believed Daniel Murphy would make a fine son-in-law. From the moment she and Daniel met at that Sunday dinner, his daughter May agreed. The wedding was planned for October 8, 1921. As the mother-of-the-bride declared, fall was the most beautiful season in the Mississippi river valley, without question.

Ever practical, Mr. Powell insisted on giving the young couple a wedding gift that they could really use: a house. May and her mother poured over the Sears, Roebuck and Co. *Honor Bilt Modern Homes* catalog, finally settling on the ten room colonial, *No. 2089, The Magnolia.* May thought the portico should be on the south side of the house so the sun would shine into their dining room and kitchen. Edwina agreed. She told Thomas that he needed to call his good friend at Sears, Roebuck and Co. in Chicago and obtain house plans that were the mirror image of those shown in the catalog. Thomas smiled and assured Edwina that Sears, Roebuck and Co. had already considered that possibility. Edwina and May simply needed to write the word REVERSED on the Modern Home Order Blank. *That simple?* Hadn't they just thought of everything, Edwina marveled.

The Magnolia cost $6,488—delivered—a princely sum in 1921, but quite affordable for Edwina and Thomas Powell. The rail business had served Mr. Powell as well as he had served it. After World War I, the nation's trains were returned to private ownership and the strategic planning he had done during the four-year conflict paid off rather well. Thomas had purchased parcels of land where he had reason to believe the railroads would eventually expand. His futurist thinking was rewarded when they were, indeed, needed for stations, rights-of-way and freight terminals. Anyway, as Mrs. Powell needed to say only once while she and Mr. Powell discussed the price of *The Magnolia*, she was not about to have her grandchildren raised in a hovel.

The Magnolia arrived in two C&NW freight cars. In the post-war depression, it was easy to find skilled workers to assemble the pre-cut lumber, guided by the seventy-five page instruction manual. Meanwhile, upon returning from their New York City honeymoon, May and Daniel moved in with the Powells. For months, the ladies used the family rail pass for furniture and home accessory buying trips to Chicago, turning a warehouse at the C&NW rail yard into a makeshift storage depot.

It all came together in June 1922, ten months after the wedding and one month before the birth of Annabelle. Marion Street, Number 1724, was ready for occupancy.

Edwina Powell was born and grew up in Rockaway, New Jersey. Her childhood was a life of privilege where shopping trips into New York City and summers at the shore were routine. She fell in love with Thomas Powell and when he followed the railroad to coal-mining country in 1875—even though convinced that she was heading for a rough and uncivilized frontier—she bravely accompanied him to Iowa. Her fears were unfounded, but she still eagerly looked forward to her semi-annual trips home to visit her sister, brother and many cousins remaining in New England.

Edwina had been mindful over the years to never let Thomas know how much she missed that life in Rockaway, but her heart skipped a beat when she first laid eyes on *The Magnolia* in the *Honor Bilt* catalog. She confided to May that *The Magnolia* was a dead ringer for her beloved family home back east. There is no question, Edwina pronounced, this was meant to be.

In the final days of construction, Daniel happened upon his mother-in-law supervising a carpenter as he installed a small brass plaque engraved *Rockaway House – 1922* at the top of the front door. Daniel gave May a questioning look. She smiled and mouthed that she would explain it later.

For Mrs. Powell, the construction of Rockaway House and all it encompassed were the culmination of a dream. She had been preparing for when May and her sister would marry and manage their own households since each had been born. The plan for May's new life was meticulously executed. Mrs. Powell left no detail to chance, from helping May select her trousseau, including a signature perfume (Mrs. Powell had a friend who had a friend who brought a bottle of the latest craze, *Chanel No. 5*, from Paris), to hiring a housekeeper.

Bridget Quinn, the youngest sister of Mrs. Powell's own beloved housekeeper, Maureen Brennan, had been recently widowed, just two years after emigrating from Ireland. Bridget needed a home, and, as Mrs. Powell coached her daughter, being so young and inexperienced, Bridget could be trained in May's style of home management and entertaining, a clear advantage. Yes, the young widow would make the ideal housekeeper for Daniel and May.

And that's how Mrs. Quinn became a member of the Murphy family.

As each of the children was born, she acted as nursemaid and nanny until May regained her strength. Mrs. Murphy told Mrs. Quinn that she was then free to hire any help she needed to keep the house running. Patricia, the daughter of a C&NW employee, came in the mornings to help Mrs. Quinn with the laundry, prepare for the day's meals and do some light cleaning. However, as far as raising the children went, Mrs. Murphy took full-time hands-on care of each one. No dissention on the matter from Mrs. Quinn or Mr. Murphy would be entertained.

In all things, Mrs. Murphy trusted Mrs. Quinn implicitly and valued her input on everything from menus to handling one of the girls when she was being difficult. Mrs. Quinn shared May's belief in discipline and respect in childrearing. She also firmly believed that Annabelle, Lauralee and Elizabeth were God's own angels as far as that goes.

But it was Daniel Jr. himself who resided in the deepest part of Mrs. Quinn's heart. From the moment Mrs. Murphy shared the news of her pregnancy to this very day, Mrs. Quinn believed it was her God-given mission to watch over little Danny. His safety and welfare were her calling.

When the doorbell rang, Mrs. Quinn looked first at her watch brooch, which she wore every waking moment and which now lay on her bedside table. It was two a.m.

No good ever comes knocking at two a.m.

She quickly slipped into her dressing gown, her hair still in its nighttime braid, slung over her left shoulder. She punched on the entryway ceiling light as she scurried down the stairs, then peeked through the narrow window at the side of the front door. As she had expected, as she had feared, there stood Dr. Burroughs, head hung, hand kneading his forehead. She took in a quick breath and opened the door.

"Dr. Burroughs. Sir, please come in." He took off his hat and stepped past Mrs. Quinn into the large reception hall. He was met with the acrid smell of carbolic acid, an odor he knew well. For a moment, Dr. Burroughs thought his nostrils had become permanently infused with the familiar hospital aroma. Then he remembered that he had just stepped into a home whose owners hoped to wash away the evil that threatened to take their young son.

"You'll need to wake Mr. Murphy." The doctor's voice was chillingly calm.

"But they're not here, Doctor. They've gone and moved in with Mrs. Murphy's people, the Powells, they have, when little Danny took sick." Across his face passed a look of confusion, then Dr. Burroughs remembered May's quickly executed relocation of the family. His eyes closed and he took a long and deep breath. Dr. Burroughs had known at the time that the move was pointless, but there was so much uncertainty—even among medical experts—about how polio was contracted, he hadn't been in a position to argue against May's fears.

"Of course. Well, then, I'll go there." Mrs. Quinn put a hand on Dr. Burroughs's arm, stopping his exit.

"If you don't mind, Doctor, I'll be goin' along as well. That's where I'm meant to be." Without waiting for his response, she hurried back up the stairs. No words need be spoken. Mrs. Quinn's older sister had buried an infant daughter many years before back in Ireland, and Mrs. Quinn was with her. Polio hadn't taken the baby but what did that matter? The cause was beside the point. Hearts were about to be broken. Dreams were about to be shattered. Someone would need to take charge. Mrs. Quinn and her sister Maureen would hold the families together. That's all there was to it.

Dr. Burroughs waited while Mrs. Quinn dressed. *Of course she needs to go along.* Having a moment to think clearly, it was inconceivable that May and the girls would face this without their Mrs. Quinn. He gave a heavy sigh and, as he had so many times before, rehearsed in his mind how to deliver news such as this.

Danny had been getting better, but this disease was so hopelessly unpredictable. Earlier the day before, Dr. Burroughs was the one who had told May to go home for the night because Danny continued to improve. After six days without leaving his side, the rest of the family needed to lay eyes upon her, he had said. May had taken the doctor's counsel and arranged for a private nurse to remain in Danny's room. She left the hospital at seven o'clock that evening, just in time to have dinner with Daniel, her daughters and her parents.

Dr. Burroughs had been roused from his own bed at midnight.

He suspected Danny had contracted pneumonia, not uncommon with such suppressed respiration. Or maybe his young heart couldn't tolerate all it had been through. With his weakened immune system, the end came swiftly. Too many questions. When he faced Daniel and May, there would be more. He wished to God he had answers, but he didn't. And he hoped May could somehow forgive him for sending her home that evening, for being absent when her son died.

Mrs. Quinn returned to the entryway, coat on and key in hand. They were leaving, her following to lock the door, when she spoke, "Please tell me, Dr. Burroughs, did he, did Danny suffer?" She broke down as she said this, reaching in her pocket for one of the hankies she knew would be needed at some time, by someone.

"No, Mrs. Quinn, Danny was gone to God in an instant. I swear to you."

"Thank you, Doctor. It's important you tell them that." They headed out together to perform this most abhorrent of duties.

Daniel and May hosted the wake at the Powell home the evening before Danny's service. They graciously greeted and thanked all who had come to pay respects to their son, who was laid in a small open casket in the Powells' front parlor. There was a toy locomotive in his hand. Surrounded by a mountain of flowers, the air was so heavily perfumed it fairly threatened to choke the mourners. Annabelle, Lauralee and Elizabeth stood by, never leaving their parents' side, never uttering a word.

The next day, the C&NW offices where Daniel Sr. worked and Danny had visited were closed and the railroad provided a special interurban train to bring the workers who lived in Clinton. A cold luncheon was served at the Powells' after the funeral at St. Malachy's, said to be one of the largest in the history of the Foresters' family business. And on April 19, 1944, Daniel James

Murphy Jr. was buried in the Irish section of the Chesterton Catholic Cemetery.

Two days later, May sat down across from her husband in the Powells' dining room. Daniel had not been to the office since Danny's death. The paper was open, in front of his face, but he wasn't reading it.

"Daniel, I'd like you to speak to Father about relocating to Chicago. I—we can't stay in Chesterton any longer." He looked at his wife's mournful eyes, now always filled with tears about to spill over.

"You're right, May. I will," Daniel said.

The discussion was over. The Murphys never returned to 1724 Marion Street.

Daniel took a post in the railroad's Galena Division with offices in Chicago. In the following years, Mrs. Powell travelled often by train from Clinton, first to help May get the family settled in the new house, then to visit and, finally, to live with them after Mr. Powell passed away.

Soon after Daniel and May took their daughters and Mrs. Quinn and left Chesterton, 1724 Marion Street was sold to the Harris family. The middle Harris boy was a classmate of Danny's, the oldest daughter sat next to Elizabeth in school. Coming from their own sizeable home, the Harris family brought two truckloads of furnishings. They had no need for any of the used furniture in the attic above the garage.

The youngest Harris boy once asked his mother about the furniture and stacks of crates, and Mrs. Harris answered that it was a very very sad story and she'd tell him one day. She'd meant to sort it all out eventually, perhaps she'd donate everything to a charity. But the opportunity just never presented itself.

In 1982, Mrs. Harris passed away at age seventy-three. Mr. Harris was able to stay in their home until just a year before his death in 2004. His children, now scattered across the country, listed the house for sale right after their father's funeral. They took any furnishings that held sentimental value for them and told the real estate agent to sell everything else with the house.

Three days later, Mrs. Sullivan was driving down Marion Street on the way to her doctor's office and spotted the For Sale sign.

Lois

It is unbelievably peaceful here. Carlene leaned back in the armchair and took a deep breath. She was alone in the sun-filled solarium. There'd been a young attorney pecking away at his laptop when she came in, but after exchanging a few niceties, he left. *Pretty cute, actually, in a dweeby sort of way.*

Lois was so weak by the time they'd gotten her settled at Rockaway House the day before, she had barely acknowledged their leaving. Carlene was awake into the night worrying about her mother, her father and herself. Finally, after two hours of tossing and turning, she sat up in bed and began reading her mother's journals. It was a bittersweet chronicle of Lois's—and Carlene's—life and sheer emotional exhaustion put her to sleep not long after that.

Looking back, this morning had turned out so very differently than Carlene had feared. What were she and her mother talking about just the other day? Carlene had forgotten what she'd learned at that seminar years ago until Lois asked her about it. *The power of positive thinking.* Maybe she should be a little more intentional about her thoughts going forward, Carlene said to herself. It was times such as these that Carlene would give anything to have some effective coping mechanisms at hand.

She reached into her tote bag and pulled out a candle warmer, a crystal pendulum, scented oils, an eye mask, a bundle of sage, a small boom box with CD player and a couple of CDs. She set them all on the coffee table in front of her. She was still amazed that she'd thought to gather these items as she hurriedly packed last Saturday night and that she'd gotten past the TSA employees at the airport without triggering a full body cavity search. *Was that only five days ago?* It seemed much longer and it seemed like yesterday.

When she first learned of her mother's terminal diagnosis, Carlene hung up from her father's call feeling as if her head was wrapped in cotton. She couldn't put two thoughts together and almost forgot to phone Rainbow and tell her of the urgent trip to Iowa. Looking back, her intuition must have kicked in because when Rainbow asked when Carlene thought she would return, Carlene had answered that she had no idea really. It could be a while.

Carlene absently picked up that morning's edition of *The Bee* from the coffee table in the solarium. Seeing the masthead reminded her of childhood visits to her father's office, usually on a Saturday when he needed to work in quiet. And that one time that wasn't a Saturday. It was a Tuesday. Tuesday, January 28, 1986, to be exact.

Like millions of children across America, fifth-grader Carlene Spaulding gathered with classmates to watch coverage of the ten thirty-eight a.m. CST launch of the space shuttle *Challenger,* carried live from NASA on a special public school satellite broadcast. The selection of high school teacher Christa McAuliffe as one of the seven *Challenger* crewmembers had turned the event into a nationwide history and science class project. Students followed the progress of her selection and training and then looked forward to the live science experiments the teacher-astronaut was going to conduct from space.

Seventy-three seconds into the flight, as a nation of children watched, the fuel tank exploded, sending the shuttle and its crew crashing into the ocean. Carlene could remember exactly how she felt, who was sitting on either side of her in that class of eleven-year-olds, and how the teacher fought to remain composed as she explained what had just happened, hoping those little minds wouldn't be scarred for life.

At six o'clock that day, Ray was still at the office, working on a special edition of *The Bee*. Carlene was on the floor of their living room, on her stomach watching CNN when Lois walked in. Your father just called, her mother said. She said he had asked her to bring Carlene to *The Bee*. He wanted Carlene to witness first-hand media coverage of what would be one of the most important news events of her childhood. It was midnight when Ray and Carlene got home. Lois was waiting up and Carlene remembered that she fixed scrambled eggs and bacon for them while Ray and Carlene related every detail of what they had done together.

From that day forward, Ray said that in all his years at *The Bee*, the editorial accomplishment he most prized was that special edition. Since 1877, *The Bee* had been a small-town local newspaper focused on small-town local news. The front page of the January 29, 1986 *Bee* was filled with the very best work of Ray's reporters: the unique impact of a national tragedy on the citizens of a small town, especially the children.

Carlene smiled as it all came back to her. Her father had been right; it was one of the most important news events of her young life. She wondered if he realized that for her it was also one of the most meaningful moments in their tenuous relationship. The memory of how horrified she was by the disaster, immediately followed by the elation and pride of watching her dad in action and working by his side had never been far from her mind.

She scanned the pages of *The Bee* as she waited to return to her mother's room. Knowing so few of the main characters in Chesterton's current day-to-day dramas diluted much of the interest for Carlene, but thank goodness some things never seemed to change: the comics page. She began to work *The Jumble* and was done in four minutes—a personal best. That gave her a bit of a boost and she opened her laptop and checked her company website. Sorting and responding to Internet orders, she forwarded them to Rainbow for fulfillment, then, just for fun, she did a little Google research on the lady she'd met on her way to the solarium, Lillian, alleged would-be child protégé.

It was true, it was all true. Lillian Sherman, now Lillian Dexter, had performed with the Chicago Symphony in 1927 at age nine. Her father had, indeed, been the luthier, working closely with Frederick Stock, the iconic music director of the Symphony from 1904 to 1942. Isaac Stern debuted with the Chicago Symphony in 1940, and, sure enough, Isaac Stern had recorded "*You Is My Woman Now*" in 1990.

"Well, I'll be damned."

"What's that, honey?" Ray walked into the solarium, picking up the paper.

"Oh, nothing, just—nothing."

"Your mom's still napping. You do *The Jumble*?" he asked as he scanned *The Bee*, open to the completed puzzle. "Me too." He took a chair kitty-cornered from Carlene. "I do it in ink—first time." Ray was sporting a smug look on his face when Carlene glanced up.

"You do *The Jumble* first time in ink? Really?"

"Oh yeah. Here's how: I do all my practice words on a scratch pad, then, once I've figured out the jumbles and answered the puzzle, I memorize them all. While your mother and I read the paper together, I fill it in, in ink, just like that! Your mother thinks I do it all in my head, lickety-split. She thinks I'm a genius." He couldn't have looked more self-satisfied and maybe even a little naughty.

Carlene was stumped. "Why would you do that, Dad?"

"Because it's sort of fun to have secrets that no one else knows, even the person who loves you most in the world, the person who knows every single other thing about you."

"I gotta be honest, Dad, that's twisted." Carlene couldn't conceal her smile as she spoke, taking the newspaper from him. "Seeing *The Bee* reminded me of the day of the *Challenger* disaster. Remember, I got to come to the paper?"

"Do I remember? I certainly do. I was so proud of you, you pasted up the front page for me. You couldn't have been more serious about it all." He glanced out the windows, thinking of that little girl on that day in 1986.

"Thanks, Dad. I was pretty proud of you, too."

"You were? Well thank you. Say, speaking of the paper, may I ask you something? I've already talked to your mother and she's fine with it."

"Sure. What is it?"

"I'm writing a guest essay for the paper. Mind you, I don't know if they'll even print it, but I was thinking of writing about what we're going through right now." He paused to gauge Carlene's first reaction.

"Go on."

"Well, honey, it occurred to me awhile back that I hadn't considered any of the issues your mother's facing or what we've faced together until now, until it happened to us. Maybe it would be of some value to other people to know what to expect. I'd like the opportunity to talk about your mother's decision and the courage it took to make it. Whataya think?"

"If you're asking me if I have any objection, I certainly don't. I'm just amazed that you're willing to share this all, but if you are, I think it'll be great, Dad, something really special. You're a very talented writer and it'd be inspiring for anyone who reads it."

"Anyway, we'll see if the young buck editor will even agree to run it . . . "

Carlene was looking down, studying the crystal pendulum in her lap. "Remember those little houses that you got to go with my train set?"

"Plasticville? Yes, but what in the world made you think of them?"

"That's how I always think of Chesterton. Little houses with little people and little cars and cats and dogs. No real problems. Like a model train layout or a still life painting."

"Your thinking's a tad bit simplistic, Carlene. It's not as idyllic as it may seem. I happen to know that one of the owners of the bookstore—the one your mother used to take you to—has terminal brain cancer. A coffee buddy of mine has a neighbor who just lost his teenage son to leukemia. Then, of course, there's *our* family, honey. Look around, Carlene. This is a vital community in every sense of the word. I don't know what's going on out in California—although I suspect it's the same there as here—but here life is far from still. It's going on, all right, everywhere you turn. Maybe you need to stop and really look around."

Carlene shifted uncomfortably in her seat. Her dad was still the champ at making a point, subtly but effectively leaving the rebuked to stew in his—or her—own juices. *When did I get so narrow minded and so incredibly insensitive, anyway? And thanks for the little smack down, Dad.*

Never one to gloat, Ray noticed Carlene's paraphernalia spread out on the table and quickly moved on to the next subject. "Hey, what's all this?"

"Tricks of my trade. I'm going to try some therapies with Mom. I think it might make her feel a little better. It can't hurt."

"Are we sure about that?"

"Very funny, Dad. Why don't you let me try some woo-woo stuff on you?" She raised an eyebrow mischievously. He looked away and cleared his throat.

"I don't know what your mother told you, honey, but I didn't mean any disrespect—"

"Don't worry about it, Dad. I'm used to scoffers. You'll be a believer before I'm done, just wait and see." She started to pack up her things. "Let's go see what Mom's up to."

"I'll meet you there in a minute."

Margaret put the vase of daisies on Lois's table. They'd been delivered first thing that morning. The card read, *Thinking of you, dear Lois,* signed *Your Merklin Way friends.* She looked over just as Lois opened her eyes, noticed the flowers and smiled.

"Oh, how lovely. We've always had daisies in our yard. Who sent those?" Margaret read the card to her. "We have the nicest neighbors. It's been a wonderful neighborhood for us to live in and to raise Carlene in. They've been so good to us since I got sick. Most of them, anyway." Lois stopped, considering whether to share her thoughts. Then again, in the past couple of weeks, Lois had adopted a new approach to situations that may or may not call for restraint. Case in point, she could only think of one reason that justified speaking her mind at that moment: because she wanted to.

"Real friends don't change, but circumstances definitely change," she elaborated. "Trust me, Margaret—the so-called friend who doesn't want to hear about the little problems in your life doesn't want to witness your dying either. Then, sometimes someone really surprises you. Someone who seems like a flake or a fly-by-night is the one who weeds your garden or leaves a week's worth of meals in your freezer." She paused to rest for a moment. Margaret agreed, her experience six months earlier had been about the same. Lois went on.

"Yup, there are cactus friends and then there are African violet friends."

"Explain that one, Lois."

"African violet friendships are high maintenance. If you don't baby 'em and tend 'em and pay constant attention to 'em, they probably won't survive. Even if you do, they probably won't survive. But for sure, those friends won't be tending to you. On the other hand, cactus friends and friendships thrive without being watered or watched and whenever you need or want them, they come running. Of course, the goal is to be a true cactus friend, too."

"So, have you found more cactus or African violets in your life recently?"

"Oh, the African violets are long gone. My energy was at a premium the past two years. I didn't have any to spare on them."

Carlene walked in and stood by her mother's bed, listening.

"Are you married, Margaret?" Lois asked.

"I was. I was widowed earlier this year." The words still had an odd sound to Margaret's ears.

Lois frowned and her brow wrinkled. "I'm so sorry. May I ask, do you miss your husband?"

"Oh yes, all the time. He was a good husband and my best friend."

Lois thought for a moment before she spoke. "I think it must be easier to be the one dying than the ones left behind. I feel bad that I'm leaving Ray alone after all these years—and you, too, honey." She smiled and nodded at Carlene. "Margaret, do you know that my dear husband does *The Jumble* in ink every day, and he thinks I don't know that he works it all out on paper before he writes his answers in *The Bee*?" She smiled at Margaret and Carlene. "Relationships are funny, aren't they?"

Carlene looked at her mother and chuckled. "Yeah, Mom, they're a riot."

Lois didn't believe she would care for any lunch. She just wasn't hungry, but she'd be glad to have the company and sit by while Ray and Carlene ate theirs. Carlene ran to the local diner and got hot meatball sandwiches and waffle fries. She and Ray sat at the table in front of the window, Lois watching them from the bed, leaning back with her head resting on the pillow.

Just the three of them. There wouldn't be any other visitors. Dear friends and close family had said their goodbyes at the dinner party ten days earlier. Between them, they all agreed they'd leave Lois, Ray and Carlene to have this time alone. Donations with little handwritten notes continued to be left at Alma's, who made a delivery whenever she saw Ray or Carlene come home for a break. Fully-cooked meals, home-baked cookies, a pie, a six-pack of pop, a vase of yard posies. Simple offerings were simple reminders that Lois and Ray—and now little Carlene—were in the thoughts and prayers of others.

"So how was your nap, Mom?" Carlene asked as she ate.

"Did I take a nap? I was just thinking I could use one."

She's losing it, Carlene thought. "I've got an idea, Mom. When we get done here, let's try some guided meditation. It'll relax you and you'll drift right off." A low-key groan came from Ray's direction. "Sorry, Dad? Did you say something?"

"No, nothing. I think I'll just run back to the house and check the mail."

"Why don't you stick around, Dad? It'll relax you, too. I'm sure you could use a little nap."

"I'm perfectly relaxed and I don't nap. I'm just not a napper—never have been." He went to dispose of the remains of lunch while Carlene prepared the room. She closed the blinds, turned on the electric candle warmer and popped a CD in the player, choosing one of her favorite guided meditations.

Ray returned and Carlene installed him in the recliner. The nurse said Lois would breathe a bit easier if she was propped up, so Carlene made sure Lois had an extra pillow behind her and then she put a light afghan over her father. With the *Do Not Disturb* sign on the door and her chair near the foot of the bed so she could see both her parents, Carlene sat down and hit the play button.

Tranquil sitar music began, followed by a mellow voice.

"*Welcome to the InagaddadaVedic Institute . . . My name is Sanji . . . Relax . . . Close your eyes . . . Join me for a guided meditation . . . A time to let your thoughts drift away as you wander to your quiet place . . . A time to refresh your mind and body . . . Now, imagine a tranquil forest . . .* "

It had been an intense twenty-four hours for all three of them. Now, given the opportunity to wind down, Sanji's familiar voice immediately triggered Carlene's relaxation response. Her head nodded and she was about to drift off when she detected a strange sound in the background. Was her CD player on the fritz? Was someone mowing the lawn at Rockaway House?

She opened her eyes ever so slightly and looked over at her mother. Lois also had one eye open. They both looked over at Ray. His head had fallen to the side, his mouth open—like a walleye on the dock, Lois was thinking—and he was snoring to beat the band. Carlene and Lois looked at each other and burst out laughing. Ray didn't stir.

Carlene spoke first. "You know, Mom, he does seem relaxed. I mean, for a guy who's not a napper."

Rockaway House

Now Lynda Wyatt understood why they shot the messenger in olden days. In a way, it had been a much more pleasant state of affairs before the mystery of the Murphys was fully solved. For Margaret and Suzi, until they met the Murphys and knew their whole story, the unknown had been titillating—maybe a little infuriating—but definitely exciting every time they hit the top of the garage attic stairs. For Lynda, that pit-of-the-stomach feeling had come whenever she tried to guess Margaret's big secret.

To finally know the story of what had led May Murphy to order all their worldly belongings yanked from the house—the home that she and Daniel had lovingly built, furnished and filled with family—was heart wrenching. It was vivid proof of the old saying, "Careful what you ask for . . ."

Yes, there was a lot to be said for ignorance.

Margaret was thinking maybe they should have just accepted the furniture as an unexpected blessing and not been so insistent about knowing why it was there. She was recalling a few occasions in the past when Ernie had turned to her and said, "Maggie, dear, did it ever occur to you that it's none of your beeswax?" So infuriating at the time, but—as was often the case with Ernie—he'd had a point.

They should have known better than to rock an empty rocking chair.

Reeling from what they had just learned, Suzi and Margaret went directly from *The Bee* to the Rockaway House garage. Bruce's trademark whistling drifted down as they walked up the stairs, neither one speaking.

At the landing, they found him unboxing Murphy family photos onto one of the six-foot worktables he'd installed. Frames of silver, wood and plaster. Small ones, snatched from a bureau or bookshelf; large ones, rescued from a piano top or mantle; and oversized ones, plucked hastily from a wall. They were the faces of Daniel, May, Annabelle, Lauralee, Elizabeth, Danny and, of course, Mrs. Quinn. These photos were taken on good days, days suitable for memorializing, days suitable for framing.

Uncomfortable with the stiff and proper portraits typical of that era, as the children grew up in the 1920s and 1930s, their mother became enamored with the new concept of informal photos. May Murphy sought out an innovative young photographer in nearby Clinton, Max Herman, and offered up her family as models for his experimental work. Max caught them playing croquet in the yard, having a game of Parcheesi at the dining room table or sharing a Thanksgiving feast. He was a bachelor whose family was in Ohio, and Max was glad to trade his talents for a seat at the Murphys' sumptuous dinner tables. Group shots always included Mrs. Quinn unless she refused to be pulled away from her domestic duty.

Those photographs further explained the census forms. In the Murphy household, Mrs. Bridget Quinn wasn't a relative exactly, but she *certainly* wasn't a servant.

Margaret, Suzi and Lynda had exhumed the stories that went with the names. Now Bruce was uncovering the faces that went with the stories and names. The Murphys were all but living back at Rockaway House.

Bruce was now practically living there himself as he spent long hours furiously cataloging each item, photographing it, putting a numbered tag on it and entering it in the database on his laptop computer. Lance had recruited a couple of CMC employees the day before, and they'd moved a few of the larger pieces down into the garage. That created a staging space upstairs for taking pictures. That was his strategy: Bruce would call Lance when a load of pieces had been cataloged. In that way, everything would be inventoried before it left the attic. Once it was all transferred to the garages below, Bruce would turn the catalog over to the commercial printer, who would create the online and paper versions.

This routine was nothing new for Bruce. Antique sales were a major part of his business. Sometimes it was due to death, but often age or disability forced a downsizing move for someone. For decades, Bruce had organized their belongings, sorting all their worldly goods into *trash*, *donate* and *sell* piles. He conducted the estate sales and auctions, often feeling uneasy, sometimes even guilty, watching as strangers pawed through the personal possessions of someone who was no longer in a position to protest.

Isn't there *someone* who cares to have these family pictures, Bruce would often think. It was sad. Like everyone else, a part of him wondered if the things he most treasured would end up like that someday, in the hands of strangers.

The Murphy Family Endowment, as he and Suzi had nicknamed the attic's contents, touched a place in Bruce even more intimate than those situations had. For the past two days, Bruce had been the designated intruder in the Murphys' lives. This was the story of a family paused in mid-reel, a half-written novel, an unfinished symphony. He'd found Daniel and May's love letters, the children's school papers, valentines, records of family finances, even Christmas decorations. These were the most personal of items, things he knew people in their right minds would never have intentionally left behind. But clearly they had not been in their right minds, had they? He'd concentrated very hard to not think about what had driven them mad and then driven them out of Rockaway House.

Suzi interrupted Bruce and gently asked him to stop what he was doing because she and Margaret needed to tell him what they had just learned. He bit his lip and briefly debated whether to ignore her. Knowing she wouldn't go away, his shoulders dropped as he sat down and listened. He had guessed it would be bad, but he had underestimated how bad. He reacted just as they had. It was hard to make sense of it.

Margaret, Suzi and Bruce were each lost in thought, each pondering some variation of the same question. By their sacrifice, the Murphys had unknowingly paid forward for the benefit of those who today walked in the halls and died in the bedrooms of Rockaway House. The two-story stucco monument was the legacy of three adults who had tried to live hard-working, virtuous, God-fearing lives. Their willingness to do anything—everything, really—to safeguard the children they were entrusted with had rendered them the unintended benefactors of the dying in another, entirely different millennium.

Margaret stepped toward the landing and said she needed to get next door and make some cookies; she really wanted to make some cookies. She'd see Bruce and Suzi again soon enough. The three of them were meeting with Rose, Lauren and Lance that afternoon to walk through Rockaway House, surveying the work to be done and making a wish list of all the new furnishings to be acquired.

Little Danny Murphy. Now there's a heartbreaker, Margaret thought. *If I dwell on what led to this day, I'll be back in bed, rolled up in a ball.* Right then and there she made a commitment: *the spirits of this family, the Murphys and Mrs. Quinn, are much more likely to rest at peace if this place becomes a lasting tribute to all they sacrificed.* As for her, that objective would feed Margaret's own spirit and keep her on track to maintain the forward momentum she'd finally achieved. *A goal. A plan.*

Bruce carefully and gently placed each of the family portraits back into the crate, put the lid on it and attached the identifying tag as Suzi and Margaret watched in silence.

He looked up and smiled. "Where do we want to store the things that aren't going into *The Auction*?"

Isobel

Isobel loved to read. When she was little, it was how she escaped the bedlam of a home with seven siblings. As a young adult, it became her flight of fancy from her wayward husband and the exhaustion of life as a single mother. In retirement, she spent the better part of her time reading. She had belonged to two book clubs at The Sunshine Retirement Village. Years before, Isobel had organized the lending library for the residents and then finally got the chance to become its most frequent patron when she quit working. She devoured fiction, nonfiction, biography and memoir—anything but romance.

Isobel's love of reading was second only to her love of music. Country, classical, American songbook, folk and definitely rock. Anything with a beat, really, and preferably with lyrics. Margaret had noticed that Isobel's clock radio was always turned on. Today it was a big band hit that Margaret heard as she entered Isobel's room.

Three or four pillows supported Isobel, the writing desk was on her lap, and *Bartlett's Familiar Quotations* was nearby. "I sure am glad you showed me this book, Margaret. It's got some good stuff in it. Listen to this: '*Anyone who believes you can't change history has never tried to write his memoirs.*' Ain't that the truth?"

Margaret was carrying a huge arrangement of roses and carnations as she walked in. "That is a good one, Isobel. Look what I have for you," she said, pulling the card and handing it to Isobel.

"Can you read it to me, please?" Isobel handed it back.

"Sure. '*Love you, Mom. See you soon.*' It's signed '*Rhonda*'. Aren't they lovely?" Margaret put the vase on the dresser.

"Jeanne would call that the FTD Guilt Bouquet. Of course, they're lovely, but I'd rather see Rhonda herself. Okay, how about this one?" With great effort, Isobel lifted the heavy book again, turned to a page she had marked with a scrap of paper and read aloud, "*What you leave behind is not what is engraved in stone monuments, but what is woven into the lives of others.*" She waited for Margaret's reaction.

"Another good one."

"I was thinking I might put one or two quotations in my obituary. What do you think?"

"That sounds like a wonderful idea. Have you chosen one yet?"

"I really like this other one, but it's pretty long. It'll probably cost an arm and leg to print in the paper, but I really like it and—what the heck—it's only money. It's from Ralph Waldo Emerson." Her voice began to tremble as she spoke the words, "'*To laugh often and much; to win the respect of intelligent people and the affection of children; to earn the appreciation of honest critics and to endure the betrayal of false friends. To appreciate beauty; to find the best in others; to leave the world a bit better whether by a healthy child, a garden patch, or a redeemed social condition; to know that even one life has breathed easier because you have lived. This is to have succeeded.'"* Isobel laid the book down, a satisfied smile on her face. Margaret sat by the bed and put her hand on Isobel's as she composed herself. "It's okay, Margaret. I know."

"Those are wonderful words." Margaret stammered a bit as she spoke. "You know, my neighbor boy's been showing me how to use my new computer and I was looking up some things about hospice care and I just learned what that is—those words from Emerson—it's his Ethical Will. It's a statement of what he believed in. You could use it for your Ethical Will, too."

Isobel really liked the idea of doing something most people had never heard of before, of being innovative and sort of shocking folks, but in a good way. "I've never seen something like that in an obituary. I am going to use it. Can I ask you to please type it up for me, Margaret? I'm sorry, I just don't have the energy to write it out." Margaret could already see that. This was Wednesday. Isobel looked like she'd lost weight since Monday and Margaret had even overhead little Lucy call her *The Incredible Shrinking Grandma.*

"I'd be honored to do that for you. Do you want me to type up this obituary and add that quotation at the end?"

"That'd be great. Then Jeanne can just hand it to Mr. Forester when the time comes," Isobel said matter-of-factly. Margaret reached into the bedside table, the familiar depository for the obit-du-jour.

"So, is this the final version—for today, I mean?" Margaret kidded Isobel.

"No, that's it. I'm done." Her meaning was clear.

Margaret took a seat as she read it over.

Isobel Ruby Baines
1931 – 2012 (assuming I finally die this year)
~~Isobel Baines leaped into the arms of Jesus today at ____ a.m./p.m. And was she ever ready to go!~~ Isobel Baines, born March 31, 1931, passed away at Rockaway House on ________. Isobel is survived by her daughters Rhonda Baines of West Palm Beach, Florida and Jeanne Evans (husband Chuck) and grandchildren Isobel and Lucy Evans, the lights of her life.
~~Isobel was divorced by that low-down dirty dog husband of hers, Stanley Baines, in 1975~~. She ~~raised her daughters on her own, doing the best she could, working~~ worked as the activity director for the Sunshine Retirement Village here in Chesterton ~~until she couldn't take it anymore (because of her health, not the people there, who were really lovely folks).~~
Her favorite pastime was being with her family, especially her grandchildren. ~~and going to the racetrack once in a while. She never bet more than she could afford to lose and she usually won!~~

Isobel was cremated and she asked that her friends and family gather to remember the good times and to scatter her ashes over the lake at Redwood Park, where she spent many happy hours, picnicking with her daughters when they were little.
And she wants to thank all the wonderful people at Chesterton Hospice who came to be friends and family. ~~when it took her so long to die. Instead of wasting good money on flowers,~~ Isobel would prefer that any memorials be made to ~~Rockaway House or the Chesterton Animal Shelter.~~ The Isobel Baines Charitable Trust for Women, Animals, Geezers and Crones.
[add my Ethical Will here]

There was no stopping it—Margaret's face broke into a huge smile as she reached the end. "What's this, Isobel? Tell me about this charitable trust for geezers."

Isobel shared her idea for the organization that her daughter Jeanne would be managing. She told Margaret how she began working right out of high school to help support her oversized family, then later on she met and married Stanley. It was a tough go for Isobel as a single mother, even with the child support Mr. Lane got for her.

She'd always wanted to go to college and become a social worker or learn how to run a retirement home like Sunshine Retirement Village. That never happened. She didn't have the time, money or energy to do more than just work every day, every week and every year to keep a roof over their heads. Isobel had never remarried. That was okay by her—she always said that marriage to Stanley had been enough fun with a man for one lifetime.

Isobel's eyes glistened as she talked about Copper, the family cat she so loved when she was growing up, and then the puppy the girls had found on their way home from school. Ellie became part of the family. To this day, Isobel couldn't go into a pet store or shelter for fear she'd bring home every pitiful stray behind bars. Now she'd be helping the pets and her trust would help people who wanted to adopt an animal but maybe needed some financial help to do that.

Then Isobel talked about how sad it had been whenever a resident ran out of money at the Sunshine Retirement Village. They still got good care, the people in charge made sure of that, but they didn't get the little extra things that people with families get. So now her trust would help those folks. Isobel's estate would provide the money to get it all started, then Jeanne would raise lots more, so that even more women, animals and old folks could be helped, she explained to Margaret.

Isobel was exhausted by the time she reached the end of her tale, but in spite of her frail condition, she made it all seem so real that when she finished, Margaret's enthusiasm for the vision matched Isobel's. What a dream come true, to do so much good, even when you're gone, Margaret thought. "Isobel, I hardly know what to say. It sounds wonderful. Your gift would certainly make a difference in a lot of lives."

Isobel smiled at Margaret's words. "You don't think it sounds conceited for me to name it after myself, do you? I just thought it would be nice for people to think of me, and it would be something for Rhonda and Jeanne and the little ones to be proud of."

"Certainly not conceited. I think it's the perfect name." Why not, Margaret thought. *Why not?*

This final version of Isobel's obituary—including the postscript of her Ethical Will—was the last detail she needed to nail down. She handed the papers to Margaret and sunk into the bedding as if she might disappear from sight altogether.

"If you don't mind, Margaret, could you please read this morning's *Bee* aloud to me?" In the past few days, Isobel had lost the strength to hold the newspaper up and read it herself. Besides, although she hadn't voiced it, she now preferred to have someone close by whenever she was awake. That the someone was Margaret, a person Isobel knew and liked, was a bonus. And whenever Isobel referred to the newspaper, she really meant the obituary page. Keeping up with the latest trends in memorials had preoccupied Isobel's time for many months and now, with the discovery of Ethical Wills and the plan to include her own, she wanted to make sure no one was beating her to the punch.

Margaret put the lap desk, paperwork and heavy Bartlett's aside and opened *The Chesterton Bee*. There was the familiar Forester Funeral Home display ad. Yes, it was the only funeral home in town, and yes, the daily obituaries were also placed by Forester's. Indeed, a few years back when *The Bee* began charging for obituaries—it had been quite the scandal in Chesterton—Harold Forester had debated whether to keep the advertising going as well. But his father and grandfather had posted a daily ad for seventy-five years before Harold ever joined the family business, and he wasn't about to kick that beehive, no pun intended. Anyway, as he told a friend recently, so many people were opting to cremate and forego funerals for "celebrations of life," there was no telling when he would be aced out by the local *Odd Fellows Lodge* or the back room of the *Tic Toc Lounge and Restaurant* downtown. Forester's needed to keep its face in the game.

Margaret scanned the paper. "Let's see what we have." Then it hit her like a slap in the face: the obituary she'd agreed to type for Isobel would be on this very page, someday soon. She glanced over at Isobel, who gave her a slight smile. *She can't possibly know what I'm thinking, can she?* Margaret shooed away the thought, stopping just short of waving her hand in front of her face and then smiled back at Isobel.

She turned to *The Bee* and began reading the salient facts of life for "*Sara Smith 1932 – 2012.*"

Margaret

Margaret hadn't had one single minute to think about the Murphys since this morning. It wasn't a subject one could sort out while doing something even as mindless as baking cookies and certainly not while hearing Isobel's life story. One family history at a time, if you don't mind. No, the unfolding Murphy saga required quiet, soul-searching alone time. When noon came, Margaret made her move, grabbed her sack lunch and headed for the rear of the Rockaway House acre lot, deep within the trees scattered in the back half of the yard, far beyond the garage. Many years before, someone had made a bench of two tree stumps. Across them was a weathered board, once painted, now mottled but smooth. *Good old lead-based paint. Nothing like a half-life of five hundred years.*

She reached into her BROWN BAG (carrying it was now a daily homage to Ernie having done the same) and pulled out her sandwich. Looking up, Margaret could just barely see the house, so she knew no one could see her. Peace and quiet.

She wanted to sort it all out, to make some sense of the Murphys' actions.

When Danny Murphy died, all the things that made Rockaway House a home instead became symbols of what could never be again, the idyllic paradigm that imploded with Danny's last breath. No matter how fervently they hoped and prayed to find peace in their grief, to find solace by honoring and mourning Danny's death—if, indeed, they had dared ask for such mercy—it would never ever be the same as it would have been if he had lived. Their belongings were part of the life from which they needed to escape, as fast as the train would take them.

Margaret had thought—at least hoped—that she'd gain some life lessons or answers from her experience at Rockaway House. Instead, it seemed she had simply raised more big questions. She in no way wished to diminish the passing of Danny Murphy, but in measuring the depth of a loss, did it matter if the deceased was a six-year-old who asked no more of life than to have breakfast with his father or a ninety-four-year-old woman eager to join those who've gone on ahead? Did the measure of loss have anything to do with the person who was dying—not their intrinsic value, because she knew that wasn't her to measure—but something about their involvement with life? Otherwise, the Murphys' loss was no more tragic than that of any of the survivors Margaret had recently met at Rockaway House.

For those left to suffer, was May Murphy's grief deeper, more profound than the bereavement of Peggy, about to lose her beloved Aunt Lil? Or of Margaret, facing life without Ernie? Somehow it seemed folly to even attempt to compare or measure grief. Maybe even a little self-righteous.

Margaret was long on questions, short on answers.

She knew one thing for sure: the most important elements of the Murphy family's history were not bits and pieces of fabric and wood and metal. It was their love, loyalty and heartbreak, the unique passions that charted the course of their lives in good times and in bad.

And yet, it *was* their material possessions that would make them memorable in the hearts and minds of so many others. Their worldly goods were poised to create the Murphys' contemporary legacy, a legacy that would not otherwise exist. Somehow the sorrow attributed to those objects had morphed into a blessing for those standing in the place May Murphy had once stood, so very long ago.

Margaret gathered up her lunch scraps and rose, ready to go inside to tackle her afternoon duties. She had an answer now, of sorts.

There was only one way to sum up the irony of the furniture and art and talcum powder so intentionally cast away now appearing as a God-sent windfall for the current inhabitants of Rockaway House: *Who in the world knows?* The key was to quit trying to reconcile the irreconcilable. It was the same as what she had asked God for and was still seeking: *acceptance.*

Margaret tossed her apple core aside for the enjoyment of the squirrels and started back to Rockaway House.

Isobel

The Isobel Baines Charitable Trust for Women, Animals, Geezers and Crones? Cameron Lane Sr. got the biggest kick out of his son's call to pass on the greetings from Mrs. Baines and to relay the news of her most recent Will revision. I told you she was special, he said to his son with a hearty laugh.

On Wednesday, Cameron Lane II returned to Rockaway House with Isobel's absolute final Last Will and Testament in hand. It included provisions for the charitable trust, appointing her daughter Jeanne as the first trustee and executive director. Getting papers signed in Isobel's room had become a familiar event, so no explanation was needed when he asked two of the staff members to witness Isobel's signature—again. Cameron was the notary.

"Well, Mrs. Baines, that's all safely tucked away. Is there anything else I can do to be of service to you today?" Cameron put the papers down and sat on the chair next to Isobel's bed. He knew this might well be his last visit with the person who had come to be his favorite client.

"So, you like what you do, Cameron?"

"Yes, ma'am, I do. Oh, sometimes the paperwork gets a little frustrating—"

"—You mean like when clients ask you to keep redoing their Wills?"

Cameron laughed. "No ma'am, I most certainly did not mean that. I meant that sometimes the practice of law can be, well—"

"—Boring?"

Isobel had him again, although Cameron had to agree this time. "Well, yes, ma'am, 'boring.' But I like what I do, even the boring parts. Why do you ask?"

"Because it's very important for you to like your work. It's a third of your life, you know. I loved working at the Sunshine Retirement Village, I really did . . . So, if you didn't do what you do, what would you do?"

"Probably the same, but spend more of my time with clients like you, Mrs. Baines, helping people to plan how they want to be remembered." *The Isobel Baines Charitable Trust for Women, Animals, Geezers and Crones* had been a test of Cameron's faith. Down the road, he'd be better at stifling any doubts he had in the viability of others' dreams. When a person has high hopes and big plans, the best thing to do was to just get out of the way.

"You're very good at what you do, Cameron, and you're a good man like your father. Just promise me you'll always remember to love what you do. I think your father loved his work."

"He did, ma'am. He has said that many times."

"Good. You do the same and you can't go wrong. You know what they say, *'Do what you love and the money will follow'*." Cameron stood up at the side of Isobel's bed, his briefcase in hand.

"I want you to know how grateful I am to know you and to call you a friend, Mrs. Baines."

"Me too, Cameron. Just remember what I said. Love what you do."

"I will never forget that—or you—you can bet on that, ma'am." It wasn't customary when leaving a client, but the obvious thing for Cameron to do right then was to lean down and give Mrs. Baines a kiss on the cheek. Cameron smiled and left just in time. As he shut the door behind him, his tears spilled over.

Nancy was coming down the hall to check Isobel's vitals. She stopped in front of the door, facing Cameron but not speaking as she waited for him to unabashedly wipe his eyes with the handkerchief he retrieved from his inside pocket. He looked a little surprised at himself, not embarrassed, but definitely caught unawares.

"My dad told me to always make sure I have a hankie to offer to a lady. He forgot to mention it's also handy when visiting a client as exceptional as Mrs. Baines." He smiled at Nancy.

Nancy had been watching Cameron since he first visited Isobel at Rockaway House. She liked this kid. "It will hardly seem like Rockaway House when she's gone. Heck, you're practically a fixture here yourself, Cameron." She smiled and he moved aside as she went into the room.

It wouldn't be long now. Isobel was winding down. She had graciously refused her dinner the night before and the same with breakfast and lunch today. No appetite. Nancy checked the water pitcher on Isobel's bedside table. For the second day, no water was missing. The nurses' aides had noted in her chart that Isobel was refusing the offer of even an occasional sip. Nancy walked up to Isobel's bedside, taking her wrist to check her pulse while she spoke.

"How are you doing, Isobel?"

She looked at Nancy with peaceful resignation on her face. In her weakening voice, she said, "Things don't always turn out the way you think they will, Nancy." She paused to take a breath. "Usually better." Isobel slowly closed her eyes and was softly snoring in a few moments.

"You are so right, my friend." Nancy tidied the covers around Isobel, closed the window shades to the afternoon sun and quietly exited.

Over the previous forty-eight hours Isobel had become increasingly disoriented, fully bedridden, barely able to raise her head, still speaking, but with arduous effort. The day before, Jeanne was just able to rouse her mother, but she couldn't say for sure that Isobel recognized her once she awoke.

There had been a time, a time that Jeanne remembered well, when Isobel's terminal diagnosis was the bad news paralyzing their lives, the unforeseen change in plans, the quick turn in the road that until then had seemed so straight and normal. Gradually, they had each worked his or her way to the acceptance stage and were prepared for Isobel's imminent death. But then, when she took so unpredictably long to get to the end of her life—

stalled on a plateau of dying with no discernible changes—life in hospice care took on its own sense of normalcy. They all—including Isobel to some extent—conveniently forgot that she was dying. Now at the end of the long reprieve she'd been so mercifully granted, they found themselves back in denial and they needed to adjust anew. *Deja vu all over again.*

Later that day, Jeanne acknowledged what could no longer be denied. She should call Rhonda and say that if Rhonda wanted to see their mother again—alive—she'd better come now. Jeanne fought the urge to skip that call, to wait until it was too late, then phone Rhonda and tell her that it had all happened so fast at the end, there just hadn't been time to summon her. *Sorry, but Mom's gone.* It would minimize the bedside drama, and Jeanne would bet anything that, given the choice, Rhonda would jump at the chance to skip all the messy parts.

Jeanne held the phone in her hand, knowing what she needed to do and what her mother would want her to do but relishing even a few minutes of postponement. Finally, she took a deep breath, dialed Rhonda's number and girded her loins for an argument.

No argument. No argument of any kind. Rhonda wasn't coming. She told Jeanne she'd rather remember their mother as she was.

Anger and a sense of abandonment were Jeanne's first reactions, then relief washed over her. Jeanne had only been jesting when she had speculated that Rhonda would prefer to stay away. Turns out Rhonda had an option that Jeanne hadn't seriously considered. *Okay, did not see that one coming, but so be it.* Jeanne would face this just as her mother had taught her, just as Isobel had faced life's unexpected twists and turns. Jeanne would focus on her mother's needs, closing ranks with her husband and daughters at Isobel's bedside.

So be it.

When Jeanne returned from making the call to Rhonda, Isobel was lying flat in bed, her eyes closed. It still seemed odd for Jeanne to find her like that, the stunning opposite of her typical animated and lively self. Isobel's eyes opened but seemed unfocused as Jeanne closed the door behind her.

"Mom?" she spoke softly as she approached her mother's bed.

"Jeanne Beanie. Is Rhonda coming?" Jeanne stopped in her tracks.

"She'll be here, Mom. I'm just not sure when." That was the truth, sort of.

"Remember that angel wrapping paper I used every year to wrap your Christmas gift?"

"Yes."

"Remember? It was red and it had an angel's face on it—her face took up the whole side of the package. Why do you suppose I pulled that paper out of the trash every year, ironed it and then used it for your present the next year?"

"I'm—uh—I don't know, Mom."

"I wanted you to know every year that the angel face would be there to greet you on Christmas morning because it's important to have some things that are dependable and always there."

Jeanne would have to think about that one for a bit. She'd always thought it was because her mother was too cheap to throw away perfectly good wrapping paper, but Jeanne liked this new explanation, that her mother was being so conscientious about making sweet holiday memories. To Jeanne, it had always seemed that just surviving was the sole objective in that tiny house, the three of them. *You just never know.*

Nancy finished giving Isobel a gentle sponge bath, followed by Isobel's favorite lotion. This was another benefit of being at Rockaway House. The staff didn't have rigid schedules for bathing and eating and most everything else. At Rockaway House, the kitchen was always open and patients could eat when they were hungry and do anything else when the spirit moved them, including bathing. Isobel had been sound asleep when the nurses' aide stopped by earlier in the day. Once she woke, Isobel had sleepily smiled and nodded at the suggestion of a sponge bath. For the residential hospice patient at Rockaway House, so it is said, so shall it be done, if at all possible.

Making a quick check of Isobel's feet, Nancy saw they were taking on a blotchy purplish color; Isobel's circulation, already compromised by her heart condition, had greatly diminished. Death was close. Isobel drifted in and out while Nancy worked around her, never speaking but smiling once when she opened her eyes and saw Nancy turn up the volume on Isobel's beloved clock radio.

Noting Isobel's vitals on her tablet computer, Nancy was moisturizing Isobel's lips when Jeanne came in the door with Chuck and the girls following close behind.

Isobel's eyes opened before Jeanne even had a chance to speak. "I have something for you." Isobel slightly lifted her hand in the direction of the bedside stand. Jeanne reached in the drawer, pulling out a brown clasp envelope, stuffed full.

"What's all this, Mom?

"Something for each of you. Your names are on them. And, Jeanne, there's one for Mr. Forester. No one open them 'til I'm gone." Margaret popped her head in the door just as Nancy left.

"Anything you need?"

"No, thanks, Margaret," Jeanne answered.

"You're all in my prayers."

"Thank you, Margaret." Jeanne watched Margaret leave and realized that the people of CCH and Rockaway House and their compassionate care had become common elements of Isobel's life as well. *But that isn't right, this is a hospice, where you come to die. So, this is really it. After all these months, all of Mother's jokes about being a "near miss," all the visits and all the time we got to spend together, this is it. Mom's time has come. All that's left is prayers and hoping that her passing will be peaceful.*

"Jeanne, are you happy?" Isobel asked in a whisper.

Tears began to fill Jeanne's eyes. "I am, Mom. We all are."

"Because being happy is the most important thing in life, honey. More important than the money, more important than a fancy car or fancy clothes, you know . . . Of course, surprises are important, too."

"Surprises?" Jeanne focused on her mother's face, hanging on her every word.

"Just remember, Jeanne, don't always want everything to be predictable and the same, you know, open your heart to whatever God brings your way."

Growing up, religion hadn't really been a part of their little household. Jeanne didn't remember ever attending church as a child, not even on Christmas or Easter. *Where is this coming from?*

"I'm not sure I know what you mean, Mom."

"Just remember to be happy, Jeanne. You girls have made me so happy and proud. I hope you know that. And don't let Rhonda get to you." She closed her eyes and her breathing was suspended for what seemed to Jeanne and Chuck like many seconds. For a moment, Jeanne thought her mother might be gone, but then Isobel loudly gasped with a quick inhale of breath.

Little Isobel and Lucy were each wrapped around a leg, pinning Chuck in place at the end of the bed. In spite of the many talks when Jeanne and Chuck had answered every possible question about heaven, Grandma's role as their guardian angel and what it meant to be dead, much like their parents, neither one was quite sure what would happen next. Jeanne and Chuck had discussed many times the wisdom of having the girls present when their grandmother died if that became an option. How could you know for sure what was best?

Jeanne wondered if she and Chuck had done enough to prepare them. She turned her head to look at the girls and peered closer, studying their faces. Young Isobel and Lucy looked sad—that was to be expected, even normal, if there was such a thing in these situations. They didn't look frightened, though, Jeanne was relieved to see. She let her breath out, and gave Chuck a half smile, knowing they'd made the right decision.

Chuck slowly moved to the other side of the bed, across from Jeanne. The girls came along, step-by-step. Now Jeanne and Chuck each held one of Isobel's hands. Her eyes were closed again and her breathing was shallow.

"Mom, we're all here with you. Don't be afraid," Jeanne whispered in her mother's ear, loud enough for all to hear.

"I'm not afraid." She breathed out a long sigh and her head fell slightly to the side. Jeanne and Chuck looked down at Isobel, now motionless. She was smiling.

And with that, Isobel McCullom Baines leapt into the arms of Jesus.

While Nancy and Sheryl prepared Isobel for Mr. Forester and for final goodbyes, Isobel's huddled family walked downstairs and into the living room. Jeanne looked around, realizing it was the first time since her mother's arrival at Rockaway House that she had ventured into this room. She could see it wasn't very cheery, but Jeanne wanted privacy and the upstairs solarium was often occupied. As usual, this space was deserted. Isobel and Lucy remained close to their father, not sure of the next move, waiting for an adult's cue.

Jeanne looked down and realized she was still holding the brown clasp envelope in her hand. She blew her nose and stuck the tissue in the pocket of her jeans, then opened the packet. "I almost forgot about this. Shall we see what Grandma left for us?"

She sat down on the couch and the girls immediately plopped on either side of her, up for a surprise. Chuck pulled a side chair close so that he could face Jeanne, knees-to-knees. He wanted to look her in the face, to reach out to her if need be without one of the girls between them.

Jeanne first pulled out a stack of smaller envelopes, bound together with a rubber band. She snapped it off and absentmindedly put it on her wrist. She spoke as she distributed the letters, "One for you, one for you and one for you." She peered down again into the big envelope, empty except for a small letter addressed to Mr. Forester. Jeanne resisted the almost irresistible urge to open the one remaining envelope with Rhonda's name on it and instead replaced it in the packet.

Everyone looked at each other, then Lucy broke the stalemate by ripping her envelope open.

"Look, Momma!" She proudly held up a photo of Grandmother Isobel with Lucy seated in her lap. There was a handwritten note on the back. "Read it! Read it!" she urged Jeanne.

"It says: '*Lucy in the sky with diamonds, I love you so. I'll be watching over you always. Love, Grandma.*'" Tears were now spilling over, running down Jeanne's cheeks. "How about you, Isobel? What did Grandma leave for you?" Young Isobel solemnly handed over her letter, intact. She nodded for Jeanne to open it.

"Let's see. There's a picture of Grandma holding you when you were a little baby. On the back it says, '*So glad you were named after me. A piece of me will always be there with you. Love, Grandma.*'" Isobel beamed, looking at her mother and father, proud to be carrying the banner of her grandmother's name.

Jeanne looked over at Chuck, waiting as he opened his personal note. He read it to himself, began to softly laugh and then read it aloud. "'*For the man who is brave enough to marry a Baines woman, I'll be here if you need to talk. Love, Mom*'" Jeanne wasn't ready to laugh, but she smiled across at Chuck. It got quiet. An awkward silence.

"Well," Jeanne said, rising. "I've got a couple of calls to make."

"I'm sorry, honey," Chuck tried to console her. "You know she was a little out of it at the end. She must have thought she left a note for you. I'm sure she meant to." Chuck's words were said to comfort his wife, but they didn't. Jeanne shrugged, took her phone and headed to the front porch.

First call, to Rhonda. Her only response was that she'd let Jeanne know when she'd be arriving as soon as Jeanne let her know when the funeral would be. Second call to Mr. Forester. He expressed his condolences and promised to be there within an hour to collect Isobel. Jeanne would give the obituary and Ethical Will—*whatever that is*—to Mr. Forester when he arrived, along with her mother's detailed instructions for her service. *God only knows what they say.* Her mother had always talked about being "laid out in lavender." *Where in the wide wide world of Chesterton would one find a lavender negligee?*

The third and last call.

The phone rang at the law firm of *Lane, Roderick, Brown, and Lane.* Jeanne waited. It was seasonably cool, but the late afternoon sun felt calming on her face and the top of her head as she sat on one of the tacky plastic chairs.

It is what it is. That was her Mom, always well-meaning but a bit flaky. *They were only notes. No big deal.*

She looked at her watch and realized it was almost five-thirty.

What if Cameron's already left for the day? I'll call him in the morning. There's really nothing for him to do now. I just thought he deserves to hear it from me, not read about Mom's death in the paper.

"Lane, Roderick, Brown, and Lane. Cameron Lane II speaking."

"Oh, hi, Cameron, Jeanne Evans, Isobel Baines's daughter."

"Yes, Jeanne." Cameron paused to take a breath. "Is it your mom?"

"It is. She passed just a bit ago. It was very peaceful."

"You and your family have our deepest condolences. You know, she was more than just a client—she was a special friend to my father and to me." Jeanne could hear the break in Cameron's voice as he spoke. That meant a lot to her.

"I know, Cameron. She thought a great deal of you. Well, I just wanted to let you know, so you wouldn't learn about it in the paper. I'll be talking to you—"

"Wait, Jeanne. Your mother gave me some instructions for you, for me to share with you at this time. It's about the trust she set up."

"I understand, Cameron. She had big dreams but that was just Mom. You know . . . " Of course Cameron already knew, Jeanne thought with a smile. She didn't need to finish the sentence.

"No, you don't understand. I have a letter from her—for you, Jeanne. I think it might be best for you to stop by. Is there any way you can come by now, I mean when you leave Rockaway House? I'm sorry to ask that of you, but I think you'll agree when—I think it's best."

A letter for me? Jeanne's head lifted along with her heart.

"I don't know, well, sure, I guess so, we were just going to head home. It'll be a few minutes before we're ready to leave here. Will you be there?"

"I'll be here whenever you get here."

They said their goodbyes to Isobel. Jeanne, Chuck and the girls were joined by staff members who had come to know Isobel well, first as their remote patient in home care and then as a resident at Rockaway House. They lit a candle and made Isobel look even more peaceful than when Jeanne, Chuck, Little Isobel and Lucy had left her side.

The girls wanted to touch their grandmother's hand and face. Was that all right, they both wanted to know. Absolutely. She wouldn't be quite as warm as usual, Jeanne explained. Grandma had left for heaven and she wasn't using her body anymore, but it was perfectly fine to remember her as she looked when she was still here. Isobel and Lucy were okay with that.

Chuck agreed with Jeanne that a stop at Cameron's office was in order. He'd seen the disappointment in her eyes, the only one without a parting message from his mother-in-law, God rest her soul. He hoped whatever Cameron had to share might ease Jeanne's hurt, even a little.

Cameron met them at the door of his storefront office, gave Jeanne a hug, and shook everyone else's hands. After they were all seated expectantly around his desk, he paused and smiled, looking from one to the other.

"I guess I don't have to tell you that your mother was an exceptional person, always full of surprises." Jeanne nodded proudly. It was the part of her mother's personality that had been sometimes frustrating but always most endearing to Jeanne.

"Don't worry about that whole trust thing, Cameron, the part in that last Will you did for Mom. That was just her, you know."

Cameron had a funny look on his face. "Actually, I think you better read this. I'll be right back." He handed Jeanne a letter, sealed, with her name on the front, written in her mother's shaky handwriting. Jeanne looked over at Chuck, then began to slowly open it. Now that she had it, she wasn't quite as keen to discover what it said.

Chuck could hear Cameron down the hall, the clanking of a heavy door and then his returning footsteps. He had a small envelope in his hand.

"Maybe you should read the letter out loud, Jeanne," Cameron suggested. The letter was typed. Jeanne figured her mother must have dictated it to Cameron.

Dear Jeanne Beanie,

I know you all thought I was nuts, having young Cameron do that paperwork for the trust, but ~~I'm not~~ I wasn't. Well, maybe I was but this isn't the reason you should think that.

I gave something to Cameron to put in a safe place. When you get the chance to check the numbers, you'll find that it is a winning Powerball ticket. You

know I didn't usually buy one of these but for some reason I decided to late last year. I bought it the day I found out I was officially dying, the day I started into hospice care.
I think it's worth about twenty million give or take and should be enough to get the Isobel Baines Charitable Trust for Women, Animals, Geezers and Crones started. Ha ha. (Wouldn't you know it, just after I won, I heard they doubled the prize to forty million dollars!)
The ticket's only good for a year and I really wanted it to be a surprise for after I was gone, which I am now. I was afraid I wouldn't die in time. I almost didn't. Ha ha again.
Jeanne, remember that you can use the money in the nursing homes for people to come to Rockaway House or pretty much anything else you think is a good idea. I trust you to know what's right, although it would be nice to use some of the money to put a nice CD player in every patient's room. You know how I love music and a lot of people feel the same.
I want Cameron to do all the legal work for the trust—he's a good boy.
If you can, have Rhonda get involved somehow. I think she feels left out sometimes and I know she can drive you crazy, but she's a whiz when it comes to real estate stuff. She'd probably need to be around here more often, but that's okay, too. See? Surprises are a good thing.
I know I always told you that a person's worth can't be measured in dollars and cents—and it can't—but having a whole lot of money is not a bad thing, when you think about it.
I love you all. I had a wonderful time and I'm so thankful for each and every one of you. And remember, "We are not human beings having a spiritual experience. We are spiritual beings having a human experience," or at least that's what Pierre Teilhard deChardin said.

Love, Mom and Grandma

P.S. Big thanks to Margaret and Mr. Bartlett.

Cameron spoke first. "Here's the ticket, dated November 16, 2011. Signed by your mom, legal as can be. I had it in the firm's safe—which is where it's going back to until we can take it to the lottery office in Des Moines, clutched in our hot little hands." He stopped and beamed at Jeanne. "Surprised?"

"She did it! Oh my God, she did it!" Jeanne choked out.

Jeanne looked at Chuck. Chuck looked at Jeanne. If it's possible to laugh and cry at the same time, that's what they did. Young Isobel and Lucy bounced on their chairs, grinning from ear to ear. They didn't have a clue about what had just happened, but as they jumped up and down giggling, they knew the energy in the room had taken a dramatic turn for the better.

Cameron seemed in control, but that's only because he'd had some time to prepare for this moment. In fact, he'd spent the better part of the previous two days thinking about little else. At two a.m. both nights, he had considered getting dressed, grabbing his sleeping bag and heading downtown to sack out right next to the safe. Instead, he got up each time and drank coffee at home until five a.m. and then came to the office. God love her, Mrs. Baines had made sure he only had to fret over the incredibly valuable little slip of paper for forty-eight hours before she passed on. It seems she'd had it all figured out. Wasn't that just like her?

Cameron did, however, have one question for Jeanne: "Who the heck is Mr. Bartlett?"

Rockaway House

Notebook? Check. Tape measure? Check. Color chart? Check. Digital camera? Check. Suzi and Margaret were in the kitchen, assembling equipment for the committee's reconnaissance mission to the first floor of Rockaway House, about to begin. Lauren, Rose and Lance would be joining them. They all agreed that the next logical step was to make a list of the work that needed to be done. Suzi and Lance would create the construction schedule because materials and labor had to be lined up ASAP, then organizing the volunteer and professional crews could begin. Bruce remained in the garage, tackling the inventory and cataloging.

Might as well start right here in the kitchen, Suzi said when everyone had gathered. To minimize inconvenience to family members, they had already decided to put a temporary snack center in the upstairs solarium during the show home. Rose said that anybody she'd spoken to was as excited about the project as they all were because, in a way, their dying loved ones would be part of helping others in the future. Don't worry, she said, they welcomed this exercise in legacy building.

So, that's just ten or fifteen more people in on "the secret," Margaret thought with a smile.

The kitchen needed only a fresh coat of paint, a day's work at most. Mrs. Quinn's rolling pin, marble pastry board and stoneware would all be prominently displayed in this room, the heart of the home. Suzi made notes as they moved through the rooms.

They squeezed into the butler's pantry. Since the day she'd helped Ray Spaulding assemble his breakfast supplies, Margaret knew this area should be permanently equipped with snacks, a microwave and a coffee maker for visitors. For purposes of the show home, Suzi would unpack May Murphy's most beautiful china and silver to display in the pantry's glass-door cupboards. They only needed a new coat of paint.

On to the dining room. With a large table already in the sunroom off the kitchen, eating space wasn't needed, but computer space was. Rose had informally polled the family members currently in residence. What type of amenities would make their time at Rockaway House more convenient or pleasant? Wifi Internet access, no question. If they could bring their laptop computers when they visited, they could stay longer and communicate better with other family members and friends of the patient.

For the show home, the dining room would be temporarily staged with the Murphys' furnishings. Afterwards, it would be fitted with semi-private computer desks with plenty of power strips and charging stations for cell phones and laptops. Lauren was no expert on IT, (Information Technology, Margaret whispered to Rose with a nod) but shouldn't it be possible to provide a printer that people could load from a flash drive or by wireless connection from a laptop? She'd check with the hospital's in-house computer guru when she got back to the office.

Lance and Suzi partnered through the rooms, making notes on the logistics needed to turn Lance's practical construction expertise into Suzi's imaginings and keeping a running tab on estimated material and labor costs.

On to the entryway. Suzi pictured the Murphys' planters and fern stands adorning the area. She looked up. *OMG, that shade isn't plastic, is it?* Sometime in the past seventy years, the original ceiling fixture had disappeared, replaced by a single-bulb atrocity. That accounted for the haunted grotto effect that greeted every visitor. *Note to self: pay a visit to Mike, Frank and Danielle at Antique Archaeology down the road in LeClaire, Iowa.*

The living room. Judging from the use the upstairs solarium got, it was clear that family members liked comfortable places to relax, have a chat or take a phone call in private. Everyone agreed they wanted more of that. Rose also hoped to use the living room for support group and educational activities in the future. She'd be talking to Lisbeth at *Under the Covers* about book events focusing on bereavement, creating an Ethical Will, genealogy or writing life stories. Maybe they'd even invite guest authors. Suzi envisioned small groups of chairs, some facing the fireplace. She'd make sure they were lightweight enough to be easily reconfigured.

The fireplace. Lance stuck his head in as far as he could. It might be possible to make it wood-burning again, but it wasn't a practical option. What did everyone think about a gas insert that looked like a log fire and would provide plenty of heat as well as atmosphere with just the flip of a switch? Unanimous agreement. He gave them a ballpark estimate and they still agreed. Thanks to Caleb Bronson, Margaret didn't need to imagine it, she had already seen the living room decorated for the holidays. It was a must-have item.

"And I think there's a fireplace on the other side of this one," Lance pointed out.

Ba-bye, office, Rose said to herself. Four years earlier, when she'd discovered the little room off the back hall, empty except for extra bedding and cleaning supplies, she didn't expect to hold onto it forever, but it'd certainly been handy while it lasted. Not having to sprint to the corporate office to send a mass e-mail or make a copy or have a private phone call had been a real time saver for Rose. *Oh well.*

Maybe, Margaret timidly suggested before they left the living room, the attached solarium could be a children's area with game tables and toys? Thumbs up. Built-in window seats would provide storage and be more kid-proof as well, Lance suggested. Suzi remarked what clever folks they were and wrote "new window treatments all around" in large capital letters on her note pad. *Those horrid roll-up shades have got to go.*

Back into the entryway with a stop at the grand staircase. It could use new carpeting and brass carpet rods, but otherwise it was fine. At one time, Lance had thought they might need to build a sound barrier, maybe install a partition at the top of the stairs, but—Lance said with a wink—he understood that someone had recently tested the soundproof quality of the first floor and it had passed with flying colors. A few weeks earlier, Margaret would have been embarrassed by his comment, but not now.

As the procession headed down the hallway to Rose's erstwhile office, Lauren took Suzi by the elbow and steered her off to the side.

"Is there any chance we'd have room for a piano for the show home? I was thinking maybe down there at the end of the living room, just this side of the fireplace?" Suzi tapped her pencil on the clipboard as she thought, then started making notes as she spoke.

"I don't see why not. I'll make a call. And I'll see about getting some of the music students around here to play during the show home. That's a marvelous idea, Lauren! How'd you come up with that?"

"Oh, I don't know," Lauren shrugged, "it just came to me."

Suzi had been mentally moving each piece of furniture from the garage into the house as they toured. Naturally, there would be room for the first floor furnishings in the show home because it had all been there at one time, hadn't it? As for the second floor bedroom pieces, they could remain on display in the garage. It seemed a shame, but there wasn't any option, was there?

She and Lauren caught up with Lance, Margaret and Rose in the tiny room on the other side of the living room fireplace. The house plans from the Sears *Honor Bilt Modern Homes* catalog had labeled it the "den." Margaret took one look and without hesitating said, "This is the meditation room." All heads turned in her direction.

"You're absolutely right!" Suzi said. "It's perfect. There really should be a place of peace and quiet. Maybe just a couple of comfortable chairs, a table, a kneeler, not an altar exactly, but a table with a candle—electric, of course—soft lighting." Rose smiled to herself. *Good idea. I like it.*

One wall held the fireplace, the opposite wall was blank and the last one had a small window. "Oh! Oh!" Suzi was having an epiphany. "A stained glass panel right there! I know just the person over at the college who can make it. Oh! Oh!" She grabbed Margaret's arm. "The tree of life! Perfect!"

Everyone thought for a moment. Lauren spoke, "I like it. It would be nice for people to be alone with God or their higher power or whatever the P.C. term is these days. Another fireplace insert, I assume?" She looked over at Lance. He nodded as Suzi furiously made notes. That left the half bath just outside, in the hallway. Suzi would decorate it with vintage items. The conference room was the only room they hadn't visited.

"Let's take a look at it, just to be thorough." Lauren led the way. It held a traditional ten-foot conference table with twelve high-backed chairs on casters. "I suppose people should see that we have this room—"

"Oh! Oh!" Uh-oh, Margaret thought, here we go. "It'll be their bedroom!" Suzi said excitedly as everyone looked at her, stumped. "Don't you see? We have all the Murphys' furniture from upstairs and nowhere to display it. We'll turn this room into a 1922 master suite!" She was moving around the room, energetically waving her arms. "We can drape fabric over this paneling. It's the perfect way to show off that incredible bedroom suite that belonged to Daniel and May Murphy."

How could they *not* make it a part of the show home display? It seemed a sacrilege to leave that set in the garage, just waiting to be hauled off by the winning bidder. "What do you think?" Suzi looked from face to face.

It was such a weird idea, it had to work. They all shrugged and nodded. Lauren was the practical one. "Any ideas on what to do with all the furniture in this room?"

"Yes, we'll take it out to the garage. We can use the table for something in the display or refreshment area. Speaking of the garage, that's our last stop." Suzi and Lance led the others out the back door and across the driveway. Lance raised one of the overhead doors and found the light switch.

"Why does this not surprise me?" Lauren said as they all looked around. "May Murphy's garage is nicer than the inside of most homes." The walls and ceilings were finished plaster, complete with oak trim. The floors were paving bricks. The stalls were open to each other, so the space was about twelve hundred square feet. Lauren stated the obvious, "I believe there's enough space for the conference room furniture."

They would meet the next day to generate a calendar leading up to the day of the show home/auction extravaganza to include all the renovation and marketing steps. Lauren reminded everyone that the event didn't yet have a firm date. Let's put that on the agenda for tomorrow, too, she suggested.

Suzi's house was back in order, post-flood, so she volunteered to hold the next meeting there. They could work undisturbed and she'd show them her plans for the launch party. Four o'clock the next day, Suzi confirmed with everyone. Plan to stay as long as it takes, she added. When dinnertime comes, pizzas will come.

The planning tour was complete and they went their separate ways, each one focusing on a different point on the Rockaway House timeline: the Murphys' past, the mountain of work to be done in the present and the dreams for Rockaway House in the future. Anyway you looked at it, this grande dame was about to get a major face-lift.

Margaret

The committee meeting at Suzi's house had begun promptly at four o'clock. It was eight p.m. when Margaret dragged in through her own door. Suzi was a woman possessed when it came to organizing an event like this. Highly productive and incredibly exhausting.

The Auction now had a firm date, November 9-11, which was just four weeks away. Lance had compiled his notes from the first floor survey and came to the meeting with an estimate of man-hours and costs to complete each room. Suzi had been to visit her good buddy Christopher Walton and now had hard costs and delivery estimates for new furnishings. With Dorrie Kelly's help, Lauren had assembled an outline of action steps for the marketing and public relations campaign. Bruce had two pages on what it would take to organize the auction. Rose had a checklist of cautionary concerns about the ongoing Rockaway House mission to be addressed as time went on.

And Margaret felt like a big ole slacker.

"I need something to do—I'm the only one without a clipboard!" They all laughed and assured her that was no accident. They hoped she'd do for *The Auction* what she now did for the Rockaway House patients and families: pick up all the loose ends. Margaret wasn't sure what that meant exactly but she gladly agreed.

Three hours and three large pizzas later, the meeting adjourned. Tired but wired, Margaret stopped at *Rex's Drugstore* on the way home. She'd gone to high school with the pharmacist, Rex "Rusty" Howell (the nickname that had stuck when red-haired Rex Jr. started working with his dad at age twelve). Like most of the people Margaret knew in Chesterton, Rusty was more than just an acquaintance. Throughout The Duration, he had gone out of his way to deliver whatever prescriptions and supplies Ernie needed on a moment's notice, no matter the time of day or night. The store was quiet so Margaret and Rusty caught up on news of classmates' and family members' comings and goings. After almost an hour, Margaret paid for the shampoo she'd originally stopped for and headed home.

She looked in the bathroom mirror as she brushed her teeth. It was almost fifty years since she and Rusty and one hundred twenty-five of their closest friends had graduated in 1963. How could that be? Right off hand, Margaret couldn't begin to remember how she had spent her time throughout those days, years, decades. Oh sure, the milestones of life, like her marriage to Ernie, buying a house, the passing of their parents, retirement and Ernie's death stood out in stark contrast to the blur of the passing years. But still, it had all gone by in the blink of an eye.

Next year was their golden anniversary class reunion. Yikes. There was no doubt in her mind it would be even more mind-numbing than ones in the past. To see the people you remembered as eighteen years old—the ones who'd moved away—suddenly reappear as sixty-eight. It was The Class Picture of Dorian Gray. No, that wasn't right, that implied the ravages of sin. What had marched across her friends' faces—and hers—was life in all of its glory. As much as Margaret hated to admit it, there was only one phrase that described the phenomenon: "It's all part of Nature's beautiful pageant." *That darn Ernie.*

She looked in the mirror and turned her head this way and that. *How long have I been wearing this hairdo? Too long.* Maybe she'd stop by *Karla's Klip & Kolor* tomorrow and get an estimate. *Ha-ha.*

Margaret lit the special candle that their niece Robin had given her for Christmas. What was she saving it for? Wasn't this aroma therapy, just like Carlene Spaulding was using on her mother—and Carlene was a certified expert in such things.

As a matter of fact, in the midst of that day's whirlwind, Margaret had run across Carlene in the upstairs solarium, reading a book while her mother Lois napped. Margaret didn't get the opportunity very often—never, really—to consult with someone from California about such things. Before she could stop herself, she was asking Carlene what she thought about communications from those who have passed on. She shared the coincidence of finding the pennies. Margaret thought they might be something special, what with the significant dates. That couldn't be just a coincidence, could it?

Carlene had to smile to herself before she answered Margaret. Many years earlier, on one of her first visits home after opening *Au Naturale!*, it had become clear to Carlene from the questions she was getting that the good people of Chesterton equated the practice of herbology with spiritualism, psychic powers, and any and all other areas of woo-woo expertise. At first it was a little irritating, then it roused Carlene's own curiosity and eventually she made space in her mind, in her store and on her website for the information and products related to all those topics. Funny how that had all worked out.

"Do you really think it's coincidental, Margaret?" Carlene paused for a moment. "Or were they pennies from heaven?"

"Pennies from heaven?"

"Pretty common, actually. Lots of people get dimes, nickels, pennies, most any type of coin. But it's the date that takes it out of the realm of coincidence."

"Oh, I don't know. It'd be nice, though, wouldn't it?" Margaret would have to noodle that one for a while. What the heck—at least Carlene didn't think she was completely out of her mind. "What about dreams, Carlene? I've had some real doozies lately."

"There's several schools of thought on that, Margaret. It may be the subconscious taking the opportunity to express itself, or simply one's imagination functioning without limitations. Of course, other theories have been suggested." Carlene stopped, waiting to see what it was that Margaret really wanted to know.

"Well, I sort of wondered about that. I've had a couple of dreams about Ernie—my late husband—and I'm never quite sure . . . Sometimes I wake up and I'm just smiling and I remember my dream and it's as if . . . " Margaret's voice faded off as she was lost in the memory for a moment. A dream like that was so crystal clear, remembering it wasn't like remembering a dream. It was more like recalling something you just experienced.

"Is it possible he's actually visiting me in my dreams, or am I just dreaming about him?" There, she'd finally said it.

"Do you mean, how can you tell the difference?"

Margaret hesitated. Carlene's question sounded loaded. Margaret was pretty sure Carlene thought it was possible that sometimes a dream is more than just a dream. "Yes, I guess that's what I mean," Margaret said very slowly.

"Some people believe that loved ones do visit us in our dreams, when our minds and hearts and souls are most receptive. When you think about it, it's difficult to imagine being able to grasp spiritual messages when we're so busy being bombarded with stimuli during our waking hours. Do you ever practice meditation, Margaret?"

"No, I've always wanted to, but whenever I try to do anything like that I can't seem to concentrate long enough. My mind's going a mile-a-minute."

Carlene laughed and nodded. "I know what you mean and it takes lots of practice, believe me. So, if your mind is too busy and your thoughts jump around like a monkey in a small cage—we call that having a 'monkey mind'—you can see how important good sleep can be. And it also makes sense that the spirit world would use that opportunity to communicate with us."

"So you believe dreams can be a visit from a loved one?" Margaret asked again.

"It's been my observation that a dream that isn't just a dream usually has a different quality to it. It's more—I don't know—vivid, brilliant somehow, and other senses are often involved, like the sense of smell. It's difficult to describe. *You* have to decide, Margaret, was it a dream or was it a visit from Ernie?"

"What's the difference?"

Carlene smiled. "The difference, Margaret, to paraphrase Mark Twain, is 'the difference between lighting and a lightning bug.' It's all the difference in the world."

Margaret was glad she'd run into Carlene. Something to think about, for sure.

Maybe she should stop by *Karla's Klip & Kolor* on the way to Rockaway House the next day, Margaret pondered. Karla always encouraged Margaret to browse the hairstyle magazines when she came in. Margaret never did but maybe she would this time. If Karla couldn't squeeze her in right then, she'd make an appointment for later in the day. With the launch party coming up, it might be nice to have a new do. And Margaret would be busy—really busy—in the coming weeks with all the preparations for *The Auction.* It'd help to not have to mess with her hair, maybe something shorter and really simple—jazzy, but simple. Maybe a little color, too, although that sounded awfully ambitious. She'd see what Karla had to say.

Margaret blew out the candle and lay back in bed. The monkey in her mind did seem to be on a break for the moment. Maybe she could make up her own sort of meditation. She could just practice breathing slower for a starter. As she recited her prayers for the night, she suddenly realized she was feeling calmer. Come to think of it, that always made her feel calmer.

Prayer as a form of meditation? Probably the last one on the planet to figure that one out.

Before the end of their visit today, Carlene had offered to give Margaret a Reiki treatment anytime Margaret was willing. She just might do that. She just might do anything she darn well pleased, for that matter.

Rockaway House

One thing was for sure, all the caterers in Chesterton (all two of them) would have an exceptionally good season by the time *The Auction* was over.

Suzi Roland had a well-practiced style of hosting an event: call the caterer, call *Whine & Cheese* and schedule an extra session with her regular housekeeping service, *Cleaning Fools.* For this occasion, she had taken an additional step: she had added her address book to Lauren Dunlap's database of supporters and she'd proofed the invitations being sent out in record time.

Delegation—that was the secret. Suzi recognized her primary function at this party as getting a community fired up to raise money for a worthy cause—read: get checks out of the pockets and purses and into the basket. She took that responsibility very seriously. Any way she could conserve energy by hiring others was fine with her.

To Suzi, the approach for dealing with the extremely short time frame before *The Auction* was obvious, and that was to make it part of the campaign. Across the top of the invitation was the *when, where* and *what time.* Over that they placed what looked like a rubber stamp impression, in bright red: RUSH JOB! With Suzi leaning over the shoulder of Lauren's administrative assistant Allie Lester, the invitations had been designed in less than an hour. The guests were invited to be part of an exciting event that would change Chesterton forever. The life-altering happening would be announced at this invitation-only party. If that doesn't get them here, nothing will, Suzi said.

Chesterton Kwik Print had the latest equipment and printed the addressees on the postcard invitations directly from Lauren's database. With the double incentive of a box of Mr. Goldberg's cookies (the currency of Chesterton second only to cold cash) and being told the reason for this affair (add another name to the list of those in on "the secret"), the owner had the postcards metered and in the mail that afternoon.

Leaving nothing to chance, Suzi had a chat with the postmistress Lucille Smith while mailing the postcards. Lucille assured Suzi that the invitations would be in mailboxes the following day without exception. Good thing, too, because the launch party was scheduled for three days later. *So, Lucille is now also in on "the secret."* Suzi was shaking her head as she drove away from the post office. It was testimony to the ethereal nature of this whole deal that it was still a secret from *anyone*—let alone most everyone—in Chesterton.

Suzi's phone started ringing the day after the mailing. Gotta love Lucille Smith, Suzi thought. Using her sweetest and most apologetic voice, Suzi told each caller that no way could she spill the beans—they would just have to skedaddle over to the party to hear the amazing news. Between phone calls, Suzi unpacked and unpacked and unpacked.

The Rolands' house was chock-a-block full, with Suzi's quick tally that there were only about twenty no-shows. Who would dare miss the launch party for *it*, whatever *it* turned out to be? For the first time Suzi could remember—ever—a secret in Chesterton had actually remained a secret. There hadn't been a major leak. She was certain of that because not one of her callers hinted about knowing what was going on and they would definitely have bragged on it if they could have.

The crowd was shifting and mingling, chattering and whispering. The rumblings were of the "What have you heard?" and "I know something, but I'd better not say" variety. The latter comments came from CCH board members and Lauren was glad to let them enjoy some pomposity—it was the least they deserved in return for their blind support of a project that was five percent information and ninety-five percent trust.

Over the past couple of days, it had been nearly impossible to take care of any Rockaway House business that was non-*Auction*, so Rose took the chance to pull Margaret aside. Someone had told Rose about Carlene Spaulding practicing Reiki on her mother Lois. Rose had asked Carlene if she'd be willing to talk to the volunteers and staff about alternative therapies for hospice patients and Dr. Bob thought it was fine when Rose asked him. You know, Rose said to Margaret, Carlene could explain the types and what they might be able to do for the patients. Maybe even volunteer some of her talents or get others on board to learn the methods.

It turned out Carlene was more than willing to help. As a matter of fact, Carlene told Rose she'd been toying with the idea of staying on in Chesterton to help her dad for a while. It was up in the air right now. She had to think about her business back in California and, well, it was all very tentative and complicated, but Carlene promised to get back to Rose soon with an answer.

Rose just had to tell someone. "So that's good, right?" she said to Margaret, nodding as she spoke. Margaret agreed, like so many other matters transpiring right now, it was very good.

Then she and Rose heard the tinkle of someone tapping a wine glass.

Lauren Dunlap had been volunteered by the others to make the formal presentation to the anxious crowd. Suzi had pointed out with a grin that since Lauren had all the accountability, she ought to have all the pleasure of announcing the plan. Lauren was fine with that—she liked being the bearer of good news for a change and she'd learned a bit from Margaret. The surest route to get people's attention was to tell a good story.

First, Lauren shared what life was like at Rockaway House on a daily basis. And then she told them about the Murphys.

The committee members had unanimously agreed it would be too much to give all the details here at the party. Just say that a personal tragedy had caused the family to abandon their possessions and move away in 1944. And say that by a strange and miraculous twist of fate, the Murphys seemed to be reaching forward in time to nurture the mission of Rockaway House for generations to come.

Everyone was obviously touched. Wow, Margaret thought, from the looks of the faces around the room, it's a good thing we didn't tell them the whole story. She wasn't sure they could handle it.

Lauren went on to explain the concept of the show home and *The Auction.* She told the crowd of eager listeners why they had each been invited: because Rockaway House needed all their help to make this event happen and to engage the entire community in the work that needed to be done. The date had been set for November 9-11, about a month away. That's why only the true leaders of the Chesterton area had been invited here—"yes, that's you"—to spread the word, to make others understand the importance of the show home and to lead the way in making it happen.

"God, she's good," Lynda Wyatt whispered in Margaret's ear.

"No kidding. Who do you think got me into the middle of all this?"

At that point, Lauren turned it over to Suzi. She went for the close.

Margaret glanced around and spotted Ray Spaulding, Lynda's former boss at *The Bee,* across the way. She gave him a wave and he started to work his way around the edge of the room, headed in their direction. Margaret shook Ray's extended hand.

"Hey, Boss." Lynda gave him a hug and a kiss on the cheek.

"Don't let Jake Elbert hear you say that, young lady."

Lynda didn't need to ask Ray how Lois was doing. She'd stopped in to visit her just before the party. In fact, Lynda had had a nice chat with Carlene, who'd told her that her father was home getting dressed—Carlene had insisted he take a break and go to the Rolands' to find out what the mysterious invitation was all about.

Lynda gave Ray a friendly elbow to the ribs. "How come you don't hang around *The Bee,* now that you're back on the staff?"

"Staff? Hardly. That essay was a one-off, Lynda." But it was true that the newshound in Ray would never fully retire. He turned to Margaret. "This is the big headline, but what's the backstory on the Murphys, Margaret? Lauren Dunlap was a bit cryptic."

Lynda and Margaret exchanged looks. Margaret shrugged and gave Lynda a smile and a nod that said, "It's your scoop, not mine."

"Hey, old Boss, old buddy, old pal. How would you like to collaborate on one of the best human interest stories you'll ever come across?" How could Ray possibly say no to that? Margaret slipped away and noticed thirty minutes later that Lynda still had Ray's ear.

As the evening wound down, Bruce and Rose were in the kitchen, having a quiet moment in Suzi's solarium when Margaret found them. "Wondered where you'd snuck off to." They smiled and Rose patted the chair next to her.

"Have a seat. We were just saying that it's all so mystical, isn't it?"

"That's the word, all right. Mystical. I think we're going to get some good coverage in the newspaper. I think Lynda Wyatt and Ray Spaulding are going to work together to do a piece." Margaret slipped out of her good shoes and massaged her feet on the rung of the chair.

"Excellent, because we've got a garage full of furniture to sell!" Bruce took a long drink of wine. "I have a feeling things are going to start accelerating at an alarming rate, starting tomorrow. We better enjoy the peace while we can."

Suzi and Stephen sent the last of their guests out the door and joined the rest of the committee in the kitchen. Suzi poured herself a large glass of wine, her first of the evening. The caterers were finishing the cleanup as she grabbed a plate of leftover finger food and dug in, then passed it around the table. Rolling her eyes, she savored the morsels, then cleared her throat.

"Okay, you're gonna love this. Jake Elbert and Lynda Wyatt were the last to leave. I just heard him say to her—and I quote—'You know, I think there might be a story in this.' And Lynda says, 'You may be right, Jake. Ray and I were just visiting about that. Why don't we all put our heads together and see what we can come up with?'" Suzi laughed out loud. By the end of the evening, they had all heard about Lynda's plan. She had the facts, Ray had the audience, and they were both talented writers. It would be a great feature, not to mention a little free advertising for *The Auction.*

Stephen Roland disappeared for a moment and returned, carrying "the basket," the vessel that held the checks, all those wonderful checks. Suzi emptied it onto the table.

"Ready, set, go!" As she read the amounts, everyone joined in, adding the cumulative total in their heads, then announcing it aloud in unison, or pretty close to unison.

Suzi read the figure on the last check and they all shouted, "Fifteen thousand four hundred!"

Oh my goodness, Margaret thought. *What have we gone and done?*

Lois

Never had anything so familiar seemed so strange.

Ray pulled the wood inlay tray from the lower cupboard in the butler's pantry, dropped the bread into the toaster, retrieved the orange from the refrigerator, popped four slices of bacon into the microwave and stood back, waiting for it all to come together. His actions were rote, his mind on other things. Yesterday, he thought he'd done this for the last time. He'd had the same thought the day before. And the day before that. *Is today the day?*

Lois stopped eating earlier in the week, but she wouldn't hear of ending the breakfast tradition, even if she didn't partake. Ray, she said with a touch of dark humor, when I don't want to share breakfast with you, you'll know I'm gone.

She'd had a sip of tea the day before, otherwise she wasn't drinking anymore, either. Lois could feel the fluids accumulating throughout her body, most especially in her lungs. Her breathing was labored and heavy.

Except for occasionally drifting off, she willed herself to stay awake most of the daytime, for the sake of kinship with her constant companions, Ray and Carlene. For all three of them, every moment was precious and every hour was a lifetime.

As usual, Ray and Carlene had compared notes when they got home the previous evening. As they sat at the kitchen table, Carlene said her mother reminded her of a ball of twine that was unwinding, just getting smaller and smaller. Ray asked Carlene if her mother had said anything that seemed a bit, well, off the mark. Sheryl, the nurse on duty, had cautioned Ray that it wouldn't be uncommon for the toxins building in Lois's system to cause delirium and confused thinking.

"You mean, is she getting loopy?"

"Well, yes."

"That's hard to say, Dad. She asked me last night if I'd seen Grandma when she came to visit."

"She did? What'd you say?"

"I said I was sorry I'd missed her. What was I supposed to say? 'You couldn't have seen Grandma, Mom, she's dead.'? Dad, just 'cause I didn't see Grandma doesn't mean she wasn't there." She caught her father's skeptical look. "Oh, sorry. I forgot you don't believe in all that woo-woo stuff. Well, let me ask you, Dad, where do you think Mom's going when she leaves here?"

Ray thought for only a moment. "If there's a heaven, Carlene, your mother will be in it."

"Agreed. So why is it so hard to believe that people in heaven can visit us occasionally?"

"First of all, what's to say your grandmother's in heaven?"

"Ouch! Dad, you and Grandma still feuding? She's been dead for twenty years. Talk about holding a grudge. Anyway, answer my question, please."

"I tend to not believe that which I haven't seen with my own eyes, honey, you know that. But I will say that the treatments—or whatever you call them—you've been giving your mother certainly seem to work. They relax her, and I'm in favor of that."

It's true, Carlene had pulled a few winning tricks from her New Age bag. The day before, she'd given Lois a Reiki treatment, an energy massage intended to relax her and heal the spirit as well as the body. Carlene introduced aromatherapy in Lois's room using a candle wax warmer and gentle hand, arm and feet massages with scented oils. Once Lois noticed Carlene's CD player, she asked her to bring some of her own favorite classical and opera music from home. While it played, Lois closed her eyes and laid back. Sure enough, Ray had witnessed it: Lois's breathing eased and her demeanor became tranquil. Okay, okay. He begrudgingly admitted he was now a believer, sort of.

Granted, it was hard to say how much of Lois's reactions could be attributed to Carlene's alternative therapies and how much to the placebo effect of having one-on-one time with the daughter she had missed so much over the past nineteen years. For Lois and Carlene and Ray, it didn't matter. All that counted was that Lois was relaxed, even serene, after each guided meditation or Reiki treatment or music therapy session.

This morning, Lois's head was slightly raised, but she couldn't sit up for breakfast. Ray arranged the tray table with the rose in a small vase he'd brought from home. He switched on the candle melting pot and Vivaldi's *Four Seasons* played softly in the background. Lois smiled weakly as she watched Ray try to swallow a few bites of toast and bacon. She raised her eyes to the opening door and Ray turned his head as Carlene walked in.

"You two are still doing this? After all these years? How precious are you, anyway?" She took off her coat, grabbed a piece of bacon and sat down in the chair by the window.

"You know about our breakfasts?" Ray ventured.

"Duh, Dad. Give me a little credit. Don't you think I noticed that I never had breakfast with either one of my parents any weekday of my entire life? I figured it out when I was about nine. To be honest, at the time I was glad to find out that this is what you two were up to behind those closed doors."

Lois smiled at Carlene. She wasn't really tracking with the conversation, but she no longer cared. The sound of Carlene and Ray's voices was like a warm wrap around her shoulders.

"Why didn't you join us?" Ray asked innocently.

"I don't know. You didn't seem to want me to—I don't know, Dad. I was nine for Chrissake."

At that, Lois did react.

"Carlene Marie Spaulding. I've talked to you about your language." Her voice was almost a whisper. Carlene looked at Ray with half a smirk.

"Sorry, Mom. I'll try to be more careful."

"Well, you better not talk like that when you get to your Grandma's. She'll put you over her knee."

Carlene cleared her throat and stood up.

"On that note, I'm going downstairs to get a cup of coffee. You two want anything?" Ray shook his head. Lois just smiled.

"Better watch it, Dad. Your favorite MIL might just show up," Carlene whispered in her father's ear as she passed him. He reached out to give her a swat but missed.

Lois's gaze followed Carlene out the door. "I don't know what we'll do when she leaves, Ray. I just don't know."

"I don't either, Lois."

"She's going to be graduating soon, you know."

Carlene made herself a cup of chai latte' and didn't even consider resisting the freshly baked cookies some dear soul had left on the counter. The sign read: Don't think about it—just have one! *God love ya, whoever you are.*

She sat down at the large table, thoughtfully sipping her latte', cookie in hand. She started to send a text to Rainbow, a marketing idea had come to Carlene this morning while she was in the shower, but now she couldn't remember what it was, so she put her phone back down. Mom's getting close, she thought. *Weaker, even a little delusional. I wonder if Dad sees how near we are to the end.* She looked out the solarium window and noticed a birdfeeder not far away with two colorful visitors. Carlene didn't see many birds in her neighborhood in California. Not that they weren't probably there, she just didn't have the chance to meet up. Footsteps at the kitchen door interrupted her thoughts.

"It's a ruby-throated grosbeak."

She turned around to find Cameron, smiling at the unexpected pleasure of finding Carlene.

"Really?"

"I don't know. I made that up." Carlene smiled back. "Mind if I join you?" Cameron asked tentatively.

"Not at all. What brings you back here?"

"A client, actually, although the one I was visiting when we met the other day has now passed away. An incredible lady, really. It's all right for me to talk about it, it was in the paper this morning."

"Haven't seen today's *Bee* yet. Do tell." Carlene was glad for the distraction and surprised at how pleased she was to see Cameron. She pointed to the chair across from her. Cameron poured himself a cup of coffee and sat down, eager to share the story of the astonishing Isobel Baines.

First, Cameron told her about Isobel's Powerball ticket, asking Carlene to please keep that under her hat, so to speak. The Iowa Lottery had leaked to the press that the winner had come forward, but in the hopes of stretching the story and selling more tickets, staff there was cooperating with Cameron in keeping Isobel's name out of the papers for a few more days.

Then Cameron told her about how he wanted to keep on working with clients like Mrs. Baines, people who wanted to make a real difference, whether or not they were people of means.

He's like a little kid, Carlene thought as she listened. "It certainly helps to have twenty million dollars to do it with," she pointed out.

Was that a note of cynicism in her voice? Cameron wasn't sure. He decided to ignore it and plow forward.

"True, but her daughter wants to use this opportunity to encourage others to support causes that echo what they believe in, which is what her mother did. It's called value-inspired philanthropy. And it doesn't matter if you have loads of money or just some time to volunteer. Pretty cool, huh?" He paused to take a breath.

Then he stopped short. He'd momentarily forgotten where they were and his tone turned suddenly serious. "I'm so sorry, Carlene. Why are you here? I mean, you must have a loved one here at Rockaway House."

"I do. My mother, Lois Spaulding."

"Wait—is your father Ray Spaulding, who used to be Editor of *The Bee*?"

"One and the same. You know my dad?"

"I do, I doubt if he remembers me. You went to Chesterton High? When'd you graduate?" It was the classic opening line in Iowa. There was a good chance you'd know someone in common.

"1993."

"I was class of 1989." Cameron racked his brain. Wouldn't you know it, he had nothing. "I'm so sorry about your mother, Carlene. How is she doing?"

Carlene was struck by his obvious sincerity. "She's dying, Cameron."

That certainly wasn't cynicism, Cameron observed. Carlene sounded resigned and tired. It was such a natural thing to do, without even thinking, Cameron reached across the table and put his hand on Carlene's.

"I am so sorry. And here I am going on and on. Please forgive me."

"No, no, that's fine. It's good to hear about something else for a change. And you put a very positive light on a life that's ended. Please, tell me more."

And so he did. He'd never regretted following in his father's footsteps and going to law school. As far as he was concerned, his dad was the noblest of men with a noble occupation. But after fifteen years of practice, Cameron was disheartened and more than a little bored. Overnight, *The Isobel Baines Charitable Trust for Women, Animals, Geezers and Crones* had brought that discouraging cycle to an end.

In the past couple of days, he'd started reading everything he could get his hands on about nonprofits, waking up in the middle of the night to jot down ideas about structure and mission statements, brainstorming over coffee with Jeanne. Cameron had found his passion and it showed.

He'd already talked to his law partners and they agreed: if Isobel's trust took all of his time, that was fine. Now he understood the expression "*Do what you love and you'll never work a day in your life.*"

"Carlene, you'd be surprised at what people want to accomplish at the end of their lives. Mrs. Baines's trust can be a part of helping them do that."

"Oh, *you'd* be surprised at what people want to do at life's end," Carlene smiled, thinking of her mother's request of her just a few days ago. *Just a few days ago? How could that be?*

"Mrs. Baines—you'd have liked her—surprised a lot of people. She wrote her own obituary and even included what's called an Ethical Will, a statement of what she believed in."

"An Ethical Will?"

"It's not a legal document. I'd never heard of it before either. It can be an essay or a letter or a collection of quotations. The Ethical Will Mrs. Baines created was a little bit of everything." He smiled as he thought of his quirky, dear client.

What Cameron described sounded familiar, Carlene thought. What about her mother's journal and her father's letters to Carlene? They spoke of what was important in life, how they wanted to be remembered and what they dreamed for themselves, for each other and for Carlene. Were those Ethical Wills?

"It's odd you would mention that. I think I might have some of those, written by my parents," Carlene realized.

"Tell me more, because that's really great if you do."

Carlene shared the discoveries she and her parents had made since she'd returned home to Chesterton. Cameron was hanging on every word, his hand still covering hers. Then she told Cameron about *Au Naturale!,* and the life she'd designed for herself in California. She'd had plans, big plans, for the business. She'd hoped to hold workshops and practice more alternative therapies with the customers and at a retirement community not far from the shop. But running the store was so exhausting. The end of each day found her climbing the stairs to her apartment and collapsing. All her inspired ideas had long ago been sidelined.

"Sounds like you're at a sort of crossroads, too," Cameron spoke sympathetically. As much as he hated to, he looked down at his watch. Okay, he still had a few minutes before he was expected upstairs. But maybe he was keeping Carlene as well. "Do you need to be somewhere?"

"Apparently, right now I need to be here," she said with a warmth that surprised them both. "I'm not sure I'd say I'm at a crossroads, exactly, Cameron. Business is really good. Admittedly, my personal life isn't all that great, but that comes with the territory." She said this very matter-of-factly with a shrug.

"I don't know much about life in California. I imagine a lot of freeways and hard bodies. I've lived in Chesterton, Iowa my whole life except when I went to college and law school—so what do I know? I have to ask, though, What is the point of being so damn healthy if you don't have time to actually enjoy life? Mahatma Ghandi said we'd be judged by our intentions, not our acts, but I'm not so sure about that."

Carlene sat up, her spine suddenly straight, her look suddenly hard. Instantly Cameron knew he'd gone one step too far. There was a tiny tug of something at the corners of her mouth. Anger? Offense? It was hard to say without asking, and Cameron knew better than to do that. Besides, he had a feeling he wouldn't be in the dark for long.

Carlene pulled her hand free. "Where I live, forty is the old fifty. I can hardly just up and abandon my livelihood in California—with all its 'freeways and hard bodies'—and come back to Nowheresville to live, can I, just because you all seem to have found some sort of Nirvana where people care about each other, and it only takes eight and a half minutes to get across town?"

It's actually ten minutes. Well, I can see my work here is done. Cameron slowly rose. "I'm sorry I've upset you, Carlene. That's the very last thing I wanted to do. It's not my place to suggest what you should do with your life—I was out of line." He picked up his briefcase. "I have a client upstairs I need to see. And I truly am so sorry about your mother. If you'd like to have a cup of coffee again sometime, here's my card." He slid it across the table. Carlene made no move to pick it up.

Cameron went for the first exit he spotted and disappeared into the butler's pantry.

Too early in the day for such drama, Carlene took a sip of cold latte', put the cup aside and sat with her elbows resting on the table, her head in her hands. Oh great, she thought, this is just great. *Why can't I keep my big gumball mouth shut? Why don't I know how to do that? Just who does he think he is?*

She was in no mood to think such deep thoughts right now. Her mind jumped to the day her father called to say her mother was terminally ill. Carlene had just gotten home from a hectic day at the shop. During her walk to pick up dinner-for-one at the nearby deli, she had spotted a couple sitting in the neighborhood pocket park. The man was reading a book; the woman was watching some children play with a small dog. Carlene was suddenly overcome with envy, the overpowering green variety that makes you do and say stupid things. It scared her more than a little. In fact, she'd quickened her steps back to the apartment above the shop—her little slice of heaven, as she was apt to say sarcastically when people asked her where she lived. Just then, the chain of events was interrupted by the phone call from her father and everything that came after his call. She hadn't revisited the scenario again until this moment.

That rush of jealousy now came back to Carlene in a flash: when she saw that couple, she'd thought of her parents, of their marriage and their life together. *Anyway, what does Cameron-la-de-da-Lane know? He's optimistic, he's self-deprecating, he's happy. How completely maddening is that?* Not to mention really good looking in a "Me, good looking? Oh, come on," sort of way. It really was off-putting.

Meanwhile, Cameron was thankful that the butler's pantry hadn't turned out to be a dead end. There were few things more embarrassing than making a hasty exit, stage left, into a closet. God forbid he had to return to the kitchen to make his escape—again. He did, however, find himself running almost headlong into Ray, who was coming through the dining room on his way to stash the breakfast gear.

"Mr. Spaulding? I believe we've met but it's been some years back. I'm Cameron Lane II. I think you know my father, Cameron Sr." He reached out and Ray set the tray on a nearby table, shaking Cameron's hand enthusiastically.

"I know your father well, Cameron. In fact, he prepared our wills—Lois and mine—about twenty years ago. And I remember you as a young man—didn't you play baseball for Chesterton? How is your dad?"

"He retired, sir, a few years after I started at the firm. Dad's doing great, making the seasonal switch from golf to football." Cameron paused for a moment. "May I say how very sorry I am to hear that Mrs. Spaulding isn't doing well." Ray wasn't surprised. In Chesterton, everybody knew everything. What wasn't read in the paper could be heard over the back fence. Ray nodded, acknowledging Cameron's heartfelt concern.

Cameron smiled warmly at Ray, then took the plunge. "So, Carlene's your daughter? We met the other day and then I just ran into her . . . " Cameron waved his hand in the direction of the kitchen. Ray nodded, not sure where this was going. "Wow."

Ray smiled. *Another piece of the puzzle falls into place.*

"Dealing with her is a bit of a high wire act, if you don't mind me saying so, sir."

"Tell me about it, son." Ray continued to smile.

He looked intently at the young man. There was something in the air, something extraordinary about this moment in time, in this place, among all the people gathered here. Ray had had this feeling only two or three times in his life. He clearly remembered one of those occasions. It was forty-four years later, and he had probably just shared breakfast with his wife for the last time. Maybe not—but probably.

A very persistent force was pulling all these individuals and little pieces of life together.

One day, in 1968, the bewildered look on this young man's face was Ray's own. The deer in the headlights. Ray pursed his lips, lowered his head and looked over the half-frame glasses he still wore from reading *The Bee* to Lois.

He didn't know where it came from, it just did. Ray put his hand on Cameron's shoulder. "I've had the blessing to be married to a Spaulding woman for forty-two years. You should be so lucky."

Ray picked up the breakfast tray and went into the kitchen to tell Carlene that her mother was asking for her.

Cameron stood still for a good thirty seconds before he gathered his wits and his briefcase and went upstairs to see Noah Smythe.

Noah

Margaret had always been a sucker for anything with whiskers and a purr, so it was fitting that she got to tell Noah that Hermione would be paying him a visit. The following day, she found Noah sitting in the recliner when she returned to his room, waiting for Fritz, who was scheduled to arrive with Hermione at two-thirty p.m.

Margaret noticed two large bouquets and a potted plant had been delivered since the day before.

"Lovely flowers, Noah."

"Yes, I can smell them, Margaret. Would you mind reading the cards to me? I've already forgotten who sent them." One was from a bestselling author, whose name Margaret recognized. Noah said he had contacted the writer and invited him to hold an event at their store when his first—of five—books was published seven years earlier.

"He never forgot that, I guess. He's a wonderful writer—he didn't need my help to make him a success. But I guess I called when he wasn't quite so popular." The other floral arrangement was from his biography group, *The Third Monday Club*. The potted plant was sent by a club he'd helped organize and had regularly recommended books to.

"You have some very loyal fans yourself, Noah. It must be rewarding to have had such a wonderful career all these years."

"Yes, yes, it has been. The store's my home and the customers are my family. I've been very blessed, Margaret. What time is it?

"Two fifteen. Any time now. So tell me how you met Hermione, Noah."

"You tell me about Maxine first."

That was a story Margaret was always glad to tell.

She had stepped out on the front porch one morning, reached down to pick up *The Bee* and heard a faint meow. Ernie happened to be out of town, so Margaret ran back inside, put on her sneakers and raced out to rattle the bushes and find the source of the plaintive cry. There, almost invisible in a patch of mint ground cover, a tiny head looked up at her. The green eyes occupied half of its face. When the pitiful creature opened its mouth, the other half disappeared.

Kitty didn't even flinch when Margaret bent down and picked it up, scrawny, wet and shivering, in spite of the July morning temperature. Margaret called the grocery store—she'd be in late today.

She fed kitty some watered down milk, got it dry and warm, put it in a tall box for the car ride and headed for the nearest veterinarian, Dr. Crown at the strip mall on Grand Avenue. He confirmed that *it* was a *she* and about two months old. It was anyone's guess how she'd wound up in Margaret's flower bed, but there was virtually no hope of finding the human owner or the feline mother. Either someone intentionally abandoned her, she'd wandered away from the litter or something had happened to the mama cat. Margaret didn't like where this conversation was clearly headed.

Did the doctor know anyone who wanted a kitten, Margaret asked. He and his assistant looked at each other, burst out laughing and pointed at the bulletin board in his waiting area, covered with notices for FREE KITTENS—REALLY CUTE! Every time Margaret tried to hand her off to Dr. Crown, he took the kitty, scratched her little head, murmured sweetly to her—and handed her back to Margaret. "Sorry, Margaret, but finder's keepers. Do you have any other pets?"

"No, and I don't have this one, either, doc. I'll take her home, but can I please put a notice on your board?"

"Sure, knock yourself out, but don't hold your breath for a call. She looks healthy. How about we give her some vaccinations as long as she's here?"

"Oh, I suppose so."

Margaret took the tiny orphan home after first leaving her in the care of the receptionist at Dr. Crown's office while she went to *Walnut Street Hardware* to get a carrier and a litter box, then next door to *The Marion Street Grocery* for kitten food. Margaret told everyone at the store about the extraordinarily cute kitten. It was obvious what they were all thinking as they smiled and nodded knowingly and said thanks, but no thanks.

"Well, I can't keep her. I'm not keeping her," Margaret assured them.

"Have you named her yet, Margaret?"

"No no no. Once I name her, that's big trouble. Ernie'll kill me."

"Nonsense, Ernie'll love her. You should name her, Margaret. You have to call her something."

Margaret tried to put the kitten in the carrier for the ride home and she pitched a hissing fit, and with those little straight pin claws of hers, there was no use arguing. So kitty rode home on Margaret's shoulder, snuggled into her neck, sleeping—or at least purring—as soon as Margaret let her be exactly where she wanted to be.

That was pretty much the way it was from then on. Margaret gave her a proper bath and after one morning of waking up to find kitty curled up on Ernie's pillow, as cute as any kitten had ever been, it was all over except for the christening. That was dealt with when Ernie got home the next day, took one look at kitty and said, "She looks like a Maxine to me. We once had a dog named Maxine and she was a heck of a dog."

"So, Noah, that little spitfire is now seven years old, fat as a pig and spoiled rotten. How about Hermione?" Noah didn't respond. His eyes were open, but he didn't seem to hear Margaret speak. Margaret tried again.

"I bet Hermione will be glad to see you."

"I sure wish she could come here. I really miss her."

Nancy and Rose had cautioned Margaret about what she could expect of Noah's behavior in the coming days and weeks. No specifics, they just knew that the brain tumor would gradually rob him of physical and mental capacity.

But there was no telling in what order and how soon, so they would all just go with the flow.

"I have good news, Noah. Hermione will be here anytime. Fritz is bringing her to visit you."

"He is? No kidding? That's wonderful!" Right on cue, there was a soft knock at the door and Fritz entered, hoisting a carrier filled to the brim with a wide-eyed orange striped cat.

"Noah, buddy, she's all yours. She's been talking my ears off all the way here." Fritz carefully closed the room's door behind him, put the carrier on the bed and opened the wire hatch. Hermione stuck out her nose, looked cautiously around, then spotted Noah and made a three-foot leap, right into his lap. He jumped in surprise, then hugged her close, burying his head in her fur, speaking her name over and over. Fritz and Margaret exchanged looks, grateful to the other for the part played in bringing about this poignant reunion.

Margaret left them alone. She'd promised Rose that the visit would last no more than an hour, and in return, Rose said that if everything went okay, there was no reason Fritz couldn't bring Hermione again, every day if he—and Hermione—were willing. Of that, there seemed little doubt.

Lois

One of the few things Lois had asked Ray to bring along when she came to Rockaway House was her Memory Box. She usually kept it on the top shelf of their clothes closet or slipped under their bed, depending on how recently she'd been looking through it. It held the most beloved tidbits of her life, the treasures that she now wanted close to her. Before Ray left the room to fetch Carlene from the kitchen, Lois asked him to put the Memory Box next to her on the tray table.

Down in the kitchen, Carlene was glad for the summons. The conversation with Cameron had left her at sixes and sevens. She had enough chaos in her brain these days without some smarty-pants, know-it-all, small town lawyer tossing in his two cents' worth of life philosophy. *Mahatma Gandhi? Give me a break.* She started to share the details of their frustrating exchange with her father, then thought better of it and went directly upstairs.

She entered Lois's room, grateful to find her mother awake, a weak smile coming to her lips as she saw Carlene.

"Hi, honey." Her voice was weedy, barely audible. Carlene leaned over, gave her a kiss and pulled a chair up close.

"How's it going, Mom?"

"I want you to see something." Lois barely raised her hand, waving in the direction of the Memory Box. Carlene picked up the cardboard carton. In a former life, it had held produce from the grocery store. It was now preserved with floral contact paper, circa 1970s. Carlene removed the lid and peered into it. *Mom and her cardboard boxes—what now?*

"Look for the folder marked 'Carlene's Stories'." Carlene did as Lois asked, gingerly removing layers of items. There was a black and white photo of Lois and Ray, she in a poufy wedding dress, he in a tuxedo. Another one, a color snapshot of baby Carlene in the arms of Lois, Ray beaming, his arm around them both. There was Carlene in her commencement gown, standing between her parents, looking none too happy. And a photo of the front of *Au Naturale!*

"Hey, when did you take this picture?" Carlene said, showing it to Lois.

"I don't remember exactly. Probably the very first time we saw your shop. We were so proud when you started your own business," Lois said matter-of-factly. Carlene looked up in surprise but didn't say what she was thinking. She kept digging and found the folder labeled 'Carlene's Stories.' It contained a stack of notebook paper. Carlene recognized her mother's handwriting, filling the pages held together with a rusting paper clip. The first page was entitled "*Mr. Pepperdo Comes to the Big City.*"

"What is this, Mom?"

In a whisper came, "Just read it."

Mr. Pepperdo Comes to the Big City

Mr. Pepperdo was a very happy farmer. He had a pig, a cow, a sheep, a chicken and a goat.

He had named each one, so he couldn't serve them for dinner, which was all right because he loved each and every one and having a steak or a drumstick that used to be named Bruno or Henrietta wouldn't have suited Mr. Pepperdo at all.

It was autumn, the leaves were falling, the nights were getting cooler and winter was coming. Mr. Pepperdo needed to go to the Big City to get feed for the cold months. He didn't want to leave his animals alone. Who would feed them? Who would make sure they were warm at night?

Carlene stopped reading, a look of astonishment on her face. "Mom! I know this story! What book did this come from? I remember this." Carlene was digging deeper in the box, looking for one of her own favorite memories. Lois just smiled, waiting for Carlene to figure it out, which took only another moment. "Oh my gosh, Mom, you wrote these." Lois nodded, still smiling. "But why?"

Lois took a long, slow breath, gathering her strength before speaking. "You were a bit of a challenge, Carlene. You didn't like any of the books I bought for you. I had to do something or you were going to be illiterate—which was not an option with your father and me—and it turned out you liked *my* stories." Tears came to her eyes as she said this. "You should have them now." Carlene looked deeper in the box. There were two more folders, more handwritten pages, at least fifty more. Lois's degree in literature had paid off after all.

Carlene couldn't speak. She whispered "thank you" in her mother's ear as she gave her a kiss on the cheek.

"You know what I'm most sad about?"

"No, what, Mom?"

"I'm sad to be leaving you and your dad. I pray every day that I won't know what missing you both feels like in heaven or wherever I'm going."

That's the only part that scares her, Carlene thought in amazement. But she could identify with her mother's focus, because Carlene was frightened, too. Lately, she'd been afraid that she might never have anyone—like her mom and dad had each other—to miss, or to miss her. "I'm sorry we didn't talk like this before, Mom."

"I wouldn't worry about that, honey. It's so much sooner than for most people." Lois gave out with a little sigh and smiled.

She accepted a few ice chips from Carlene and didn't take her eyes off her daughter's face as Carlene moistened her lips with Vaseline.

"Should I keep digging in the box, Mom?" Lois nodded. The next envelope in the stack was labeled *Memorial Plans.* Carlene started to put it back but Lois shook her head.

"No, honey, bring that one out. Your Dad won't talk about this. I need you to do something for me." Carlene opened the envelope. Simple instructions, carefully organized, exactly what Carlene would expect of her mother. Lois wished to be cremated and have her ashes buried in the family plot, where she and Ray owned two spots, right next to her parents and younger brother who had died twenty-five years earlier. She'd made a list of songs and readings for her memorial service, some from the Bible, some from her favorite authors and poets. She suggested that the retired minister from the Chesterton First Christian Church, a neighbor, could officiate. Lois chose him because he knew her, so he wouldn't have to begin with "I'm sorry I never got to know . . . " Every time Lois heard someone say that at a funeral, it gave her the willies.

"I don't really care about having a service, to be honest with you, but, well, I think there should be one, don't you?"

Carlene nodded in agreement.

Lois's obituary was there, neatly typed. All that remained was to insert the date of her death, and it was very nearly time to check that last item off her to-do list.

Carlene finished reading and put the papers back in the envelope.

"I'll handle this, Mom. Don't worry." That was what Lois wanted to hear. She sighed in relief.

"I love you, Carlene. Remember to be happy."

"I love you, too, Mom. I will, I promise." Lois drifted off.

Carlene turned on the music, Puccini's *La Boheme,* put a fresh lavender wax pod in the candle warmer and opened the paperback she had begun reading on the plane. She and her father had agreed before leaving home this morning that one or the other would stay with Lois 24/7 from now until the end. Ray couldn't bear the possibility of Lois being alone when she died and Carlene agreed. She'd stashed this book and a change of clothes in her bag before she left the house that morning.

Ray returned to the room not long after Lois fell asleep. Carlene looked up as he came in, thinking her father seemed to have aged ten years since her return to Chesterton, and that he looked like he could use a mid-morning nap. He settled into the recliner but didn't put his feet up. Carlene studied his face while he studied Lois's. Once she was sure he wasn't planning to doze, Carlene spoke up.

"Mom shared her memorial plans with me, Dad. I told her I'd take care of it. I will." Without speaking, Ray nodded his appreciation, his gaze never leaving his wife's face.

"Your mother looks like the day I married her."

Carlene caught herself before speaking. Lois's face was puffy and stretched, more so in just the past twenty-four hours, and her color had a yellow/gray tinge to it. Her hair had been shampooed the day before, but it was unavoidably stringy and matted. Not that any of that bothered Carlene, it just didn't jibe with her father's observation. She thought hard before she spoke, trying to be sensitive to her dad and also conscious of what the nurses had reminded them: *the hearing is one of the last things to go.*

"I'm a little concerned about how Mom looks, Dad. But you don't think so?"

"Carlene, I hope you'll get the chance to know this one day. When you love someone, you can see their beauty no matter what changes, no matter how old or how sick. Even in the dark you can see their beauty. They never really change."

That's good to know, Carlene thought. *If I do ever get the chance . . .*

"I told your mother while you were downstairs, I just heard that my guest column is going to be published in *The Bee.* Thought I better let you know—it'll be in the paper sometime in the next few days."

"Hey, good for you, Dad. I'm really glad you did that."

In 1959, when Ray got his journalism degree, all he had wanted to be, all he had imagined himself being, was a columnist for a great metropolitan newspaper. As it turned out, when it came to being a columnist, Ray was a great editor. At age seventy-five, he had supposed that was never going to happen, most especially with a thirty-five-year-old making the editorial decisions at *The Bee.* He had first viewed the acceptance of his guest essay as nothing more than a lucky break and a chance to check an item off his own Bucket List.

The editor who replaced him, Jake Elbert, had phoned to tell Ray of the firm publication date. Then, just as he was about to hang up, Jake casually mentioned that some of the readers of *The Bee* might enjoy a regular column about the issues of aging and discovering all the joys of senior life (Ray thought Jake might have been mocking him a little with that last part).

Ray had replied, "I'm no expert on senior life, but I'm sure as hell an expert on *my* life," admitting to himself that those two topics were now one and the same. And the deal was struck. Young Jake was no dummy. Ray's guest column was a great piece of journalism, and it would hit all the right buttons for the readers of *The Bee.* His name alone would sell papers. And, seriously, if one more person said to Jake, "You really oughta think about having Ray Spaulding do a column. He's still around, you know," he'd spit.

"Actually, Jake—he's that young editor—asked me if I'd write a regular column for the paper," Ray shared with Carlene. "A perspective on getting old, well, older. For some reason, he thinks I'm demographically qualified to do so," he said with a grin.

"Really, Dad? That's wonderful! You've always wanted to be a columnist, haven't you?"

"I have. I didn't know you knew that. Did your mother tell you that?"

Carlene shook her head. "I always knew you were an excellent writer. I'm glad you're finally getting to live your dream." Carlene looked out the window down Marion Street. "I'm sorry I left you two alone for nineteen years."

"You have nothing to be sorry for, honey. And we weren't alone. We had each other and a full life. Actually, I think maybe it was you who was alone. But you're not anymore, are you?" Carlene could see that her father had an expectant look on his face.

She shook her head. *Not if I don't choose to be.*

Ray Spaulding was born in Chesterton, Iowa. He had left only once, and that was to go to Iowa State Teachers College, down the road in Cedar Falls. He came home from college and he never left again.

"Everybody needs a dream, Carlene. It was important to your mother and me that you get the chance to follow yours. Some dreams seem to happen on their own, some get put off, some are just never meant to be. And sometimes the pursuit turns out to be the dream. I was the editor of *The Bee*, just a small town paper, but I kept the members of a community in touch with each others' lives for forty-three years. That was never my dream—or at least I didn't realize it—but I did it, and I think I made a decent go of it.

"When I started, I was just glad to have a job, then it became a career, and—I don't know—maybe it turns out it was my dream. Now I'm finally getting around to something on my wish list, you might say. Your mother said it would happen in its own good time."

"She's pretty wise that way." Carlene kept looking out the window.

"You sure everything's going okay with your business? If you need some help, your mother and I aren't exactly destitute. We could—"

"—Dad, I'm fine, the business is fine. Actually, Rainbow, the woman who's watching it right now, made an offer to buy me out. I'm sort of considering that. I'd keep on managing the Internet business, though, which is where the real money is."

Ray just shook his head and smiled. "*The real money*"? Their little flower child had grown up to be a sophisticated, savvy entrepreneur. He couldn't be more surprised—or proud. Of course, that didn't mean he was done handing out fatherly advice.

"Sometimes our dreams need a slight kick in the butt."

"Oh yeah? Where'd you get yours?"

"Your mother, of course. She's a true friend and a life partner who never doubted that I could do anything I put my mind to. After a while, she got me believing it, too." Ray inserted a significant pause before going on. "Young Cameron Lane seems like a go-getter . . . with decent manners."

"Nice segue, Dad. Let's talk about something else."

Margaret

Really, Margaret thought, somebody should write a book on soup therapy. And she didn't mean a twelve-step program for people who have an unhealthy relationship with soup. This soup therapy tome would showcase the restorative benefits of making soup.

Margaret already knew how it should begin: assembling all the ingredients. *Hey! It's a sort of meditation because you have to give it one hundred percent of your attention or you're likely to leave something out.* Or, worse yet, forget to buy the item in the first place and have to make a trip back to the store. Ernie had been famous for coming home with everything but the one thing he'd been sent for. That was okay, he loved all the people at the store and they were always glad to see him. Now they missed him. They often said that to Margaret. Sometimes she believed those people missed Ernie as much as she did. I suppose, she thought, in their way they do.

Broth, tomatoes, onions, carrots, celery, potatoes, beans. Each one ready to play its part in the symphony of tastes and smells. Then, of course, there was the creative side of the process. Turkey, beef or chicken? Meatballs, ground meat or sliced sausage? Italian seasoning, oriental or the Mexican family of spices?

Cutting up vegetables, now that's truly therapeutic. Mindless and at the same time grounding. It appealed to Margaret's sense of order to assemble the soup, bit by bit, then enjoy her creation throughout the day as the house filled with the smell. Slow cookers may have been meant to provide the convenience of "fix it and forget it," but for Margaret the temptation was too great. Every hour or so she would remove the lid and give the pot a good stir, releasing even more of the enticing smells. It worked to tease the senses and glory in the making of a well-assembled culinary mélange.

Like most of Margaret's best ideas, the next one came when she least expected it. *If a pot of soup makes my house smell good, wouldn't it do the same at Rockaway House?* She'd ask Rose if it was okay. She'd assemble the soup at home, then let it stew in the Rockaway House kitchen. Soup ingredients and a loaf of crispy bread from Mr. Goldberg once in a while. Now *that* would be a good use of some of the insurance money. *Free soup!*

Margaret gave the pot one last stir and started out the door. Then she stopped, walked back to their bedroom and stood for a moment in front of their wedding picture.

"It's a new chapter for me, Ernie. Not a better chapter, but a new one. I love you and I miss you."

She had just enough time to treat herself to a chai latte' on her way to Rockaway House.

Lois

Ray couldn't have been more shocked when he walked into Lois's room that morning. There was Carlene with breakfast for two laid out on the tray table. Lois was barely awake, her eyes half closed.

"Well, will you look at this, Lois. Who knew?" He kissed his wife and daughter in turn. Carlene stood, ready to leave. "Why not join us, Carlene? I think she's old enough to sit at the adult table, don't you, Lois?" He winked at his wife.

Lois opened her mouth to speak, then stopped, nodded weakly toward the water glass and Carlene picked up a wetted sponge, dabbing it on her mother's lips, dripping a bit into her mouth. Lois tried again.

"I can check this off my Bucket List," she whispered.

They had an unforgettable breakfast. Ray and Carlene carried on a lively conversation as Ray skimmed the headlines in the copy of *The Bee* he'd brought from home, reading aloud to his wife and daughter. Lois had a wistful look on her face. Almost angelic, Carlene thought.

She was so relieved. Carlene had insisted she take the first night shift and had slept in the fold-out recliner in her mother's room, sending her father home at nine-thirty. The night had been a bit rough, but no need to tell Ray. Lois's rasping breaths had awakened Carlene from her light sleep at least once an hour. Each time Carlene got up and held her mother's hand, spoke softly to her and Lois would smile back after her breathing calmed, then drift off.

Carlene hesitated several times, then about three a.m. she finally got the nerve to ask the night nurse if her mother's symptoms were what was called a "death rattle." The nurse, Crystal, said she'd like to get ahold—like around the neck ahold—of the person who'd first used that term. Yes, Lois was actively dying, but that sound was caused by the fluids that were building up in her throat, making her breathing even more difficult and labored. Crystal gave Lois medication that might help dry the secretions, then she confirmed during her four a.m. bed check that the end was very close for Lois. Her feet were cold and mottled with practically no circulation.

With each episode, Carlene was terrified that her mother would not be able to hold on, that she would pass away with Carlene alone at her side. But about half-way through the night, a peace descended on Carlene and she realized that if that were to happen it was because her father was meant to be spared. If not, if her mother made it through the night, then that's what was meant to be. But still, she was so relieved when morning came and her dad arrived.

One time during the night, Lois had looked over at the corner of the room, smiled and nodded. When Carlene asked her mother if she saw someone there, Lois whispered, "Just Mama."

Stick around, Grandma. Your favorite son-in-law will be here soon. Carlene hadn't decided whether to share that good news with her father. *She's ba-ack . . .*

"Well, I'll be damned," Ray suddenly exclaimed. "There it is." He folded over the newspaper and held it in front of Lois and Carlene. The column was entitled "*Saying Goodbye*." Byline: *Ray Spaulding, former Editor of The Chesterton Bee.* Lois smiled, then she and Ray shared a lingering look.

Carlene opened her mouth to congratulate her father. She heard her mother take in a quick breath, then release it ever so slowly. Carlene instinctively looked her way, just in time to see her mother's eyes peacefully close.

Ray's voice was a whisper. "Carlene, I think your mother just passed."

Carlene wasn't so sure. She put her hand gently on the center of her mother's chest. No breath. No heartbeat. Her mother was gone. Lois's face relaxed, her lips turned in the most subtle of smiles. Carlene leaned over, kissed her on the cheek and whispered in her ear, "I love you, Mom."

Ray was holding Lois's hand and softly sobbing. Carlene went around to his side of the bed. He let go of Lois while he and Carlene embraced. Then Carlene stepped back, smiled and looked directly at her father.

"Headline, Dad: **World's Best Mom Passes Away**." Ray's mouth dropped open and stayed that way as Carlene excused herself to let Sheryl know.

"Why, that little stinker. All these years, Lois . . . "

Sheryl returned with Carlene. "You have my sympathies, both of you, Carlene, Ray. I'm glad it was so peaceful for her. God bless her. Sometimes it's quick like that, the heart just stops."

Sheryl had spoken to Carlene the day before about the rituals surrounding a death at Rockaway House. Now was the time for Ray and Carlene to honor Lois's body for the final time, if they chose to.

Carlene put an arm around Ray's shoulders. *When did my father get shorter than me?* "Dad, I'd like to help prepare Mom's body for leaving, if you don't mind." Ray was a little surprised, but he was fine with that. He left to call friends and family members. Sheryl brought a basin, washcloths and towels to the room. She helped Carlene undress Lois, then Carlene proceeded to gently bathe her mother's body, applying scented oils and brushing her hair. All the while, Carlene spoke to her mother, thanking her for the childhood she had enjoyed, for the wisdom Lois had shared and for the unconditional love she had always demonstrated. Lois's favorite music, Mozart's *Eine Kleine Nachtmusik* was playing softly in the background. Carlene was thinking about what her mother had said and what Carlene had promised to her. Maybe it was time for her to choose happiness. Perhaps she had put it off long enough.

With Sheryl's help, Carlene dressed Lois in a gown and the bedjacket she'd given to her the Christmas before, placed Lois's hands on top of the covers, tucked a handkerchief in her sleeve and opened the door.

Ray arrived just as Carlene turned back to the bedside.

"I called Harold Forester. They'll be here in about an hour. I thought we could talk to him about the services when he gets here."

"I'll handle that if you want, Dad."

"No, no. I want us to do that together, Carlene. I don't know, I just couldn't talk to your mom about it. I was never as good about facing reality as she is—was. She was the strong one, you know."

Carlene realized what her mother had considered in planning to have a memorial service. There's no way her father would recognize on his own how many Chestertonians would want to pay their respects to Lois—and Ray. As he always had, Ray underestimated the importance of his role in the community and the deep affection the subscribers of *The Bee* had for him—and for Lois. The people of Chesterton had long forgotten what it was like to know Ray Spaulding without Lois Spaulding at his side. As Lynda Wyatt had said to Carlene when she visited last, *Your dad's a fixture in this town—and so is your mom.*

Carlene smiled to think of her mother making this last set of plans for the benefit of her life partner. It was so like her.

Ray sat next to the bed, holding Lois's hand. Staff members stopped in to say goodbye and to give their condolences to Carlene and Ray. Then, at last, they were alone with Lois for the final time.

"I've been thinking about this day for almost two years," Ray admitted to Carlene. "I know life will go on, I just can't picture myself in it without her by my side. But how can I possibly deny your mother her peace, no longer being tied to a body that was just plain worn out? So if I'm really honest, I have to admit that it's me I'm sad for. My grief is one hundred percent selfish." Ray leaned over and gave Lois a final kiss.

"I wanted it all and, come to think of it, that's just what we had. We had a helluva run, didn't we, Lois?" Carlene came to his side of the bed and put an arm around him, her first hero, and still her number one.

"You have a lot left to share with others, Dad. Mom was right, everything happens in its own good time."

Harold Forester came and took Lois away. His son Hank was working part-time with his dad and came along. He drove Ray's car to their home so Ray could ride with Carlene, and then young Hank walked the three blocks back to the funeral home.

As Ray carried the carton with Lois's few possessions from Rockaway House into the kitchen, Carlene trailed behind him, hugging the Memory Box.

"I've got to make the rest of the calls, Carlene. Did your mother leave an obituary that I need to get over to *The Bee*?" It was a rhetorical question. Of course she had. Carlene reached into the box and retrieved the remaining envelope.

"Here, Dad."

Ray sat down at the kitchen table. He looked over at the empty chair across from him. He could count on one hand the number of times he'd sat alone at that table over the past four decades.

"Dad, I need to run an errand, and then I'd like to talk to you about a conversation I had with Rose Sears at Rockaway House. I'd like you to consider whether you and I could live together, for a while anyway."

Ray looked up. Astonishment, then relief, then joy passed across his face.

"Sure we can, honey. As long as you understand this is a tofu-free zone."

Carlene leaned over and gave him a hug and a kiss.

The offices of *Lane, Roderick, Brown, and Lane* were on Main Street, across from *Under the Covers* and *Whole Latte' Love.* Carlene took a big breath and approached the entrance. She had no idea what time it was until she saw the little "Be Back At" clock hung on the door. The plastic hands were set to one o'clock. She looked at her watch and saw that it was half past noon.

"Only in Chesterton, Iowa, would a business actually close over the lunch hour," she muttered with a smile as she turned to wait in her car. Then she heard footsteps and there was Cameron, coming across the street, a to-go salad and soda in his hands. She waited to speak until he got to the door, right in front of her, and then she didn't need to.

Cameron looked at Carlene's face and quickly unlocked the office, juggling his lunch to hold the door open for her.

He set down his food and turned to face Carlene.

"She passed just now, Cameron." Then she broke down. These were the tears she had held back while she bathed her mother, while she helped her father make funeral plans and then while she drove him home and got him settled. They flooded out with choking sobs.

Cameron did the only thing he could do. He held her, letting her cry. When she had calmed down, he stepped back, reached into his pocket and pulled out a plain white handkerchief.

"My dad told me to always make sure I have a hankie to offer to a lady."

Carlene loudly blew her nose in a very unladylike manner and wiped her cheeks. She offered the handkerchief back to Cameron. He declined it with a shake of his head. She looked in his eyes, hoping he was going to speak first. He wasn't.

"Were you thinking about offering to come over to my parents' house to be with Dad and me?" she said, speaking barely above a whisper.

Cameron took his time answering. "No."

"Because, I was just going to say that if you were thinking about offering to come over to my parents' house to be with Dad and me, I just wanted to let you know that I would be very grateful for that kindness."

Cameron tried to keep a straight face. He really did.

Rockaway House

Margaret recalled that at the launch party Bruce had said, "We better enjoy the peace while we can." Margaret and Rose had nodded like they knew what he meant because they thought they did, but they hadn't.

For instance, Bruce had about a million things on his checklist these days, trying to pull everything together. Ten days into it, he had finally decided on a hybrid bidding arrangement, probably never before done. The once simple, silent, in-person auction had morphed into an enormous, online, out-of-control Frankenstein monster. And didn't that just fit the way the whole *Rockaway House Heritage Show Home and Auctionpalooza* had evolved up until now?

People began to complain immediately, but Bruce didn't care. Those were the rules and if anyone wanted to be a buyer, this is how is how they had to do it. Bidding could be done in person, of course, anytime up to the end of the show, which was six p.m., Sunday, November 11, 2012. For remote buyers, the bid could be submitted by mail or by e-mail, but this was not a sophisticated eBay operation, where offers could be raised in split-second intervals. If someone out-bid you before the bell rang, you were most likely stone cold out of luck.

The running bids would be published on the website—updated hourly—so anyone who wanted to raise an existing price could do so, but remote bidding ended at four p.m. on Sunday. Once four o'clock Sunday came, that was it. If more in-person bids came during the last two hours, remote bidders were out of luck.

Bruce was a worrier, so he'd already considered the possibility of a buyer not performing. He gathered from all those *Don't bid unless you intend to buy!* warnings on eBay that bidding and paying were two different things. He'd do whatever he had to do to make this system succeed because he wasn't about to get to Monday after *The Auction* with a bunch of furniture and without a bunch of legitimate buyers. No problem. The winners had until six p.m. on Monday to show up with a cashier's check or cash—and a truck. And Bruce wasn't suffering any excuses or cry babies. For any item not claimed and paid for, the runner-up on the list would be contacted to get to Rockaway House—toot sweet, as Suzi would say—cash in hand.

True, it was a bizarre process, but then, so was the whole event. Bruce said, who would dare be a big donkey about rules when it was all for a good cause? Anyway, people would bid outlandish prices for things in the name of charity. That was his plan and he was sticking to it.

Meanwhile, Margaret had started surfing the Web in earnest (the biggest reason she wasn't getting much sleep) as soon as it was for sure that *The Auction* was going to happen. She was gung ho to use her newly-acquired computer savvy to help promote it and after a week and a half of trying to figure it out on her own, she called Lenny, her computer tutor and new best friend.

How difficult was it to create one of those Facebook pages, she wanted to know. No biggie, came the response. Cookies were coming out of the oven as she spoke. Did Lenny happen to be free right now?

Margaret could have sworn the doorbell rang before she hung up the phone.

The Facebook page could be very simple, Margaret explained to Lenny, nothing fancy. Margaret figured it would be helpful for people to read the story behind the event so she asked Lynda to e-mail over the feature that she and Ray had written for *The Bee*. Margaret wanted Facebook visitors to be able to access it from "the cloud" (wherever that is). Also, it was best if they could visualize what Rockaway House looked like, so she got Suzi to e-mail the same picture they were using in the other marketing materials. And, of course, the point was to get tickets sold and bids placed, so they would need a link to Bruce's official website.

Oh, and put a Google map and directions to Chesterton on there, too, Margaret added. People might end up in Ohio or Idaho without some concrete guidance.

Lenny was a bit taken aback with Margaret's mastery of these techie terms as she ticked off the list of features—and more than a little impressed with his own skills as a coach.

Take the pebble from my hand, Grasshopper, he said to Margaret with a smile. She had no idea what he was talking about.

It took Lenny about forty-five minutes to pull it all together and publish the page. Margaret sat next to him at the kitchen table, watching in amazement.

"Anything else, Mrs. Williams?" Lenny asked.

"What happens now?"

"Well, you hope someone will want to be your friend. I set it up so anyone can follow you and like you. Hey, I'll be your first follower." He picked up his phone—never more than an arm's length away—and touched the screen until he had the Rockaway House Facebook page in front of him. "There! You have one *Like*!" Margaret went back to the page on her computer and, sure enough, it showed *1 likes.*

Hot dog, Margaret thought.

Margaret was trying very hard to not get all obsessive about the Internet. She didn't constantly check her e-mails, which was a temptation easily overcome because you could count on one hand the number of people on the planet who had *her* address in *their* address book. Most of the spammers hadn't even bothered to find her. But this morning Margaret wanted to see that spanking new Facebook page just one more time before she left for Rockaway House. How cool was it that she was involved in an event that had a Facebook page—thanks to her and Lenny—and that she could now visit it on her very own computer?

She hit the power button and waited. Then she went to the *Favorites* where Lenny had placed a link to Facebook. She double clicked and signed in.

"What in the world is all that?" She leaned close to the screen as she scrolled down. There were comments, hundreds—who knows, maybe thousands—of them right underneath the post that contained the link to Lynda Wyatt and Ray Spaulding's story in *The Bee.* Just below the picture of Rockaway House, it said "*23,135 likes, 15,251 talking about this.*" Margaret snatched the phone off the kitchen counter.

"Lenny, tell me again what it means if people are talking about you?"

Things went completely bonkers after that.

It had all begun this way: three days before the night that Margaret got 23,135 *likes,* Ray and Lynda's story appeared in *The Chesterton Bee*, circulation 4,273. Margaret read it while she ate breakfast. She already knew all the characters, and she already knew what happened to them, and she already knew how the story ended and she still cried. So did Rose and Lauren and Suzi and Bruce and every other person who read it. Jake Elbert said it was some of the best writing he'd ever had the privilege to edit, not that it required much editing.

Jake had a buddy at *The Des Moines Register*, a friend from college. Jake sent him the story by e-mail. Any interest, he queried. *Big* interest, the friend shot back. *The Register* reprinted the story the following day, which immediately put it in front of the folks at *USA Today*, a sister publication to *The Register*, both owned by the Gannett Company. *USA Today* reprinted it the day after that. The AP picked it sometime later that afternoon. Margaret didn't know any of that because she subscribed to and faithfully read *The Chesterton Bee*, but certainly not *The Des Moines Register* or *USA Today.*

Margaret was blown away but no one was as pleased as Bruce at the unexpected publicity bounty. While researching the furniture, he'd also researched Rockaway House and when he heard that Lynda Wyatt was writing the Murphys' story, he shared with her what he had learned about the Sears, Roebuck and Co.'s *Honor Bilt Modern Homes.* Lynda had included it all—she'd loved it, it was off-beat, like the rest of the story. Bruce had hoped upon hope to pull in Chicago bidders and he thought the Sears house angle might do the trick. It did the trick all right.

Suzi had naively put her home number on all publicity and her phone was ringing off the hook. She hired her sixteen-year-old niece to do nothing but retrieve and write down the messages in every spare moment she had. At fifty cents a pop, it practically broke Suzi's bank. But Suzi was afraid her voice mailbox would otherwise fill up, and folks simply had to get through.

Most were for tickets. They had advertised a Sneak Peek admission that got you into the house two hours ahead of the general public on the first morning, from eight to ten a.m. There'd be a line waiting to get in, right?

Maybe some people would think it was worth an extra charge to avoid standing in it. The committee certainly hoped so because regular tickets were $20 a head but Sneak Peek tickets were $50.

The invitation-only party at Suzi's house was Friday, the night before the show home started. Those people were paying $250 for a glass of semi-cheap wine, a cheese cube and the opportunity to be the first to get inside Rockaway House.

On the afternoon of the day that 15,251 people started talking about *The Auction* on Facebook, Suzi didn't bother to use the phone, she just walked across the driveway and, without saying a word, grabbed Rose and Margaret from inside Rockaway House. She marched them out to the garage where Bruce was sorting the furniture into "going in the house" and "staying in the garage" groups.

"Emergency committee meeting, my friends." Suzi punched Lauren Dunlap's number, now on her cell phone speed dial. She had called ahead from the house, making sure Lauren was in her office and available. Once Lauren was on the speaker, Suzi addressed them all.

"We've already sold 2,700 tickets. First, we have to cut off the Sneak Peek sales, or there won't be time for them to get in and out by ten a.m. Second, we need to seriously consider extending this for a second weekend."

No one said a word. Their good fortune in promotion and publicity had turned into a gigantic dilemma. And they didn't need Lauren to remind them that the patients and family members were still the top priority at Rockaway House, which she did, anyway.

Rose quickly responded. "You know, I've been keeping the family members and staff—especially the medical staff—closely posted on everything that's going on. I've constantly checked with them about whether they're bothered by the progress or the noise or anything. I gotta tell ya, nobody's got any complaints at all. In fact, the family members are all excited. They feel like they're a part of this. It's very rewarding for them, to make even the slightest sacrifice, like moving their kitchenette upstairs, to help out. There's no problem on this end." That was good news.

Margaret was making some mental calculations as she listened. "Suzi, are you telling us you've already sold $54,000 worth of tickets?"

"No, because that doesn't include the Sneak Peek prices. $54,000 plus."

Margaret still had a flip phone and couldn't have sent a text message to save her life, but she'd picked up some lingo while hanging out with Lenny. "OMG."

"OMG is right. Well, do we do this a second weekend?"

Lauren said it all depended on whether they had the volunteer staff to work it and would Bruce be able to let bidders know that *The Auction* would be extended? Yes and yes.

From the beginning, the operation had required oodles of detail, pin perfect organization and ironfisted resilience. Bruce had focused on assembling the best team of Type A+ volunteers he could find. His crew of ladies with attitude (he affectionately called them The Hell's Belles) had built a detailed database of the bidders, including e-mail addresses, so it would be easy to send out a notice of the extension. They were—can you believe it?—now turning away volunteers, so no problem there. And, as luck would have it, there was one more weekend on the calendar between *The Auction* and Thanksgiving.

"Well, then that's it. We carry it over to Saturday, November 17 and Sunday, November 18. God have mercy on our souls," Suzi proclaimed. Lauren clicked off and they all went back to work.

Rose was right, there was definitely no shortage of volunteers. True, some were motivated by a wish to see the furniture or a peek at the inside of the house ahead of time, but if they were good workers, why not? But most were there because a loved one had been in hospice care at the end of their life or they wished they had been or they were just now grasping how important the hospice mission was to their community. No doubt about it, the word was out.

A week later, Margaret was watching Lance and his assistants bring down another load of cataloged furniture when a gray-haired gentleman walked up the driveway.

"Are you Margaret, ma'am?"

"I am." Margaret extended her hand. "And you are?"

"Paul Thornton, Margaret. My wife Mary Pat was a patient here at Rockaway House. She passed away eight months ago."

"I'm so sorry, Paul. Did you say 'Thornton'?"

"Yes, ma'am. I stopped inside and they said to talk to you. Before Mary Pat got sick, we had a big backyard garden for thirty years. Actually, I'm a master gardener. I don't mean I did it for a living or anything, I was a carpenter for a living, gardening was just a hobby, but I'm pretty good. I moved into a little apartment after Mary Pat died, so I don't get much chance to dig in the dirt, and I just wondered if you could use some help with the yard, you know, for the show home."

"Are you for real? I can definitely use some help, Paul. Let's talk." *Thornton? Whoa.*

The whole RUSH JOB theme was kitschy and worked for Suzi's purposes, but it was wreaking havoc with Margaret's slight OCD. She'd volunteered (or she'd been volunteered—she could no longer keep it all straight) to pretty up the outside of Rockaway House, and if anyone had asked, she wouldn't have minded telling them that she was struggling with that. All those times Ernie had tried to get Margaret interested in the yard work were coming back to haunt her.

Sure, it looked all right, but she wanted it to look much more than just all right. There were lovely brick-bordered flowerbeds, filled only with mulch. It was way too late in the fall to do any serious planting and even if it wasn't, the beds wouldn't amount to more than little sprouts with big intentions for the spring. Margaret needed a Plan B, and everyone else was so focused on the *inside* of Rockaway House, the redecorating, the details of *The Auction,* the exhibits and the activities in the garage, no one was interested in discussing the *outside.* She led Paul to the picnic table just off the driveway, they sat down and she asked him if he (please God) had any ideas.

"Well, when my wife and I were first married, we didn't have much money for major landscaping or, you know, hardscaping items like benches or things like that so we sort of camouflaged our yard until we could afford more."

"Talk to me."

"We sort of drew the eye away from the bare parts with inexpensive mum plants and did container gardens and this time of year we would have had pumpkins and maybe a scarecrow. I don't know, it sounds sort of silly, now that I say it."

"Silly? It sounds absolutely inspired! I actually have a budget, what I don't have is ideas and time. What are you doing right now, Paul, I mean *starting right now?* Can you go with me to *The Farm and Home Center* and load up?" She didn't wait for his answer, she was already headed in Lance's direction to borrow one of the CCH trucks.

Paul watched her go and wondered what in the world he'd gotten himself into.

Margaret couldn't believe her luck. The cavalry had arrived. Tons of mums, a mountain of pumpkins, corn stalks, lots of cornstalks, bales of hay—the old-fashioned rectangular ones, not those super ginormous round ones they make nowadays—and a couple of park benches. The more Margaret and Paul talked on the way to the store, the more ideas they came up with.

Lance was driving. He was fairly sure Margaret didn't have much experience behind the wheel of an extended cab pickup truck. And no offense to Mr. Thornton, who seemed like a very nice guy, but Lance was not about to loan the company vehicle to the first well-meaning volunteer who strolled up the driveway, even if he did appear to be heaven-sent and no matter how thrilled Margaret was.

In two hours, they were back at Rockaway House, unloading supplies and assembling whatever tools Paul needed to get started. Was he hungry or thirsty? Margaret showed him the area in the garage set aside for volunteers where he could help himself to sandwiches and drinks. She turned him loose.

Pleased to note that her calls were now always put through, no matter what got interrupted, Margaret phoned Lauren Dunlap. Lauren eagerly answered the phone and wanted to know how it was all going, hoping there was a mini-crisis that required her immediate appearance at Rockaway House. Margaret told her it was going great. Then she got to the point.

"Is there some money in the budget for front porch furniture and maybe a few pieces for the patio?" Margaret asked hopefully. Those areas looked so bare and were hardly the welcoming face that they wanted Rockaway House to be wearing.

Lauren thought that was very doable. She'd make a call and get back to Margaret. Great! Margaret told her she'd be on her cell phone, quickly making sure she had it with her and it was turned on.

Good enough. Margaret had unlimited faith in Lauren's ability to make things happen and she was eagerly anticipating a little buying trip. Glancing over to see that Paul Thornton had already plunged into his project, Margaret headed down the driveway to the house next door. Suzi could use a break, Margaret knew that for a fact. For the past couple of days, she'd looked as if the top of her head was going to blow off any minute now.

Meanwhile, Lauren was on the case and had punched another number as soon as she hung up from Margaret's call.

"This is Lauren Dunlap. May I please speak to Christopher? Thanks . . . Christopher, Lauren Dunlap at Chesterton Community Hospice. How are you? . . . Good, good. Say, Christopher, your mother is such a dear. She has been so generous with her time as a director, you know. And, of course, I don't know how we can ever express our gratitude for your generosity in helping us to buy all that new furniture at wholesale . . . Yes, well, your mother told me just the other day that if there's anything, anything at all that we need for the show home, I'm to give you a call. I can't even tell you what a relief it is to know that we can turn to you . . ."

What a day. Margaret lowered herself onto the new front porch furniture and gave out with a long sigh. That Christopher Walton was certainly personality-free, but he made up for it with a great warehouse. It hadn't taken Margaret and Suzi any time at all to pick out two settees gliders, matching chairs and a couple of tables. They were reproduction 1940s metal furniture, the kind with little holes punched in the backs, powder-coated in white. Their cushions made Suzi think of William Morris wallpaper and they were perfect for Rockaway House. Now there was an inviting conversation group on each side of the front door and a dining set on the patio.

Margaret looked out over the terrace. It was adorned with an assortment of pumpkins and gourds, clustered on top of hay bales. The corners were filled with great tall corn stalks that had been skillfully bundled by Paul Thornton. The way it looked to Margaret, he was as much an artist as a master gardener. Yellow and orange and scarlet mum plants marched along the edge of the sidewalk leading up to Rockaway House. Margaret thought it looked like the center aisle of a church. An immense oak tree, probably a resident of the neighborhood a century before Edwina Powell browsed through that Sears catalog, guarded Rockaway House and filtered the afternoon sun into its living room. Its boughs now sheltered a slatted bench, inviting someone to enjoy the natural peace. The flowerbeds were sprinkled with more colorful potted mums. Paul would plant them once the fundraiser was over, before the first frost came.

The chair cushion was warm from the sun. *Nothing like a toasty bum on a cool afternoon*, Margaret thought gratefully with a smile, as she slowly glided forwards and back. *This feels so right.*

Victoria

A.M. bulletin issued. Magda shut down the laptop computer and stood up from the kitchen table. Each morning she dutifully sent out a group e-mail to friends and family awaiting news of Victoria's condition. Magda had long since given up sending messages that implied a cure was still at hand or that Victoria was on the mend. She focused now on the reality of the situation. This morning's report was that Victoria continued to be comfortable and that the staff at Rockaway House had figured out how to keep her pain at bay, something Magda had failed to do when Victoria was still at home. Magda didn't really say that last bit, but she didn't need to, did she? Wasn't that already obvious to everyone?

She scanned the numerous incoming e-mails expressing words of support, promises that she and Victoria were being remembered in prayers, requests for Magda to call if there was something they could do.

How about you just do something to help without me having to ask you?

Magda hastily chided herself for being so ungrateful. Their friends had been wonderful, all in all. She couldn't have imagined going through this without those who had shown their love and empathy, time and time again. *Let's face it. There's no pleasing me today. I'd bitch if my ice cream was cold. Isn't that what Victoria sometimes says?*

Magda had no intention of responding directly to each individual. *Really, what would be the point of sending out a mass e-mail if I'm expected to answer twenty incoming messages? Anyway, the unvarnished truth would be the same for everyone: It's almost over. If you want to see Victoria, you'd better beat feet over to Rockaway House.*

Sorry again. That was unkind. And untrue. It's too late. Three weeks earlier, Victoria had made it clear that open visiting hours were closed. She didn't like being seen so helpless and so weak. She dictated to Magda a list of people who were still allowed to see her. Magda needed to give all others the message that Victoria simply wasn't up to company.

Magda was glad to pass that on.

For Magda, visitors while Victoria was still at home had come to mean making coffee, keeping an assortment of snacks on hand and constantly washing up cups and saucers. She'd finally rebuffed her inner hostess months before Victoria went to Rockaway House and made a trip to Sam's Club, coming home with a freezer full of cookies and disposable cups and plates. *Screw the environment.* She'd never looked back.

Magda slowly mounted the stairs at the rear of the Rockaway House kitchen. Family members had been advised to use the back entrance once the redecorating project began. Magda thought the whole idea of the show home was intriguing—it made her think of the days when she and Victoria were sweating gallons of equity into their little bungalow. There was a tiny part of Magda that wanted to poke her head into the downstairs rooms to see the "before," but at the moment she didn't care enough to do it. Her attitude toward most everything right now was best described as indifference.

Her focus rested entirely on maintaining low expectations.

Magda thought it best to not hope that Victoria was alert and capable of a meaningful conversation this morning. Not that Magda didn't care one way or the other or didn't want Victoria to know she was there, but Magda was tired of getting her hopes constantly and consistently dashed. She wanted to just sit peacefully at Victoria's bedside for a while. Yes, some peace would be nice.

But that wasn't the plan.

Rona, the nurse on duty, was hurrying out of Victoria's room as Magda approached the door.

"Magda, Victoria's in a lot of pain right now. I've got Trish on the phone with Dr. Gold. I'll be back in a quick sec with some relief. Maybe you can help her calm down a bit." Magda started to ask a question but Rona was rushing to the nurses' station, already out of earshot.

Magda apprehensively opened the door to Victoria's room.

"Magda! Thank God you're here!" Victoria reached out to Magda, her arms moving spastically, reacting to the amplified pain that followed each movement. Magda stepped quickly to her bedside. Victoria grabbed at Magda's arm. "Can't you make this pain stop? Please? We still have those sleeping pills at home. You have to go get them and bring them to me. You have to do this for me, Magda. Please." Victoria was slowing contracting into the fetal position, too delirious to recognize that each movement was probably adding to her misery.

She's crazy with pain. Please God, she didn't mean that. They'd talked about this many times on their own. Then again, while they signed their advance directives, their attorney had explained all about assisted suicide. Not that either Victoria or Magda thought it seemed like a good option, but that didn't matter, it was illegal. No exceptions.

Magda willed herself to take a calming breath and put her hand gently on Victoria's arm.

"Vic, take deep, slow breaths. Remember what we learned in yoga? Let's do that now. The nurse will be right back with something."

"Please, please, Magda. God will forgive you. You have to make this stop. Please," Victoria moaned.

Magda began to cry. She could feel a burning sensation crawling up her neck and settling at her temples. *God? She doesn't even believe in God. How many times has she said she expects to go nowhere when she dies? God will forgive me? Easy for her to say.*

"I would do anything for you, Victoria, but you can't ask me to do that. I'm so sorry, Vic, I'm so sorry."

Victoria peered intently into Magda's eyes and Magda didn't know if her look was disappointment, resentment or resignation. "It hurts so much. I don't want to live anymore, Magda. Why can't I die now?"

"I don't know, I don't know. But we'll get through this together. Just breathe like me. In. Out. That's better." Was Magda becoming delusional, too, or was Victoria calming down a bit? Just then Rona returned with a hypodermic in her hand.

"Here we go, Victoria. This will do the trick, sweetie." She gingerly eased Victoria's arm flat onto the bed, and injected the drug into the semi-permanent catheter that had been placed in Victoria's arm weeks earlier. It was a portal for drugs to directly enter the bloodstream. The morphine could take effect much more quickly than with a pill or a shot into the muscle.

Victoria's breathing and involuntary thrashing slowed down almost immediately. Rona stayed at her side for a few minutes, checking her pulse and watching her body language. No one spoke. Victoria's eyes closed. She was out. Magda visibly relaxed as Rona stepped back and motioned for her to follow into the hall.

"I'm so sorry that happened, Magda. It's what we call breakthrough pain. We have her on a regulated schedule of meds, but sometimes the pain just beats us. We just can't anticipate when acute pain like that will occur. That should keep her comfortable for a couple of hours at least. Hopefully, longer, then the morphine patch we have on her should be sufficient. If not, we'll address it just as quickly next time." She looked at the ashen faced Magda. "I asked her just before you arrived and she said that on a scale of one-to-ten, her pain was a fifteen." Rona gave Magda a sympathetic smile.

"That sounds like Vic. She doesn't mince words."

"We assume the patient is the best judge of how much it hurts. Are you okay? Relaxation and distraction can go a long way in pain relief. You did good, Magda."

"Really? Yes, yes. I'm fine now. Thank you."

Margaret had just checked in at the nurses' station and walked up as Magda was about to go back into Victoria's room. "Can I interest you in a cup of coffee in the kitchen, Magda?" she asked.

Magda hesitated and looked to Rona for direction.

"Victoria will probably sleep for a while now. We know where to find you if need be," Rona said as she gently steered Magda away from Victoria's door.

Magda shrugged and walked at Margaret's side along the hall and down the back stairs. "Whenever I come this back way, I always imagine what it must have been like to be a servant in this home, to be a part of the family that built this house," Margaret involuntarily chattered. Magda didn't respond.

In the kitchen, Magda took a seat in the solarium as Margaret got them each a coffee and a cookie and joined Magda in the morning sunshine. She waited for Magda to speak first.

Magda took a bite of cookie and a sip of coffee. "Thank you, Margaret, this is good. Just now, Victoria asked me to kill her."

Once again, her experience as a hospice volunteer was of little use to Margaret in knowing how to respond. Her time at Rockaway House hadn't included this situation—until now. She thought for a minute. She thought about what might have comforted her a few months earlier.

"I know she was in a lot of pain. That must have been very frightening for both of you."

"The thing is, we talked about this over and over. We agreed that we would never ask the other one to do that and then she . . . "

"I think it's one of those things that, even if we try, we can't really imagine what it might be like. That's probably why it's good that we make those promises ahead of time." These were the sort of things that only made sense in hindsight, never in real time, Margaret had figured out last spring.

Magda looked into her coffee cup as she spoke. "When our dog got sick, we kept her at home for as long as possible. We even gave her daily insulin shots. Then one day, she couldn't eat anymore and we knew it was time. Why can't we be that compassionate with human beings?"

"Good question, Magda. We do what we can to relieve pain, and then we leave it to God to decide when life should end. That's just how it is here and now. I'm not sure I would want the responsibility to have it any other way. You're Victoria's health care proxy?"

"Yes, and she's mine. Come to think of it, I guess I better get myself a new one."

"Well, she trusted you to make the right decision when the time came and you didn't fail her, Magda." Now Margaret had a question. "I never thought before about an unrelated person being able to be a proxy, but that's nice that you can, isn't it? So, you and Victoria are roommates?"

"Yes, we own a home over by the community college."

"Sometimes I think it'd be nice to have a roommate—besides my fat, lazy cat, Maxine. It's sort of weird living alone after so many years of being married. Ernie and I were married back in 1971."

"Victoria and I have been together for—well, next month would have been our twenty-fifth anniversary." Margaret smiled and nodded, then stopped, mid-nod. Her eyebrows furrowed as she grasped the meaning of Magda's words. Magda, staring out the window, was oblivious to the perplexed look on Margaret's face.

If you asked her, Margaret would describe herself as a liberal on most social issues. But politics aside, when it came to homosexuality, Margaret felt precisely the same as she did about heterosexuality: she didn't care to hear what or how often anyone was doing anything to anybody. She had always considered that topic to be placed squarely in the None of My Beeswax column.

Not that she'd met that many same-sex couples until now. Actually, Victoria and Magda—assuming they were—were her first. Or were they her first? If she'd misinterpreted this situation, who knew how many others had gotten past her?

Then the true implication of Magda's words washed over Margaret. It was one thing to lose a dear friend, but it was a whole other ballgame to lose a spouse, a life partner. What Magda was going through was what Margaret had gone through when Ernie was dying. There was no difference whatsoever and that cast a whole new light on this conversation.

While Margaret worked through her epiphany, Magda's head was somewhere entirely different. Her thoughts had moved on—or back—to other things.

"I thought I was all done being angry with Victoria—I know it sounds awful that I'm angry with her at all. It doesn't make sense, I know," Magda interjected apologetically. Then, "Anyway, whatever, I'm mad all over again."

Margaret didn't think it sounded awful. She thought it sounded very human. Magda's comments prompted Margaret to think back on her own most confusing, exhausting times while being Ernie's caregiver. She remembered desperately wanting consistency in her life while he was dying, for there to be no more shockwaves even if it was only to know that an emotion had been dealt with and stowed.

"I know what you mean. Some days I would get so mad at Ernie and it was so irrational. As if he wanted to be sick! I think sometimes it's just that you'd like to be the one being taken care of even if only for an hour—not that you want to die, even though you'd change places in a heartbeat if you could, which makes it all the more confusing. Truth is, it's just not your turn and you know it can't be. And then I'd feel so guilty, well, for even sleeping when Ernie was close to the end. I felt bad that I wanted to sleep! And then I'd get mad at myself for being so out of control. Looking back, none of that was rational." Margaret waited and Magda slowly nodded as if she hated to agree but she did. "And yet I wouldn't trade that time for anything in the world, Magda. I'd gladly be that tired again every day if I could have just five more minutes with Ernie."

Magda looked up, surprised, because that's exactly how she felt. If Margaret understood her, maybe she wasn't crazy after all.

Then again, maybe we're both nuts. "Yes! Victoria wants to talk about her funeral plans because she wants to make sure everything's done ahead of time for me, and I just don't want to talk about that stuff. Then I feel bad because I know it gives her some sense of control to handle those details. She was always *Marge in Charge* at home. That is, she used to be."

"My Ernie was the same. He met with Forester's and made all the arrangements ahead of time, even paid for it all. I had no idea until the hospice nurse called over there the day he died. That was a big relief, though. I really appreciated that, you know." Margaret's own thoughts wandered and she reeled herself back to the moment.

"Tell me about your life together, Magda. What do you two like to do?"

Magda told Margaret about buying their house, a sad little student rental, and spending every evening and weekend for months, making it a home. She told Margaret about the last trips they'd made, gambling in Vegas, gawking at the Grand Canyon, hiking in Arizona.

"When Victoria was still getting chemo, we spent hours watching old movies. I'd get funny ones for us to watch, like *You Can't Take It With You* and *Young Frankenstein* and we'd sit in bed together and laugh, really laugh." Her voice broke a bit and she absently rubbed her temples as she recalled those times. "But once we knew we weren't going to beat the cancer, we got a different attitude about our life. While Vic was still feeling pretty good, we went out to dinner more often and we had friends over for game night and we bought some toys we'd always wanted." Magda smiled as she said this.

She told Margaret about their splurges. When watching old movies became the only thing Victoria could enjoy, Magda had insisted they invest in a big-screen television. Right after that, Victoria was adamant that Magda upgrade from a spinet to the baby grand piano.

"Those are wonderful memories," Margaret said.

"Yes."

"Sometimes it helps to call on those kind of memories when times get rough." Margaret let Magda sit in silence for a moment. "Would you like to go back upstairs now, Magda?"

"Yes. Yes, I would."

Victoria was still sound asleep. Magda folded into a chair and read the book she'd brought from home, looking up at Victoria every few minutes, wishing very hard that she would wake up. A few hours later, when Victoria did wake up, she actually felt like visiting. They reminisced about their life together and about their lives long before they met.

Victoria couldn't imagine why but she was remembering little bits of nothing, how when she was little, she put her pajamas under the pillow when she made her bed each day, and made wishes on the first star of the evening. Magda told about being in high school plays. She was Eliza Doolittle in *My Fair Lady* and the caterpillar in *Alice in Wonderland.* She still couldn't believe she'd done that. Victoria said she wished she'd known Magda then. Magda agreed, she would have liked Victoria to see her perform.

Victoria was quiet for a moment. Just as Magda thought maybe she was drifting off again, Victoria spoke.

"When we made that trip to the Grand Canyon, you didn't want to go, did you?"

"No," Magda said.

"No, I didn't think so."

Victoria told Magda she was sorry she'd asked her to get the sleeping pills. She didn't know what she was saying at the time.

Could Magda ever forgive her?

Magda said not to worry, she already had.

Margaret

People don't change. Take Rusty Howell at the drugstore. He was a really nice person, just the same as in high school. Most people were, the same, that is. Occasionally someone had a genuine transformation and a real jackass became a great guy—not usually the other way around, thank goodness. Unfortunately, mutation at that level was pretty unusual and even more remarkable if it lasted. Margaret knew that for sure. She'd been on every diet known to modern man. Permanent change was a tough nut to crack.

Then there was that long conversation with Magda, Victoria's partner, and that was further confirmation of Margaret's theory. Anybody could see that relationship was a bit lop-sided, probably always had been. Clearly, Victoria had been the one driving the bus for years. Now that she was dying, nothing had changed, except maybe to ratchet up the intensity. Margaret thought Magda seemed a little disappointed at the predictability of it all, and more than a little confused about her own role going forward. Margaret shook her head. *That happens a lot.*

We like to think that people become more gentle, nicer, more in touch with their inner kind person when death is near, Margaret reflected. *They don't. They're what they've always been, except maybe more vivid.* That was neither good nor bad, it's just the way it is. Margaret had seen a few folks hope to the very end that their loved one, the patient, would have a deathbed conversion and suddenly say all the things they'd always wanted them to say and adopt all the attitudes they'd always prayed they'd have. Time and again they were disappointed.

Better to understand that each of us has a distinctive approach to life and that doesn't change just because death is so near. Better to respect and appreciate the singular nature of each person and tailor care to those unique needs. *Viva la difference.*

It also hadn't gone unobserved by Margaret that those final days and hours are when these unbendable traits are sometimes first noticed by loved ones. It was a fascination to her—no different than when she experienced it herself in caring for Ernie—that there are still new things to learn about a person, even if you've spent the better part of your lives together. Dying had a way of bringing out the very best and worst in people. More than Margaret would ever have guessed, it was an exceptional learning experience to be present at a life's end. The traveler and the bystander.

Margaret stepped out her front door to retrieve the mail and noticed the yard was neatly mowed and trimmed. Lenny had been there. This time, he'd been able to bag the fallen leaves with the mower but one good rain or one windy day would put an end to that shortcut.

She looked up at the home across the street. The couple was piling their young family into the minivan, mindfully strapping the children into the back seat. The husband gave Margaret a friendly wave. Margaret waved back and remembered how she used to wish, once in a while, that her life with Ernie had included children. She didn't think that anymore. She and Ernie had lived the life they were meant to live, and she still was. She had people at Rockaway House who relied on her contribution to their lives and her presence at their dying. In turn, there were people at Rockaway House who Margaret could call, if she needed something. Nope, things were as they were meant to be.

This time next week, Lenny'll have to get out the rake, she thought as she walked back from the mailbox. Maybe, as Ernie used to, he was hoping for a couple of windy days to shift the rest of the leaves over to the neighbor's yard. Better be careful with that wish, she thought with a smile. If it got too windy, Lenny would end up raking Margaret's leaves from his own yard and not getting paid to do it.

The day he rakes, I think I'll pitch in. Raking leaves had been one outdoor chore she'd shared with Ernie every fall. It'd be good to do that again, to be outdoors in the fresh air. That mildewy, mossy smell of leaves reminded her that winter was next on the agenda. Margaret couldn't imagine living somewhere that didn't have a distinctive change of seasons. That's how spring and fall cleaning got done. That's how furniture got rearranged to face the fireplace. That's how closets got cleaned out.

The closets. Today was the day.

Getting rid of some of Ernie's things was symbolic in ways that Margaret couldn't even put into words. It had to do with moving on, the whole physical versus spiritual thing. It had to do with trying to glean something good out of something bad. Not to mention that cleaning out closets was what she'd done every fall for her entire life. That's just what she did, so it also had to do with being some version of normal again.

Who knew a bunch of stuff could have such mystical implications?

Two hours later, Margaret had three thirty-gallon bags of clothes in the trunk of her car, ready to be dropped off at the men's shelter in Clinton. An entire box of nothing but shoes was now in the corner of the garage, including that brand new pair of men's house slippers, still in the bag with the receipt. She'd scored them in the after-holiday sales, December of 2011. *Free slippers.* She'd completely forgotten that she'd stashed them away for Ernie's birthday coming up in July. He would have been seventy-one on that summer day. *Lucky Ernie, he'll forever be seventy.*

Ernie's yard shoes were right beneath the slippers. Margaret wouldn't bother to ask Lenny what size sneakers he wore. First, she could see that his gunboats would never fit into Ernie's size nine and a halfs. Second, Margaret knew darn well that no self-respecting teenager would wear anything that wasn't the latest style—whatever that was—so no need to put him in the embarrassing position of kindly refusing.

No, she'd let the Universe choose the path that Ernie's shoes would next walk.

Rockaway House

The attention span of a gnat. Lauren thought she remembered her mother once describing her that way. Or was it Helen Sullivan who said it? Lauren preferred to think of herself as high-energy, but she had to admit that when she was under stress, she became a little, well, frenetic.

She was in her office by the crack of dawn on the Thursday before the first *Auction* weekend, but she didn't plan to stay for long. By eight a.m., she had disposed of everything in her In box and had already bolted for Rockaway House. Starting in the garage, she checked on the educational exhibits and briefly watched as the caterers set up tables and chairs. Bruce was zipping around, directing his many volunteers as they began to move items onto the driveway. With partly cloudy skies and a zero chance of rain, it was a safe staging area until time to start taking things into Rockaway House.

Lauren watched them, with growing admiration. She was a numbers person and she knew exactly what everything associated with *The Auction* had so far cost. She also knew none of it would have been possible, logistically or financially, if not for the thousands of volunteer hours. What had she read just the other day? There are 450,000 hospice volunteers providing 21,000,000 hours of hospice service every year in the United States. *And these folks count for a good portion of that.*

Now she was stationed at the windows in the second floor sunroom, looking down on the activity below, the anthill of workers. Just that morning she had thought to call Dorrie Kelly and have her get a photographer/videographer there for the day to record all the last-minute preparations for the show home. Lauren was already fantasizing about the board of directors' meeting where she would report the final tally from *The Rockaway House Heritage Show Home and Auction*. The DVD of this day could be a big part of that.

Lauren's cell phone vibrated. It was Allie. There'd been a call from the chief financial officer of CMC. He had a question on a Medicare reimbursement issue. I'm on my way back, Lauren said with a sigh. Thank goodness she'd have that video later to see everything she missed.

After all the work, all the hours—the endless hours—the pizzas, the cold coffees and the warm pops, the day had finally come. Bruce, Suzi, Lance, Rose and Margaret had carefully inspected the inside of Rockaway House first thing that morning, before Lauren had even gotten to her office.

Everything was completed and it was magnificent.

Lance was embarrassed by the praise and hugs that just kept coming. The smallest detail had been attended to as planned and Lance and his dedicated staff and volunteers had gotten it all done—right on schedule! Not quite on budget, but Suzi had shrugged that off. In her experience, she pointed out, it was prudent to double the estimated time and costs. Since they didn't have double the time to spare, might as well quadruple the expenses! But, with all the in-kind donations they'd gotten, the end-of-the-day budget had hardly budged.

The Murphys' exquisite arts and crafts rugs had been thoroughly aired and vacuumed and were back in Rockaway House. Carpet runners (thank you, again, Christopher Walton) wound throughout the house, guiding the guests and protecting the floors. A week earlier there had been a great debate: to rope or not to rope? In the end, they roped. Without soft barriers, not only would people be tempted to sit down on the furniture and pick up every knick and knack, but it would take unmanageably long to tour the house. They needed to get people in and out, toot sweet.

Once everyone agreed that the interior was ready, they gave Bruce the go-ahead. This was always Suzi's favorite time in any decorating or rehabilitation project: the move-in. Bruce directed the order of the pieces as his crew of über organized minions formed a continuous loop, carrying, depositing and returning for more. Suzi and Margaret were stationed inside Rockaway House. Margaret stood back, watching as her friend directed the people who were doing the heavy lifting—those infinitely patient people.

Right there. No, no, maybe to the left a bit.

No, I thought that would work against that wall but it really doesn't.

How in the world did the Murphys fit this all in?

Let's try over here. Perfect!

Bruce was incredibly organized. He sent the furniture in by rooms, the same way he'd had it arranged in the garage. In ninety minutes, it had all been moved and set in place. Suzi took another hour to put accessories atop the furniture while Margaret went to work setting the dining room table for ten: the Murphys, the Powells, Mrs. Quinn and Mr. Herman, the photographer. Margaret used May's best Noritake china. After all, she was setting this table for Thanksgiving dinner.

Three days earlier, Margaret had called Suzi from *The Farm and Home Center* as soon as she'd spotted their gorgeous mum plants—did Suzi want some for inside Rockaway House? *Oh! Oh!* came the answer. Margaret took that as a big *yes* and they were now distributed throughout the interior.

Each room in Rockaway House had been adopted by a local civic group or circle of friends that took responsibility for providing the plan and materials for an autumn decor. There were cornucopias, more pumpkins and gourds and loads of bittersweet (which grew at a secret location in the timber on the property owned by one of The Hell's Belles). These clusters of volunteers had been waiting on the front terrace—and no one would call them infinitely patient—for Suzi to let them in.

Margaret and Suzi banned Bruce from the property until the last silver dessert fork and mini gourd were in place. Just before fetching him, the two walked throughout the first floor, adjusted the lighting, flipped switches to ignite the fireplaces, fluffed the drapes, tilted the blinds just so, made sure each article was perfect and then finally led Bruce in, with arms linked between them, his eyes closed.

"Okay, you can look," Suzi said.

Eyes open, hands to face.

"Oh my," was all Bruce could muster. He turned this way and that, slowly walking from room to room. Suzi and Margaret followed him, in a way seeing it for the first time themselves. When the tour was over and they were back in the entryway, Bruce looked at Suzi, then at Margaret.

"When I thought about what this furniture would look like in here, I never saw this—I couldn't have imagined this, but this is just how it looked for them, isn't it?" Group hug.

The day had gotten away from Lauren. Rose had stopped by the corporate office to ask what Lauren thought about using more alternative treatments with the patients such as music and pet therapy, Reiki and acupuncture. Right behind Rose, Jeanne Evans, Isobel Baines's daughter, had called to see Lauren. Although Cameron had carefully guarded the secret until after Isobel's funeral (well, except for telling Carlene that day in the Rockaway House kitchen, but he'd been severely smitten, so who would blame him for that?), there'd been a story in *The Bee* and the tale of Isobel's Powerball ticket was now all over town. Lauren was clearly excited to hear what Jeanne had to say to her.

As Jeanne explained to Lauren, Carlene Spaulding had spent some time with Isobel, doing guided imagery with her. It was very calming, Isobel had commented several times, and that was the sort of thing Jeanne wanted her mother's trust to initially focus on for hospice patients. Lauren liked the idea as well and she had pulled Rose into the conversation by speakerphone. The three of them scheduled a time to talk more the following week.

Throw in some regularly scheduled meetings and routine tasks and it had been a very exhausting—and highly rewarding—day. But Lauren wasn't too tired to top it off with a trip to Rockaway House to check things out.

The front door was locked. Rockaway House had never been locked before nine p.m. as long as Lauren had been around. It made sense, though, with all the valuables and publicity. Lance had already upped the patrols considerably in the past ten days and there'd been a security guard on the premises 24/7 for weeks. Lauren rang the bell and got buzzed in by the nurse on duty upstairs.

She gasped as she entered. She hadn't walked through Rockaway House since the work had been completed, almost a week earlier, and she'd purposely taken the back stairs during her brief visit this morning, not wanting to spoil the surprise for herself. A week earlier, the house had been filled with window treatment installers and the cleaning crew. With so many busy bodies buzzing around, Lauren couldn't really see what the house looked like. Now she could, and it was breathtaking.

Rockaway House was peaceful like a home the night before Christmas, ready for the excitement that was about to explode within its walls. Lauren walked slowly down the entry hall and started her private tour in the former conference room. *That Suzi, what a visionary.* Who would have thought this twenty-first century office space could be transformed into an elegant 1920s bedroom? Lauren gingerly moved aside the posts and rope blocking its double-door opening and stepped in. She went from piece to piece, running her hand across the heirloom quilt, touching the perfume bottles and silver comb, brush and mirror set. *That's May's monogrammed manicure kit.* There was a lovely nightgown laid out on the chaise lounge at the foot of the bed. Their clothes, Lauren realized with a little gasp. *The Murphys left most of their clothes behind.*

As she walked through the first floor, Lauren had the same thought Bruce had voiced: Rockaway House was the Murphys' home once again.

There was the baby grand piano at the end of the living room. In all the commotion of the past few weeks, Lauren had completely forgotten about asking Suzi to see about getting one for the show home. A small framed sign sat on a crocheted doily. The piano was on loan from the McClaren Brothers Music Company. A parade of Chesterton High School students was scheduled to play background music during the tours. Suzi hadn't said a word to Lauren since the day she suggested it. *Bless her heart.*

Lauren ran her hand across the high gloss top. She loved the piano, any piano. If she played very softly—pianissimo—surely she wouldn't disturb anyone. Then she had to smile, remembering Margaret's stunt at that board meeting. The *Overture of 1812,* no less. Board members still mentioned it and laughed whenever Lauren came across them. Cissy Peters had gone on and on about it at the launch party. Lauren was convinced it was one of the unique touches that had helped them raise over $15,000 that night.

She sat down on the bench, lifted the keyboard cover and lightly ran her fingers across the keys, cool to the touch. Tenth grade, that's when Lauren had quit taking piano lessons. She'd had to choose between that and—what was the social activity that had been so important? Lauren couldn't remember now.

Maybe I should take some piano lessons over at the college and brush up. Winter's coming. It never hurts to plan a distraction.

Noah

Hermione was one of many visitors Noah had at Rockaway House. Since that first time, she and Fritz had been there every afternoon along with a stream of people who considered Noah and Lisbeth their good friends. Naturally, most were local customers of *Under the Covers*, but there were also the booksellers who had called on Noah and Lisbeth for almost three decades, hawking their publishers' upcoming releases, and the authors who credited the couple for a portion of their success. Sometime over the years, those relationships had turned from professional to personal. The folks who owned the other storefront businesses near the bookstore were neighbors in every sense as they paid their respects to Noah and offered their help to Lisbeth. Noah's apartment building held more dear friends. Each and every one wanted to make sure Noah realized he was in their thoughts and prayers.

Those who came to say goodbye didn't notice the changes in Noah occurring daily, sometimes hourly. The staff, Lisbeth and Fritz could see that the cancer was boldly defeating Noah, physically and mentally. His speech was sometimes slurred. More and more often he didn't make much sense, using the wrong word or dropping off in the middle of a sentence, never to return. Noah was bedridden, his muscles too unreliable for him to stand or even to swing his legs to sit on the edge of the bed. His mind could no longer be trusted to focus on where he was or what he was doing. Lisbeth sat as close as possible, always in touch by holding his hand through the side rails or at least laying her fingers on his arm.

Other than checking in at the store for a short time each morning, she was spending every waking hour with Noah, leaving Molly to mind the business. For the past twenty-four hours, Noah's eating was limited to an occasional taste of ice cream or a sliver of lemon babka. He had no appetite, even for his favorites. Lisbeth looked at him and thought that overnight his pajamas had become two sizes too large.

A few days earlier, Lisbeth had asked that she and Noah be left alone at the end of each day, and the staff was there to gently shoo out any others once they saw that Noah was winding down. This day, their time alone came early. It was only six o'clock and everyone else had gone home.

"I'm leaving my share of the store to you, Lisbeth."

Here we go again, Lisbeth said to herself. "Why, Noah? I told you I'd buy your partnership interest from your estate. Then the money can be used for whatever you say."

Lisbeth could hardly believe that Noah was using what little conscious thought process he had left to address this topic once more; that they were still arguing over this same stupid bone of contention. It seemed to Lisbeth that they had endlessly discussed business continuity for *Under the Covers*. More accurately, she had patiently listened to all of Noah's plans for a smooth, nearly imperceptible, transition at the store.

Since the day of his diagnosis, there had been many frank conversations about how Noah's absence would impact the bookstore, conversations all initiated and dominated by Noah. For thirty years they had functioned in parallel, equal but separate, performing the tasks they were each best suited for. With his cancer came Noah's realization that Lisbeth needed to handle his jobs or at least be familiar with them. During the first week of The Plan, he had prepared lists and meticulous instructions for performing his daily, weekly, monthly and even annual duties.

He had even found his own replacement.

The daughter of a long time customer, also a visitor to the store since childhood, would graduate in the spring with a business degree. She was a passionate bibliophile and, before Noah even got sick, she had timidly proposed through her mother that she would love to one day be considered for employment at *Under the Covers*. As Noah had since worked it all out, she could help at the store over the Christmas and spring breaks, a sort of trial run for everyone concerned.

Indeed, they had talked *about* and *around* but not exactly *through* the issue of Noah's impending death. Lisbeth knew every excruciating detail about how the *business* would function without Noah. But, like other subjects they had tacitly agreed to circumvent over the years, the topic of *life* without Noah had vigilantly and intentionally been avoided. What Lisbeth longed for was to have her best friend please share his plan for how she was to cope with having her morning cup of tea alone, as one of many examples. It was hard to say for sure, but she was now afraid the opportunity for that meaningful two-way conversation had forever slipped away.

"Lisbeth, my piece of the business was only ever on loan to me," Noah tried to explain. "Like the books. Like everything. What do we 'own' that we aren't just borrowing for a time, just acting as stewards?"

Lisbeth marveled at how Noah was speaking clearly and with purpose. He was so coherent this evening.

"Really, Lisbeth, I've been very lucky. I haven't had even one seizure and I just lost my vision. What's it been, a week now?" It had been six weeks, but never mind that. "Last night I dreamt I could see again. I wish I could, just one more time. I'd like to see your face, Lisbeth, just one more time." He reached out as he spoke. She guided his hand to cup her cheek.

"Well, I can still see you, Noah, and you look the same as the day I met you in the library." As he felt her smile, he smiled, too. Over the decades, they had each thought countless times of that moment and how their lives had been dramatically changed by a seemingly random meeting.

"What library?" He was gone again, but his palm remained against her cheek.

"The Chesterton Library, Noah. Remember when you worked for the awful Miss Rhoades? Weren't you lucky that I rescued you from her?" That had been their banter over the years: Lisbeth rescued Noah versus Noah rescued Lisbeth.

"Thank you, Lisbeth."

"For rescuing you?"

"For my life, for everything . . . You know I love you, Lisbeth." It was a statement, not a question. "I always have. I always have."

He was back. She was pretty sure he was back.

"I love you, too, Noah."

"I know that. I always have."

Lisbeth hesitated before responding. *What does that mean?* That Noah knew she had kept her deepest feelings for him at the back of her mind and, after so many years of denial, successfully hidden even from herself? Early on, she had been afraid that passion between them would jeopardize the friendship, business partnership and perfect synchronicity of their ideal life together. It had seemed too high a price to pay.

Or was this just the brain tumor talking? Did it even matter? Twenty-nine years earlier they had come to an unspoken accord. She'd accepted long ago that it had worked out as it was meant to—exactly as it was meant to.

"Yes, Noah, I have always loved you. And I have always known that you love me."

"With all my heart, dear Lisbeth." He seemed totally lucid. It didn't really matter, but Lisbeth still hoped he knew what he was saying, that these words were coming from a place of conscious intention.

She lowered the side rail and dropped her head down to his hand, now lying limp on top of the bedspread. She wept for the loss of her friend, the loss of her partner and the loss of her love. There was no longer any reason to wear a mask.

She raised her head up. Noah's face was turned in her direction; he seemed to be looking right at her. She leaned forward and kissed him on the lips—for the very first time. He kissed her back, sweetly, slowly.

Noah smiled and softly spoke, "Will you please raise the blinds, so I can see the sundown, Lisbeth?" Without thinking, she instantly rose and did as he asked.

And then he stopped speaking.

As the evening went on, Noah became fidgety and anxious. Lisbeth asked if they could give him something to help him relax. After a single dose of an anti-anxiety drug, Noah seemed settled for the night. Lisbeth was debating whether she should stay with him when she found Crystal at the nurses' station, bringing medical charts up to date after rounds.

"Crystal, may I interrupt you for a moment?"

"Of course, Lisbeth. What is it?"

"I was wondering if you think I should stay here with Noah tonight. I mean, do you expect . . . " Lisbeth couldn't figure quite how to put it.

"I believe he'll be fine tonight, Lisbeth. Of course, you're welcome to stay and I can't say for sure—I wish I could—but he has a bit more time with us, I think. You can stay if you want. I'll be glad to get you some bedding for the recliner." Crystal waited. It was clear that Lisbeth had more than one concern.

"I'm his health care proxy, you know. We're really the only family the other one has. I want him to be comfortable, but I don't want to ask you to do anything that would make him—well—die before he's supposed to." She'd finally spit it out.

"And we wouldn't let you do that, Lisbeth, so don't worry. He isn't having any pain now. Sometimes brain cancer's like that. If he does start to have any pain, we'll do whatever we can to relieve that. We can sedate him if necessary, but we'll just take it as it comes." She paused, watching Lisbeth's face relax a bit. "If you're worried that relieving Noah's pain or helping him to relax might make him die sooner, I can tell you that's not usually the case. We'd never do anything with the intention of hastening someone's death—that's not what hospice is about."

Lisbeth's tight shoulders visibly relaxed.

"Did you and Noah ever talk about the end of his life and what you might need to decide on his behalf?" Crystal asked.

"Yes, well, as much as we knew how to, I guess. He told me he didn't want me to do anything that would prolong his life once he couldn't talk and that he trusted me to do what I think is best." At this, Lisbeth's lip trembled. Nancy reached across the desk and patted her arm.

"Then you'll be fine, won't you? You know what he wants, that's what's important."

Maybe. And since Noah was apparently going on ahead of her, Lisbeth had recently been thinking more and more about her own end of life. With an out-of-state brother as her only family, the answer wasn't obvious to her. "What if Noah didn't have me, Crystal? What about people who don't have anyone to be with them or to look out for them?" she wondered aloud.

"Some people have what's called a professional guardian, a person—a stranger, really—who volunteers to look after them. The court appoints the person as the patient's proxy. But usually we just take our cue from the doctor who knows the patient, and hopefully we can talk about it with a patient when they come here, before it's too late. We make sure they have a Living Will when they arrive, if they can still make those decisions, then we know what they want. If not, remember, once you come into hospice care you've already made the decision to forego life prolonging measures."

"Oh, yeah, that's true. Okay. Well, thanks, Crystal. I think I'll go on home and get some rest. I'll be back in the morning. And, you know, if anything goes on during the night or if he asks for me . . . " Lisbeth wasn't ready to share or even admit her guess that Noah would not be speaking again.

"Of course, Lisbeth. We have your number. You get some rest."

Lisbeth walked down the back stairs and out the door onto the parking lot. She started her car and the jazz station from the University of Iowa came on the radio. It was a favorite of hers and Noah's—they often turned it on in the store if they got busy with customers and didn't have time to attend to the CD player.

She sat and listened for a few minutes, struggling to gather her thoughts. If she closed her eyes and concentrated, she could still feel Noah's lips on hers. Her heart was soaring and her heart was breaking and her head just might explode.

Rockaway House

She couldn't help it, Rose Sears was taking it all very personally. Since the day her husband James died, she'd wanted to establish a place and time to formally memorialize patients who passed in CCH care. Since the day she'd joined the staff, she'd planned to make it happen. She hadn't so far. There was always a fire that needed to be put out, an expanding role for volunteers, a new federal regulation to implement. When Rose first heard Suzi's idea for *The Rockaway House Heritage Show Home and Auction*, she made up her mind. *This is the place. This is the time.*

As difficult as it was to hold it in, Rose waited until the second meeting of the committee to spring her idea on the others. Suzi, Bruce, Lauren, Margaret and Lance were all there and before they tackled the first item on the agenda, the price of tickets for *The Auction*, Rose sat forward on her chair and boldly spoke.

"I think we should find some room in the budget for a memorial garden in the backyard. And I think we should have a remembrance ceremony sometime during that first weekend." Everyone waited for the "So there!" that seemed inevitable to follow Rose's definitive speech. They looked around the table at each other and then Suzi spoke.

"That's a great idea, Rose. Right, everybody?" Agreed. "Tell us more. How much do you need?" Rose sat up straighter and spoke with even more self-assurance.

"I was thinking maybe a simple flower garden with a bench so people had a place to sit, and I thought maybe people could buy bricks for a little patio with the name of their loved one inscribed or even plant a tree with a plaque. I'm not sure what that would cost, so we can decide if we want it to be a fundraiser or just a memorial." She took a quick breath. "And I thought we could have a ceremony dedicating the garden before the house opened on that first Sunday morning. Maybe have the bench there and the outline of the area, at least. I know we don't have much time to get it done—especially with everything else we're doing—but it'd be a start, wouldn't it? Oh, and I found these." She handed Margaret a small pink heart, about two inches across. It had the texture of stiff felt.

"What is this?" Margaret asked as they passed it from one to another.

"You plant it and it turns into wild flowers. I thought maybe it's something we could use in the spring for a little ceremony and let each survivor plant one."

Everyone thought the little heart and the bench and the memorials were touching and very fitting. They appreciated the sentiment and Rose's heartfelt passion, but mostly they gladly welcomed the chance to think about something other than the business end of this massive undertaking and they were glad to be reminded of what was at the heart of it all.

Suzi moved that the Chesterton Community Hospice Remembrance Garden be dedicated at eleven a.m. on the first Sunday of *The Auction*, a motion that passed unanimously. (The Sunday tours didn't start until one p.m. For most people in Chesterton, Sunday morning still meant church.) Now it was an official item on *The Auction* schedule of events.

Rose sat back, a satisfied look on her face. Seven years ago, she'd promised herself and James that she would do this. Now she had.

Well done, Rosie.

You're welcome, James.

Five and a half weeks. That was the measure of time from the afternoon that Margaret first showed Suzi "the stuff" in the garage attic to this day, the start of *The Rockaway House Heritage Show Home and Auction*. Nobody in their right mind would have bet that it could be done. But they didn't know who they were dealing with, did they? It was clear that Suzi, Margaret, Bruce, Rose, Lauren and Lance were a force to be reckoned with.

Friday night was the party at Suzi and Stephen's for those willing to pay the price to get the first look at the finished project. The garage would also be open to view the exhibits about hospice care and CCH's mission and to inspect the auction furniture that didn't fit back in Rockaway House.

It was a short party and that was fine with the antsy guests. Given the option to skip it entirely and go directly next door, they would have. Two hundred of them filed energetically out of Suzi and Stephen's, down the driveway and back up the Rockaway House sidewalk. By then it was eight p.m. and all the antique lamps, sconce lighting and chandeliers were ablaze.

You could hear the collective intakes of breath as they filed through the door. Margaret trailed at the rear of the crowd with Suzi, who was closely timing how long it took to get through the house. The day before, they'd strong-armed Lance and a couple of his workers to act as proxy ticketholders, but being there under protest, it was hardly the same. Everyone moved on to the garage to see the displays and place their bids and the evening ended by ten o'clock.

The committee members compared notes. They'd heard nothing but praise for the house, for how it looked and for the organized way *The Auction* was being conducted. So far, so good. The real test would come the following morning.

Chesterton Police Chief Lee Butler showed up an hour after the doors opened on Saturday. The City of Chesterton had granted emergency parking on both sides of Marion Street for the weekend. There was plenty more space in the high school lot, serviced by a fleet of golf cart shuttles to Rockaway House, piloted by members of the FFA chapter at Chesterton High. They weren't charging for rides, but there was a bucket labeled "Rockaway House" on each dashboard for goodwill donations.

Chief Butler assured Lauren he was there to make certain everything was going smoothly. Lauren smiled and told him what a dear he was for being so diligent and further responded with, Yes, Lee, you need to pay admission and get in line just like everyone else. He begrudgingly headed to the garage to buy his ticket.

Mayor Howard Randall appeared not long after Police Chief Butler. He, too, was concerned that his city was making the best possible impression on the regional media sprinkled throughout the area. Lauren tried not to think about the mayor's behind-his-back nickname, "H. R. Pufnstuf," as she thanked him for his conscientious oversight and assured him that everyone concerned had heard nothing but praise for Chesterton. The Mayor beamed, acknowledging the inferred recognition of his role in that. "Right over there, right behind Chief Butler," Lauren said as she smiled and pointed him to the long line in the garage.

Bruce, who was commandeering Auction Central, was still assisting with registrations and talking up the Murphys' furniture to potential bidders. The other committee members, basking in the glow of the well-oiled operation, meandered throughout the area, listening to the comments and addressing any little glitches. There was Carlene Spaulding in line, talking to Lisbeth Jones. Margaret had to smile, thinking how Lisbeth chose to support the event when she could just as easily have snuck downstairs to see it anytime she wanted. The two women were renewing a friendship that went back decades to when Carlene visited *Under the Covers* as a child with her mother. Carlene and Lisbeth had met again when Lisbeth attended Lois's funeral. Margaret stepped over to say hello, and overheard Carlene asking Lisbeth if she would look at some unpublished children's stories Carlene had come across. She'd tell Lisbeth all about it when she came to the store.

Larry and Holly Everest Lang were in line, laughing and visiting with the people ahead and behind them. Margaret gave them a wave from the driveway.

Inside Rockaway House, Rose saw Lauren whisper something in Suzi's ear. An hour later, Rose was standing with Lauren when Suzi came up and said, "You wanted to know if Mr. McClaren showed up? He's over there." Suzi discretely nodded in the direction of a distinguished looking elderly man, full head of snow white hair, three-piece pin-striped suit, a cane hung over his arm. He was standing near the baby grand piano, smiling and listening to a medley of 1940s ballads being played flawlessly by a Chesterton High School senior.

"Pay attention, Rose, if you don't want to miss some great dinner theater," Suzi whispered and nodded in the direction of Lauren, who was zeroing in on Mr. McClaren. She glided over, touched him gently on the arm to get his attention, then introduced herself. His eyes twinkled as Lauren said that she hated to interrupt Mr. McClaren's enjoyment of the music, but she just had to take this opportunity to personally thank him for the loan of this incredible instrument. She wouldn't bother him anymore. She glided away. He watched her go.

That's how the whole day and the next slipped by, smoothly and gracefully. Rose's remembrance garden became an official part of Rockaway House heritage on Sunday morning. At the brief ceremony, people gathered around the quaint area that Paul Thornton had whipped into shape with very little notice. He'd laid a ten by ten patio, but assured the committee that the paving bricks were set only in sand, so they could be easily replaced with memorial stones as they appeared. There were already three engraved bricks, courtesy of Rose and Margaret. One was inscribed with the name of James Sears. The other two were for Ernie Williams and Danny Murphy.

Although everyone thought it should be her, Rose wouldn't speak. She was sure she couldn't, but she did have a poem she thought was fitting, just one stanza from *The Fallen* and she asked Lauren to please read it in her place.

They shall grow not old, as we that are left grow old.
Age shall not weary them, nor the years condemn.
At the going down of the sun and in the morning
We will remember them.

Then Lauren invited everyone to join in a moment of silent prayer and reflection. Afterwards, the committee members hugged Rose and thanked her for making this a part of *The Auction.* It was a touching reminder of what Rockaway House was all about. Another Murphy-inspired legacy. Between sniffles, Rose said she was the one who was most grateful, for all that Rockaway House had meant in her life.

The joyous clamor of the first weekend of *The Auction* had passed. At seven p.m. Sunday night, Rockaway House sighed, as human beings do at seven p.m. Christmas night. The participants are exhausted, the hubbub has passed and all that's left is to look back and savor the new memories.

Except, Christmas isn't usually followed by an encore Christmas a week later and *The Auction* would be. The organizers needed to get their second wind and gear up for Round Two, the hubbub was only taking a breather, and more new memories were waiting to be made. That's okay, they all agreed. They could pull it off in the knowledge that it had unquestionably been an outstanding success so far—and as long as they had five days for their feet to recover.

Eleven p.m. Margaret had never been inside Rockaway House this late before. She'd told the others to go on home and she'd check the lights before she left. Homer, the security guard, had locked the doors and Margaret knew he was checking on the garage area. He'd be circling the house and watching out from his vehicle in the driveway for the next eight hours.

Margaret went from room to room, turning off the ceiling lights, leaving a table lamp on here and there, as they always had, for anyone who wandered downstairs during the night. She was just leaving the living room when a sweet wave washed over her. She stopped and stood still.

It was *Chanel No. 5.*

Margaret could all but see May Murphy standing on the far side of the room, looking back at Margaret. It would be clear from the look on May's face that she saw Margaret not as an intruder but as a welcome guest in her home. Margaret could only imagine May's delight at being once again surrounded by the precious belongings that had made this house a safe and nurturing haven. At one time, they were the furnishings that she and her family had sat on, slept in, eaten at. Then they were the furnishings that she and her family had abandoned because the memories they evoked were too painful to bear.

May would smile in appreciation that somehow the new inhabitants had found a way to negate the fear and pain that drove her family out almost seventy years earlier. It would truly be the Murphys' Rockaway House again for a while. The furniture might be there only temporarily, but Margaret felt sure that the spirit of love and loyalty and laughter that had made Rockaway House a home was back to stay.

She switched off the overhead light in the entryway and then turned to look back, just before she walked out the front door.

"You're welcome, May. My pleasure."

Victoria

It had been such a peaceful interlude. The hospice team had gotten Victoria's pain relief meds just right, so she was awake at least part of most days and Magda could understand nearly all she said. Victoria's blood pressure was stable, and there were no clear signs that she was actively dying.

Magda was thinking a lot clearer these days and she reminded herself that there were also no hard and fast rules for this game and that Victoria's tranquil state didn't mean the dying process had been postponed. In fact, Magda thought maybe she better ask Sheryl if she should stay for the night.

"You're certainly welcome to, Magda. If you think it's important that you be with Victoria at the end, it could be any time. But you need good rest, too. What would you like to do?"

Magda decided to split the difference: she'd go home, get a shower and then come back to Rockaway House later in the evening and sleep in the recliner.

Once home, Magda sent out the now twice-daily mass e-mail, read the incoming notes and sorted the snail mail.

Just a quick nap, just to rest my eyes.

She took the kitchen timer with her to the living room and laid down on the couch, using her afghan for a pillow.

Something woke her. Magda lay very still, holding her breath. Maybe the sound had been in a dream, but she didn't think so. It wasn't an intruder, she was pretty sure of that. She wasn't afraid. For some reason she thought the sound was familiar. Was it Victoria? She thought it might have been Victoria. Had she called out from the guest room?

Magda rolled over to check the baby monitor. No baby monitor. Then Magda saw that she was on the couch, not in bed. She looked down on the floor—the kitchen timer was still set for sixty minutes. She'd forgotten to push the START button. She quickly glanced at her watch. *Two fifteen.*

Magda sat up. The very next moment, she knew that she needed to get to Rockaway House. *Right now.* She grabbed her car keys and purse and raced out to her car. She wanted to go back and check the lock on the front door but she didn't dare take the time to do that.

Crystal was setting the receiver back down just as Magda arrived at the nurses' desk, out of breath.

"I was just phoning you," Crystal said calmly. "Victoria's very restless. She's asking for you and we think she might be close to passing away, Magda." Magda was well past Crystal by the time she spoke the last words. Magda didn't need to hear them, she already knew.

Once inside the room, Magda looked immediately at Victoria. Trish, the nurses' aide, was at her bedside. Victoria didn't acknowledge Magda's presence until her face was right above hers and Magda was holding her hand. Then Victoria looked up at her, smiling sweetly.

"You're here. I held on. I knew you'd come. I called for you."

"That's why I'm here, I heard you, Vic. It's okay now, I'm here." Magda lowered the side rail and got as close as she could, laying her arms alongside Victoria, her face close to hers. "It's okay for you to go, now, Vic. I'll be fine," she spoke through her tears.

"I know you will. I'm going to go ahead, but you'll come later, right?"

"Yes, I'll see you someday, my dear one. You can go now, you need your rest."

"I think I will. I love you, Magda."

"And I love you, Victoria."

Magda reached across Victoria, holding her every so gently, still wary of causing her any pain even in these final moments. Victoria looked into Magda's eyes.

"I know now what it was all about." Victoria spoke so softly that Magda leaned closer to hear, as close as she could get. She felt Victoria's last breath softly whisper past her ear. Magda was about to ask Victoria to repeat her words when she realized that was no longer an option.

Magda put her head down on Victoria's chest and softly wept. Trish stepped back and silently left them alone.

Why did she say that—what did she mean? What am I supposed to do now?

Rockaway House

One flight up from *The Rockaway House Heritage Show Home and Auction*, it was business as usual for the living and dying.

A family had made the difficult decision to bring the father, age fifty-two with terminal pancreatic cancer, from continuous home care to Rockaway House for respite care. It was the wedding weekend of his twenty-five-year-old daughter. The date had been scheduled and rescheduled twice. Each time it had seemed he could make it, each time his condition had deteriorated.

No one expected it, no one ever considered it happening, but he died during that brief stay at Rockaway House. Two of his business partners had offered to sit with him during the ceremony, so the family would know he was with loved ones. He passed away two minutes before his daughter's wedding began. There was no question in anyone's mind: he wanted to be at the church to get started as her guardian angel. When they broke the news right after the ceremony, she agreed, that would be just like her dad to do that. They celebrated his life even as they celebrated the marriage.

A forty-three-year-old patient had lived in the brain injury wing of the Good Shepherd Care Center in Chesterton since suffering a massive stroke fifteen years earlier. She had long accepted being a quadriplegic with more grace than seemed possible, and then she decided she no longer wanted to live. She wanted to join her parents and brother in the afterlife. Declining food and water for a week, she was moved to Rockaway House and passed away peacefully with her family at her side ten days later.

If Margaret had been surprised when Edward Everest died during his first night at Rockaway House, she'd be shocked when she heard about Mrs. Francis. She'd hardly gotten settled in her room—her son had left to get her a cup of tea—and she was gone. Just like that. Now Rose was in the solarium with her son, trying to make him understand that it wasn't the move to Rockaway House that had killed his mother. He hadn't done anything wrong by bringing her here for care, it was just her time. Sometimes it happened that way.

During *The Auction*, everyone associated with Rockaway House thought often of the striking contrast between the solemnity of the upstairs and the social atmosphere of the downstairs. It was a thought-provoking paradox, a stark reminder of the cycle of life at Rockaway House, a pageant that spanned days for some and was reaching across centuries for others.

The second weekend of *The Auction* was even more successful than the first. Initially, although Rose had welcomed the chance to educate the public about volunteer opportunities, she considered it little more than a fringe benefit of the fundraiser. Not so. Using the inquiry form available at the CCH garage exhibit, applications had been pouring in. They would talk later, she told Lauren and Margaret, but Rose envisioned a series of events at Rockaway House where people could come and learn more before they committed to volunteering. It looked very promising, though, very promising indeed. Lauren even commented that patient referrals had taken a bit of a jump in the past month, probably due to increased public awareness. They hadn't anticipated that.

On Sunday night of the second weekend—the official end of *The Auction*—Suzi brought a bottle of champagne from home and the committee raised a glass to the event, to the Murphys and to themselves. But for Bruce and his volunteers, some of the most intense work was yet to be done.

At eight a.m. Monday morning, movers would arrive to bring the furniture out of the house and back into the garage. The winning bidders, notified by e-mail Sunday evening, would line up to collect their loot beginning at noon. There was nothing complicated about the rules of the game: Show up with photo ID and cash and take the item away. Thanks to The Hell's Belles, the records were meticulously organized, and the anxious winners were efficiently sorted out and attended to.

About two o'clock, Margaret stepped out to the driveway and wasn't surprised to see that the evacuation was running smoothly, a constant parade of furniture and small articles being hauled and carried down the driveway to waiting cars, vans and trucks. For the out-of-town buyers, Chesterton's own Hardie Moving and Storage (a sponsor of the show home) was available with shipping services.

Bruce wasn't budging with any guesstimate of proceeds. Some bidders might not show and, in that case, they would call the second highest bidder, so it could go on for an additional day or so. Margaret had to smile, watching Bruce move at warp speed, overseeing the operation and taking cash from the hands of his volunteers, each payment inside a small envelope with the name of the bidder and the catalog number of the item. A commercial safe had been delivered by First National of Chesterton, a very serious-looking depository, and an off-duty policeman was shadowing the perpetual-motion Bruce and his loot. The officer, far from serious-looking, was, in fact, smiling—no, smirking.

Margaret backed away from the action, and no one noticed as she opened the small door next to the garage stalls. She stepped through the simple, unadorned entrance that barely seven weeks earlier had been the portal to a miraculous series of events. She walked purposefully up the stairs, looking down once to confirm that her footprints in the dust were gone, long gone.

Back at the CCH corporate offices, Lauren had just returned from her own visit to Rockaway House. By the time she'd gotten there, the first floor was empty except for a few pieces of furniture. They were keeping the china cabinet to display some of the Murphys' small belongings and the bookshelves and library table were now permanently at home in the conference room. Most of the wall art and photographs were staying and Lauren had held back a variety of Murphy possessions for a tableau she was planning to put in the lobby of the Chesterton Medical Center. She could envision a large screen monitor playing the video of *The Auction* activities on a continuous loop. Oh, and at Margaret's suggestion—inspired by Caleb Bronson's party in September—they had kept all of the Murphys' Christmas decorations. Suzi was already salivating over the idea of staging Rockaway House in vintage yuletide finery.

Walton's Furniture would be making the big delivery any minute now. Christopher Walton himself had called Lauren to confirm the time and to tell her—and it wasn't just because his mother told him to, although she had—that he would be there in person to supervise delivery and placement of the new furnishings. He made it clear that he wanted to see this project through to the end, the very end.

I'll bet he does, Lauren thought with a smile.

Before the new rugs and furnishings could come in, one last item had to be moved out: the McClaren Brothers baby grand piano. Lauren had asked Suzi to please hold off on having it collected. She wanted to make that call herself.

Lauren took a deep breath and dialed the number.

"Good morning, McClaren Brothers Music Company."

"Good morning, this is Lauren Dunlap at Chesterton Community Hospice. May I please speak to Mr. McClaren?"

"Yes, one moment." Lauren's fingers tapped out a simple tune on her desktop as she waited.

"Samuel McClaren here. May I help you?"

Lauren identified herself, reminding him of when they met. There was no need; Samuel McClaren knew who she was. He well remembered meeting Lauren Dunlap at the show home. She was that charming young lady who made a point of thanking him for the loan of the baby grand.

Had Mr. McClaren considered donating the piano to Rockaway House, Lauren asked. That would be quite a legacy for McClaren Brothers Music Company. How many years was it that his family had been in business?

Over sixty-seven years. When he and his two brothers started the music store, Samuel was a twenty-year-old bachelor. Now he was an eighty-seven-year-old bachelor and the last surviving McClaren brother.

"I mean, it's used now, isn't it? Just between you and me, Mr. McClaren—may I call you Samuel?—you can't really sell it as a new piano, now can you? Not that anyone would need to know, but I'm just saying . . . Are you still there, Samuel?"

Samuel hardly heard Lauren speaking. At that moment, his thoughts were focused on another time long before this fall day in 2012, because that piano, in that room, with that young lady playing those songs during the show home had had such a familiar air about it.

Rockaway House was not so very different from the Chesterton home Samuel grew up in. He'd graduated in the Chesterton High School Class of '43. Lauralee Murphy was meant to have been in the class of '44. The story of

Danny Murphy had been long forgotten by Samuel McClaren until he read Ray Spaulding's account in *The Bee* three weeks earlier. For the first time in sixty-eight years, Samuel thought about how disappointed he was when Lauralee left town with her parents just two months before her graduation. To be honest, he supposed he was more heartbroken than merely disappointed at the time, but that was so long ago, who could recall for certain? The Murphys were a lovely family and Lauralee was a beautiful girl. What if Danny Murphy hadn't died? What if the Murphys hadn't moved?

Samuel forced his focus back to the present and thought, there was a time when he wouldn't have been so easily manipulated, when he wouldn't have continued to listen to someone with such a transparent motive, even someone as charming as Lauren Dunlap. Samuel would have said that his deliverymen would be there to pick up the piano within the hour. And then he would have hung up the phone and that would have been the end of that.

"If I give that piano to Rockaway House, can I at least get a receipt for tax purposes?"

Lauren giggled into the phone. "This is incredibly generous of you, Samuel—so unexpected!"

"Young lady, fifty years ago you wouldn't have gotten that piano from me so easily."

"Are you sure about that, Samuel?"

Margaret heard the rumbling vibration and looked down from the garage apartment's kitchen window. It was the Walton's Furniture truck. To think, this all began with her dream of two Barcoloungers. *Who'da thought?* Just one quick look around the attic and then she'd leave to watch the delivery.

This is a cute apartment.

She wondered if it had been Mrs. Quinn's living quarters before the furniture was relocated and she'd moved into the big house for the massive cleaning. So much Margaret still didn't know and never would.

Now that all the furniture was gone, the rooms in the apartment didn't look smaller or larger, they just looked deserted and lonely. Lance had the water running again and had replaced the plumbing fixtures, so Bruce and his crew had facilities and a working refrigerator over the past few weeks.

Margaret quickly walked through the rooms and even stuck her head into the unfinished attic area. She had to admit she was hoping to get a whiff of *Chanel No. 5*. It didn't happen, but that was okay. She knew in her heart that May Murphy had moved on as well. She no longer needed to nudge them to uncover the story and her family's legacy. May's work there was done.

Really a decent-sized apartment. I wonder . . .

Margaret headed downstairs for the finale of the rehabilitation drama. She wanted to see Suzi in action. Talk about good dinner theater. Margaret hurried across the parking lot and in the back door of Rockaway House.

She watched in amazement as the weeks of planning came to life around her. The techies were doing their thing, installing charging stations and printers in the former dining room, now the computer center. The inviting conversation areas in the living room and the children's play area in the bright solarium came to life. In the butler's pantry, May Murphy's treasured china and silver were on display permanently in the upper cabinets, while a modern coffee maker and microwave sat on the counter for the use of family members.

And the meditation room was more inspirational than any of them had imagined. The stained glass window lent just the right touch. Margaret thought how many times she could have used a place such as this nearing the end of Ernie's life. Somewhere quiet to have a rational thought and a visit with God. *Check your monkey mind at the door.*

She turned to find Lauren Dunlap at her side in the doorway.

"I wanted to let you know that the piano is staying," Lauren said.

"Really? That's wonderful. Now all we need is someone to play it!"

Lauren left Margaret's side and went out the back door to the garage. Bruce's operation was in full swing and Lauren was amazed to see how many of the sold items were already gone. The four car stalls, once jam-packed, were now vacant except for one, half-full. She walked through the empty space.

Really a decent-sized building. I wonder . . .

Lauren punched Cissy Peters's number on her cell phone.

Rose was coming out of the kitchen as Margaret walked in. "There you are! Just the person I wanted to see!"

"Isn't this exciting, Rose? Can you believe all that has happened in less than two months?"

"No, my friend, I cannot. What are you doing right now? Can I talk to you for a minute?" Margaret nodded and followed Rose upstairs to the nurses' mini-office, at that moment, the only place with any privacy.

"Here's the deal, Maggie. I've talked to Lauren and with the money we expect to come in from *The Auction* and some other changes they're making at corporate—that I'm not privy to but who cares since they're good for us—I'd like to offer you a paid position. You'd be a sort of community liaison, working between us and the people of Chesterton, part public relations, part public education. The whole auction thing has made us realize what a poor job we've done up until now of getting our message out into the community, but there's a corporate commitment to fix that. You can still do your concierge thing, too, if you want to, I mean I'd like you to. Whatdaya think?"

What do I think? What could she be thinking?

"I don't even have a college degree, Rose."

"So, that's one more thing you and Steve Jobs have in common. I'm not looking for someone with a degree, I need someone with a brain and a passion for the mission of hospice. Would you agree you do, you know, have both?"

This job sounded like it went against everything Margaret held dear: independence, no commitments, not getting her heart bruised on a regular basis, not answering to others, not having others answer to her, learning to bite her tongue, or exposing her soft underbelly to criticism, to name just a few.

"I'll do it!" she heard herself say.

"I'm afraid we can only afford it as a part-time position to begin with."

"That's fine—I only want to work part-time. There's a bunch of other things I want to do." Margaret was thinking about joining a book club; she'd seen in the paper that Rolling Hills was looking for volunteers for their activity programs; and Jeanne Baines Evans had told her the other day about embellished scrapbooking as a type of Ethical Will. Margaret had some thoughts about her life with Ernie that she wanted to get down on paper, and she'd always meant to try her hand at scrapping.

Then there was that file of hospice ideas she'd found on the Internet. A lot of them would make great programs to get the community more involved in CCH. She'd come across a template on how to really organize a platoon of cookie bakers, and she wanted to talk to Rose about companion services for patients during caregiver meetings.

What a relief, Rose was thinking. Lauren was pushing her to get the new liaison program up and running ASAP, but Rose's own duties were already overwhelming and expanding. She hoped Margaret would have some ideas on how to get started right away.

"Rose, I already have some ideas on how to get started right away."

Thank you, sweet baby Jesus.

Noah

Three hundred twenty-seven. That's how many biographies and autobiographies *The Third Monday Club* had read and discussed. One per month for over twenty-seven years. While they examined the lives of the famous and infamous, the club members inevitably became travelling companions on their own life journeys. Marriages, mini-breakdowns, divorces, wandering career paths, grandchildren and health crises were among the mile markers they'd passed along the way.

The one thing they had never before encountered was a dying club member. Noah was their first.

Two out of the group, Sandy and Reuben, called Lisbeth early in the morning. They offered to spell her at Rockaway House for a couple of hours, so she could take a break. Trusting their solemn promise to stay by Noah's side in her absence, Lisbeth left as they arrived, eager to get to the store. There was a shipment of new releases to be logged in. Lisbeth couldn't help thinking that Noah would freak out if he knew readers were being deprived of their favorite authors' newest works.

Sandy and Reuben were more than just founding book club members, they were Noah's two favorite members—not that he played favorites. The three of them—all confirmed singles—had spent many evenings away from the bookstore cooking gourmet meals at Sandy's condo or taking an occasional weekend trip into Chicago for a show or trekking to Minneapolis for a concert. They knew each other exceptionally—actually, frighteningly—well.

For most of the day following that evening of Noah's final words, he seemed not unconscious, but semi-conscious, at least that's what his friends wanted to believe. Although his eyes remained closed tight, everyone agreed that he smiled when someone squeezed his hand and gave a tiny shrug of his shoulders if he got a kiss on the cheek. Lisbeth's only concern was whether he was comfortable and pain free. She was satisfied that he was.

As Sandy and Reuben sat on opposite sides of Noah's bed, looking across his still form, they began to play a game the three had perfected over decades of studying life stories and drinking wine: *Name and Defend.* Naturally, they included Noah.

"Okay, my very very favorite was *The Life and Times of the Thunderbolt Kid* by Bill Bryson," Reuben began.

I laughed so hard I thought I'd pee my pants. Of course, I'm prejudiced, since Bill Bryson's from Iowa and he did that event at the store for us back when the book came out. God, I remember his fans started lining up the night before. That was an unforgettable day for Lisbeth and me.

"Well, sure, if you're going for milk-out-the-nose humor, but for historical perspective, you've got to consider David McCullough's *John Adams.* Right, Noah?"

Sandy and Reuben both leaned forward, willing Noah to respond. Sure enough, there did seem to be a tiny upturn at the corners of his mouth.

Face it, Reuben, she's got you on that one.

"See? Told you!" Sandy pointed and crossed her arms in a superior manner.

"All right, then I submit Bryson's biography of Shakespeare."

Lazy thinking, Reuben, old man. She's not gonna let you get away with that. Three, two, one—

"Oh, okay, Alex, I'll take 'Books by Bill Bryson' for $400. This is a serious discussion, Reuben, not a game of Jeopardy. Remember when Noah suggested Einstein's bio by Isaacson? Everybody in the club loved it, and it's still one of my favorites."

"Well, sure, isn't there some kind of law that everyone has to like every bio written by Walter Isaacson? How about Frank McCourt's *Angela's Ashes*?" Reuben suggested.

Come on, you two, just because I'm dying? The only thing more depressing than that book was the movie. Why not nominate The Bell Jar? Let's pick the pace up, shall we?

"You cannot be serious, Reuben. How about we bring some chicks into the competition? Catherine the Great or Cleopatra are on my list." Sandy leaned back smugly.

Thatta girl. Reuben?

"I swear to God, Sandy, if you say *Jane Austen: A Life*, I'll puke."

"Please, Noah, gimme some help here. We'll leave the discussion of the incredible, indelible contribution of Miss Jane Austen for another day. Two words, my friends: Julia. Child."

Game, set, match. I love you two, I really do, but please go on without me, I need to rest. Lisbeth'll be back soon.

Noah's head dropped slightly to the right. Reuben stood and leaned over him, speaking in a whisper, "I think he's gone to sleep, Sandy. What do you think?"

She whispered back, "What do I think? I'll tell you what I think: if that little game of pseudo intellectual ping pong didn't put him to sleep, nothing will." They sat in silence for a moment. "Reuben, how are we going to have book group without Noah? I'm not sure we can do it." Her voice cracked. "Is it okay to talk about this in front of him?"

Reuben shrugged. "I have no idea."

Neither one had noticed Nancy, the day nurse, slipping in the door.

"It's definitely okay to be talking in front of Noah. Noah, I'm going to check your vitals." Nancy stepped to the head of the bed, put a digital thermometer briefly in Noah's ear and then took his pulse. "The hearing is the last to go. I always tell the patients what I'm doing anytime I disturb them or touch them because I always assume they can hear me. I think it's just plain good manners. And I'm sure Noah would want to know how much you're going to miss him." She smiled at Sandy and Reuben. They looked at each other and nodded.

"You're right. A minute ago, he seemed to be responding to us. I think he just nodded off. Although, it could have been the company." Sandy rolled her eyes and tilted her head in Reuben's direction. Reuben didn't notice. He had stood and was wandering absently around the room, studying the items Noah had chosen to bring with him to Rockaway House.

"Hey, here's Noah's Word-a-day calendar. Let's see what we have." They waited as Reuben read it to himself. "Whoa. *Omphaloskepsis*—that's a mouthfull. *Navel-gazing. A favorite pastime of postmodern philosophers, especially when used facetiously to refer to the habit of mentally considering everything while ignoring the real world. Contemplation of one's navel as an aid to meditation.* Hey, let's read this one to Noah when he wakes up. Nothing he loves better than a pretentious postmodern philosopher." Nancy joined in their laughter. She didn't really get the inside joke, but she was always glad to recognize the joy and humor in a life well-lived. She pulled up the covers at the end of the bed and briefly checked Noah's feet for signs of diminished circulation. So far, still warm and pink.

"I'll see you two later. Buzz if you need anything."

Reuben continued his tour of the room. There was a framed photo of Lisbeth and Noah with Bill Bryson in the middle, standing in front of *Under the Covers*. Noah was gazing over the author's head, smiling down at Lisbeth. She was looking up at Noah, also gazing past Bill Bryson. Only the author was looking into the camera.

"That's right, Bill Bryson did an author event at the store, didn't he? I remember now—I was out of town on business. I was so disappointed. Did many people show up?" Sandy couldn't remember. She liked Bill Bryson well enough, but she certainly wasn't going to stand in line for hours on end to get his autograph.

Reuben moved on. The collection of Dylan Thomas poetry, a catnip mouse—well-chewed—and a picture of Noah's parents. From their attire, Reuben guessed it was taken in the late 1950s. "Hey Sandy, look at this. Noah looks just like his mother. You look just like your mom, Noah." Noah's parents looked very young and very happy. Reuben showed the picture to Sandy and she smiled and nodded in agreement.

Each morning Molly got a report on Noah's condition from Lisbeth when she stopped by *Under the Covers* on her way to Rockaway House. That day, Molly got a double dose when Lisbeth returned to unpack the book shipment. At Molly's insistence, Lisbeth took a few moments to have a cup of tea. For the first time, Lisbeth admitted to someone that she could feel in her heart that Noah was very close to the end. She broke down and sobbed, another first in Molly's presence.

As soon as Lisbeth left again for Rockaway House, Molly activated the phone tree. Within an hour, every person who cared about Noah and Lisbeth knew that the time they had been dreading for almost nine months was quickly approaching.

Lisbeth never thought it was her place to limit visitors to Noah, but she hadn't needed to for the past week. With few exceptions, everyone had already said their goodbyes. The scores of friends had gracefully accepted that there simply was not enough space at Rockaway House for all of the people who cared about Lisbeth and Noah to huddle together. So naturally, everyone now made a beeline for *Under the Covers* instead.

Molly was blowing her nose for the umpteenth time that morning when the bell on the front door first jingled. They just kept coming and they didn't come empty handed. It was Iowa; their arms were laden with food and libations of all manner. And it was more than convenient that *Whine & Cheese* was just two doors down.

Some said they were worried about Molly being alone, others admitted they didn't want to be by themselves at a time like this. One of the neighbors helped Molly push Noah's clever rolling shelves aside and they set up folding tables, the ones they kept for author events. They were soon covered with snacks, plenty of liquid refreshments, and babkas, oodles and oodles of babkas and cookies.

Everyone had stories to share and, as befitted bibliophiles, they spoke eloquently and emotionally of their lanky friend. By sharing his love of books and of life, Noah had made each one of them laugh, cry and think. "Newcomers"—those who had been patrons of *Under the Covers* for ten years or fewer—were captivated by the recollections of the "old timers," tales of the store's early days. In the beginning, the Chesterton Chamber of Commerce didn't see how Noah and Lisbeth's idea for a spring afternoon book festival would be good for neighborhood business. Now in its twenty-fifth year, the festival goes on for a week, with book signings and author appearances spread throughout the downtown Chesterton shops and restaurants.

Countless children had visited the store on countless field trips throughout the years. For every one of them, there were two remarkable highlights: The Story Lady (Lisbeth dressed up as a gray-haired fairy godmother) and The Book Wizard (Noah dressed up as, well, a wizard). Three of those children were now successfully published. One of them, Alice Minard, was an award-winning children's author. She drove the two and a half hours from Chicago at breakneck speed as soon as Molly's call came that morning. When Alice arrived, she stood on a chair and told the crowd about writing her very first book, complete with illustrations. She was eleven years old at the time.

Noah had reviewed it for her, giving Alice constructive and encouraging ideas. Then Noah made a Xerox copy of the handwritten book and asked

Alice to autograph it for him. He told her he wanted to own the very first First Edition of her work. The cheesy black and white manuscript was still displayed in a shadowbox hanging on the wall of *Under the Covers*—one of Noah's proudest possessions. Which is why, Alice stopped to blow her nose and then concluded, every one of her more than fifty bestsellers was dedicated *To Noah, The Book Wizard.*

More memories called for more toasts, which called for more wine, but the very nearly boisterous crowd grew silent as Mr. Goldberg, owner of *Babkas 'r Us*, shared how close he had come to shuttering his doors after only six months in business. He couldn't understand it, but at the time no one in Chesterton had the foggiest notion of what a babka was. Then that tiny woman who opened this bookstore about the same time he was about to close his bakery—that would be Lisbeth—came into his shop and asked if he would consider baking cookies for her to offer at their self-service coffee bar. For a reasonable discount, she would post a prominent sign advertising where they had come from.

In a few months, Mr. Goldberg would celebrate thirty years in business, specializing in babkas—and cookies. He raised his glass to Noah and Lisbeth and cried like a baby.

Sandy and Reuben headed for an early lunch when Lisbeth got back to Rockaway House. Alone with Noah for a short time over the noon hour, Lisbeth tried desperately to get him to acknowledge her in some way. He just wouldn't. Holly, the nurse on duty, examined him and said he was probably in a semi-comatose state. Whatever the label, he was unresponsive. Never opening the book she had brought along, Lisbeth sat at his bedside, gently stroking his hand.

As he and Sandy finished eating, Reuben said he felt like they should head back to be with Noah and Lisbeth. What did Sandy think? She agreed, they should head right back. They arrived behind Fritz and Hermione and ahead of Sally and Ronnie, two members of *The Second Thursday Club.*

Once Noah had become unable to sit in a chair, Hermione had taken to spending her visits on the bed, which was fine with Hermione. As long as Noah was awake, she stayed close to his head, glad to accept his affectionate chin scratches and until the evening before, he was still able to reach out to her. If he drifted off, she invariably went to the end of the bed and reclined, converting Noah's legs to a sort of kittyfied chaise lounge. And that's where she was now, comfortably ensconced at Noah's feet, leaning on his leg. The crowd of visitors was no impediment to her naptime and she slept soundly with an occasional snore.

Sally and Ronnie hadn't intended to hold a formal meeting of *The Second Thursday Club*, but Sally said that since they hadn't been able to reconvene after that first get together and since she and Ronnie happened to each have a book with them, why not? Lisbeth couldn't argue with that.

There was no discussion of where everyone should sit as they gathered their chairs around the bed. Noah had never passed up an opportunity for book chat and there was no cause to dismiss him as a group member now.

Sally had just started reading *Tuesdays With Morrie* the day before. She didn't want to say out loud that she was hoping it might help her to better understand what Lisbeth—and Noah—were going through. Ronnie laid *The Next Place* across his lap. A friend had given it to him when Ronnie's mother was dying, five years ago. Noah's dwindling life had made Ronnie think back on that time and he had found the book in the "to keep always" section of his bookshelves.

Sally, Sandy, Fritz and Reuben didn't recognize Ronnie's choice but Lisbeth smiled, she was familiar with both books as favorites of Noah's.

"What is that, Ronnie?" Sally picked it up from his lap, opened the cover and leafed through the pages. "This is a children's book."

"Well, yeah, it could be, I guess. I didn't want to bring something terribly literary, I wanted to share something—well—nice, sort of hopeful. What do you think, Lisbeth?" Ronnie was half-embarrassed, hoping the book wouldn't upset her.

Tuesdays With Morrie? I didn't see that one coming, but okay. I definitely like Ronnie's choice. Lisbeth and I sold about a gajillion copies of that over the years.

Lisbeth said she thought it was an excellent choice and so was *Tuesdays With Morrie.* As they all knew, Noah had remained very positive throughout his illness about how he would spend the rest of this life and where he would be going on from here.

"Did anybody see the movie about Morrie? I liked that, too," Reuben chimed in. Sandy peered at him over the top of her Peepers.

Seriously? she thought to herself. *If Noah could speak, this would not be happening.*

Now wait just one minute. I'm supposed to be the one with dysphasia. No one brought As I Lay Dying? or A Grief Observed or Death Be Not Proud? Please tell me that one of these otherwise literate people brought some Dylan Thomas with them.

"Wasn't Dylan Thomas one of Noah's favorites?" Sandy said, trying to bring the conversation back around, up to what she knew were Noah's standards.

Yes, yes! Finally!

Sally spoke one line from memory, "*Rage, rage against the dying of the light.*"

Thank you, Sally . . . Wait! Oh. My. God. I know what that means—I know what that means. No, no, I really know now what that means. "Grave men, near death, who see with blinding sight, Blind eyes could blaze like meteors and be gay, Rage, rage against the dying of the light."

". . . but what did Thomas write after that?" Reuben was asking. "Anybody know?" He was forever the seeker of obscure details, the one who most often answered his own questions. "I think it was that 'play for voices' thing he did. I bet Noah could tell us what it is. Hey, if we had a copy of that, we could perform it!" As Reuben spoke the words, all heads instinctively turned to acknowledge Noah.

And then it happened.

Noah opened his eyes and slowly, deliberately looked at each face, the faces of the friends who encircled him with their embracing energy of loyalty and empathy. Those who had come to lift him up and to comfort his Lisbeth. In witnessing his dying, they bore witness to his life and for that he would love them forever.

He paused when he got to her.

Everyone except Noah had stopped breathing. Still he looked at Lisbeth. Two seconds passed. Three. Finally, his raspy voice broke the silence. His words were deliberate and unhurried.

"Dylan Thomas's last work was *Milk Wood.* And the last line is 'The End'." Noah's gaze never left Lisbeth's. She was transfixed, her eyes wide open and locked onto his. He smiled at her and Lisbeth's face slowly relaxed into an identical expression, as they seemed to share a sacred, secret joke. As if in slow motion, Noah's eyes closed and he died.

There was a slight, almost imperceptible movement in Sally's peripheral vision. She looked away from Noah's face in time to catch sight of Hermione opening her eyes. She raised her head in Noah's direction, stood, arched her back in a stretch, walked to the head of the bed, curled up in the crook of his arm and went back to sleep.

No one spoke or even breathed. Then, like slowly turning up the volume on a radio, faint gasps were joined by muffled sobs and hushed voices as they began to comprehend what they had just heard and seen.

"Could he—was he seeing us?"

"Well he was sure as hell seeing Lisbeth."

"That was amazing. Just amazing."

"He's gone. Oh my God, he's gone. Lisbeth, we're so sorry."

"What should we do now?"

Without a sound, Sandy slipped out the door and went to the nurses' station to let Nancy know. Then Sandy phoned Molly, so she could break it to the crowd at the bookstore. Molly said, please tell Lisbeth they would be toasting Noah—again—as soon as she hung up the phone.

Reuben picked up Noah's favorite book from the bedside. Lisbeth was still holding Noah's hand, tears streaming down her cheeks, a serene smile on her face.

"Lisbeth? Is it okay if I read Noah's favorite poem?"

They all knew the poem and the poet that Reuben meant.

Lisbeth nodded, her gaze never leaving Noah's face.

He looked younger to her now, his features relaxed in death. In fact, he looked just like that day in 1983 when she had first gazed up at the lanky man on the library step stool. She thought he was handsome in a professorial way.

It had taken Lisbeth two trips around the stacks before she found the courage to step up and say, "Excuse me, may I bother you for a moment?"

Reuben interrupted Lisbeth's reverie. His voice quivering at times with an emotional timbre, he was determined to do this thing for Noah and every other person there:

Do not go gentle into that good night,
Old age should burn and rave at close of day.
Rage, rage against the dying of the light . . .

Everyone except Lisbeth was standing with heads bowed as Reuben read the poem. When he finished, he closed the book and laid it back on the bedside table. Then he was the first to say goodbye, leading the diminutive procession. In choked whispers, there were comforting words to Lisbeth and farewells to Noah as each person stopped, leaned down and gave him a kiss or a pat on the arm or half a hug.

Moving as one in their communal grief, they filed out of the room, disappearing to the upstairs solarium. Without speaking, they collectively granted that this should be Lisbeth's time to be alone with Noah, to say her private goodbye.

After all, everyone knew they had been best friends for all these years.

Rockaway House

How much do they pay to have the lawn mowed, Margaret asked Lauren. How about snow removal, how much does that cost, she wanted to know. Does Lance spend much time at Rockaway House doing odd jobs, a lightbulb here, a jammed garbage disposal there?

Lauren patiently answered Margaret's questions as well as she could, then finally dared to pose one of her own.

"Margaret, for heaven's sake—cut to the chase. Why are you asking?"

Margaret told Lauren about Paul Thornton, master gardener, carpenter and handyman. She wondered if it might make sense to swap out the living quarters above the garage for his services around Rockaway House. He'd be an extra pair of eyes for security, too. For Paul, it would mean having a yard and gardens to tend again. Margaret was almost positive he'd like the idea.

She'd already decided to donate all of Ernie's power tools and yard equipment to Rockaway House. Someone there could use them, she couldn't. Anyway, every time she saw a hedge being trimmed or a flower bed being spaded, it would be like Ernie getting one more chance to putter in the yard.

Lauren thought Margaret's suggestion about the apartment made a lot of sense. Yes, it really did make sense since the board had decided two days earlier to move the hospice administrative offices into the Rockaway House garage. That made use of otherwise empty space and put everyone who had the goal of providing the highest quality hospice care possible in proximity. Whether tackling the mountain of paperwork, raising money, or giving hands-on patient care, they were a team. You couldn't really be a team if you weren't sharing the same space, could you? It also meant the receptionist in the new location could handle deliveries and manage admissions and discharge paperwork. That would give the caregiving staff at Rockaway House more time to be, well, giving care.

Oh, by the way, Lauren said to Margaret with a smile, from now on the board of directors will be having *all* their meetings in the Rockaway House conference room.

The unspoken deadline for completion had been "in time for the holidays" and Lance Wilson set some sort of record getting the new office space ready once Lauren gave him the go-ahead. Staff moved in just before Christmas, which made the new digs all the more inviting, thanks to Margaret's most recent effort at community involvement: the Seasonal Decor Committee. The offices and the interior of Rockaway House were beautifully adorned with the Murphy family decorations and the committee was available to do the same in the home of any hospice patient. You had only to ask. Most of the members of the committee had been Hell's Belles (although Margaret did make them deep six their former nickname) who were bitten by the hospice volunteer bug while helping Bruce with *The Auction.*

The Auction. When the dust had settled, when the revenue from *The Auction* and the tickets and the donations (of which there were many after all of Suzi and Lauren's arm-twisting) was counted against the expenses (of which there were few after all of Suzi and Lauren's arm-twisting), the net proceeds far exceeded Bruce's original estimate. So far, in fact, that CCH would soon have its own foundation, no more having to beg funds from the CMC. The cornerstone of the hospice foundation was the *Murphy Family Endowment*. It assured the financial security of the Chesterton Community Hospice and the jewel in its crown, Rockaway House, in perpetuity. Margaret loved that word, 'perpetuity.' From then on, she always used it when she told the story of the Murphys and she told the story of the Murphys every chance she got.

The second official donation to the *Murphy Family Endowment* had been the personal library of one Noah Smythe. And what a library it was. Lance installed floor to ceiling bookshelves on one whole wall in the living room. There was a self-serve checkout system and patients and family members were loving it. Noah had also given the executor of his estate—Lisbeth, of course—carte blanche to make charitable donations with a generous portion of his assets. In light of what Hermione's visits had meant to Noah, Lisbeth asked Margaret's help in setting up a special fund to care for the pets of patients and to establish a formal pet therapy program through the CCH. The certified pets and their humans would also visit hospital wards and nursing homes. Following Hermione's example, pets now regularly came to see their family members at Rockaway House, and it was therapeutic for everyone concerned, including the staff and volunteers.

And, speaking of Hermione, Margaret had finally gotten up the nerve to talk to Rose about a resident cat. Noah's friend Fritz would have loved to keep Hermione but he already had a dog (the reason she was left alone in Noah's apartment in the first place) and Lisbeth was allergic. No hard feelings, Hermione was fine with the new arrangement at Rockaway House. She had the run of the place and, if not being cuddled by a patient or family member, she could be found basking in the sun in a comfy chair.

"I'd love to talk about this more—and we will—but I have a commitment over at Rockaway House. I need to run." Lauren hung up the phone, threw on her jacket and eagerly headed across the parking lot. It was noon and for the past five weeks, she'd been playing the piano there every other day over the lunch hour, without fail. Magda Stark played on the in-between days.

People were beginning to gather in the kitchen for Margaret's soup du jour. The staff and volunteers had dropped whatever they were doing to open the door of any room where the patient didn't object to hearing the live concert that would soon be drifting up the stairs.

By the time Lauren retrieved her music books from the piano bench and was seated, eight or nine family members were already settled in the kitchen solarium and in the living room, TV trays holding their soup bowls and crispy bread. Once a week or so, Mr. McClaren made a point to sample the Rockaway House fare and listen to Lauren play. (Cameron Lane II had been recently asked to amend Mr. McClaren's Will to include a generous bequest to Rockaway House.) Various bereavement support groups had moved their meetings to one o'clock on some days. They'd quickly discovered that more newcomers were inclined to attend after joining in the midday music and fellowship.

Usually Lauren included Scott Joplin, Cole Porter, maybe a little Sammy Kahn and now, of course, seasonal selections. She would take requests, provided she could locate the sheet music. Sorry, she often apologized, I don't play by ear, never could, but I'll find the music on the Internet—be here day after tomorrow and I'll give it my best shot. After a couple of weeks, Mr. McClaren always seemed to have some surplus sheet music to donate each time he visited.

Margaret made sure first floor doorways were all open, so those in the kitchen could hear the music—including her, if she got delayed by her baking and serving duties. As Lauren began to play, Margaret was at the stove, taking out a pan of brownies—always best to serve them *a la mode* while they were still warm. The notes of *O Holy Night* wafted into the kitchen, and Margaret headed to the living room, leaving the brownies cooling on the counter.

She glanced to her right and saw—how could it be for the very first time?—the lighted **EXIT** sign at the end of the hall leading to the back door. She stifled a giggle. *You'd think so, wouldn't you? But the people who come to this home never really seem to leave.*

Margaret stopped and leaned against the frame of the living room's open French doors. A fire was blazing at the far end beyond the piano.

She closed her eyes.

She could see clearly that it wasn't Lauren Dunlap at the piano at all, it was Lauralee Murphy. Seated primly at the keyboard, she was giving an impromptu recital of the Christmas piece she had learned at her last piano lesson. Together on the settee, her sisters Annabelle and Elizabeth were pouring over a fashion magazine that Daniel had brought home as a surprise. Danny was curled up on the bench in the inglenook, reading a comic book, his father was in a nearby armchair, feet on a stool, his eyes closed. May Murphy was sitting near a floor lamp, darning one of Daniel's socks.

Looking up, May gazed around the room, putting her hand to her cheek, nearly overcome by gratitude for the family she and Daniel had been blessed with. Margaret could sense Mrs. Quinn in the kitchen, standing right in the place Margaret had stood a few moments earlier, kneading dough that would rise overnight, ready to bake into cinnamon rolls the next morning.

How extraordinary, Margaret thought. Rockaway House could sometimes be visited by anger and denial and conflict. A moment later, it was a refuge of love and acceptance and redemption. Maybe not so surprising for a house overflowing with people who were facing some of life's most intense and passionate moments. When it was all said and done, in the end, Rockaway House was a safe harbor for witnessing and validation, for all who sought shelter there.

And it had taken a family from another century to transform it into everything it was meant to be.

"Welcome back, Daniel and May," Margaret whispered under her breath. "And thank you."

Margaret

Houses have faces—at least Margaret had always thought so. Over the past months, the facade of Rockaway House had gone from steadfast and determined to embracing and nurturing. True, its physical demeanor had been softened by fresh landscaping and welcoming touches, but more than that, its spirit had been renewed.

Margaret stopped her car at the end of the driveway, much as she had that September day on her first visit. She looked up at the grande dame. Rockaway House was like an elderly lady awakening from a nap. To her amazement, she finds she is completely refreshed and feels almost young again. It's not that she'd ever lost her will to live, but it's liberating to know that others now acknowledge her inner vitality and the significance of her presence.

Margaret knew what Rockaway House knew.

Not so very long ago, Margaret had chosen to dwell in the past—the saddest part of the past—because that's all she seemed able to remember. Now she was choosing to move beyond that point in time. She could visit yesterday whenever she wanted, to savor the memories and the lingering images in her heart and mind. And she had no doubt she would from time to time because those memories weren't "somewhere else"; today held a piece of each and every yesterday.

Rockaway House now seemed like a second home to Margaret. She finally understood what Ernie was feeling when he'd come home from being on the road for a few days, brimming with stories about the terrific people he'd met or old chums he'd reconnected with, his eyes sparkling. They were folks who began as customers and had become his friends and his "work family." They lived in homes sprinkled across the countryside where he would share home-cooked meals, lie down if he took sick, spend the night if weather turned nasty without warning. What Margaret had felt as she listened to Ernie's stories over the years hadn't been jealousy—she just didn't get it. Now she did.

From the vital retiree who chose quality of life over quantity to the head-strong woman who found compassion and spirituality at life's end. Each one had faced death as each had faced life: with a one-of-a-kind attitude, a perspective that came from a unique history and a unique relationship with life that made for a unique relationship with life's end.

Last September, Margaret had not yet met any of these folks, she had not yet stepped into the lives of these incredible characters. She hadn't known—couldn't have imagined—how each one would have a part in changing her life forever as their own lives drew to a close.

She parked her car and walked in the front door of Rockaway House, its entryway no longer forbidding and dreary; it was now bright and airy. Meandering through the first floor, Margaret saw three young children playing

Chutes and Ladders in the solarium, two people having an intimate conversation in the corner of the living room and an older lady knitting as she sat in the inglenook, warmed by the fire. Hermione, now bored with chasing the ball of yarn, was asleep at the woman's feet.

Margaret passed through the kitchen. A volunteer she recognized smiled and waved as she pulled a sheet of cookies from the oven. Margaret smiled back and shook her head at the wonder of it all as she went out the back door onto the parking lot.

She watched in silence as Paul Thornton slowly stood from finishing the first of the spring plantings, the perennials that would fill in between the mum plants, the mums that would be a welcome annual reminder of the show home event. He put his hands in the small of his back, stretched and then approached the door that led to the second floor of the garage, above the hospice offices.

Margaret stared as Paul removed his shoes, holding onto the door handle for balance. He pulled out a pocket knife and meticulously scraped the mud and dirt off each sneaker before putting it back on. His hand was on the knob and he started to open the door, about to go upstairs to his apartment.

"Say, Paul, what size shoe do you wear?" Margaret called over to him.

"Hey, Margaret, hi! Nine and a half, most days. Why do you ask?" Paul smiled at her.

"You know, I think I might just have something for you."

This book is a work of fiction.
These, however, are facts:

- About seventy-five percent of people wish to die at home. About twenty-five percent do.
- Less than twenty-seven percent of American adults have executed advance directives and communicated their wishes for end-of-life care.
- Forty-four percent of Americans now die under the care of a hospice provider (1.5 to 1.6 million patients treated annually).
- Medicare currently pays for 89 percent of hospice care.
- 450,000 volunteers provide 21,000,000 hours of hospice service each year in the United States.
- The estimated value of unpaid personal caregiving in the United States is $450 billion, approximately the same as the entire Medicare budget.
- Over 120,000 people are waiting for the donation of an organ to save their lives.

Medicare website for hospice information

www.medicare.gov

National Hospice and Palliative Care Organization

www.nhpco.org

Information on organ donation

www.organdonor.gov

To my readers

This is fiction and any of the names of people or places I used are either totally fictitious or I am using them in a fictitious manner.

I probably don't need to tell you this, but because **EXIT** is a work of fiction, some of the things I included may not completely jibe with your own experiences or those of people you know or have known.

Everything in this book is provided for entertainment or general informational purposes only. To avoid any possible misunderstanding, it is not meant to save you a trip to a doctor or even to an attorney. When in doubt, please check it out.

The author

Attorney Jo Kline Cebuhar is author of the award-winning books **Last things first, just in case... The practical guide to Living Wills and Durable Powers of Attorney for Health Care** and **SO GROWS THE TREE – Creating an Ethical Will – The legacy of your beliefs and values, life lessons and hopes for the future**. She is also the former chair of Iowa's largest hospice organization. **EXIT–A novel about dying** is her first book-length work of fiction. She lives in West Des Moines, Iowa with her husband John, two cats (neither one of which is named Macavity) and a nearby forest of critters.

To contact Jo: jcebuhar@msn.com

www.**SoGrowsTheTree**.com

Thank you. Thank you. Thank you.

Attribution and gratitude to these individuals,
folks who know what it means to leave an Ethical Will:

George Eliot for *The Lifted Veil*

George Gershwin for *Summertime*

T. S. Eliot and Andrew Lloyd Weber for *Macavity The Mystery Cat*

Victor Young and Will J. Harris for *Sweet Sue*

Charles Tazewell for *The Littlest Angel*

Edward Lear for *The Owl and the Pussycat*

Harold Arlen and E. Y. Harburg for *Somewhere Over the Rainbow*

Laurence Binyon for *The Fallen*

Mitch Albom for *Tuesdays With Morrie*

Warren Hansen for *The Next Place*

Dylan Thomas for *Do Not Go Gentle Into That Good Night*

David Ben-Gurion

Pericles

Henry Wadsworth Longfellow

Ralph Waldo Emerson

Made in the USA
San Bernardino, CA
15 October 2014